By Elizabeth Hand

Waking the Moon
Glimmering
Winterlong

Published by HarperPrism

It is so hard to dream posterity
Or haunt a ruined century
    W. H. Auden, "Hell"

GLIMMERING

A Novel by

ELIZABETH HAND

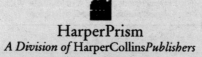

HarperPrism
A Division of HarperCollinsPublishers

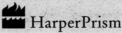

HarperPrism

A Division of HarperCollins*Publishers*
10 East 53rd Street, New York, N.Y. 10022-5299

This is a work of fiction. The characters, incidents, and dialogues are
products of the author's imagination and are not to be construed
as real. Any resemblance to actual events or persons,
living or dead, is entirely coincidental.

Grateful acknowledgment is made for permission to reprint excerpts.
"The Waste Land," in *Collected Poems 1909-1962* by T. S. Eliot, copy-
right 1936 by Harcourt, Brace & Co., copyright © 1964, 1963 by
T. S. Eliot. "A House Is Not a Motel," by Arthur Lee,
published by Grass Roots Music BMI.
"Starry Eyes," by Roky Erickson.

A hardcover edition of this book was published
in 1997 by HarperCollins*Publishers.*

ISBN: 0-06-101216-5

HarperCollins®, 📖®, and HarperPrism®
are trademarks of HarperCollins*Publishers* Inc.

Cover design by Richard Hasselberger
Cover photograph © 1997 Shinichi Eguchi
Cover photograph © Gene Mydlowski

First HarperPrism mass market edition printing: March 1998

Printed in the United States of America

Visit HarperPrism on the World Wide Web at
http://www.harpercollins.com

❖ 10 9 8 7 6 5 4 3 2 1

For Christopher Schelling—
Amicus usque ad aras
And for my brother Brian,
who is already planting palm trees
along Lakeshore Drive
With all my love

Four voices just audible in the hush of any
Christmas:
Accept my friendship or die.
I shall keep order and not very much will happen.
Bring me luck and of course I'll support you.
I smell blood and an era of prominent madmen.

—W. H. Auden, "Blessed Event"

"*Fin de siècle,*" murmured Lord Henry.
"*Fin du globe,*" answered his hostess.
"I wish it were *fin du globe*," said Dorian with a sigh.
"Life is such a great disappointment."

—Oscar Wilde, *The Picture of Dorian Gray*

CONTENTS

PROLOGUE

Afterward he would think, *We should have known it was coming. Should have seen it in the fiery darkness above the Palisades, or traced it in the flaming contrails left by disintegrating jets as they plunged into that watery cleft between the Battery and Liberty Island. Fingerprints upon a windowpane, etched in August ice; crocuses blooming in December, then November; peepers waking in the February mud to sing, too early by far; to sing again next spring, and then never to wake again.*

We should have known, I should have known, he thought, pounding his hands against the glass until it broke and there was blood then to worry about as well, blood to worry about again; blood and a hole in the sky, the fabric of the world rent, and we the living should have known what would stream through that shimmering gap, we should have remembered before they returned to remind us: we the dying at the end of the world should never have forgotten the dead.

Rubric

I.

In June 1996, an emergency meeting of the United Nations World Council on Carbon Dioxide Emissions and Global Warming was held in Rio Gallegos, Argentina, to discuss the unpredicted and potentially disastrous rise in global temperatures during the previous eighteen months. In a desperate effort to stabilize the atmospheric concentrations of carbon gases, the European Union, allying itself with Trinidad, Tobago, New Zealand, and Australia, led the push for ratifying the 1991 UN climate treaty and the earlier Montreal Protocol. This revised treaty, very narrowly passed despite the vocal and hostile opposition of the United States, China, and Russia, provided for immediate worldwide implementation of an involuntary cap on emissions, as well as an international ban on CFCs and HCFCs. In a concession to pressure from the conservative governments of the U.S., Japan, Russia, and China, the council also passed a bill that permitted limited industrial use of the experimental refrigerant and heating agent bromotetrachloride, or BRITE.

II.

In the early 1990s, BRITE had been developed in Finland as a substitute for chlorofluorocarbons and hexachlorofluorocarbons, and had been used in experiments to mine gas hydrate in the Arctic. The polar regions' vast deposits of gas hydrate, with their frozen stores of methane, held the potential to provide twice as much carbon energy as the fossil fuels that had helped cause the rapid degradation of the ozone layer. BRITE appeared to have no adverse environmental effects; unlike CFCs and HCFCs, it degraded in the upper levels of the atmosphere. It was also relatively inexpensive to produce.

By the end of 1996, BRITE was in common use throughout the industrialized world.

III.

In March 1997, during an American gas hydrate–mining expedition off the Ross Ice Shelf in Antarctica, a massive series of ocean floor avalanches occurred, releasing a sudden, almost inconceivably vast store of methane from the hydrate reservoir. The Antarctic deposits alone contained over three times the amount of methane found in the atmosphere; methane has a greenhouse effect eleven times that of carbon dioxide. Along with the loss of life and scientific equipment in Antarctica, three thousand canisters of BRITE were destroyed, their contents voided into the atmosphere like smoke.

The gas hydrate explosion had the misfortune to occur at the same time as a massive solar storm, predicted some three days earlier by NOAA's newly launched Hermes X-ray satellite. Solar physicists at NASA's Jet Propulsion Lab cheered as the first images crept across their monitors: the sun's corona disappearing as a billion tons of gas spewed forth. Three days later, this river of solar particles streamed into the Van Allen radiation belt like a celestial lava flow, even as the Ross Ice Shelf collapsed.

This disastrous confluence of events created a surging electrical current that altered the earth's magnetic field.

Transformers exploded; circuit breakers shut down; satellite transmissions were lost as an early night descended upon the world's cities. Fifty kilometers above the earth, the sun's ultraviolet rays began a complicated pavane with bromotetrachloride.

IV.

On March 26, 1997, the glimmering began.

PART ONE

Come as You Are

CHAPTER ONE

March 26, 1997: At Lazyland

On the night of his fortieth birthday, John Chanvers Finnegan stood upon the balcony of his Yonkers mansion and watched the sky explode above the Hudson River. It was the end of March, an unusually warm and beautiful day in early spring; though all the days now seemed lovely and warm, bathed as they were in the vernal glow of a dying century. From the house beneath him came the sigh and hum of conversation, an occasional *ritornello* of raucous laughter—Leonard's, Jack thought, and allowed himself a melancholy smile. He had come outside, not so much to be alone, as to savor the notion that everyone he loved best in the world was there with him now: his surviving friends, his ex-lover, his grandmother, his brothers. From here he could listen to them all, see them even, if he leaned over the balcony and craned his neck to look back at the house.

But he didn't do that. It was enough, to know they were there; enough to sip champagne from a crystal lily, and listen.

The house was called Lazyland. It had been built in 1884 by the department store entrepreneur Myles Finnegan, Jack's great-grandfather. Just four years earlier, in 1880, Myles had worked in Stevens' variety store on North Broadway in Yonkers, stocking shelves and sweeping the day's detritus of torn paper, bent nails, and broken glass out onto the sidewalk. One rainy morning in September his employer, suffering from an attack of gout, sent Myles in his place to the import warehouse of a toy wholesaler in Brooklyn. There Myles was to inspect the company's selection of new and unusual items to sell at Christmas.

"Here," the importer said, pointing to excelsior-filled crates in which nestled papier-mâché crèches from Salzburg's *kristkindlmarket*; porcelain dolls from Germany; English lead soldiers and French soubrettes of colored paper, with lace roses and spun-glass hair. There were boxes of tin flowers and images of the Christ Child cast in wax, silver-embossed cardboard animals from Dresden, and little metal candleholders to clip onto fragrant pine boughs. Myles, tall and dark and lean, with an expression of perpetual surprise, had big bony hands more accustomed to handling cartons of dry goods than these fragile toys. He wondered aloud if there wasn't anything *new*.

The importer turned, affronted, from admiring his painted lead battalions. "These I just received yesterday."

Myles shook his head. "*Different*," he said. "I wonder now, haven't you anything different? Unusual, I mean—" He fingered a doll's tartan gown and tried to look knowledgeable.

"Unusual?" The importer nodded eagerly, suddenly blessed with an idea. "I didn't understand that your employer is looking for the *unusual* this season. Has Mr. Stevens seen these?"

He took Myles's arm and led him to a darker part of the warehouse. Overhead a single gas lantern cast a fluttering light, but on the floor beneath there seemed to be myriad candles glowing within a row of wooden boxes: a cache of rubies and sapphires and golden orbs that made Myles suck in his breath, amazed.

"What is it, then?" he whispered.

The importer tilted his head. "These are Christmas

tree dressings from Sonneberg." He stooped and very carefully removed a blown-glass dog, held it up so that it turned gleaming in the gaslight. "Lovely, aren't they?"

"They're beautiful," breathed Myles Finnegan. He knelt beside the rows of boxes, took first one and then another of the brilliant confections from their paper wrappings, and raised them to the light.

"They reflect the candlelight, you understand," the importer explained somewhat officiously. "It reduces the cost of buying many candles, which as you know are so expensive right now . . ."

His voice trailed off. He did not offer to Myles Finnegan that the ornaments had been in the warehouse for some months, having proved impossible to sell. They were too expensive, too fragile; no one but German immigrants would want them, and who amongst the poor Germans could afford such frivolities?

Myles continued to gaze entranced upon the shining glass figures. He thought of the Christmas tree in his employer's house, the only one he had ever seen. Magic it had been, with the sweet wild smells of wax and balsam, and Mr. Stevens's children shrieking with delight as they pulled their gifts from the dressed boughs; but to see a tree glittering with such things as these! He drew a multicolored teardrop close to his face, saw within its glorious curve his cheeks streaked gold and green and crimson and his eyes ashine like stars. "How much?" he asked.

The importer quoted a figure seven times what he had paid his business counterpart in Sonneberg. But Myles proved to be more astute than that; they argued and dickered for fifteen minutes before agreeing upon a price that Longfellow Stevens would not consider too dear.

Unfortunately, when the crates of ornaments arrived

some weeks later, Mr. Stevens reacted much as the importer's other customers had when shown the pearls of Sonneberg.

"I can't sell these!" he fumed. "*Glass!* Mr. Finnegan, what were you thinking?" He kicked angrily at a carton, then turned a red face upon his employee. "I have no use for them. Send them back."

"He—he won't take them, sir." Myles swallowed. "It was the agreement we made, we would take them at this price—"

"We? *We?*" roared Longfellow Stevens. "*We* agreed to nothing! As of this week your employment is terminated, Mr. Finnegan!"

Myles stared at him, too stunned to be angry. But when Mr. Stevens began talking of withholding his wages to pay for the shipment, Myles spoke.

"I'll take them, then. The Christmas boxes."

"You will *not.*"

"In place of my wages." He was already bending over the cartons, light as the egg panniers that came daily from Flatbush. "I'll take the Christmas dressings."

And he did. Late in November he took them in a borrowed wagon to Getty Square, and hawked them to the well-dressed shoppers along South Broadway. In two days he had sold them all, and returned to Brooklyn for more, and then again a week later for the rest of the importer's stock. By January of 1881, Myles Finnegan was well on his way to being a rich man. By January 1882, after the first of his many visits to Lauscha, where the glassblowers who supplied Sonneberg lived, he *was* a rich man. And by the following year he was very rich indeed, having purchased Stevens' Variety and renamed it Finnegan's: the flagship store of what was to become a vast American retail empire, built upon blown glass and candlelight. It wasn't until the 1930s that Finnegan's first

Sparkle-Glo factory opened on Long Island, mass-producing Christmas balls; but by then the family fortunes were well in place.

While he was still in high school, Myles's great-grandson Jack could look out from the attic window at Lazyland, across the Hudson to the Palisades, and read atop the cliffs there the defiant legend emblazoned on the abandoned factory, like a thought untethered from a dream—

SPARKLE-GLO

Lazyland belonged to Jack now, even though his grandmother Keeley—Myles's only child, who had been born there in 1899—still held formal title to the house. Upon her death the mansion would pass to Jack. The thought made him almost unbearably sad, even though his grandmother had only a few months ago celebrated her ninety-seventh birthday, and Jack himself had never expected to see forty.

"Hey, Birthday Boy."

Jack turned, smiling, and raised his champagne flute. "Hi, Jule."

"I wondered where you were." Jule Gardino, Jack's oldest friend and sometime legal advisor, ducked as he passed through the doorway. "Hey, nice night, huh?" He propped his elbows on the balcony beside his friend, blinking at the muzzy violet light, then pointed in mock excitement. "'Peter! I can see your house from here!'"

Jack laughed: the tag line from an old joke. "Here—"

He grabbed the bottle of Veuve Clicquot from beside his feet and handed it to Jule. Jule swigged from it, wiped his mouth, and took another gulp. "Whooee! Thanks—"

"Everyone behaving downstairs?"

Jule shrugged. "Leonard dropped trou and showed Grandmother his *apadravya* again."

Jack took the bottle from Jule and refilled his glass, laughing. "I guess I better get back down, then."

"No hurry." Jule draped an arm around his friend and stared out across the sloping lawn. "Mmm. Daffodils?"

Jack nodded, gesturing with his champagne. "And hyacinths. And lilacs. And the apple trees are budding."

"Wow. Amazing."

Below them stretched the grounds of the little estate, two acres upon a hillside overlooking Untermeyer Park and, below that, the Hudson. The park had years before fallen into decay. It was haunted now by crack dealers and *fellahin*, teenage runaways who drifted to the City, then north, until they reached the no-man's-land that was Yonkers and the southernmost reaches of Westchester County. From Jack's balcony at Lazyland one could glimpse the ruins of other estates, mansions that had belonged to Van Cortlandts and Van Rensselaers and McGuires and Phillipses. All had been abandoned. Those who could afford to had fled. Those who could not had been driven out by the gangs, by the drive-by shootings and random bombings, the murderous attacks of *fellahin* and cranks; or by the sight of mange-ridden coyotes staggering north from the wastelands of the Bronx, and south from the woodlands bordering the Saw Mill River and the Sprain Brook parkways. Two months ago the house nearest to Lazyland, a shingle-style Victorian whose elaborate dormers could once be glimpsed through the new green of oaks and tulip trees, had been forsaken by the maharani who bought it only five years earlier. Jack had watched her go, and the sad small parade of sons and housekeepers who followed the stooped middle-aged woman in her yellow sari and high-heeled sandals. The men got into their cars, the housekeepers clambered into three rented Ryder trucks; the maharani and her eldest son and his wife stood for several minutes staring up at the gilded silhouette of their manse *cliquant*. Then they left, for Canada, Jack thought. Two nights later their house burned to the ground; only one fire truck responded to the emergency call. Now Lazyland stood alone upon the hill.

Jack sighed, poured the last bit of champagne into Jule's glass. All about them trees rustled in the gentle night wind from the river. The air was fragrant from the flowers blooming in the grass below; but there was also the fishy reek of the Hudson, the charred damp smell of all those other ruined mansions, and the omnipresent scent of marijuana smoke and carrion from the *fellahin* encampments. Overhead a few faint stars shone in the deepening violet sky; far below the Hudson stretched, a swath of black and indigo flecked here and there with gold.

"Nice," Jule murmured, sipping his champagne. He looked at his old friend and nodded. "You oughta do this more often, Jackie. Get out more. Or have people in."

Jack smiled sadly. "All the people I used to have in are dead, Julie." He turned and leaned against the balcony rail, stared for several minutes at the twilight. "Do you remember my fourteenth birthday?" he finally asked. "At Saint Bartholomew's?"

"Was that when you and Leonard—"

"*That* was sixteen. No—don't you remember? The world was supposed to end," Jack said wistfully, turning to stare down at the unruly patches of daffodils that were like a yellow mist settled onto the lawn. "A two-headed cow was born somewhere, Mahopac, I think, and there was something about a baby born with a caul. The *Herald Statesmen* had a big article on it, about how everyone thought the world was going to end on Good Friday. March 26, 1971. And that was my birthday."

Jule shook his head. "I don't remember. Did we do something? I mean, was there a party?"

"No." Jack tapped the rim of his glass against his lower lip. "That was the whole thing. It was this beautiful, beautiful day—like today, actually—and I was with you and a couple of other people. Don't you remember? We all had to go to afternoon Mass in the auditorium, because it was Good Friday, and afterward there was like fifteen minutes before the next period started, and so we sat outside on that little hill overlooking the lake. *Everyone* was there, I mean, practically the whole school was outside, and we all just lay on the grass. I don't really remember anything about it at all, except that someone gave me a Hostess cupcake with a candle in it and we were talking about how the world might end.

"But I thought, *You know, this is it—I am perfectly happy. Right now, on my birthday, on this beautiful day with my friends—if this really is the end of the world, I don't even care, because right now I am perfectly happy.*"

"And was it?" asked Jule. "The end of the world?"

Jack smiled. "No." He set his empty champagne flute on the broad railing and turned to leave. "And I've always been kind of sorry."

The darkened glass of the doorway threw back his reflection. Jack caught a glimpse of Jule gazing at him fondly. He dipped his head slightly in embarrassment, knowing what his friend saw: a tall spare figure, with the Finnegans' ridiculously patrician Celtic profile—straight sharp nose, a strong chin deeply cleft (legacy of a childhood bicycle accident), high broad forehead with its sweep of blond hair yielding at last to grey—so at odds with the melancholy cast of his pale blue eyes and his boyish, rather mannered, swagger. Those big knotted hands jammed into his pockets, his head always tipped a little to one side, as though he were listening for something. Larksong, a distant train, the dying strains of "Telstar": one of those dreamy sounds that would keep Jack long awake when he and Jule and Leonard were all boys of a summer night, lying side by side by side in a rope hammock beneath the stars.

Now there was nothing so nostalgic as that to hear. Only a far-off drone, the weary exodus of buses and automobiles from the City, the sound of broken glass echoing up from the *fellahin*'s thickets of sumac and brambles. Jule smiled reassuringly, as though Jack had said something that needed a reply. Then he set his empty glass upon the balcony and started back inside. He didn't notice that Jack had taken a step back out onto the balcony, and was standing there with his head cocked. Jule ran right into him.

"*Owff!* Christ, Jack—"

"Listen."

Jack stood, frozen. One hand clutched the jamb above him; the other bunched into a fist inside his pocket. "Did you hear that?"

Jule shook his head. "Uh-uh."

"Shhhh! Listen!"

Jack strode back out to the railing. Dimly he was aware that something was wrong; the way he had once felt when there had been a fire in his dorm at Georgetown, and he had to be carried from his room in a smoke-thick stupor. An abrupt tingling in his hands and face, a sort of psychic shiver. As though every nerve in his body was firing, trying desperately to send him terrible news, and for this one split second he had not yet heard.

There it was again. From somewhere down the hill toward the river, a girl's voice, screaming.

"Oh, shit." Jule groaned. "Here we go again. I'll call 911—"

Jack shook his head. "No—"

His mouth was dry, his eyes unfocused. *What's wrong, there's something wrong—*

"No, Jule. Wait. There! It's—"

And now Jule felt it, too, Jack could tell. His friend stood in the doorway with his head thrown back, eyes rapt as he stared up at the sky. From down the hillside came a man's voice—

"Fuck! Jesus fuck—"

—and a sudden burst of sirens: home systems, car alarms, car horns, police sirens, a whooping shriek from Saint Joseph's Hospital. Voices everywhere, from every direction: like the wind rising before a hurricane, an approaching storm of wings. Jack thought of the night Harvey Milk was murdered: it had been like this, all of San Francisco yelling and guns being fired, car horns and heaved bricks and breaking glass.

But now there was no outrage; not even fear. Just amazement, a sort of horrified disbelief. And, after a moment, distant explosions—first one, then another, and still more, like a string of demonic firecrackers; and then flames streaming upward from electrical power plants in Bergen County. Jack clutched the rail and stared out across the river. For an instant he saw burning towers, transformers and blazing pylons like lightning poised between sky and the familiar pointillist array of lights upon the Palisades.

Then the lights went out: everywhere.

"Jule! *Jule*—"

From downstairs, Jack heard Jule's wife Emma cry out for her husband, and Leonard's fey tones abruptly gave way to a howl.

"Jack? Where the hell *are* you? *Jackie!"*

Jack Finnegan said nothing; only stood, and stared. On the western horizon, above the Hudson and the dark shelf of rock that was the New Jersey Palisades, the sky was erupting into flame. An immense molten globe, brighter and huger than anything he could have imagined. And Jack could imagine *many* things. Nuclear disaster, gas explosion, stray weather balloons, terrorists bombing Bear Mountain, 757s shot from the sky like geese, forest fires, mustard gas—

This was none of these. This was—

Jack shook his head, out of breath, heart pounding though he hadn't stirred. This was—

What? A star? A nova? The Northern Lights? But Jack had seen auroras, boreal and hyperboreal; auroras and Saint Elmo's fire and the magnetic image of his father's brain, the tumor pulsing there like a candle flame.

But not this, never this! a rapture of gold and black and emerald green, sheets of flame leaping from the cliffs as the vast globe grew, flattening as it stretched across the horizon, as though it were an inconceivably huge and swollen camber being crushed by an even huger hand. Within twenty-four hours the news would start to drift in, garnered from shouted conversation with *fellahin* and Jack's ancient shortwave radio: the terrible confluence of a solar storm and the collapse of the Antarctic ice shelf, the atmosphere ignited like grease—

—but now Jack only stared at the spectral sky, the coruscating heavens, and knew it had come at last. What they had all been waiting for, consciously or not— the whip coming down, the other shoe dropping, the sound of sixteen hooves beating measured and far off upon the tarmac, still distant but not for long. The sound of something chipping at the earth as though it were an egg; the sound of the fabric of the century being torn.

The world had changed, changed utterly, and was

no longer his, or humanity's. It had been occupied, they had all had been seized, were all possessed, strange particles charged by what loomed above them; all now shivering beneath the severed heavens; all now aglow, and glimmering.

CHAPTER TWO

1999: Natal Astrology

Actually, it would have been easier for Jack Chanvers Finnegan if the world had ended that night at Lazyland. And so, of course, it did not.

That was a bad year, 1997. The tenth anniversary of his acquiring the AIDS virus—and he thought of it as an acquisition, like a bad investment. Say, a forged Artaud notebook, or a painting mistakenly attributed to Thomas Cole—the year his dear friend and former lover Eric died. Nineteen ninety-seven was the year his grandmother fell and broke her hip. It was the year Jack developed full-blown AIDS; the year the glimmering began.

After that first night at the end of March, it was weeks before things returned to normal. Though, in fact, "normal" was gone forever, at least for people like Jack; in other places, of course, they'd never gotten word that normal had ever been there at all.

Miles above the earth, the filmy ozone veil had in places deteriorated from three millimeters in thickness to less than one. The chlorine-based chemicals that for decades had been kept in check by this, now floated like so many toxic feathers into the uppermost levels of the atmosphere. There they fell victim to devouring ultraviolet radiation, which rent the CFCs into chlorine atoms. These free radicals could each destroy a hundred thousand ozone molecules, momentarily linking to form chlorine monoxide before flying apart again and continuing their rampage. Added to the atmospheric stew were independent molecules released from BRITE, as well as the ceaseless solar rain no longer deflected by a fragile ozone parasol.

One relatively benign side effect of all this was the disruption of television broadcasts worldwide. What had once been the stuff of tight-lipped television news reports—food riots, looting, cannibalism in Laos and Kansas City, Bible school vans set on fire by anti-Fundamentalists, killing hail in Orange County, starving migrant workers storming a locked-gate enclave in the Napa Valley, war between the Koreas, children dying of dysentery and cholera in Minneapolis, Amarillo, London—became stories repeated in line at Delmonico's and the Grand Union, where Jack walked in generally fruitless efforts to get fresh vegetables, bread, dented cans of tomatoes and chili, the *New York Times*. Eventually power was restored, but never for long; and so at Lazyland they grew accustomed to eating by lamp-light, or in the dark. When the power did come on, when the television managed to lock onto a station broadcasting news from a studio that looked reassur-ingly like normal life, with reruns and talk shows and music videos that belied the coruscating heavens out-side, they might forget to eat at all.

"One gets used to anything, even dying," Jack's grandmother Keeley used to say when he was growing up. He recalled that now, a *lot*: when he was thinking of complaining about a ConEd bill delivered by moped courier (an electric bill! when waking to find the power on was like winning at fucking Lotto!), or about the bonfires that could be glimpsed each night from Lazyland's windows, sullen flames where the *fellahin* squatted and played their boom boxes or, when the music failed, sang hoarsely while beating upon empty metal oil drums.

Still, life went on ("That's what *life* does," Keeley

snapped at him one night, during one of Jack's sinking
spells), and Jack watched it, mostly on TV, when the
TV worked. Amazed at the compelling illusion of
canonical American Life cast there: talk shows, baseball and football games (though the cameramen
avoided crowd shots of Wrigley Field, which had been
severely damaged in the riots), reruns, and a few tentative, new episodes of the most popular sitcoms, which
Jack found himself analyzing obsessively for what they
might tell him of the world outside. Recycled advertisements were, gradually, replaced by new ones;
apparently not even intimations of apocalypse could
interfere with sales and production of Coke, Pepsi, Big
Macs, Miller beer. Jack thought of the old joke, about
what would survive a nuclear holocaust. Cockroaches
and Cher; and it seemed that there would be plenty of
junk food for them to eat. Not that Jack ever saw any
of it.

That was 1997. By 1998 he had grown accustomed
to life under wartime conditions; that was a bad year,
too. Nineteen ninety-eight was the year during which
Jack was certain that *The Gaudy Book*, after a century,
and more incarnations than the Dalai Lama, would
finally expire. And while he had never confessed it to
anyone—not even Jule, not even Grandmother
Keeley—for his entire life Jack had believed that his fate
was tied inextricably with that of his family's magazine.
If *The Gaudy Book* died, so would he.

In September, the *New York Times* had run a sad little front-page piece, a preliminary obituary embalming
The Gaudy Book in three inches of newsprint and electronic lettering. Travelers on the Infobahn (Leonard
amongst them) had chortled, seeing this as another
death spasm of The Written Word.

Still, the magazine continued to limp along. There

were a few thousand stalwart subscribers: Jack imagined them as silver-haired toffs sitting upright in deck chairs aboard the *Titanic*, *Gaudy Books* firmly in hand, reading from the Slings And Arrows feature while the band played "God Save the Queen." And there were dwindling loans from Jack's own dwindling finances, the last copper pennies from what had been one of the great fortunes of the twentieth century. Leonard had helped, too, improbable as that seemed; but then,

"It's the least he can do. The bastard." Since high school Jule had suspected Leonard of the worst of intentions, and time had proven that Jule was usually correct. "If I were you, I wouldn't have anything to do with him."

Jack tilted back in his chair. They were in the carriage house, the office of *The Gaudy Book*. "I know, I know. But . . ."

His voice trailed off. Jule snorted in annoyance: Jack had never quite gotten over an intense relationship with Leonard that had seen him through his twenties. "But nothing." Jule gazed with distaste at one of Leonard's prints, framed in silver on Jack's desk. It showed the charred carcass of an Antarctic snow petrel, now extinct. "He's gonna fuck you up again, Jackie, you know he will. Don't do it, Jackie. Don't talk to him."

Jack stared at the ceiling through half-closed eyes. After a moment he shrugged. "Well, anyway, he has this idea to help bail me out. I just want you to look over the proposals and make sure I'm not liable for anything."

He handed Jule the thick folder Leonard had sent via bike courier that morning. His friend took the package and stuck it into his knapsack, then stood to go.

"Right." Jule pushed a lock of longish greying hair from his forehead, grimaced, and tugged at his shirt collar. "God, I hate fucking court appearances. The phones are dead, so you can't call anyone, you get down to the courthouse and you're fucked 'cause the DA couldn't get a fucking message to you that the case has been dismissed. I haven't had a decent haircut in a year. Do I look like an asshole?"

Jack laughed. "You look very nice, Jule. Emma pick out your tie?"

Jule looked wounded. "No, she did not."

"I figured." Jack pointed with his pencil. "It's got something on it."

"Shit! Really?" Jule stared down in alarm.

"Ha-ha. Made you look."

Jule glared at him, then started toward the door. "Later. Don't sign anything till you hear from me."

"How long will *that* be?"

"Who fucking knows? Maybe tomorrow if the phones are up, maybe a week. See you, Jackie."

When Jack was alone again he sighed. On his desk scattered bills and manuscripts, collection notices and invitations to charity dinners formed a jagged white plain, like a field of broken ice. He picked up a small card, hand-lettered in pale blue ink on Crane's stationery.

Dr. Peter Fulbright and Ms. Anna Herrin-Fulbright
request the honor of your presence at the
1998 HARLEQUIN BALL
Proceeds to benefit
The World Wildlife Fund Genome Project

Jack tossed it into an overflowing wastebasket. It had been a decade since *The Gaudy Book* could afford a secretary, or even an ambitious high-school student, to help him in the office.

"Well." His chair thumped noisily as he leaned forward and swept the papers off his desk and into a cardboard box. "Time to re-ordure."

The office was filled with paper. Boxes and filing cabinets, wastebaskets and piles of unopened manila envelopes. A moosehead with antlers draped with ticker tape from the 1974 St. Patrick's Day Parade. Two IBM Selectric typewriters with old contracts still sitting in them; the Underwood typewriter on which Jack had learned to write. There were also several Macintosh computers that had been difficult to service even before the glimmering, and a Telex machine that occasionally sputtered to life with strange queries from readers in Bangkok or Iowa City. Leonard Thrope found it all very quaint. He had never stopped mocking Jack's refusal to invest in nascent technologies when he had the chance.

"Netscape, man! I *called* you about that! And Evans Laboratories, you were *crazy* not to go with them!"

Now, perversely, Leonard wanted to save Jack's magazine. Once Jule gave the go-ahead, he organized the special *Memento Mori* issue and its concomitant exhibition at the Whitney. It was the biggest-selling issue of *The Gaudy Book* in twenty-three years, and the most controversial show ever mounted at the museum. And, despite Jule's best efforts—he was a very good man, but a rather bad lawyer—there *were* lawsuits, as there inevitably were if Leonard Thrope was involved. These came in the wake of Leslie Harcourt's unassisted planned suicide (a ticketed event and a sellout), but Leonard handled them with his usual flair, half ringmaster, half dominatrix, and with his usual phalanx of attorneys. When the smoke cleared, there was a multicolored paper check on the breakfast table beside Jack's coffee cup, holographed blue and brown like the fragment of a morpho butterfly's wing.

$289,747.32, To Be Paid to the
Order of The Gaudy Book. Memo: Mori.

Enough money to keep the magazine afloat for perhaps another year.

"And we'll *bury* it then, Jackie!" Leonard crowed. He
leaned across the breakfast table for the powdered milk.
"But now I have to go."

Jack nodded at his friend, then started as the phone
rang on the wall behind him. "Hello?" He cleared his
throat nervously; it had been a week since the phone
lines were up. "Ah, hello?"

But of course the call was for Leonard. Three species
of Madagascan forest-dwelling frogs were to become
extinct. The last of their kind, they had fallen prey to a
fungus within the protected crystal walls of their habilab
at the Ampijeroa Forest Station. Was Mr. Thrope interested? A very rich, anonymous patron would arrange for
air transport to Mahajanga on a private Learjet supplied
with black-market fuel.

"Another job for the Angel of Death." Grandmother
Keeley regarded Leonard coldly from the other side of
the breakfast nook. "How can you stand it?"

Leonard smiled. The placebit in his front tooth
winked from ruby to gold. Jack stared at it resentfully,
wondering if *he* would be more cheerful if he could
afford implants that would pipe a steady flow of serotonin and melatonin and vitamin K into his beleaguered
body. Probably not. Wistful melancholy was Jack's
default setting, as cheerful chaos was Leonard's.

"Oh, Keeley. *Please*," said Leonard, and sipped his
coffee. Real coffee, just as the small yellow brick he
had given Grandmother was real cheese. Despite the
faint odors of Bedlam and decay that trailed after
him, Leonard was always welcome at Lazyland. He

set his coffee back on the table, and for a moment let his hand rest upon Jack's. "You *know* that I don't kill them. Ramo Resorts International does it for me. In Africa, at least. Excuse me."

He left the room to make several quick calls from his own phone, then found Jack again and kissed him.

"Now, now," said Leonard. "Don't look like that, you'll see me soon enough."

Jack smiled wanly. "I know. Thank you, Leonard, for—"

"Shhh." Leonard placed a scarred finger on Jack's lips. "Bye, Jackie."

From inside, Jack watched as Leonard slid into the limo that would take him to White Plains Airport. At the top of the winding drive the limo paused in front of Lazyland's security gates, then swept through as they swung open. Jack waited to make sure they shut securely again and returned to the kitchen. He picked up the phone to call Jule, to tell him that Leonard had come through with the check; but this time the line was dead.

Now it was almost two years later, early spring of 1999. But Jack still winced at the memory of how Leonard saved *The Gaudy Book.*

"What is it, dear?" His grandmother took another sip from her whiskey sour, put the glass back upon her side table with its collection of glass millefleurs and knitting needles.

"Hum? Oh, nothing." From the kitchen Jack could hear the comfortable rattle and clink of Larena Iverson, Lazyland's venerable housekeeper, clearing the dishes. "You know. Things. Leonard."

Grandmother Keeley scowled. "That *dwarf.*"

Contempt sharpened the word into something stealthy and menacing. In fact Leonard, while slight, was not at all dwarfish. Instead he had the supreme self-confidence and feckless daring of all those youngest sons in fairy tales—all those legendary Jacks whom John Chanvers Finnegan so painfully failed to be—joined to the lithe body of a circus acrobat and the scruples of a heroin dealer. Dark as Jack was fair, with black curly hair and hazel eyes and an intoxicating laugh, Leonard was the nimble demon who sat on his friend's shoulder whispering *Drink it! Eat it! Do it!* between glasses of vintage Taittinger and lines of bluish cocaine.

This evening Jack could have borne the diversion of listening to Leonard's advice, if only to ignore it. He had been so tired these last few days. Not mere physical exhaustion but that deeper, sadder fatigue he had glimpsed in others, those friends who had gone before him and died before their time. He had seen it over and over again. You could live for years—five, ten, nearly twelve years if you were Jack Finnegan and could afford to keep up with the drugs, if the drugs were still being manufactured; seemingly forever if you were Leonard Thrope.

But then one day it happened. You began to die. In spite of the drugs, the acupuncture therapies, the shiatsu massages and fungus teas and wave after wave of chemicals and vitamins; in spite of everything, you died. One day you were home with your geraniums and cats and a hundred bottles of medicine. The next you were in ICU with flowers brought up from that vendor in midtown who was the only person who had fresh flowers anymore. Then you were gone, and they were holding white roses at a memorial service and trying not to notice who else had a rattle in the throat and shaky hands.

And it was worse, now, of course—everything was worse. The experimental AIDS vaccine that had been given via lottery mutated into the petra virus, whose hosts were immune to HIV but died of other things. Even the drugs that worked no longer worked, because who could afford them, and the glimmering interfered with the labs producing them, and the factories that distributed them, and the doctors who no longer went to their offices because they couldn't get gas for their Mercedeses and Range Rovers.

". . . dear?"

Jack started, looked up shamefaced. "I'm sorry, Grandmother? What did you say?"

Keeley smiled sadly. "I said you looked tired, my dear. Why don't you go to bed early?"

"I think I will." Jack nodded and sank onto the couch beside her, leaning back with his eyes closed. "I don't know why I'm so tired."

His grandmother took his hand and squeezed it. She had recovered from her broken hip—miraculously, Jack thought—but it had left her more frail, dreamier, than before. Still, her grip was strong and limber as a girl's; her skin smelled of almond oil and Chanel No. 19. "I feel the same way. It's this weather—can't decide whether it's spring or winter still."

She let go his hand and reached for her drink. Her last remaining vice, along with the single cigarette she would smoke later, leaning out her bedroom window in deference to her grandson's health. Leonard brought them for her, and when he was visiting insisted on joining her when she smoked, much to Keeley's annoyance. He liked to suggest other bad habits she might enjoy.

"There's IZE; I know you can't have tried that. Or heroin—I could teach you to shoot up! I could probably get a cover feature out of it," he would say thoughtfully, watching the Japanese dirigibles make their test flights through the crimson air above the river. " 'Former Deb Now Centenarian Junkie . . .' "

Now Jack watched as Keeley drank her whiskey. "Up in Stonington they call it March Hill," she went on. Her pale blue eyes went to grey, the way they did whenever she spoke of the family's summer cottage in Maine, long since sold to developers to keep *The Gaudy Book* alive. "Every spring the obituaries come, and you read them in the paper, so many of them it seems, and the old folks say, 'Oh old Virge, you know, he didn't make it over March Hill.' "

The luster dimmed in her gaze. Jack knew she was thinking of her husband James, who twenty-six years before had not made it over March Hill. "Ah, but what am I saying? It's just the weather, Jackie. Spring snow, that's all." She patted his hand. "You go to bed now; Larena will help me later. Go on, now."

Jack yawned and draped an arm around her thin shoulders. "You sure?"

She kissed his cheek and shoved him gently. *"Go."*

He went. Behind him he heard his grandmother calling to Larena and the housekeeper's plaintive reply.

"Yes, Keeley, I am *coming."*

Jack smiled in spite of himself. He slung his hands in his pockets—it was always cold at Lazyland—and nodded as Mrs. Iverson bustled past him. He had this, at least: loving grandmother and faithful retainer, guarding him in his castle from the storm outside. In the middle of the entry room he paused, listening to make sure Mrs. Iverson had not fallen. Her health was more precarious than Keeley's, though at eighty-nine Larena was a full decade younger. Then he walked to the broad curving staircase.

At its foot he paused. To one side of the stairs

loomed Lazyland's grandfather clock. *The* grandfather clock, so-called to distinguish it from the dozens and dozens of other clocks that Jack's grandfather James Finnegan had collected. Grandmother clocks and case clocks, gallery clocks and shelf clocks, cottage clocks and tourbillion watches. A clock with a white mouse that ran down its side when it struck one. A gold and velvet-encrusted clock that had been made for the Shah of Turkey. An Athenian water clock. They filled the house not with staccato ticking but with a gentle undercurrent of sound like waves upon a beach. Jack usually did not notice them at all, any more than he noticed the sound of his own breathing or the even beating of his heart.

But it was difficult to ignore the huge grandfather clock, especially if you were standing at the foot of the stairs. James Finnegan used to joke that he would like to be buried in it. In fact it would have swallowed him, with room for his Irish setter Fergus, too. The clock dated from the early nineteenth century, but its face had come from an eighteenth-century astronomical clock he had found in a wooden box of oddments purchased at Christie's in 1937. The main dial had dragon hands to tell the hour, tiny golden salamanders on the twelve concentric hour-position dials, sun and moon effigies, moonballs, indicators to indicate the hours of light and darkness, the month and day and year, mean and solar time, and a Julian perpetual calendar.

There was also, just beneath the clockface, a holy-water font that had been in the same box. Jack's grandfather (with absolutely no evidence whatsoever, save that manufactured by a sentimental nature; he was a famous weeper at weddings) decided the clockface had come from the High Court Monastery in Vienna during the reign of Empress Maria Theresa. Sadly, the immense clock itself had not worked for some years now. Jack's best efforts to keep Lazyland's clocks running could not duplicate the love that James Finnegan had lavished upon them. Their gears rusted, their levers warped, without his nimble, nicotine-stained fingers to soothe them.

The font was quite old, fourteenth- or fifteenth-century Italian, of very fine blue-glazed porcelain aswarm with adipose cherubim and small flowers like violets. When his grandfather was alive, it was always filled with holy water from Sacred Heart up on Broadway. Whenever he visited Jack would take some and flick it onto his forehead; not from any sense of spiritual devotion but because it was such a heady novelty, to be in a *house* that had holy water. Back then Lazyland was always filled with priests, their shouting laughter from his grandfather's study and their marvelous smell, frankincense and cigarette smoke and Irish whiskey, the crisp retort of their street shoes on the highly polished wooden floors. Whatever private sorrows and torments they endured, they had never shown Jack or his brothers anything but kindness and how to throw a football so it soared.

But then they had failed to save his grandfather during his brief final illness. After that there were no more priests at Lazyland, except for old blind Father Warren. Grandmother Keeley drove them away, Jack's mother said. Jack always thought of the picture of Christ driving the moneylenders from the Temple: Grandmother wielding a cat-o'-nine-tails, as myriad black-clad figures fled out onto North Broadway.

So, no more holy water. For years a fine film of dust had clung to the ancient porcelain, and Jack had been able to invoke the ghost of a scent from his childhood. Now even that was gone. Still, he couldn't resist probing the font with a fingertip.

Nothing, of course. He smiled wryly and began the long ascent up curving staircases to his room on the third floor.

For most of his life he'd taken those stairs at a run. A habit carried over from childhood, when he and his brothers and cousins would race up the first set of broad golden oak steps, kept polished to a near-fatal slickness by Mrs. Iverson, and then continue in a sort of exhilarated terror up the second, darker, narrower curved stair, like the innermost chamber of a nautilus. A twelve-point elk shot by Jack's father was mounted high above these steps, its glass eyes sanguine with the glimmering's reflected glow. As he approached the third-floor landing he felt the same primal dread that had gripped him as a boy: that huge grey muzzle with its blackened lips, the long shadows of the elk's tines, like dead tree limbs. Jack shuddered, heart hammering and chest tight from the effort of climbing, and took the last few steps two at a time.

His bedroom door hung open. He bumped against it, staggered to his bed, and collapsed, one hand automatically switching the light on the nightstand as the other grabbed his inhaler. He gave himself two jolts of his asthma medication, then pulled the drawer open and scrabbled amongst his stockpile of bottles until he found the alprazolam. He took one pill, swallowing it dry, and flung himself back upon his pillow.

After a minute the inhaler began to take effect. He breathed slowly, deeply, then opened the nightstand again and took out a bottle of over-the-counter cold medicine from Emma's private stash—she had a huge closet full of drugs she'd been hoarding since the glimmering began. Emma had told him to use this instead of sleeping pills, and so he swallowed two capsules, chasing them with the dregs from last night's water glass.

Too late he wondered if this perhaps had been a mistake, one of those badly mixed pharmaceutical cocktails that would send him to Saint Joseph's in the middle of the night. But within fifteen or twenty minutes he felt better. He could breathe again; soon the alprazolam would calm him. Maybe he was just sick (*of course* he was sick! he could hear Leonard shrieking); maybe he just had a cold. Without moving from the bed he nudged his shoes off and heard them drop onto the worn old oriental rug. He sighed and yawned, stretching luxuriously. The yellow light from his bedside lamp gave everything a sweetly nostalgic look: burnishing the dark arabesques of the walnut sleigh bed, showing off the cobwebs and dust filigreeing the old Indian headdress hanging on the far wall. More than a few of its regal feathers had been purloined over the years by Jack and his brothers and cousins, to be used for quill pens and darts. Other than that, nothing much had changed.

It had been his father's childhood bedroom, the room where Jack had always slept during childhood visits, and it was his room now. A small tucked-in spot on the third floor, catty-corner to the airy nursery attic and the other bedroom, the one where his cousins used to sleep. The walls held a framed picture of dogs playing poker, an exquisite black-and-white print of one of Leonard's flower studies, a photo of Jack's aunt Mary Anne, who went to California in 1967 and disappeared, a painting by the San Francisco artist/activist Martin Dionysos, who had briefly been Leonard's lover. Beside the window hung a spavined pair of wooden snowshoes. The floor still bore round scorched scars like bullet holes, where Jack and his brothers lit Black Cats on the Fourth of July.

Now it was March. Outside the wind railed at the eaves. Even with the two old Hudson Bay blankets pulled up to his chin, and a nearly new down comforter (his Christmas present from Jule and Emma), Jack felt cold—Lazyland was famously uninsulated. As boys, he and Jule and Leonard had sat in this same room and watched snow sift through the walls, covering the floor like fine white silk. Things were no different tonight, save that he was alone.

Once again he yawned, reached for the tipsy stack of magazines and manuscripts that held his bedside reading. No matter that the written word was dead (Leonard and the other mori artists had held its funeral at the Cathedral of Saint John the Divine, where copies of *The Gaudy Book*, *The New Yorker*, and the *Paris Review* were ignited within a brazier, their ashes dispersed in the adjoining cemetery); hard-copy submissions for *The Gaudy Book* continued to arrive whenever the mail got through. Jack tried to draw solace from them—"the claustrophobic, fascistic tyranny of the written word," some HARDWIRED wag had called it—but it was difficult. He recalled his grandfather railing, "Don't they teach these kids to *read* anymore?"

But of course now they *didn't*. After all these centuries, children finally had shaken off the yoke of inauspicious words and replaced it with whatever it was they did with their goggles and retinal implants and drugs, so many drugs even Leonard couldn't keep up with them. Jack preferred not to know. Jack preferred to hide within the failing fastness of Lazyland and muddle through his manuscripts, waiting to die.

Which it didn't seem he was to do this evening. The alprazolam kicked in, its sedative effect boosted by antihistamine. He felt a pleasantly perverse sensation of febrile drowsiness. Emma, who had done time as a freelance chemist working with local motorcycle gangs before attending medical school and becoming a neurosurgeon, had explained to him once how the drug worked.

"These gates in your brain, the gates are on the neuronal membranes, and the Xanax, I mean the alprazolam, it closes the gate on one of these neuronal channels, and that causes a, a hyperpolarization of the postsynaptic neuron. So *that* neuron *doesn't* fire, d'you see?"

Emma got very excited, talking about how psychotropic drugs worked; especially since Emma and Jule's daughter, Rachel, had been killed by a drunk driver three years before. It was like listening to a recovering addict rave about Narc-Anon. "And all across your *entire brain*, that particular neuron doesn't fire—it's like a pinball game, think of it like a pinball game: it's all about gates, gates opening and closing, so only certain balls can get through, only certain *perceptions* get through . . ."

Right now Jack felt as though all the balls were at rest. He had a disturbing momentary glimpse of them as eyeballs, the reflected sheen of falling snow upon their moist curves; but then that, too, faded. He dropped the unread manuscript upon the nightstand and within minutes was asleep.

Much later he awoke. A sound had disturbed him, but he waited to open his eyes, uncertain if he was asleep or dreaming. His various antidepressant and antianxiety drugs had an odd side effect on Jack. They made him feel curiously detached from his dreams, the emotions he experienced while asleep weirdly inappropriate, almost fetishistic, so that he would find himself being aroused to orgasm by the sight of a stone, or moved to tears by the smell of lighter fluid. Sometimes these bizarre emotions would carry over into his first waking moments. So Jack had learned to lie in bed and purge his mind of whatever strange fragments it had acquired during the night.

He was sure that he had heard something. The wind, maybe, nudging around the chimneys. He had almost drifted back to sleep when he heard it again and was shocked to full wakefulness, as though someone had yanked the covers from him.

It was a flute. No, not a flute. Something more primitive, a wooden instrument like a recorder or panpipe. He could hear the faint intake of breath between the notes, and the notes themselves, rich and plangent and somehow *solid* in a way that other sounds were not, rising into the air like bubbles of earth. The tune was simple, almost childish—four notes played over and over again, with a sweet refrain.

Yet for all its simplicity there was something terrifying in the music. It was like a recessional, like the subdued yet ominous tolling of a bell sounded at the end of the Latin Mass. With a muffled cry Jack sat bolt upright in bed, his heart pounding.

The room was still. The sound of wind had died, and the rattling gutters; but the piping music went on. Jack snatched at the bedclothes. The air was so cold he could feel his lungs tighten; he grabbed for his inhaler and sucked at it gratefully. After a minute or two his breathing eased. He shut his eyes and tried to slow his heartbeat, but it was keeping pace with those four notes—

Ba *dum* ba dum, ba *dum* ba dum . . .

He opened his eyes: nothing. Whatever light there was seemed to come from the veil of snow covering the floor, and from the wide many-paned window overlooking the lawn. As he stared the window shuddered,

though there was still no wind. The sound of the
recorder grew louder, as though whoever was playing it
was moving slowly, oh so slowly, and with each step
drew nearer to the house.

"Shit." Jack swore beneath his breath, shivering. He
had had dreams like this: waking dreams, walking
dreams. All his life he had been plagued by nightmares.
But there was no comfort knowing that, because with
dreams there came dream logic, inexorable and dreadful. And so he found himself sliding from bed and walking to the window.

Beneath his bare feet the snow was dry and fine as
dust. As he walked it moved in slow eddies, like breeze-
blown sand. The window's pallid glow grew brighter,
even as the music grew louder. But always it was a sere
lonely music, the echo of another song like the echo of
ice booming upon the great river.

At the window he stopped. His entire body shook
with cold, so that he had to brace himself as he leaned
forward to look out.

Below him the lawn shone with a dull blue gleam.
Dead grass pierced the new snow, black spines like scattered bones or teeth. Overhead the glimmering showed
through the cloud cover: greyish waves chased by crimson flares, an occasional burst of brilliant orange. Now
and then the sloping hillside would be slashed with iri-
descence, like the glimpse of gold within a pocket, and
though the snow had stopped, the air glittered fiercely.
The piping music seemed to come from everywhere, the
way the wind sounds during a hurricane.

Jack shuddered. Dread clenched his bones like grippe.
His eyes watered from the caustic light, and there was an
acrid taste in his mouth, a smell like wet ashes. He was
backing away from the window when something on the
lawn began to move.

From the tulip trees and overgrown sumac at the bottom of the garden a figure crept. A child, maybe twelve or thirteen years old. Barefoot, shirtless, wearing only some kind of loose dark trousers and clutching something in one hand. Jack could not tell if it was a boy or girl. As it stood it raised its hands before its face. Wisps of white-blond hair fell across its eyes.

"Hey," Jack whispered. *"Hey—"*

It did not seem to notice the cold at all. It stood up very straight—unnaturally so, like a child in a wedding party. Then, with exaggerated slowness, the child began to pace across the lawn. Its feet left no mark upon the snow, and while the scraggy trees cast wavering shadows, the terrible child had none at all.

The haunting music swelled. Its echoes filled the room like water filling a sealed-off chamber, and even so the monotonous notes inundated Jack, driving out breath and blood and matter until, with a grunt, he slid forward, his hand smashing against the window.

Dull pain shot through his wrist. He cried out and found that he could breathe again. He brought his wrist to his mouth and nursed it, lifted his head to gaze outside.

On the lawn the child still marched and played its reed pipe. Beneath the poplars something else moved. Jack gasped as another figure emerged, much taller than the child; then another, and another; until there were six in all. Jack cried aloud.

"Holy Christ."

They were men; they had once been men. Tall and emaciated and naked in the snow, so thin the glimmering washed across their pale flesh like rain. Each bore within his hands a huge pair of antlers, raised so that they seemed to spring from his skull. They moved in an awkward stooping walk, shoulders hunched beneath the weight of those great horns. As Jack watched they followed the child across the lawn, until the child stopped. The six men bowed to it, each in turn. The thin piping music rose above them like smoke as they took their places, forming two rows of three with their antlers raised above them like tree limbs, and began to dance.

It was like nothing he had ever seen. A weird loping dance, the two rows moving backward and forward, heads alternately raised and bowed so that it seemed the horns must tangle and be wrenched from their skeletal hands. And yet the antlers never touched, their bodies never touched. Their feet left no sign upon the snow, and their movements made no sound. The motions were grotesquely childlike, almost crude; yet at the same time so terribly, horribly *real* that Jack felt as though he had never seen dancing before; as though this was dancing, this was *The Dance* from which all others had been wrung. The music of the reed pipe spiraled and wailed, the child stood as though frozen; the hornéd men moved back and forth like the shuttles of a loom. Above them the antlers curved like the spires of some unearthly cathedral. And like light falling from a cathedral window the flesh began to fall from their bodies, in small bright blades of gold and green and red, until only their bones remained, unearthly white and unconquerable, moving across the snow.

In his room Jack watched. Terror and beauty ravaged him; he could feel the boom of blood in his head and a softer throbbing in his chest, as though the child played him as nimbly as its flute. Still they danced, the hornéd men, with steps careful and measured as automatons'. They might have been part of some infernal timepiece ringing the changes.

But then, very slowly, he became aware that the

music was diminishing—he sensed rather than heard it, like warmth stealing back into his hands. He leaned forward, blinking as at an unaccustomed brilliance, and saw that the dancers had paused. The child bowed its head. Then, as slowly as it had arrived, the child turned and retraced its steps, pacing back across the lawn. When it reached the shadows of the trees the skeletal dancers followed. They moved now with a more somber grace, no longer rocking back and forth beneath the weight of those heavy racks. Indeed it seemed that the antlers had somehow grown and become part of them. All their bestial power had fused with the frail bones of men. As they walked light clung to them, light falling from the sky or rising like mist from the ground. When they reached the shadows of the tulip poplars they were clothed in it. They did not turn their heads or in any way look back to where Jack sat and watched them. And yet he knew that *he* was the reason they had come here: vision or dementia or the exalted remnant of a dream, they had come for him.

The last shining form dipped its head beneath the branches and disappeared. The music died away. Alone in his room stood Jack, robed in light and burning with fever, his pale eyes huge and glittering with the glory and horror of what he had seen. He was still there next morning when the housekeeper came to see what had kept him from breakfast.

"Jack? What is it, Jack? Are you sick? Good Lord, he isn't—"

And he shook his head, unable to tell her No he was not dead nor even sick, but burning, burning, burning.

CHAPTER THREE

Trip Takes a Fall

He would die at Hell Head.

Trip Marlowe knew that was how the obituaries would begin. Never mind that no one from away knew that Hell Head was where you always went to die, if you were from Moody's Island. For sure it was where you went to die if you were a Marlowe. It was where his father had gone when Trip was six years old, and blown his brains out with a thirty-aught-six; where Trip's mother had gone a year later, to dive into the whirlpool and never be found. Hell Head was where the island children went on Halloween, daring each other to stare into the black water at low tide and glimpse the bones there, the bones he had never seen but they were there, for sure Trip knew they were there. Trip Marlowe knew all about bones.

He was twenty-two years old and the Voice of The Last Generation. That was what some flack on Radium had called him, after Trip's first album—the one that originally came out on Mustard Seed, the one that got him six Dove Awards and an Emmy and his face on a zillion home pages and the cover of *OUR* magazine— was bought and rereleased by a Xian subsidiary of GFI Worldwide early in 1998. The album was called *LIVE FROM GOLGOTHA*. Trip stole the title from an old banned book in the hard stacks at Olive Mount Bible College. His best friend, Jerry Disney, had found the novel; God only knew how it got there. Trip never read the book—Trip didn't read, except for the Bible and furtively hidden copies of Matrix comics—but he liked the title, and he knew how to use it. Even as a child on Moody's Island, where he sang in the choir at the Fisher of Men First Harbor Church, he had always possessed what the people at GFI called marketing savvy. For instance, it had been Trip's idea that alone of all the children in the choir, he should wear red when they performed.

"It'll make me stand out." He hoped he didn't sound as nervous as he felt: he had already dyed his white choir robe Deep Scarlet, using a packet of Rit Dye from the Moody's Island Beach Store. "You know. When I sing."

"You *already* stand out," said John Drinkwater. He was the choir director. A skinned stick of a man who wouldn't allow his own kids to use the computer in the broken-down trailer that was the island school. But he sounded amused. "But sure, okay. We'll try it."

It was August the first time Trip wore the red robe. They were singing at the Grace Fellowship Baptist Church over to Jonesport, not a long drive; otherwise, probably he would've passed out from the smell of Rit Dye. Deep Scarlet came off on Trip's hands, his skinny freckled arms and chest, and even his face. But it was so hot inside the church, the choir's singing so pure and exalted, that no one at Grace Fellowship even noticed.

"Probably they just thought your face was all red and you were goin' t' pass out." Jerry Disney fanned himself with his own crumpled-up robe and stared out the bus window at rows of boarded-up gas stations and abandoned shopping malls. "I sure thought I was."

After that he always wore the red robe. When Trip grew out of it, John Drinkwater had his wife sew him another one, with fabric that came all the way from Bangor. And when Trip grew out of *that* one, John

Drinkwater had his wife make him a dozen, in various sizes, "So's you won't ever have to be without."

He'd been Tripp Marlowe then, a golden star in heaven's crown, for sure the star of the Fisher of Men Children's Choir. Summer and winter they traveled inland, to Bangor and Caribou and Presque Isle, and up coastal Route One to Calais, which was practically Canada. Twenty-four children and their chaperones crammed into the church's old blue school bus, where the stench of ethanol vied with that of squashed peanut-butter sandwiches and the Dignam twins, who always had to go to the bathroom. John Drinkwater sat in front behind Mrs. Spruce, who drove, and even after they sang themselves hoarse at church suppers and Christian Coalition fund-raisers, country fairs and weddings, funerals and baptisms; even at twelve midnight, when the littlest children were so tired they lay across their mothers' laps and wailed, John Drinkwater made them sing some more.

> *Jesus is my friend and always will be*
> *Jesus walks beside me every day . . .*

Exhausted as they were, the children sounded beautiful. Outside might be nothing but ravaged forests left by bankrupt paper companies, or the potato-field waste-land of Aroostook County; but inside the bus it was heaven. Even the poor bleary-eyed mothers would take a break from rummaging in paper sacks full of molder-ing apples and bottles of Coke, to lean back in their seats and smile and clap in time.

> *Don't expect me to cry*
> *For I will never die!*
> *Jesus is the sun who shines for me . . .*

When the hymn was done they kissed the children, smoothing the boys' buzz-cut hair and adjusting the girls' dirty pink headbands, and told everyone how wonderful they sounded.

"Like angels, now then, hush, let's try and get some sleep."

That was what the mothers said as the bus jounced over the bridge to Verona Island, or as it sat with the engine turned off in Bath, waiting for the foot traffic at the ironworks to clear.

But later, when the children finally passed out in their mothers' laps, those chaperones who were still awake would turn to each other and nod toward the back of the bus where Trip always sat.

"Isn't he cunnin', that one? When he sings! If only his mother could've heard him. He could be a star, you know. He really could be a star."

It was Trip they spoke of, of course. He heard them and tried not to be proud, and it wasn't so hard, because he didn't *feel* proud, not really. It wasn't like the way he felt at school, when someone told him he'd done a good job with an assignment he'd spent too many hours trying to understand. Because he *worked* at that, he *worked* at school, even though he knew it was useless. He was smart, he knew that, he wasn't like the Dignams. But reading was difficult for him, and there never seemed to be a point to it.

So he just kept on singing. When he outgrew the children's choir he joined the church's praise and worship band, part of the youth group for teenagers. He was seventeen when John Drinkwater told him he might be able to go to college on a music scholarship. That was before John Drinkwater realized that there wasn't anywhere Trip Marlowe *couldn't* go. Not with a face like that; not with a voice like that.

Because if you were to take a cruse made of ice and drop it, the sound it would make, the sound of cold and crystal shattering—that would be the sound of the children's choir. That would be their voices.

But the glitter in the air, the arcs of light and color and the stunned silence thereafter—*that* would be Trip Marlowe.

He had thought he would never fall. And, falling, he had never for an instant believed that he might crash. That the scattered pieces would be *him*. That there'd be no one there to catch him, no one there to help him gather what was left. Which was just Trip Marlowe, another little broken idol.

Once, there would have been someone there to hear him. John Drinkwater, at least, or Jerry Disney, or, for a few days, the blond girl. Now there was no one. When an angel falls, John Drinkwater said, it falls alone. Nobody but Satan hears it hit the ground.

Only of course that wasn't true. Because Trip was sure that everyone on God's green earth would hear the explosion when he crashed and burned. He'd been the first Xian artist to receive full media superstar treatment, with his "Don't Forsake Me" video in constant rotation worldwide, an interactive disc, global concert tours, and Trip's face on the cover of every mainstream magazine and gracing computer screens from Salt Lake City to Beijing. It was the face that did it, of course. Equal parts choirboy and catamite, his strong jaw offset by that full lower lip with its hint of a pout, those slanted electric blue eyes; the faint golden stubble on his chin and his yellow hair, like the sky streaked with emerald and bronze, the simple gold chain and cross nestled against his chest. John Drinkwater had a fit when he saw Trip's dyed hair. Peter Paul Joseph, the president of Mustard Seed Music, only nodded, his thick face impassive but his eyes sharp and bright as needles.

"The kids'll eat it up," he drawled, and gave Trip a look that made the singer's flesh prickle. "Hope you're ready for it, Trip." Then, to John Drinkwater, "He can paint his face blue for all I care. But not the dancing. None of that jumping into the crowd stuff. You understand, Trip—gets out of hand. You could get hurt."

To make sure it didn't get out of hand, Peter Paul Joseph hired a manager for the band. By then they were calling themselves Stand in the Temple. The manager was Lucius Chappell, a lean young man only four years older than Trip, with lupine eyes and a Maltese cross tattooed onto his shaved skull. He had put himself through law school managing another Xian group, and eventually signed them to a major label. When Trip and the other band members saw their morality clause, it was Lucius who had drawn it up, and Lucius who presented the signed document with a flourish to Peter Paul Joseph.

"Let the games begin," Lucius said. His smile revealed white teeth glittering with tiny silver crosses that to Trip looked like miniature gravestones.

"Damn cracker," Jerry muttered disdainfully; but Lucius just laughed.

At Trip's insistence, John Drinkwater stayed with the band. There was a pretense of giving him duties, like checking everyone into hotels. But really he was just Trip's moral support, his last threadbare lifeline to Moody's Island. It was Lucius who made the arrangements, Lucius who knew how to get fuel for the tour bus and food for the crew, Lucius who somehow got through to booking agents and reporters and on-line magazines when the phone lines were down and the rest of the world seemed paralyzed.

"I got connections," Lucius would say, raising his eyebrows and grinning to show his cruciferous enamel.

He did, too. Not just with an extensive network of Christian compounds with impressive stockpiles of ethanol, petroleum, and advanced information technologies; but with radical Xian groups like Blood on the Door, which targeted women who had had abortions, and the Blue Antelope Fellowship, youthful preservationists whose firebombings had already killed twenty-three legislators who opposed various endangered species acts. In fact, Lucius's outside interests took up much of the time in which he should have been monitoring Stand in the Temple. Refueling stops provided opportunities to talk to the pro-life radicals, who in some parts of the South and Northeast controlled much of the black market in firearms as well as fuel. There were cranks, too, with real metal spines protruding from their skulls alongside spiky hair, and metal chastity belts dangling from their waists and groins. Onstage Trip avoided their eyes, meth-crazed and staring, and tried to filter out their manic shrieks when Jerry struck the opening chords of a song they recognized.

It proved more difficult to avoid Blue Antelope. Radical Xian environmentalism was Chappell's pet cause, and Blue Antelope was its army. During and after performances, he arranged meetings with local members and insisted that Trip greet them. The organization's demographics were similar to those of the band's ideal audience: young, white, rebellious Christians who had co-opted the term "Xian" from their neo-pagan counterparts. Their manager even encouraged Trip to write songs inspired by Blue Antelope.

"They've got money, man!" Lucius rubbed his fingers together and leered. "*Many* talents, Trippo—not to mention God on our side."

"Uh, I'll think about it," Trip demurred, wondering

how good it would be for album and ticket sales if word got out they were writing songs for the terrorist group that had firebombed an Arizona hospital because its new temporary wing encroached upon a nesting site of the blue-throated hummingbird.

"Where does he get off with this 'our side' shit?" Jerry fumed; but Trip had other things to think about. Because, busy as he was with Blue Antelope, Lucius Chappell wasn't paying much attention to Trip's gyrations onstage.

So:

No dancin' in Anson! Trip wailed in Texas, his long arms and hands swaying above his head as he rocked back and forth in one spot onstage. *No dancing in Lansing! No waltzing in New Paltz! No moshin' in Tucson!* During each performance he'd stay resolutely in one place, at the very edge of the stage, blue eyes flaring as his hands moved, sinuous and suggestive as one of those Javanese dancers he had seen on the Great Big World Channel in a hotel outside Austin. *Wayang-wong*, their dance was called; it had impressed the singer mightily.

The band almost always stayed in Christian-run hotels or hostels. Mustard Seed wanted to ensure that their artists were not exposed to the wrong kind of people. Even more insidious was the wrong kind of video programming: since the glimmering began, television had become a sort of deranged *pachinko* game.

Usually, Trip wouldn't be able to pick up any stations at all. Other times he'd find himself watching local news, and the fat friendly weatherman would suddenly be displaced by heaving thighs and breasts, mass atrocities in Nigeria, entire city blocks evacuated because of abandoned cars, a reasoned discussion of filmed suicide by a panel of mori artists.

"Shoot. *Talking*." Jerry Disney shook his head in disgust as the blurred image of a mass grave abruptly changed. He stood and walked to the door. "I'm gonna go *eat*."

That was how Trip was left alone in a hotel room in Terre Haute. Onscreen, the mori artists disappeared. The Disaster Channel flickered in and out of sight with a quick look at a mud slide in Arizona, the heroin overdose of a singer Trip had opened for once in Boston, an unsuccessful surface-to-air missile strike against a commuter 707. Then the channel changed again. The moss-grown ruins of a pagan temple filled the screen.

". . . ritual in Probolinggo, Java," a woman's voice said softly. Trip sat on the edge of his bed and stared transfixed at the retrofitted Magnavox.

On the temple steps stood a beautiful young man wearing mask-white makeup and silks stiff with pearls and glass beads. From his head rose a crown made of tropical flowers and long blue-black feathers. It trembled as he danced, his bare feet sliding across a cracked stone platform strewn with leaves. Behind the dancer the sky rippled mauve and grass green. The narrator, her voice sibilant and hushed as a child's, recited in perfect, Oxford-accented English:

> King Klono, the wanderer from afar, has come to
> Java seeking the Princess Chandra Kirana. He has
> seen her only in his dreams and fallen in love with
> her, but his love will destroy him. He wears red to
> show his passion and gold because he is a god; but
> even gods die if they forsake their kingdoms for
> the base hungers of the world. So did the
> Victorious One, the Buddha, warn us: "Enticing
> magicians are performing; fear the beguiling, hyp-
> notizing phantoms of the Kali Yuga"—that is to

*say, the final age that is now upon us: the end of
the end.*

The end of the end. Trip was still repeating the words
to himself when the television reception blipped out
completely.

That night he wrote a song, staying up until John
Drinkwater knocked at the door to wake him the next
morning. On the bus he taught Jerry and the others the
chord changes. They even had time to practice before
that night, their very first New York appearance. The
Beacon had its own power supply, and it took the road
crew longer than usual to set up. In the green room,
Trip and the rest of the band went over the song by the
wavering light of a sodium lamp, then joined hands for
a final prayer. When Stand in the Temple finally took
the stage, Trip was shaking so hard his teeth hurt from
chattering.

"This is, uh, something I wrote last night. A song—a
song about the age we live in." His body mike gave a
weird hiss to the words, as though he was speaking from
a room that was on fire. "The End of the End."

The words were mostly nonsense, cribbed from the
bible John Drinkwater had given him long ago. *I possess
the keys of hell and death, I will give you the morning star.*
But the melody was eerie, even coming out of Jerry
Disney's poorly tuned electric guitar. Four chords echoing again and again, with Trip's voice whispering the
refrain:

"The end of the end. The end of the end . . ."

The audience went crazy for it, and finally Trip did,
too, diving into the crowd and letting them catch him,
letting them carry him, hand to hand and mouth to
mouth, girls kissing him and boys, too, their hands like
feeding starfish as he swam across them until Jerry finally

pulled him back onto the stage, killing Trip's body mike in the process. He lost his cross, too, the chain yanked from around his neck by an eager fan. Lucius bought him another the next day, elbowing amongst Russian gangsters and silver-masked drug dealers down in the jewelry district.

"Here," he said, draping the chain over Trip's head. An elaborate Abyssinian cross dangled from it, larger than the other one, at once more archaic and fashionable. "They'll *notice* this one."

That was how it started, the end of the end, the beginning of the end. When Trip started dancing, everything changed. Within a week, Stand in the Temple became the first Xian band ever to hold the Number One slot on *Billboard International*.

CHRISTIAN RIGHT's DARLING TURNS SALOME! shrieked the *New York Beacon*. XIAN STAR WALKS ON WATER! CHECK RADIUM @ Z.RO FOR PIXNFAX!

And later, when his first single was released and his picture appeared everywhere, silvery blue threads streaming from his eyes like tears, TRIP TAKES A TRIP! The holographic cover showed Trip posed as a blond Christ in Gethsemane, the image saved from smarminess or cries of heresy by the sheer intensity of Trip's expression as he gazed upward at a golden bar of light slanting down from the sky. It was an expression that was at once exultant and doomed. The music's apocalyptic mood suited those days of wrath: the web downloaded two million copies in twenty-three hours.

His audience grew. There were still the church groups bused in from suburbs and compounds and housing projects, and the mainstream alternative fans; but now there were others, too. Blocks of tickets were bought by Blue Antelope and other progressive fellowships. Trip could recognize the former by their masks. No demure white surgeons' masks or the simple black crosses favored by mainstream Christians, but colorful representations of African elephants and pandas and the blue antelope, which was the first African species to be extinguished by humans, hunted to death for dog meat. And, of course there were droves of new fans who were obviously either newly anointed Xians or just old-fashioned heretics out for a good time listening to bad news.

> *More confusions, blood transfusions*
> *The news of today will be the movies of tomorrow*
> *Cause the water's turned to blood*
> *And if you don't think so*
> *Go turn on your tub . . .*

In vain Trip argued with Xian talk-show hosts and church leaders. "It's not just *me*, you know." On-line and onscreen his boyish tenor was soft, almost pleading: if you had no visuals, you might think he was only thirteen or fourteen years old. "Some guy gets onstage and moves around, what's the big deal? It's these times, everyone's so repressed—I'm just trying to, ummm, put some tension, some *joy* into it. I mean, even if it really is the end of the world, I don't think Jesus meant for us never to have a good time."

OUR ran a sidebar—GIVE US THAT GOOD TIME RELIGION!—and sales continued to soar. During their second, fateful New York engagement, Lucius Chappell spent a lot of time speaking quietly and intently on the phone. A&R people started showing up backstage after the shows. Messages from entertainment moguls began appearing on Trip's knee top. Foot and bike couriers arrived at the Stamford Four Seasons where the band was staying, their faces hidden behind masks, glinting the metallic green of a beetle's wing or striped like yellow

jackets, black and atomic gold. The couriers bore contracts, T-shirts, vacu-sealed bags of coffee. When these
offerings were ignored, corporate flacks in ragged Xian
garb would flag Trip in the street and offer to take him to
lunch. And one afternoon Trip got a surprise visit from
Peter Paul Joseph in his Stamford hotel suite.

"We don't want to lose control of what we've got
here," Peter Paul said. He wore a plain white surgeon's
mask over his mouth and nose, something he seldom
bothered with back in Branson. "Trip. Your—our—*success*. Bringing the Word to all these kids. We're talking
about a very special situation here, and we just have to
be *very careful* about not losing control." He dabbed at
his forehead with a handkerchief.

Sprawled in his chair facing Peter Paul, Trip didn't
laugh—he was too polite for that—but he did smile,
tightly, a very controlled smile that didn't show any
teeth. "Sure," he said in his soft voice, then lowered his
head, one hand shading his eyes. "I understand."

The next day he called Agrippa Music, the subsidiary of GFI Worldwide that had distributed *LIVE
FROM GOLGOTHA*. "This is Trip Marlowe. I—I want to
talk to someone about signing."

The someone who returned his call was A&R head
Nellie Candry, who was (to put it mildly) taken aback.

"Of course we'd love to, Trip, that would be *awesome*, I mean it would be *better* than awesome, but you
have to go through the proper channels with these
things."

Trip could hear her voice catching, that tightness in
the vocal cords people got when they were nervous or
excited. He felt a quick surge of guilt. "I'm sorry. I didn't
mean to, like, go over someone's head or something—"

"No! No—" The tremor in her voice eased and Trip
relaxed, slumping down onto the hotel bed. "It's just

that—well, we should really talk to your attorney, find out the terms of your contract with Mustard Seed, things like that. I mean, I assume they control the rights to everything you've done so far—"

"Just *LIVE FROM GOLGOTHA* and the singles. I mean, we haven't actually recorded anything else—"

He heard her take a breath. "Right! We'll have to iron that out. But there's always a way around these things, Trip, so don't worry. I'll get someone in Legal on it right away. *Right away!*"

Trip didn't tell her he didn't have an attorney, except for those employed by Mustard Seed. Instead he arranged to meet her in the hotel lobby bar that evening at eleven-thirty.

"Eleven-thirty?" Nellie laughed. "In a *bar*? Isn't that kind of weird? For you, I mean."

Trip shook his head: it was one of those rare occasions when Lucius had booked them into a fancy secular hotel, and he was curious to check it out. "It's a good time for me," he said. "I don't have a show tonight. I'll see you later." And he hung up.

It actually *was* late for him. Lucius never bothered to check, but John Drinkwater enforced a strict ten o'clock curfew on those nights when Trip wasn't performing. This wasn't for reasons of propriety, so much as to ensure that Trip, a lifelong night owl, would get enough sleep. Trip's onstage shenanigans notwithstanding, John Drinkwater could no more imagine his protégé doing something truly outrageous—drinking, smoking, drugs, girls—than he could himself.

That night, John's good-night call came at 9:17. Two hours later Trip went down to the lobby. His long green-streaked hair was shaved in the front, and he had a new cruciform brand on his forehead, still raw and red in the center. He wore black denim jeans, faded to steel grey, and a lumpen wool fisherman's sweater that had been his father's. He drew the attention of the hotel's few ostentatiously dressed guests. It was impossible to read the expressions behind their masks, those artfully minimal Noh-like carapaces favored by the rich; but their conversation fell silent as he passed, and he could glimpse their eyes tracking him from inside their glittering shells.

Still, no one seemed to recognize him: that's why they were staying in the secular Stamford Four Seasons, and not a church-owned place. He walked quickly, heart pounding as he glanced around for Lucius or John Drinkwater. But the lobby was nearly empty, save for uniformed bellhops and a lone woman waiting by the front doors, dark eyes regarding him suspiciously from behind her extravagant floral mask.

He had to show ID to get into the lobby bar, a roomy alcove overgrown with tropical plants. The golden retriever held by the security guard sniffed Trip apologetically, tail wagging.

"Enjoy your evening," the guard said, and waved him past.

Just inside the lounge a discreet gold-lettered sign read *For your health and safety, this area has been treated with Viconix*. Little bamboo pagodas held tiny birds, finches and weavers that chirped plaintively as Trip passed. Hidden lanterns cast a twilight glow upon the overhanging branches and sent ripples of indigo and black washing across an elaborate fountain shaped like a dragon. There was a smell of rain, of newly turned earth, and the ubiquitous vanilla scent of the Viconix enzyme.

"Trip."

He started. The voice came from behind a thicket of bamboo. When Trip peered around it he saw a youngish older woman sitting at a small glass table. She had short dark hair, very chic, and was heavily made-up: chalk white skin, eyes elaborately kohled with swirls of red and blue and yellow, mouth a crimson minnow's-curve. She wore a long-sleeved billowing silk dress, sand-colored, and a wide-brimmed straw hat. A rubber man-drill mask lay beside her wineglass. Except for the enzyme-treated gauze that lined it, exuding the smell of vanilla, the mask resembled the sort of thing kids on Moody's Island used to wear at Halloween. At the woman's side sat a very thin blond girl who would not meet Trip's gaze.

"Trip! Hi, Nellie Candry." Extending a hand gloved in topaz silk. "And this is my daughter Marzana—"

"*Marz*," the girl murmured. Trip caught a defiant glint in her eyes as she glanced up at him.

"—*Marz*, my daughter Marz. She's actually my foster daughter," Nellie went on in a conspiratorial tone, as though the girl wasn't there. "I mean, you can tell, 'cause I'm not like actually *old* enough to be her real mother. I was supposed to get *another* girl, I went over to Poland the week after the earthquake and—this is *incredible*—the other girl is *dead*, everyone at that particular orphanage was dead but *Marz*!"

Nellie leaned back in her chair and stared covetously at the girl beside her. "So I like bribed everyone I met and brought her back. Isn't that *amazing*? Not only that, she *loves* your music, and I thought, what the fuck, what's the good of being A&R if you can't do something like this, you know, bring the kid along so she can meet you. I didn't think you'd mind. Oh! *please*, Trip, have a seat, have a seat—"

He sat. Nellie was asking him something, what he wanted to drink; he gestured weakly with one hand, nodding when he heard papaya juice but still not looking at Nellie, looking only at *her*—

The blond girl. He had no idea how old she was—
fourteen? sixteen?—that was a part of him that never
had the chance to develop: girl radar, boy radar. But
she was so thin she looked younger, not childlike but
childish. Hands so long and pale and slender they
were like bundled birch twigs; a white chip of a face
with no makeup. Even her lips were pale, and her
cheeks. The tiny indentations to each side of her delicate nose looked almost surreally dark, as though they
had been daubed with black powder. A fringe of white
corn-silk hair fell across her brow. She batted at it nervously with one hand, and he saw that her nails were
bitten to the quick. On her right hand she wore a
ring, a plain thin band of dull gold. Trip couldn't tell
how tall she was. She looked tiny, and he would have
thought she really *was* a child were it not for the kingfisher flash of her eyes, oddly vigilant and twilight
blue.

"Trip? Here's your juice."

A gloved hand pushed something across the table to
him, and he took it, drank it, but tasted nothing. He
heard nothing, saw nothing except the girl staring back
at him, staring at him with such wild intensity that his
face flushed and he could feel himself growing hard, so
hard so suddenly that he moved awkwardly to hide it
and nearly spilled his drink.

"Trip? You okay?" Nellie's voice dipped in concern.
"We could do this tomorrow—"

"No—no, this is good, this is fine . . ."

If he had looked up, he would have seen a flicker of
satisfaction in Nellie Candry's dark eyes as she glanced
from Trip to the blond girl, and heard a very soft sigh as
she leaned back in her chair. Somewhere in his head a
lisping voice warned him: *fear the beguiling, hypnotizing
phantoms of the Kali Yuga . . .*

But it was too late. He was bewitched.

They talked. Rather, Nellie talked, Kabuki makeup belying her excited tone.

"You know, I was *at* Todd and Haiko's show, when all the girls were wearing these——" She held up the mandrill mask, made a face, and laughed. "I mean, talk about revolt into fucking *style*! The Surgeon General oughta give those guys a medal—you know, fashion fucking *matters*. It can *save lives*." The mask fluttered in her hand as she motioned for their waiter. "Do you have irradiated skim milk? Trip? More juice?"

Trip nodded. Ceaselessly, restlessly, after a while not even pretending to look at Nellie or pay attention: he was simply riveted by the blond girl. She sat scarcely two feet away from him, but he might have beheld her upon a television screen. She seemed that distant, that detached; that unreal. She continued to stare at him with those feral eyes, every now and then tilting her head to regard something else, a slight movement in the lush branches above them, the clatter of a dropped glass like a gunshot at another table. But mostly she just stared back at him: two enchanted children, and not a word between them spoken.

"Well, Trip," Nellie Candry said at last. Her gaze lingered on the boy. It was a look Trip might have recognized if he had seen it, a certain affinity with Lucius Chappell's avid gaze; and if he had been less moonstruck, he might have wondered, too, at the mandrill mask, the discreet tattoo of a running antelope revealed on Nellie's wrist where the silk glove cuffed above a spur of bone. "This *has* been enlightening. I guess I'll just have Legal call someone tomorrow at Mustard Seed. You said you didn't know who——"

"I'm sorry." Trip wrenched his head around, forcing himself to look at her. "I mean, probably I could get a name for you——"

"*Please*. Not to worry." Nellie's fingers curled around a blinking plastic chip: somehow the check had been taken care of, his second empty glass replaced with a full one, and all without him noticing. "This will work out fabulously. Now—"

She slid the mask over her face, immediately was transformed into a simian goblin. As she stood Trip found himself stumbling to his feet, his hand outstretched imploringly; not to say good-bye but to beg her to stay, to leave the girl at least for another moment—

"Marz, would you mind waiting for me a few minutes?" From a pocket in her loose dress Nellie pulled a phone. "I've got to send a message. Trip—"

She turned to him. The rubber mask muffled her voice. "It's been great talking to you." Her hand when he shook it was small and fine-boned. She lifted the mask so that he could see her smile. For the first time, Trip realized that the heavy makeup covered a network of scars, gashes that began beneath her eyes and extended to her jaw. Petra virus. Embarrassed and slightly horrified, he looked away as Nellie went on. "I'll touch base with you tomorrow. And Marz—right back."

Immediately he slid into her empty chair, the one nearest to the girl.

"Hey," he said.

The girl smiled tentatively. "Hi."

"So." Trip cleared his throat. "She's, like, your mother?"

The girl stared at the empty glass in front of her. Her expression clouded, and she brought a hand to her mouth, started nibbling at her thumb. After a moment she spoke again, in a sullen tone. "Yeah. She's okay, I guess." Her voice was heavily accented; it made his skin break out in goose bumps. "I am supposed to be dead, you know."

"Oh," said Trip.

He was close enough that he could smell the sweet-ish fragrance that clung to the fine white hair brushing the nape of her neck. Without thinking he took one of her hands. The other remained at her mouth, where she continued to chew her thumbnail. In the room around them Trip could hear soft voices and the sleepy twittering of the caged finches, the plink of water in the fountain. He thought that probably he should say something but had no idea what. He had practically no experience whatsoever with girls, except those heavily chaperoned at church outings; a big deal had been made of his signing a vow of celibacy along with his morality contract. Virginal as a nun at twenty-two, Trip Marlowe had never really understood what the big deal was all about.

Until now.

He squeezed the girl's hand. She didn't squeeze it back, but smiled at him with devastating sweetness. Her skin was the bluish white of skim milk, the hollow of her throat lavender-grey. When she tilted her head her eyes caught the light and glowed violet. "So," Trip said, and coughed self-consciously. "Marz. Your real name is Marzana? Is that, uh, Polish?"

She shook her head. "They called me the hyacinth girl," she said. Her voice was raspy, with a slight lisp. "So—just Marz. Okay?"

He nodded. "Sure. Listen—" He took her other hand, the thumb still damp, and held it tightly on the tabletop. "Could you—you want to do something? Like see a movie or something?"

Marz laughed. "It's kind of late—"

"I mean tomorrow. I could meet you somewhere, pick you up. John Drinkwater could come with us, from my church. So you can tell her—Nellie, your mother—"

"I don't know." The girl slipped her hands from his.

He tried to catch her gaze but she looked away, very deliberately. "Plus I just met you. I like your video, though. But yeah, okay."

He met her the next afternoon in the city, in Nellie Candry's office at Agrippa Music. He told himself he couldn't believe it was so easy. In fact it was almost the hardest thing he'd ever done. He lied to John Drinkwater and Jerry and Lucius, telling them he wanted to go to the city to visit one of the museums, the one with the dinosaurs. John was surprised but not suspicious, and instantly said no.

"By yourself? You crazy, Trip? You *never* been in the city by yourself."

"I won't walk—I'll take taxis everywhere," Trip protested, trying not to sound desperate. He'd been up all night, figuring out what he'd say. Now his heart was beating so hard he was afraid John would hear it; he was afraid John would know he'd jerked off three times already, thinking of her. "Or get me a driver like we did in Austin—"

"You want to go to the city?" Lucius raised his eyebrows. "By yourself?"

The manager looked over at John Drinkwater and shrugged. "Hey, there's always a first time, right? I turned Alabaster Jar loose in San Francisco once, turned out okay. And Trip's not like Jerry. He's not gonna get in any trouble."

He turned back to Trip. "Sure, you can go, man. I'll call Skylark Limo and get you a driver. Just—I dunno, don't flash it all around *who* you are, okay? And don't make a big deal out of it with the others. And *definitely* don't tell Mr. John Paul Tightass Joseph."

To Trip's amazement, John Drinkwater sighed and agreed. "Okay. You're a big boy now, you can take care of yourself. I guess. Here—"

John took out his wallet and carefully counted ten twenty-dollar bills. "Now put those in your shoe, in case you get mugged and they take your credit card. And tell the driver to have you back here by four. We got a show tomorrow, and I've got some stuff to discuss with you all."

He walked Trip to the door of his hotel room, his hand on Trip's shoulder. "And listen—"

Trip halted. He looked at John's face but couldn't meet his eyes. "You be careful, okay? Use your head, don't do anything stupid." And John hugged him, his unshaven cheek brushing Trip's as he kissed him on the forehead.

The limo arrived, petrol-driven with an array of small solar cells atop it like so many black parasols, and monstrous tires, the better to hydroplane through the messier parts of the Merritt Parkway. The interior was clean but worn, smelling strongly of Viconix and stale cigarette smoke. The uniformed driver was a former marine whose Medal of Honor hung beside her ID card on the dashboard. Her mouth was hidden behind a utilitarian blue-and-grey mask embossed with the limo service's logo.

"You going to the Pyramid?"

Trip shrugged and glanced nervously back at the shining outlines of the Stamford Four Seasons, fading into the rubescent streets behind them. "I guess. The GFI building?"

The driver nodded. "That's the Pyramid. Ever been there?"

"Uh-uh."

"It's something else, man. Like Disney World, ever been to Disney World? But this Pyramid, miracle they even got it *built*, you know? All this shit coming down, they still throw that thing up in two years. Fucking

Japanese, man, they can do anything. It'll be a few hours before we get there. Want to hear some music?" Trip shook his head. "Sure? Okay. Let me know if you want anything." She pressed a button and disappeared behind a plasmer shield.

He dozed most of the way, exhausted by expectation. He didn't wake until they were on Riverside Drive, stalled in traffic beside a park, trees holding on to withered brown leaves, swing sets with no swings, some kind of playground structure that had been so vandalized its original purpose could only be guessed at. Broken blacktop and scuffed brown earth, no grass; but there were benches, and there were people: lots of them, faces protected from killing sky and viruses by hats or cheap plastic masks. Even through the car's closed windows Trip could smell smoke, meat cooking—meat! The scent made Trip dizzy; he couldn't recall where he had last smelled meat. Was it Austin? A radio blasted music that sounded like gunfire. Mothers watched children, dogs strained at leashes. A group of men and women sat cross-legged in a circle, chanting, heads tilted to the sky so that he could see the soft fleshy outlines of faces beneath their masks. Along the edge of the cracked sidewalk, people sold things from rickety card tables or blankets laid upon the ground. The crimson sky gave it all a harsh, premonitory glow.

Sudden loud tapping at the passenger window. Trip edged nervously into the center of the car seat as a maskless woman pressed her face against the glass.

"I will pray for you," she shouted. She had sun-ravaged skin, grey-blond hair, and a red dot in the middle of her forehead. "Pray for me—"

He stared after her as the limo lurched forward. Several well-dressed black men in suits and ties and kente-cloth robes crossed the street in front of them, tending a small group of children. Boys on Rollerblades swept past, and the men smiled, calling out names: Robert, Fayal, Assad.

Trip turned away and watched as the park slid by them. On the broken sidewalk a man was selling coffins made of plywood, with a small and more elegant model of carved pine set atop them with a sign: Will Make To Order. Children hawked plastic shoelaces. Where the sidewalk trailed off into rubble, there were people selling food. Canned goods mostly, but one woman had a case of peanut butter. Trip stared longingly at the red and blue jars, touched the pocket where his wallet formed a reassuring square. Another woman was selling water from a blue five-gallon container, measuring shots into a chipped plastic mug, filling milk containers and those Day-Glo plastic drinktubes that kids wore around their necks.

Then the hired car turned onto a side street where the alleys had become canals, the main avenues a yellow churn of taxis and hired vehicles. They were approaching midtown. The driver lowered her shield and pointed out a few landmarks to him: Grand Central Terminal's sandbagged facade, the never-completed Disney towers. Trip rubbed his eyes and mimed interest.

His mouth was dry, his palms damp. The limo stopped abruptly, in front of a seemingly endless line of other limousines and expensive hired cars. The driver smiled and adjusted her mirrored sunglasses.

"Okay. Here she is. Got any idea how long you'll be?"

It took him a minute to grasp the fact that *here* was the headquarters of GFI Worldwide Inc. He stuck his face against the window and peered upward, but could make out nothing but some kind of flashing marquee and, above that, a blinding slant of glass or metal that reflected the rippling sky. Beyond the line of waiting limos an immense crowd passed in and out of enormous revolving doors, like a huge deck of cards being endlessly shuffled.

The Pyramid itself was so huge it seemed almost extraneous, a monolithic backdrop to the street. He thought of what he had heard someone say on TV, shortly after the Pyramid opened but before the first waves of failed terrorist attacks directed at what had, so far, proved to be an inviolable structure. That it was like a hive, that the Pyramid had been constructed with hivelike precision and efficiency and speed. That, despite the myriad restaurants and boutiques and studios inside, despite the theaters and offices and all the *galleria* trappings of upscale commerce, it did not seem to have been designed with human beings in mind.

"Sir?"

Another moment before Trip remembered that *he* was "sir." "Uh, I dunno. I mean, probably not long. I'm just picking someone up. We're going to the museum."

The driver nodded, then popped her door and slid into the street. An instant later Trip's door opened and, with a flourish, she beckoned him out.

"They're expecting you, sir? Security's tight here."

Trip's throat contracted. "Yeah." His voice came out in a whisper, but the driver, at least, seemed satisfied. She smiled again and pointed at the building's immense maw, the doors changing color to keep pace with the rainbow sky.

"Well, I'll be here!" Once more she took her place behind the wheel. Trip swallowed, shoved his hands into his pockets, and forged on into the building.

He had to go through a metal detector and a crowded disinfectant chamber, where a yawning woman in a surgical mask gave him a perfunctory blast of Viconix.

"Any recent infections?" She glanced at his face and hands. A masked guard held a dog that sniffed Trip perfunctorily. Trip smiled at the dog; then, as the guard motioned him on, went through the door, into the Pyramid. And outside.

He gasped, stopping so quickly that he was immediately buffeted by more people hurrying by.

"Watch it, asshole," someone hissed. Trip stepped aside, blinking in amazement.

Overhead, the sun was shining, radiantly, in a blue sky. Golden sun like the first day of summer vacation, sky so brilliant it was like blue paint thrown into his eyes. A faint warm wind was blowing, just enough that Trip could feel the hair on the back of his neck stir. The breeze smelled sweetly of earth and pine needles, and fresh water. Beneath his feet the ground felt uneven. But it was all there, branches of trees moving against very high thin white clouds, light exploding behind leaves and limbs in a thousand rayed parhelions. There were people everywhere, hundreds, perhaps thousands of them, walking and running and talking animatedly. Most of them were expensively dressed and masked, in what looked to Trip like evening clothes, or outfits for a costume party; but other people were wearing ostentatiously casual outdoor clothing, the kind you bought at L.L. Bean once upon a time, or from catalogs that pretended to outfit expeditions.

And in all of it there was not the cacophony of sound he might have expected: instead all those voices spiraled up and out of earshot, like doves loosed in an auditorium. He stood with his mouth open, as though to catch rain upon his tongue, his eyes closed because you can't look into the sun. He felt dazed with unthinking joy. It wasn't until someone else elbowed him, though with an apology this time, that he opened his eyes and began looking around with intense curiosity, suspicion almost, trying to figure out how it was done.

At first he couldn't tell. But as his eyes grew accustomed to the light he began to get a fix on the immense space soaring above him. Somewhere, very very high above the trees, above the clouds even, and the radiant sun, there seemed to be wires, or catwalks, or some kind of grid that moved in subtle ways, so that his eyes were never quite able to focus on what was there. And when he turned to look around him, he saw that in the distance there were numerous mezzanines and balconies and glass elevators that did not climb any walls—there were no walls that he could see—but crept along glowing green cables that slanted above the crowds like a spider's draglines, moving toward some unimaginably distant apex. When he looked down he saw earth, and stones. There was a faint purl of running water, the smell of crushed ferns. But he saw no pebbles, no twigs or fallen leaves. And when he began to walk, very slowly, as he used to on the beach at Moody's Island looking for shells, he saw that all the stones were fairly large, and flat. When he tried to nudge one with his foot it didn't move. None of them did. He strolled past several trees, white birches with great masses of granite grouped around them, like benches, where people sat and laughed. Ferns grew beneath the trees, and moss; but when he looked carefully he could see that the ferns were set in some kind of elaborate planter, designed to look like stone. So were the trees. As he went on he began to notice other things—faucets poking up from the ground like mushrooms, cables threaded along tree trunks like vines. After a few minutes even some of the people wandering through the atrium, or sitting casually on rocks, started to look odd to Trip: they smiled at him, but their gaze remained on him a little too long: if he glanced back they would still be staring at him, and only pretending to have a conversation. He wondered if they were security guards, or if someone in this vast complex actually paid people to sit around in mountain-climbing gear and look as though they were enjoying the great outdoors.

This thought brought Trip to his senses, sort of. He tried to look purposeful, jostling into people until he found an information kiosk where he was directed to yet another glass booth from which enclosed walkways radiated like the arms of a sea star. He went inside and sat on a patchwork sofa as yet another security dog nuzzled his legs, waiting as a guard buzzed Nellie Candry's office.

"You're all clear." The guard watched Trip sign a log-book, then pointed him down one of the enclosed walk-ways, to an elevator. A minute later Trip got off at the thirtieth level, dizzy and slightly nauseated by the ride.

"*Welcome to Agrippa Music,*" a voice announced. Trip opened his mouth to respond, snapped it shut when he saw there was no one there. "*Bien venu à Agrippa Music,*" the voice went on, repeating the wel-come in Japanese and German and Spanish. "*Living in the Light . . .*"

Everywhere he looked there were video screens showcasing various Agrippa acts. It took him a moment to find the door, cobalt glass with AGRIPPA MUSIC spelled out in shifting holographic letters. Behind it a young man sat monitoring phone calls and a CD carousel.

"Hi!" he called cheerily as Trip entered. Silvery plas-mer implants hid his eyes, but he didn't wear a mask, and his smile seemed genuine. "You must be Trip Marlowe! Come on in, come on in!" He adjusted his body mike and announced, "Nellie? Your date's here," then gestured at a chair. "Sit down, honey, she'll be right with you."

Five minutes later Trip's heart sank when Nellie Candry stepped into the reception area, alone.

"Aren't you sweet to ask Marzie out!" she said, then laughed. She wasn't wearing a mask today, or heavy makeup. Beneath a sheen of light foundation her scars had the silvery roughness of beech bark; the cicatrices left by petra virus gleamed like lacquer. "Hey, don't worry—she's upstairs, waiting for you. Did you think you were going to be stuck with *me*?"

"He should be so lucky!" the receptionist cried as Nellie pulled Trip through another door.

"So. The Museum of Natural History." Nellie grinned as they padded down a hall carpeted with thick spongy black rubber, the second life of a hundred old steel radials. "Is that where you nice Xian boys go on a first date?"

Trip tried to smile. "Yeah, I guess. I've never been, actually. I wanted to see the planetarium."

Nellie laughed again; it made the vertical gashes on her cheeks move in a strange way, as though they were composed of a different material than the rest of her face. "The planetarium! God, that's great! Real James Dean, huh?" Trip looked at her blankly. "You know, *Rebel Without a Cause*? Oh shit, never mind. They never finished the renovation there, you knew that, right? Here we are."

They turned a corner, and she took him by the arm.

"Listen," she said in a lower voice. They stood in a softly lit alcove before a set of black glass doors with *Nellie Candry* etched in gold script. "I just want you to know this is a *really nice thing* you're doing. It really means *a lot* to Marz. She's had a hard time in the last year or so, coming from a war zone, you know? She and

I are still getting used to each other, and she hasn't really made any friends at the Brearley School yet. So it's a pretty big deal that someone like you would take her somewhere. She's just a kid, you know?"

A flutter of panic in Trip's chest: how old *was* she, anyway?

Nellie rattled on. "But I figured, well, we're nice guys, right?" She cocked her head and gazed at him with those disconcertingly lovely eyes. "Us Christians. I mean Xians. You especially. I mean, I probably *wouldn't* let her go out with that guy from Slag Hammadi, you know?"

Trip blushed, but already Nellie was steering him through the black doors and into her office. There were posters tacked to the walls, rollaway stands holding video monitors and VCRs and, surprisingly, piles of old-fashioned silver film canisters. In one corner leaned some kind of staff, topped with a grotesque wooden mask and deer's antlers.

"My secret life," Nellie confessed. She paused to rub a strip of acetate between her fingers. "I started out as a maker of documentary films. Then I got sick—"

She grimaced. Trip looked away from her scarred face, to her hands, and noticed that she wore a dull gold ring like Marzana's. "—though actually, I've got another film project I'm working on now. This A&R stuff, it's just a day job, you know? Not that I don't take it *seriously*," she added, grinning. "Okay, Marzie! Company!"

Nellie edged past Trip and slid behind a tiny banana yellow desk strewn with IT discs and promotional gadgets: Viconix dispensers, crucifix penlights, body gloves. Atop her telephone perched a snowy owl mask. "Here he is. Now, if you guys can hang here for just a minute—"

"Hey," said Trip, trying to keep his voice from breaking. "Marz. Hi."

Marz lifted her head and peered out from between the arms of the chair in front of Nellie's desk.

"Hi," she whispered.

A long fringe of corn-silk hair hung across her eyes. She wore very tight, white jodhpurs, a fuzzy lavender sweater, and a hugely oversize raincoat of transparent pink vinyl that made a crunching sound when she moved. Her feet were clad in pink plastic mules with bunnies on them.

Trip shook his head. It was the end of March, and freezing outside.

"Aren't you going to be cold?"

Marz shot him a disdainful look. *"No."*

Nellie laughed. "What'd I tell you?" She pointed a finger at Trip and smiled triumphantly. "You'll take better care of her than me—*I* told her to wear that coat."

He sat uneasily, staring at the blond girl. Nellie was asking him questions—had he ever made an IT recording? had he ever been to New York before? had he ever done drugs? IZE?

This last was odd enough that Trip looked away from Marz, startled. "Drugs? Jeez, *no.*"

"Never?" Nellie tilted her head, her eyes unreadable: was he being tested? She picked up several 8x10s, black-and-white photos of blank-faced people standing in line, and fanned herself with them. "A lot of people don't really think of IZE as a *drug*, you know. I mean, they practically had FDA approval before—"

Her hand waved disdainfully at the wall with its square of dark protective glass. Outside the glimmering could be glimpsed only as arabesques of black and grey moving above the skyscrapers. "—before all *this* came down."

Trip hunched his shoulders. He wanted to leave. This woman was acting fucking *bizarre.* "Uh, yeah. I guess. But I don't do drugs. I mean, I'm not just saying that. I never, *ever* did anything. My father was an alcoholic and he, like, killed himself. I signed a pledge when I was in sixth grade, and I've kept it."

Nellie smiled. "Of course. I read that somewhere, or no—I saw you on *Midnight*, that's it. Well, that's great, Trip, really!" Her eyes grew soft as she leaned across the desk, smoothing the photos and setting them aside. " 'Cause a lot of these bands, they're just cashing in on the whole Xian phenomenon, just riding the wave—but you feel like the real thing to me. I think you're just going to get bigger and bigger, Trip. I think you're going to be *huge*."

He nodded, forcing himself to smile; then let his glance ride back to Marz. She stared at him, eyes narrowed, and very slowly licked her upper lip.

The phone rang. "Okay!" crowed Nellie, cradling the receiver in her palm. "Off you go, kiddies. Marz—be good—"

They left. Even with her head down and eyes blanketed by her hair, Marz managed to navigate the Pyramid lobby with enviable ease. At her side Trip tried desperately to think of something to say. He did remember to let her go first into the limo, the driver holding the door open for them.

"The museum?" she asked. Trip nodded, and they were off.

The limo let them off in front of the planetarium's unfinished new entrance, hidden behind plywood and rusted scaffolding. Trip told the driver to come back in three hours. Then he scrambled out behind Marz, stepping on her raincoat so that she lurched forward against the curb.

"Oh—hey, I'm sorry, I—"

He tried to grab her arm but came up with a crackling handful of vinyl. As the car pulled away he found himself staring down at her small pale face, nestled in its bright pink wrappings like a marzipan sweet.

"It's okay," she said, and, turning, she headed toward the entrance. For a moment he just stared, blinking as though stunned by the chill morning light slanting down between grey buildings, the sight of the girl's gumdrop coat flapping around her white-clad legs. Then he hurried after her.

He paid for their tickets, and they stood in line for the first show of the day. The planetarium complex seemed not so much unfinished as partially excavated from an archaeological dig. There were yawning pits crisscrossed by boards and metal catwalks, monolithic objects—kiosks, dioramas, monitors, IT booths—strewn seemingly at random throughout the cavernous space, and a fine layer of sawdust and grit overall. Trip felt as though he were lurching around inside of someone else's movie, doing simple things—buying tickets, waiting behind the worn brass stanchions—without actually sensing the two slips of paper in his hand or the rough velvet rope beneath his fingers. He had never been on his own like this before, not in a city. Was it okay to pay with a fifty-dollar bill instead of a credit card? What would happen if he took off his heavy old pea coat? Should he give Marz her own ticket, or hold them both? There were only a handful of other people waiting to get in, an annoyingly convivial family whose masks identified them as part of TeamAmericon! and a small school group wearing uniforms and wrist monitors, desert boots and tiny ID implants that glowed on the backs of their hands.

"So." He coughed nervously. "You ever been here before?"

Marz shook her head. "No," she murmured. She was

staring hungrily at the school group. Trip watched her face, the way her tongue flicked out to lick her lower lip and her strange violet eyes as she watched the children elbowing each other and sniggering behind their hands at their cabal of chaperones. Her expression was sad yet intense; after a minute she looked up at him.

"I used to wear one of those monitors." She leaned back so that her arm stuck out from its plastic wrapping, displaying a wrist so thin Trip marveled that anything could have remained there without sliding off. "When Nellie first brought me over. But I was allergic." She traced a circle where the flesh still held a greyish shadow, like the stain left by a cheap metal bracelet. "See?"

Trip nodded, reached with a tentative finger to stroke the smooth soft skin inside her wrist, then to touch the simple gold band on her ring finger. "Did it hurt?"

"No." She glanced at the schoolchildren. The line started to move, the children arranging themselves in an orderly row alongside their teachers. "I wish I still had it."

Trip handed their tickets to a solemn usher, and they went inside. The huge dimly lit space reminded him of a cathedral he had visited once, barely occupied and chilly as this place was and with the same whisper of ambient music and rustling papers. It smelled faintly of vanilla and balsam disinfectant. He took Marz's hand and led her to the far side of the room, where no one else was sitting, and they took their seats in a middle row.

The program started, an energetically produced but intrinsically dull explication of the atmospheric effects that produced the glimmering and which now seemed to be giving birth to still more and stranger celestial events. There was a protracted discussion of millennial cults and prophecies through the ages. Trip yawned and scrunched way down in his seat. Beside him Marz did the same, her raincoat popping explosively.

"I better take it off." She giggled. "Before they throw me out. That happened once, you know."

She dropped the raincoat over the row of seats in front of them. In the middle of the room the aged Zeiss planetarium moved up and down like an avid mantis, a huge ungainly mechanism covered with round lenses and bulging optics. Overhead the dome with its spectral colors faded to a night sky, and a woman's recorded voice began intoning the names of various constellations.

"*Aquarius,*" she said. "*The water-bearer.*"

Trip stared at the false sky. He had not seen so many stars since he was a boy in Maine. Everywhere else he had traveled, the sky had been either poisoned by the glimmering or given a sickly yellowish cast by crime lights and mall lights and glowing smog. Here inside the planetarium it was as though he were back on Moody's Island. Suddenly he felt homesick. Even the chill bite of air-conditioning made him think of home; even though he had always hated it there, the rancid smell from the fish-processing plant and the buckled floor of the grimy little Half-Moon trailer where he lived with his grandmother.

"It's so cold," a voice came in his ear, so soft it might have been his own thought. But then a small, very cold hand plopped on top of his. Not moving, not curling its fingers around his, just lying there as though it had fallen from the sky. He could feel the ring on her right hand, the slender band of gold like a chip of ice burning against his knuckle. Glancing sideways he saw the girl gazing at the dome, her mouth slightly open. Then, very slowly, she turned and looked at *him*, not saying anything, not moving her

hand from where it lay atop his. Just staring at him
with those strange shadowed eyes, and smiling.

Afterward Trip recalled that moment and knew it for
the one in which his life was cleaved in two. Sitting there
in the make-believe night, with make-believe peepers
crying and make-believe stars, and the warm sweet dusty
scent of the girl beside him with her face upturned. The
Zeiss whirred and slowly spun about. Stars like spray
washed across her cheeks as the astronomer spoke their
names. Algol in Perseus, Regulus in Leo, the winter sky
tumbling into spring and Corona Borealis rising to shine
upon her brow with such brilliance that he had to blink
and look away. When he glanced up again she was staring at him. The pixie light gave a strange luster to her
skin, as though it were made of some brittle nacreous
material that would splinter into dust if he were to touch
it. But all he wanted to *do* was touch it. His lips were
parted, and he was breathing hard, his heart pounding,
hands unsteady, until suddenly he leaned over, crushing
her arm into the seat rest as he kissed her. Her mouth so
small and hot it was like some warm liquid spilling into
his, her fine hair like pollen filling his nostrils until he
had to draw back, sneezing. Before he could catch his
breath she was tugging at his hands, pulling him gently
but irresistibly toward her. He kissed her everywhere,
not just her mouth but the fine soft flesh of her cheeks
and chin and jaw, her throat, with its pulse beating like a
trapped bird, and the rough, gnawed tips of her fingers.
He could hear her gasp and feel her heart knocking in
her chest; smelled her, a hot pungent scent like the
inside of a winter barn. But for all that she did not stir,
not once she had pulled him to her. He closed his arms
about her—he almost felt they could have circled her
twice, she was so small and thin—but she did not
embrace him. When he kissed her, her mouth parted, he

could taste her fluid sweetness like melted chocolate. But her lips and tongue did not move. Her hand did not stir where it lay upon her thigh, with the golden ring winking softly in the darkness. Trip had never kissed a girl before. In a horrified rush of embarrassment, he realized he must be doing it wrong. Abruptly he pulled away from her.

"... *the star Fomalhaut. Above it you can see Aquarius, perhaps the most ancient of all the constellations, with its alpha star Sadalmelik resting almost exactly on the ecliptic, the celestial equator. Sadalmelik means 'Beloved of the king' in Arabic, and Aquarius shows up in all kinds of ancient myths, including several deluge myths that predate the Biblical story of the flood. As an astrological sign, it is associated with air, and danger. Now if you follow my pointer to the north ...*"

The blond girl's eyes were wide but without expression. Her arm still lay upon the velvet seat rest. As the projected stars crept across the dome her eyes would hold their light and for an instant seem to candle with passion or curiosity. Gazing at her Trip felt gooseflesh break out on his arms and the back of his neck: she was that strange, that lovely.

"Who are you really?" he whispered. But then the dome grew pale, the lights came up, and he was blinking painfully. "Oh," he said, neither disappointed nor relieved, just confused. "I guess it's over."

"I want to see it again."

Trip laughed, thinking she was joking, and started to reach for her raincoat.

"Really," the girl said. "I want to see it again. Can we stay?"

Trip looked around, shaking his head. "I don't think so. I mean, yeah, we can see it again. If you really want to. But we'll have to get tickets ..."

He waited for her to say *Jeez no, once is enough, it was so boring!* Instead she slid down in her seat, the front of the chair folding up so that her legs hung over it like a child's. "I like these seats. Let's just wait here, okay?"

He stared at her. Then, "Okay." His throat was so dry it hurt to speak. "If you want."

"I do," she murmured, smiling; and he knew he was doomed.

No one cleared the room after the first show. Marz remained half-hidden in her folding seat, but Trip sat bolt upright beside her—that way, he thought, if anyone confronted them it wouldn't look like they were trying to sneak in without paying. Trip's amazement at his own obliquity had faded to a sort of stunned bewilderment. He still had a hard-on, but he did none of the things he'd been taught to do in such a terrible circumstance: think of his mother, recite some bit of Scripture, get up and leave the room and wait until he was married to her to touch the girl again. Instead he found himself staring at the white skin above the cleft of her lavender sweater, the way her legs hung over the edge of her seat and her pants bunched up at her crotch. A flush had spread across her cheeks, the skin so fine that he could see the cellular array of crimson dots, as though she had been spattered with red ink. Her eyes were closed, her mouth barely parted; she looked as though she were asleep. He thought he would go mad, watching her. He was certain he would come in his pants if he stayed there looking at her, but he no longer cared. Dimly he was aware of the soft drone of music, doors opening and people entering, another school group from the sound of it. Still he couldn't wrench his eyes from the girl.

The school group took their seats on the other side of the room. The music paused, then swelled. Overhead the dome grew dark. A panpipe wailed as sheets of green and gold swept across the sky. Without a word Trip grabbed the girl by the shoulders and pulled her toward him.

She was as passive as before, but he didn't care. He thrust his hands under her loose sweater, kneading roughly at her flesh until he found her breasts, so small he could cup each in a palm, feel her nipples burning the flesh of his hands. He kissed her; her mouth moved slightly beneath his, and she moaned. He drew back, gasping, but before he could touch her again she slid from her seat to kneel on the floor in front of him.

"What?" Trip whispered hoarsely, shaking his head. *"What?"*

Of course he knew what she was doing—he may have been a virgin, but he wasn't an *idiot*—but this was so far beyond anything he had experienced that for one awful moment he was certain that he had gone insane. Then he heard the soft shirring sound of his fly being unzipped. He felt the girl's fingers fumbling with the loose fabric, and then the exquisite softness of her hair brushing across his cock as she withdrew it from his shorts. He couldn't breathe. He sat absolutely rigid in his velvet seat, every atom of his body keeping time with his heart, as he stared straight ahead and felt the girl's small hot mouth close upon him. His hands clenched upon his knees as her tongue fluttered up and down the length of his cock. He moved his head imperceptibly, gazing down upon the silvery corona of her hair, like another star blooming between his legs. For an instant he caught the violet flicker of her eyes as she raised her brow and stared up at him. Then he came, exploding into her mouth as she lowered her head, and her fingers pressed against his groin. He felt as though his heart had burst; he must have cried aloud because suddenly she was back in the seat beside him, making soft *shushing* noises as she stroked his cheeks and kissed his mouth, silencing him. He pushed her away, gasping for breath, then quickly pulled her back.

"You," he whispered. Her hair was like water in his hands as he kissed her, the soured sweetness of her tongue and her small teeth clicking against his. He kept his eyes open, because he had never seen anything like this before, could never in his life have imagined this strange girl with the white hair and amethyst eyes, curling into his lap with her delicate fingers flexed against his chest, moving the heavy gold cross aside to feel his heart beat. *"You . . ."*

She tilted her head to gaze at him, unsmiling. Her eyes were wide. They caught the reflected shimmer of the constellations processing slowly across the dome: Canes Venatici, Coma Berenices, Virgo. Her mouth was parted so that he could see her small front teeth, a spark of saliva glinting upon her lower lip. She stared at him, her chest moving in time with his and her hands pressed against his belly; but her expression was coldly, almost malevolently, ferine. It should have frightened him. Instead he was getting hard again.

". . . most famous are those of the sixteenth-century French medical doctor known to us as Nostradamus. His prediction that 'in the New City the sky burns at forty-five degrees' has been interpreted by many as a warning of the destruction of the ozone layer here above Manhattan and of the atmospheric disturbances that followed . . ."

Trip scanned the rows in front of them. They seemed to be empty, as were the two rows behind them. On the other side of the circular room, he could barely make out the dim shapes of schoolchildren staring raptly at the dome. From hidden speakers the astronomer's calm voice droned on.

". . . also spoke of plagues that would devour man and

*animals alike. Millennial cultists such as the Wheel of Light
and the New Puseyites believe that Nostradamus's references
to 'The Last Conflagration' dovetail neatly with the famous
apocalyptic visions of Saint John the Divine, and that these in
turn point indisputably to the celestial special effects dubbed
'the glimmering' by Stanford astrophysicist Francis
Partridge. Scientists, of course . . ."*

"Come here," Trip whispered. He slid from his chair
to the floor, crouching so that his head was below the
level of the seats in front of them. The blond girl sank
deeper into her chair, so that her disembodied head
seemed to rest upon the points of her skinny knees.
"Come *here*," he repeated more urgently.

She went to him. Without a word, seemingly without even moving. One moment she was there above
him. The next he was staring into her huge eyes, and
her hands were upon his knees.

"Hey," he whispered, startled. "I—"

She shook her head, raised her hand, and brushed it
across his lips. Her fingers smelled of earth, her touch was
oddly damp. But her mouth when she leaned forward to
kiss him was hot as before, and tasted like buttermilk. He
put his arms around her and drew her to him, clumsily.
She was so frail, he could feel her bones like the spars of a
kite. If he handled her roughly it seemed that her skin
might tear.

"Marz." He took her face in his hands and kissed her
cheeks, her eyes, the wisps of hair at her temples.
"Marz—"

"Shhh," she said, then murmured, *"I love you."*

She tilted her head, staring at him. Her hair held the
restless sheen of leaves in moonlight. Her pale eyes
gleamed as she drew away from him, and he could see
her pupils, not swollen and black as they should be in
this darkness but mere specks, like the dark pistils at

the heart of a myrtle blossom. Her gaze unnerved him, it was so detached, but before he could say anything or even look away she smiled, her little white teeth glinting.

"Come here," she whispered.

Trip's breath caught in his throat. He started to back away, but her hand closed upon his wrist, surprisingly strong. "No. *Wait*," she commanded, and letting go of him she dipped her head and in one smooth motion pulled off her sweater, dropped it on the floor beside her. Then she leaned forward and took his hands in hers.

"Like this," she murmured.

He shook his head desperately, glancing up at the rows of seats, the spinning stars overhead. "Hey—n-no, we can't, I'm—"

"Don't be afraid," she whispered. He wanted to pull away, but she was too close, she was everywhere, it was too late. He was lying upon her, and she was unbuttoning his shirt, so that he could feel her flesh against his, so warm and yielding it was like floating in a tepid pool. Then her hands were tugging at his pants, unzipping them and pulling them down until his cock sprang out, nestling between her thighs. He groaned and pressed his face against her throat, tasting her skin, the soft prickle of her hair falling across his mouth. He moved his hands slowly, as though trailing his fingers through still water, until he found her breasts. Their nipples hardened beneath his cupped hands, and he thought of plucking flowers from the water, hyacinths and wild iris. A sweet musky scent filled his nostrils; he moaned, and seemed to hear from very far away a childish voice saying *They called me the hyacinth girl*.

The musky fragrance grew stronger, choking him. Trip tried to raise his head but could not. The girl's hands had tightened around his back and she was pulling him close, her legs coiling around his, the heat of her groin pushing against his cock. She was making mewling sounds, *unh unh unh*, like a small frightened animal, her eyes shut tight as she buried her face against his breast. Her scent was everywhere, his legs were trapped by hers but it didn't matter, she had found him somehow, her cunt another greedy mouth upon his cock as she swallowed him, and he could feel the sharp jolt of her hipbones against his as she thrust against him, again and again and again, until with a hoarse cry he came inside her.

"What is that noise?" From across the room, a child's whisper repeated, "What is that noise?"

Trip gasped, in a panic yanked at his trousers, shoving the girl aside and fumbling for his shirt, his fly, buttons, and zipper. For a moment he crouched in the narrow space between rows, holding his breath and waiting for some terrible rector to descend and make public his disgrace. But no one appeared. The planetarium show continued without interruption. Someone on the other side of the room loudly blew his nose, and several children giggled. He heard the muted hum of a child monitor, the clash of cymbals accompanying a nova bursting overhead. Finally he started to grope his way back into his seat, but stopped when he saw the girl already there, gazing at him.

"Oh man," he said, and sank back down. She looked so tiny, sitting there; so small. So goddamn *young*.

She's just a kid, you know.

Shame like a fever surged through his entire body; he actually thought he might pass out. He had to lean against the other seats to steady himself as his stomach churned with guilt and fear. Had he gone *insane*? John

Drinkwater's face loomed in the darkness before him,
and Peter Paul Joseph's plump pale hands, holding Trip's
morality contract and the results of a lab test.

*For the lips of a strange woman drip as a honeycomb,
and her mouth is smoother than oil: but her end is bitter as
wormwood, sharp as a two-edged sword.*

Trip moaned under his breath, grinding his knuckles against the rough carpet. He knew nothing about
her: but Nellie Candry had the scars from petra virus,
and the girl had come from some foreign place . . . He
could *die* now, just as surely as if he had walked into a
radiation chamber; bones and blood poisoned, and all
his magic gone, that clear white veil he had carried
about himself for twenty-two years torn beyond all hope
of repair.

*Woe is me! for I am undone: because I am a man of
unclean lips . . .*

Yet even as he groaned he could feel once more the
girl's moist warm skin, the lilac musk of her hair seeping
into his nostrils, and her small mouth pressed against
his. The stars shifted in the sky above him, the
astronomer's voice purred on.

"*. . . along with the glimmering an increase in the
sightings of other previously rare phenomena, parhelia or
sun dogs and the refracted moonlight called paraselenae
which sometimes appears in the darkness . . .*"

Darkness which may be felt.

He raised his head and forced himself to look at the
girl staring down at him. Her sweater had slipped from
one thin shoulder, and he could see a small bruise there,
like a dark thumbprint. Otherwise, she seemed utterly
composed. He had expected her to be angry, or even
scared, her white childish face gazing at him from a chair
that was too large for her. Instead she hunched defiantly
down into her seat. Her eyes opened wide, wider than he

would have thought possible, until it seemed they held neither iris nor pupil, only an awful empty whiteness like that of a winter storm. Her mouth was open as well, a black crescent starred with tiny sparks where her teeth caught the dome's light.

Gazing at her Trip held his breath. His hands grew cold, his cock shrank to a damp spot between his legs. He glanced away from her, then back again. Still she stared at him, her expression unchanged. He began to shiver, hugging himself. Above him the stars faded, and with them the reassuring recorded voice of the planetarium's narrator. For an instant the room was absolutely black, save for the dull crimson lozenge of an EXIT sign. Trip could hear snorts and nervous laughter from the schoolchildren, their teacher's loud *hush*. In the uneasy silence the air-conditioning's soft breath became the measured sound of waves receding from an infinite shore. He forced himself to stare at the darkness where the blond girl sat, trying to muster up some memory of what he had felt just minutes before. But his desire was utterly gone. In its place he felt a desperate sort of queasiness, a growing certainty that if he were to extend his hand to her chair, he would find it empty, the velvet upholstery chill to the touch.

He felt like an idiot, but that's just what he did, willing his hand to be steady as he groped tentatively at the seat. There was nothing there. His neck prickled, his breath came fast and shallow as his fingers ticked along the edge of the chair, the plush cloth like cool skin, but she was not there, she wasn't there, and in a horrible moment of clarity he knew that she never *had* been there. He made a small groaning noise, both hands now clutching at the empty seat, and looked around frantically. Could she have left without him seeing? Had she crawled over the back of the seat and fled? His fingers clawed the soft velvet as he started to pull himself up. His chest heaved, and his mouth opened to call out for her, when he saw in the darkness before him two pale glowing orbs. At first he thought they were astral images projected upon the blank curve of wall behind the rows of seats. But then they moved closer to him, slowly but irrevocably, and he knew that they were her eyes.

"*No,*" whispered Trip.

In the air before him they floated, and he had no hint whatsoever of a face or body or even a sensibility behind them. Only those two deathly white globes, devoid of any markings that might have tethered them to a person, a place within the sky. A bit of nonsense spurted into his consciousness, something he had heard or read in school—

> *Who is the third who walks always beside you?*
> *Who is that on the other side of you?*

—and then the air was split by the ringing thunder of a gong. The dome blazed white and gold, the constellations suddenly visible in all their primal glory. Not stars and nebulae, pulsating variables and spiral galaxies, but horned beasts and the alchemical furnace, a crow bearing a chalice to a dying god, a man doing battle with a serpent. Superimposed across this radiance was an immense rotating wheel, crisscrossed with a multitude of brilliant silver lines, and the words AS ABOVE, SO BELOW.

"SUPERSTITION DIES HARD," a voice rang out. No longer the soothing, uninflected tones of the astronomer, but a man's voice, boomingly confident.

"EVEN THE HIGH-RESOLUTION IMAGERY OF THE HUBBLE AND DESCARTES TELESCOPES CANNOT DESTROY CENTURIES OF IGNORANCE AND

FEAR. YET EACH DAY CONTINUES TO BRING US
NEW DISCOVERIES, NEW SKILLS, AND NEW TOOLS
TO MASTER THE UNIVERSE. ASTRONOMERS AND
ASTROPHYSICISTS PREACH A GOSPEL OF HOPE,
NOT DOOM. WE MUST LOOK NOT TO THE DISTANT
PAST BUT TO THE FUTURE AND A NEW MILLEN-
NIUM: A NEW LUMINIST AGE FOR HUMANITY.
OTHERWISE, WE ARE NO BETTER THAN ANIMALS
GROVELING IN THE NIGHT."

The glowing shapes of the constellations faded. In
their place a scarlet banner of words rippled across the
dome, speared in place by a cold array of stars.

**WHEN THE WHEEL OF TIME SHALL HAVE
COME TO THE SEVENTH MILLENNIUM,
THERE WILL BEGIN THE GAMES OF DEATH.
—MICHEL DE NOSTREDAME**

A hiss as the words burst into flame and then faded
into darkness. In their place another banner rose, its letters stark as steel against the dome.

**FEAR IS THE MAIN SOURCE OF
SUPERSTITION, AND ONE OF THE
MAIN SOURCES OF CRUELTY.
TO CONQUER FEAR IS THE
BEGINNING OF WISDOM.
—BERTRAND RUSSELL**

Trip gaped as the letters grew more and more brilliant, until the entire dome was a dazzling aureole. He
shaded his eyes: had this happened at the earlier show?
If so, he had no memory of it whatsoever. Maybe that
was what sex did to you. With one last fanfare of gongs
and drums, the planetarium went dark. Almost imme-

diately the house lights came up. Trip blinked, and found himself staring into Marz's waifish face.

"Hey." He scrambled to his feet, confused, and bumped painfully against the edge of her chair. "Ouch. Where'd you go?"

She shrugged. "Nowhere. You know. Here."

Trip waited for something more in the way of an explanation. She said nothing, just stood and leaned over the seat in front of her to retrieve her raincoat. Her jodhpurs were slung so low about her narrow waist that when she bent he could see the top of her ass. To his shame and amazement, his cock began to swell again. A giddy wave of desire swept through him. When Marz turned around he grabbed her and kissed her, the raincoat crushed noisily between them. Her mouth parted for him, but she felt limp and all but weightless. He might have been kissing a cloth doll. On the far side of the room someone snickered. Trip drew back from Marz, blushing, and stared at the floor.

"I guess we better go," he mumbled, and took her hand. She nodded and followed him out of the planetarium, dragging her raincoat behind her.

The limousine was waiting outside. A thin icy rain nicked at the cobbled sidewalk, but the blond girl didn't put on her raincoat. Silently the driver emerged to hold the car door open for her. Trip waited until she had slid all the way over to the far window before he stepped inside. They sat without speaking at opposite ends of the car as it drove crosstown, music droning from the speakers.

"Check out the dinosaurs?" the driver asked as they swung into traffic. Trip shook his head. The driver shot him a disbelieving look. "No dinosaurs?"

"No," Trip snapped.

The driver shrugged. "Next time, huh? Where to now?"

Trip sighed, and gestured weakly. "Back to GFI, I guess."

They started crosstown. Trip stared out the smoked glass at the flood of yellow cabs turned livid by sleet slanting down from a distempered sky. Just a short time ago he had seen it all for the first time, sitting beside Jerry Disney in another hired car and laughing in amazement at the legions of taxis (private cars were outlawed now, except on weekends, when the affluent fled the city and the streets were jammed with decrepit vehicles of every type), the buses with kids hanging from the doors. Kids everywhere, some so young Trip was aghast that they could be running around untended. More feral children than he had ever seen in Nashville or Austin or even Seattle, begging and skating and stumbling out of icehouses, pink and orange wires tangled in their purposefully disheveled hair, or accompanying the youthfully middle-aged and wary, who paid them to serve as escorts and so deflect the attentions of other young caitiffs and thieves. Runaways and prostitutes, John Drinkwater said—though some of them looked Trip's age, so they couldn't really be called runaways, could they?—but Jerry told Trip that they were *fellahin*.

"That's an Arab word," he explained in his usual superior tone as they stared out their hotel window at a dark-haired boy in kilt and football helmet, panhandling on the sidewalk. "I saw it on Radium. It means, like, *whore*," he added, staring in disgust as the kilted boy leaned into the window of a cab.

Actually, the original meaning was closer to *peasant*, as Trip learned when he mentioned this newfound bit of

esoterica during *his* interview on Radium with Lotte
Sa'adah. But as Lotte said,

Hey! whore z-head *fux populi* wtf! f*ck! whatever! so
ok areet?!

Back then even the numberless runaways had
seemed exotic—romantic even, because pitiable—to
Trip. Now, with a girl he barely knew slouched silently
at the other end of the hired car, the mere notion of the
fellahin seemed more sinister. Trip dug his hands into
the pockets of his jeans and sank farther into his seat,
glaring resolutely out the window.

It was late afternoon. Sandbagged sidewalks were
jammed with pedestrians and cyclists crowding subway
entrances and storefronts to keep out of the rain. In the
tiny bright aperture between skyscrapers Trip saw a
writhing shape like an amoeba, one of the city's solex
shields come loose. And he glimpsed the brass-colored
capsule of one of GFI's famous fleet of dirigibles, fresh
from its factory in Northern Japan, moving slowly across
the sky and towing a rippling banner.

NEW ZEALAND/MALAYSIAN PEACE TALKS!
LOVETT-FORBES WEDDING!

As the car crawled uptown, the sidewalks became
thickets of metal trusses, where new protective shields
were being installed in corporate buildings, the reflective
sheets of solex rippling in the wind as workers struggled
to hold them. Trip cracked his window and smelled steam
and roasting garlic and exhaust, a faint sweet memory of
rain on new leaves. Between restaurant awnings well-
dressed men and women scurried like ants. Some wore
sunglasses, despite the freezing rain, or wide-brimmed
hats. Many more had the blank silvery gaze that came
from plasmer implants. They walked with exaggerated

caution, as though drunk. When the hired car stopped at a light, Trip stared at one woman who sat astride a black horse extravagantly caparisoned with metal spikes. The woman's elegantly masked face tilted upward, so that the rain streamed down her cheeks and pooled on the collar of her black rubber shawl. Her eyes, like her mount's, were silvery grey, their gaze fixed upon some distant spire. In the ten minutes that Trip watched them, neither woman nor horse once blinked.

After nearly an hour they reached the GFI complex. Trip and the blond girl said not a word to each other, though once or twice Trip responded briefly to a question from the driver. The rain had stopped by the time the car pulled beneath the huge solex awning that fanned out across Fifty-third Street. Ribbons of pink and orange streaming across the sky made Trip look up, past the solex shield. At her end of the car the girl shrugged on her rain-coat and looked at him.

"Thanks," she said. The driver held the door open, but Marz remained inside, staring at Trip. Her eyes appeared sun-dappled as pansies, her expression so remote she might not have seen him there at all. Trip waited for her to say good-bye, wanting desperately for her to be gone. He himself could say nothing, could only stare miserably at his hands on his knees. When after a minute he looked up he saw through the limou-sine window a glister of pink vinyl disappearing through the Pyramid's revolving doors.

The ride back to Stamford took several hours. Trip stretched across the backseat and slept, awakening as they hydroplaned onto the Hutch. Flooded fields and golf courses reflected the early-twilight sky, calm pools of gold and violet with drowned dying trees rising from them like scaffolds. They passed onto the Merritt Parkway and the alluvial plain that had been

Connecticut's gold coast, its abandoned shorefront con-
dos and mansions now given over to the rising Atlantic.
In the gold-slashed dusk Trip could see lights flickering
from the upper stories of some of the houses, and on
dilapidated barges and houseboats. He opened his window; the car filled with the low-tide reek of fish rotting
on the strand, the faint and sweetly ominous sound of
drums and singing children.

It was after six when he got back to the hotel. John
Drinkwater collared him in the hall, already dressed in
the disturbingly stylish hempen suit he insisted on
wearing when Trip performed.

"Where have you been?"

Trip pushed past him and into his room. "I need to
take a shower."

"You don't have time! We have to go *now*, Jerry
needs a sound check on—"

Trip shook his head. Without a backward glance he
started for the bathroom, peeling off his shirt as he
went. "He can go, then. You too. Get me another car—"

John grabbed Trip's arm, his voice rising. "Hey! You
were supposed to be here *two hours* ago! You listen to
me, Trip—"

"No." Trip whirled, yanking his arm back so hard
that John staggered away from him. "I'm taking a
shower, okay? *Okay?*"

He shouted the last word, spun on his heel, and
stormed into the bathroom. John Drinkwater blinked
before recovering himself.

"Eight o'clock, Trip!" he yelled as the door slammed
shut. "You go on at eight o—"

"I'll go on when I'm fucking ready!" Trip's voice echoed
through the suite, followed by the roar of water.

John stared at the bathroom door, shaking his head in disbelief. Then he walked to the phone and called the concierge.

"I'll need an additional limousine for Mr. Marlowe. Tell the others to go on now, and we'll meet them."

He hung up and started for the door, but stopped when he saw Trip's shirt crumpled on the sisal rug. For a moment he stared at it, then stooped and picked it up. Tentatively he brought it to his face and inhaled, breathing in the stale odors of lilacs and sweat, and a fainter, muskier scent.

"*Hah.*" John Drinkwater stared at the shirt, then flung it back onto the floor. *Women*, he thought balefully, and stalked from the room.

Trip's performance that night was off-kilter, almost frenzied. At first Jerry and the other musicians were nonplussed, but after the first three songs they seemed to catch Trip's frantic buzz, segueing from a rave-up cover of "Walking with the Big Man" into "The End of the End." Trip crouched bare-chested at the edge of the stage and sang in a soft moan, his bare skin glistening in the spotlights. John Drinkwater stood in the wings and watched in silence. When Trip finally walked off, the front of the stage was heaped with crosses and flowers and T-shirts flung there by fans, and a single broken-spined Bible.

Backstage, an exhausted Trip made straight for the door that led outside, where the limos waited to bring him and the others back to the hotel. But three teenage girls and their parents stood beneath the EXIT sign, beaming as he approached. In the shadows nearby, John Drinkwater stood in his hempen suit.

"Hi, thanks for coming to the show, hi," Trip mumbled. The girls giggled and held out copies of *LIVE*

FROM GOLGOTHA for him to sign. Trip glanced at John Drinkwater.

"Kind of a short set tonight, huh, Trip?" one of the fathers asked in a conspiratorial tone. He lowered his surgeon's mask apologetically, looked slightly askance at the cross branded on Trip's forehead. "Uh, I hate these darn masks—"

"Yeah, me too," murmured Trip. He scrawled his name across the disc and shoved it back at the girl, shot her a quick smile. "Kayla, huh? Pretty name."

The girl's father shook his head. "You look tired, Trip," he boomed, clapping Trip's shoulder with a powerful hand. "Singing takes it out of you, eh?"

Trip forced another smile. The girl, rosy-cheeked and golden-haired, plucked her surgeon's mask from her face and smiled beatifically. "These are for you," she said, and shyly thrust a fistful of lilacs at him. Trip took the flowers, his smile frozen; they were limp and warm and greyish, wrapped in damp shreds of paper towel.

"Th-thanks." He glanced at the outside door, then at John Drinkwater. "Thanks again," he croaked. "Uh, I better go—"

On the way back to the hotel, Trip deliberately sat between Jerry Disney and their bass player. That didn't stop John Drinkwater from giving them all a brief lecture on the perils of the road, along with a reminder of the terms of their morality contracts. Trip looked contrite, but when they got to the Four Seasons Jerry cornered him in the hotel lobby by a bamboo grove.

"That was some crazy shit you pulled!" he exclaimed exultantly, punching Trip's arm. "Man, I almost swallowed my gum—"

Trip went cold. *He knows!* he thought, and saw the blond girl's luminous eyes staring at him from between the yellow leaves. But then Jerry grabbed a bamboo stalk and rattled it. "'Walking with the Big Man!' I forgot I even *knew* that song!"

"Yeah," Trip said, relieved. "Yeah, it sounded good."

"It was *fucking great!* We gotta put that on the next album—maybe *live*, huh? LIVE FROM GOLGOTHA LIVE! Oooweee—" Jerry spun in place, laughing. "This is *so great*—"

Trip watched his friend. *The next album* . . . He thought of Nellie Candry, of Agrippa Music and Mustard Seed's army of red-faced lawyers back in Branson. He thought of Marz, then looked down at the limp bundle of lilacs. "I'm going to bed," he announced, and headed for the elevator.

"Boston tomorrow, Trip!" Jerry yelled after him. "College boys and girls! We're gonna be *wicked* big stars! *Wicked* big!"

"We already are," said Trip, as the elevator door slid shut.

Once in his room, Trip moaned and collapsed into an armchair.

"Jesus God." He stared dazedly at the pathetic handful of lilacs he still clutched. *The grass withereth, the flower fadeth* . . . "Poor things," he murmured.

Since the glimmering began, flowers no longer thrived, especially early-spring flowers like lilacs. These looked puny to begin with, but he didn't have the heart to toss them away. So he put the lilacs in a tumbler of water on the table beside his bed, shoving aside one of John's *Guideposts* discs to make room. Then he took another shower. Afterward he walked dripping from the bathroom, drying his hair and tossing the towel onto a heap of dirty clothes as he made his way to bed. Suddenly he stopped.

When he'd put the lilacs in their glass, the flowers had been lank and grey, their leaves dark and curled as discolored ribbon. But now the stems were supple and thick as his finger, the heart-shaped leaves fresh and green. Above the rim of the tumbler the blossoms frothed, so rich a purple they fairly glowed. The scent of lilacs was everywhere, and the soft monotonous buzz of a bumblebee. He stared openmouthed, then gingerly plucked them from the tumbler.

Lilacs. Trip closed his eyes and inhaled until he was dizzy. He saw his grandmother's trailer on Moody's Island, crowded by the ancient lilac trees that were the sole remnant of the farm that had once stood there. The bee droned past him and he twitched involuntarily, then sank back onto the bed. He pressed the blossoms to his face, heedless of water running from the stems onto his bare chest. The wind blew warm as blood, the trees moved slowly against a sky so purely blue it made his heart ache, a sky he only saw in dreams now. He knew he was half-asleep, but he made no move to get under the covers, or to put the flowers back into their glass. Instead his fingers tightened upon the mass of blossoms, crushing them against his cheeks and eyelids until he felt their sweet moisture seeping into his skin. With a groan he watched as the wind rose and the trees thrashed, the sun's warmth fading as one by one the stars sprang out against the blue. The bee's humming ceased, and the pattering of leaf upon leaf. The air Trip breathed grew cooler still as he flattened his palms against the broken blossoms and moved upon the bed.

Beyond the broken tracery of limbs and sky a darkness stretched. True night, black and fathomless, with no spectral glare to rend the shining arcs of constellations as they passed above him. Cassiopeia, Corona Borealis; Andromeda and Dagon and Berenice's Hair. Stars like salt spilled upon a plate; yet they were *people*, too—Trip could see the gleaming spar of the hunter's elbow as he bent his bow and the severed tail of the great serpent where it writhed in Ophiuchus, and Spica, the shining spear of wheat clutched within Virgo's hand. As he watched the Maiden turned. Her hand drooped, the bright cluster of stars upon her breast burst into a shower of violet rain. Amidst the stars a small figure straightened and shaded her eyes, as though gazing into a great distance, then resolutely began to walk toward him. Beneath her feet the darkness churned into sand, the stars to rubble and flecks of dust. As she drew closer he could see her face, small and pale and unsmiling, and her hands swinging loosely at her sides. She was naked save for the aniline glitter of her raincoat, the streaming bands of gold and green and amethyst that bloomed around her, blotting out the sky.

"My feet are upon the New City," she whispered, and the words licked like flame against his ears. *"And my heart beneath my feet."* She was so close upon him that he could feel her warm breath upon his cheeks. Dimly he heard a bell ringing somewhere, a muted thump, and someone calling his name. *"But we who were living are now dying, here at the end of all things; for a foolish man bears our world away with him, who did not speak one word to the king concerning the anguish that he saw."*

The smell of lilacs flowed from her like water from a jar. She knelt between his legs, arms outstretched to embrace him, and with a hand as light as rain brushed the flowers from his cheeks. "Do you remember nothing?" she asked.

He started to reply, but she kissed him, her mouth cool now and sweet as sap. His arms enfolded her, and he drew her in, her fine hair a mist across his eyes as she moved against him. When he came it was like falling into sleep, a long slow shudder and the girl's sighing breath tangled in his hair. For a long moment he lay there, trying to hold in his mind the image of stars and green trees, the odor of lilacs and rain falling upon a withered land.

Then he woke. There was a pounding at the door and John Drinkwater's recorded voice echoing from the telephone with his 6:00 A.M. wake-up call. Trip rose groggily from his bed, brushing leaves from his hair and chest as he stumbled to his feet; and looked out upon his room to see lilacs, twigs and limbs and heaps of lilacs: lilacs everywhere.

He never saw the girl again. They were unable to get enough fuel for the bus to drive them to Boston, so Lucius arranged a morning flight from Westchester Airport. A hired car drove them; their equipment would, hopefully, follow.

At the airport Trip and John Drinkwater and the others sat in the crowded, yet comparatively quiet and well-appointed first-class terminal, with its smells of stale vanilla and ersatz coffee. There Trip watched impassively as airport health security surrounded a well-dressed Asian man whose mask fell away to reveal the garish cicatrices and facial tics of petra virus in its secondary, infectious phase. Lucius Chappell averted his eyes. Jerry Disney made a disgusted sound and headed for the bathroom. John Drinkwater lowered his head. His lips moved, praying—*Lord, grant Thy love and healing grace upon those who suffer*—and Trip felt a small surge of love for him. Meanwhile the Asian man stood wordlessly as his briefcase and roll-along were taken and sheathed in protective latex. He waited with the starkly composed expression of utter despair as the orange-suited men pulled a transparent hood over his head and bore him away. Shortly thereafter someone whose mask and silvery eyes were embossed with the NatLink logo informed Lucius that their plane was ready to board. As it turned out, it was the only flight that would leave New York that week.

CHAPTER FOUR

Between Planets

For nearly two weeks Jack passed in and out of fevers, in and out of ER and ICU, in and out of consciousness. There were glimpses of white-masked faces floating in the burnished bubble that was Saint Joseph's jury-rigged AIDS ward, a terrifying memory of sudden darkness and frightened screams, flame and shouted curses and the horrific certainty that he had somehow missed his own death and plunged straight into hell. But that was just the first minutes of the first blackout, before the hospital's emergency generators kicked in and the ward's sodium lights began to glow. Jack missed the next few blackouts, being too busy manufacturing his own. His fever soared and dipped. When he was conscious he felt giddy and exalted despite the excruciating pain that gripped his bones; felt himself wheeling far above the blue-and-white hospital building and looking down upon Untermeyer Park, the broad ruddy sweep of the river, and the Palisades, where he could see cormorants nesting, and bald eagles. These flights would be interrupted by someone taking his temperature, his blood, fecal samples, and swabs of spit and tissue from inside his mouth. His upper arm ached from repeated stabbings with a hypodermic needle; his hands, when he could feel them, were cold, and his feet. This did not prevent him from flying—jumping, actually—after the first few forays he realized he could move faster and farther if he leapt into the air rather than attempting to pump his arms like wings. So he would leap, bouncing as upon a trampoline and holding his breath until he began to hang up there, each time a few moments longer, and at last he did not fall, he was there once again above the world, between feedings and fevers, between planets.

Sometimes within the coils of cloud and star he saw faces that he knew. His brother Dennis; Jule Gardino; Leonard, but it was the Leonard of long ago, his sloe eyes brimming and his mouth close to Jack's. He saw his former lover Eric, too, which confused him but filled his heart with such joy that he shouted, and was confused again when the nurses came. And once his aunt Mary Anne drifted past, long blond hair and paisley wrappings trailing behind her. Sometimes he heard music. Another man in the ward had a boom box; the nurses fiddled with it relentlessly, until they found a working broadcast band. What spilled out then was like what was going on inside Jack's head, "Gimme Shelter" and *La Traviata*, *Rent* and old Ajax commercials, a man shouting about Jesus and a withered hand, Sandy Becker and the murdered pope. During his flights the music faded, and sometimes the carnival light as well. It was then that he would see a great unblinking eye moving slowly across the heavens, like a hot-air balloon that had lost its gondola. The eye terrified him: it grew slowly larger and larger, until it filled the sky, turning slowly as it stared down upon the world, its black pupil opening into the abyss. He would wake screaming, barely conscious of cool hands in worn gloves pushing him back onto the cot and the hot sting of a needle in his upper arm.

Then a day came when a new voice cut through the babble. A woman's voice, half-familiar, but it wasn't until he heard his doctor arguing with her that he realized it was Jule's wife, Emma.

"Are you fucking *crazy*? That much morphine for *two weeks*—"

"Six days," the other doctor's voice protested.

"—you goddamn *bastards*, you're trying to kill him, aren't you? You fucking *cannibals*."

There was a clatter and the sound of scuffling, a shriek and then feeble applause from one of the other cots.

"—sterile, you're not *sterile*!" the doctor cried.

"I'll sterilize *you*, you son of a bitch—"

What happened next was mostly pain, experienced at varying speeds, as Dr. Emma Isikoff shouted and waved her cellular phone and stalked between cots, yanking up patients' charts and scanning them by the uneasy glow of the sodium lamps. "'Morphine.' 'Morphine.' *Morphine*!" she read, and in a rage threw the last chart so that it fluttered onto an IV pump. "What, is this *Verdun? You're killing them*!"

Jack still hadn't managed to do more than shake his head admiringly, when Emma commandeered a wheelchair from somewhere, lifted him, and deposited him gently on the frayed vinyl seat, thick with duct tape and newspaper padding. The trip from the hospital to Lazyland was a blur, barely glimpsed through the filthy, barbed-wire-framed windows of Emma's Range Rover. And the next few days were horrible, more fever and convulsions from the abrupt morphine withdrawal, and a new regime of herbs and antibiotics administered by Emma.

"Remember that scene in *Gone with the Wind*? That's what it was like in there." Emma was a neurosurgeon on the staff at Northern Westchester, where (apparently) sick people were treated like gold: when the power went they operated by candlelight and never lost a patient. "Next time you have a seizure and go to the emergency room, I want you to call me, okay? Jesus."

Jack smiled. Emma's shift—nine days on, four days

off—allowed her to stay with him. Which was lucky, since Keeley was too frail to serve as nurse, and all of Jack's brothers were too far away or, in Dennis's case, too burdened with their own children to help out.

The terrible illness turned out to be flu. It had not progressed into pneumonia ("No thanks to *them*," Emma snarled), which almost certainly would have killed him. Paradoxically, the morphine might have helped, by forcing him to rest.

"But no more drugs, understand? Unless *I* give them to you. And I'm taking these," she announced, the bottle of alprazolam clutched in her fist like the scalp of an enemy. "I mean, are you totally insane? I told you these interact with tricyclics, not to mention you could get *sleep apnea.* I thought you were on fluoxetine! Jesus!" Emma was small and round and blond as a newborn chick; Leonard called her Doctor Duck. She shoved the alprazolam into a pocket and pulled another bottle from his nightstand. "Who gave you *these*? *Not* Dr. Kornel, *tell* me Ed Kornel did not prescribe these—"

Jack gestured weakly. "Leonard," he croaked.

"Leonard! *Leonard*!" Emma actually jumped up and down in fury, blond curls shaking and floppy sweater rising to give him a glimpse of her round white stomach. For an instant Jack thought she would explode, like Rumpelstiltskin. "If *Leonard Thrope* told you to jump off the—"

"Emma. *Please.*"

Emma stopped and took a deep breath. She smoothed her frizzy aureole of yellow hair, opened her voluminous leather sack, and dropped the bottle into its maw. "Okay. Okay. Leonard wants to kill you and take pictures of your rotting corpse, that's okay with me. Okay? But not on *my* watch. If you are going to pop whatever street dirt Leonard gives you, Jackie, then *I* am

going to stop coming to save you. Because I don't want
to be the one talking to the ambulance crew. Understand?"

"Okay," he whispered. "But," he couldn't resist
adding, "you know, I've taken them before and nothing—"

Emma fixed him with a glare from her ice-blue eyes.
"You are playing *Russian roulette* with your body, Jack—"

I thought it was pinball; but Jack only nodded.

"—but anyway here. I brought you these." She
placed a number of small brown glass dropper–bottles
on his nightstand, each with its hand-lettered label in
Emma's miniscule penmanship. "Skullcap, that'll help
you sleep only not too much because it can cause bad
dreams plus there's a possible reverse effect of insomnia.
Valerian, blessed thistle. More echinacea. Here's some
goldenseal. And garlic." She dropped a fat papery corm
in his lap.

Jack grimaced. "Jeez. Vampires now, I'm worried
about vampires?"

"Jule said you were having bad dreams."

"And indigestion will help me?"

Emma gathered her things: stained white linen
jacket, Zabar's shopping bag, leather purse. Thus burdened, she leaned over and kissed Jack's forehead, let
her hand rest there a moment. He remembered seeing
her do that to Rachel when she had chicken pox, not so
much testing for fever as she seemed to be seeking to
draw it out through her palm. Doctor Mom. Doctor
Duck.

She hesitated, then asked, "Dreams. What did you
dream, Jack?"

He shook his head. "Nothing," he lied. "Just—you
know. Some nightmare I don't remember. Night terrors."

Emma nodded. "Rachel used to have those," she

said. She always made a point of talking about Rachel. It made Jack uncomfortable, this false bravura; after two years he preferred Jule's unrelenting drunken grief. "Has Julie told you about what he's—dreamed?"

Jack moved the garlic to the side table. "No," he said, curious. "What kind of dreams?"

Emma eyed him thoughtfully. "Just—dreams," she said finally. "I better go, sweetie. I wish I could stay—"

"Hush—" He held out his hand. She took it, and for the first time he saw tears in her eyes, a terrible weariness there. "You're my angel, Emma." He coughed, covering his mouth with his pajama sleeve.

She bent to kiss his forehead. "Lots of rest, lots of fluids—no alcohol!—and please, *please*, watch your meds. Okay? Okay."

He watched her go, hearing her cheery good-byes to Grandmother and Mrs. Iverson as she descended through the house. Then he crawled back beneath the covers and fell asleep.

A week later Leonard arrived. It was eight-thirty on a Friday morning. Jack was always slightly unnerved at the way Leonard kept these businessman's hours; such discipline gave weight and credence to Leonard's work, which even after all these years Jack preferred to think of as a repellent hobby, like Leonard's penchant for S/M and body piercings.

But Leonard *was* a businessman, the very modern avatar of artist as financial entrepreneur—even his T-cell count was part of his portfolio. As such he traveled via a vast seal-grey diesel-powered limousine that belched foul smoke and was reputedly a gift from a Russian heroin overlord. And Leonard traveled with an entourage, an amorphous group of followers which changed with current fashions—this week young and blond and pale, trembling from amphetamines and IZE excess; next week playing host to a half dozen street people with the dull crimson eyes of birds of prey, who left the leather interior of the limo flecked with scabs and dead skin and spit.

Jack shuddered each time he heard the car entering Lazyland's compound. He had long since forsaken going outside to greet his friend, for fear of finding himself face-to-face with lepers flown in from Bangladesh or some convicted serial murderer sprung from prison by Leonard's army of legal counselors. Instead Jack tracked Leonard's current cult status by means of outdated tabloids glimpsed at Delmonico's or patter overheard on TV. Leonard himself he always recognized, because in twenty years Leonard had not altered his uniform of gold and black leather. Though the gold was more subtle now, the leather was cracked and faded as old gesso, and Leonard's flamboyant mane of curling black hair was streaked with grey and braided into a single long plait.

"Jack? Oh Jackie-boy!"

Leonard's voice echoed up through the house, his footsteps pounding as he took the stairs two and three at a time, as he always had. In his bed Jack moaned.

"*Please,* Leonard," he called out into the hallway, coughing for effect. "I'm *sick*—"

"Of *course* you're sick. That's why I'm here!" With a thump Leonard gained the third floor. Jack heard the familiar *boom* as his friend slid across the slick wooden landing and crashed into the wall opposite. Then, grinning like Mister Punch, Leonard's head popped through the open doorway. "Please say you're glad to see me, Jackie."

In spite of himself Jack laughed. "Christ, Leonard. *What* is that—?" He pointed in revulsion at Leonard's back.

"It's a *leopard skin*. D'you like it?"

Leonard whirled so that Jack could admire him: his slight rangy form in its cracked leathers, hair braided and ornamented with an array of tiny bones—Jack knew better than to ask about *them*—hands and cheeks so tattooed, scarified, beaded, bruised, and bedecked with light implants that the press had named him The Illuminated Man. Mirrors hung everywhere from his clothes. His left eyebrow had been shaved and replaced with a series of chips representing the weighing of souls in the Egyptian *Book of the Dead*. A sleek camera bag hung from his waist. Draped over his shoulder was a huge if moth-eaten pelt, complete with eyeless mask and dragging tail and two front paws tied loosely about his neck, like a sweater.

"Leopard?" Jack repeated, horrified. "Aren't they endangered?"

Leonard pranced to the bedside, his small feet in their steel-toed boots scuffing at the oriental rug. "*Snow* leopard, Jackie. *Not* endangered. *Extinct*." He unlooped the two immense paws and let the pelt fall to the floor with a thud. "It was a gift."

"Right." At least it wasn't a human head, which was what Leonard had worn to the opening of the last Whitney Biennial. "So that makes it okay—"

"Oh hush. Here, I brought you a present."

Jack instinctively yanked the covers up around him as Leonard thrust his hand into a pocket of his leather kilt. "Wait a minute—okay, here it is—"

Jack peered into Leonard's open palm and saw a small highly polished stone, incised with a few random-looking lines. "It's a kind of dream-catcher," Leonard explained. "I got it in Nepal. One of the priests gave it to me, because I was—well, Jule told me you had been having nightmares. I figured you could use it more than me. I'm *used* to bad dreams."

Leonard put the stone into his friend's hand and closed Jack's fingers around it. Then he gently raised the hand to his mouth and kissed Jack's knuckles, one by one. "I'm sorry you're sick, sweetie," he said softly.

A creak as the door behind them opened wider. Jack craned his neck and saw his grandmother standing there, immaculately dressed in a Lagerfeld woolen suit and white silk blouse. Behind her stood Mrs. Iverson, a meek shadow in blue moiré, breathing heavily—she seldom ventured above the second floor.

"Jack dear. I heard voices—" Keeley's cane struck the floor with a resonant thud. She stepped carefully into the room, bringing with her the subdued scent of Chanel No. 19. Her narrowed gaze showed she knew exactly who his visitor was. "Oh. *Leonard*. I didn't hear you come in."

Leonard grinned, light glancing from his ruby placebit. "Hello, Grandmother."

"What are *you* doing here?" she demanded.

Leonard stared at her admiringly. "God, she's amazing! She just *never gives up*." He raised his voice and pronounced with exaggerated slowness, "It's Leonard, Grandmother—Leonard Thrope! You remember, Jackie's old friend from Saint Bartholomew's—"

Keeley raised a hand as though to strike him. Before she could, Jack swung himself from bed, shuffled to her side, and kissed her. "Shut up, Leonard. Grandmother, I *told* you not to come all the way up here—"

"*Pog mo thóin,*" Keeley spit. She glared at Jack. "I told *you* I don't want to see him—"

Leonard's eyes widened. "Hey! She just cursed me in *Gaelic*."

"Okay, he's leaving, he's leaving. He just dropped by on his way out of town, that's all—" Jack walked Grandmother back out the door, past Mrs. Iverson

watching everything with her customary, slightly
stunned expression. "Come on, Grandmother, I'll help
you downstairs—"

"No! Back to bed, you." Keeley drew herself up and
motioned at the housekeeper. "Larena—"

Mrs. Iverson took Keeley's arm. Jack hovered over
the two of them, clutching his bathrobe closed. Despite
his grandmother's protests, he followed them down to
the second-floor landing. There he steered them into
Keeley's bedroom, kissed her, carefully shut the door,
and went back upstairs.

"I think she secretly likes me," said Leonard.

Jack sank into a weathered armchair by the window.
"You asshole. You give my grandmother a heart attack
and I'll kill you."

Leonard stooped to pick up his leopard skin.
"Hating me's what keeps her alive, Jackie-boy. What is
she, a hundred?"

"Ninety-nine." Jack sighed, shielding his eyes from
the window. "She'll be a hundred around Christmas."

"A century baby! I should do something—"

"*Forget it*, Leonard."

"Huh." Leonard sniffed, turned to look disdainfully
at the painting by Martin Dionysos that hung beside
the window. An abstract sunstruck landscape, all greens
and yellows and sea blues that stood in Stagiritic opposition to Leonard's own icy aesthetic. "God, I *hate* that
picture."

Jack ignored him, gazing out at the distant river,
turned to molten green and gold by the spectral display
overhead. Like sunspots, the glimmering came and
went, flaring up for weeks at a time; then receding, so
that for a day or two, or an hour, one could almost
imagine the world was as it had been. No one seemed
able to predict when it would be active, or what caused

the remission. Jack imagined masked scientists aboard icebreakers in the Weddell Sea peering up through telescopes, watching as the ozone hole above them dilated like the pupil of some malevolent eye. "Jeez, it's busy out there today, isn't it?" he said absently.

"Yeah. I heard there's a heavy-duty UV alert. I had to cancel a morning shoot out at Rikers. That's how come I'm here—"

Jack turned from the window. "I should have guessed."

Leonard looked aggrieved. "I was going to come yesterday—"

"I'm *kidding*, Leonard. Yesterday I felt too sick to see anyone—this is the first day I've gotten out of bed, really." Jack stood by the old chair, his fingers tracing the whorls on one wooden arm. "I'm sorry your shoot got canceled. What was it?"

"Hmm?" Leonard looked distracted. "The shoot? Nothing big."

He fell silent and stared thoughtfully at the picture of Aunt Mary Anne on the wall. At last he said, "I have something else for you, Jackie."

Jack's heart sank as Leonard sat on the bed and pulled his camera bag up beside him. "Something else?"

"Don't look at me like it's a horse's head." Leonard unzipped a side pocket, reached inside, and withdrew a small cloth pouch. He let it rest in his palm for a moment, as though weighing it. In a low voice he said, "Come here, Jackie."

Jack didn't move. His eyes were fixed on the window, the fey light flickering there like so many fish darting in the shallows. In the silence he could hear Leonard's breathing, the soft ticking and tocking of Lazyland's clocks. But something else, surely there was something else . . . ?

He cocked his head and listened, suddenly uneasy. Not at all sure what it was he listened *for*, but certain it must be there. The echo of a voice, the piping of a distant flute—

He heard neither. Only a soft *fumpp fumpp* as Leonard tossed the small cloth pouch up and down in his palm.

"Jackie," his old lover repeated. Jack felt his neck prickle with gooseflesh. "Come here, Jackie."

He stood and crossed to the bed.

"Sit." Leonard patted the comforter beside him. Jack sat. Leonard looked at him and frowned, as though he'd been sent the wrong model for a shoot. Finally he said, "I was planning to give this to you. But I was going to wait—"

He hesitated. "—to wait just a little longer. Then Jule called me and said you were so sick—"

"It was just the fucking *flu*, Leonard," Jack broke in. He felt anxious and angry and aroused, as he usually did when Leonard visited. "You didn't—"

Leonard hushed him, touching a finger to Jack's lips. "He *said* you were really *quite ill*; and so I decided this was not the time to be patient."

"Oh, *right*. Leonard Thrope's famous patience—"

Leonard ignored him. He stood, peeked out into the corridor, then closed the bedroom door.

"You're not going to smoke, are you?" Jack tried not to sound peevish.

"No." Leonard settled back onto the bed. He looked so serious that Jack's anxiety began to churn into fear.

"Now," said Leonard, "I want you to listen to me very carefully. You know I was in Tibet, right?"

Jack nodded. His gaze was fixed on the little bag in Leonard's hand.

"Well, I *met* someone there—"

"Congratulations," Jack said coldly.

"Don't be an idiot. I mean, I met a *very extraordinary* person, someone who—well, someone who just may have been the most important person I've ever met in my life. The most important person *any* of us might meet . . ."

Jack suppressed a groan, thinking of all the other Most Important People in Leonard's life, from the Dalai Lama to Gunther, Leonard's personal scarification artist.

"Don't you look at me like that." His tone startled Jack: not Leonard's usual imperious command, but something that held a warning in it. Not just for Jack, either. Leonard himself looked distinctly uncomfortable, almost frightened. And *that* worried Jack most of all, because Leonard Thrope made his art, and his living, by not being afraid of anything.

"Jackie, I am doing you a favor," Leonard went on in the same quiet voice. "A very *big* favor. I think." He glanced down at the cloth bag.

"Oh." Jack swallowed. He imagined any number of horrors that Leonard might have brought back from Tibet—scorpions, a mummified penis, a chunk of uranium. "Well. Maybe you shouldn't have."

Leonard sighed. His fingers closed around the sack. For an instant Jack's heart leapt: he wouldn't be able to part with it, after all. But then Leonard let out his breath and, leaning forward, opened Jack's hand and placed the cloth pouch inside it.

"Okay. There—I've done it. It's yours, now."

Jack made a small sound and tried to shove the thing back at Leonard. Leonard shook his head.

"Hey! Relax, Jack—it's not a goddamn monkey's paw—"

"Leonard, I don't really—"

"Just open it, okay? For chrissake." Leonard stared at his friend in disgust. "And be *careful*—"

Jack looked down at his open palm. The pouch lay there, small and oddly heavy.

"Open it," Leonard urged.

The pouch was closed with a narrow strip of leather. Jack teased it loose, his heart beating much too fast. He turned so that Leonard would not see how his hands trembled.

"Right," Jack whispered. Now the pouch was open. He tilted it above his palm, half-expecting something to spill forth, bones or stones or magic beans. But whatever it held was too big. Jack bit his lip, then stuck his finger and thumb into the pouch and pulled whatever was inside, out.

"There!" Leonard grinned triumphantly, the same expression he'd had when he first talked Jack into visiting the Anvil with him oh, a hundred years ago.

Jack shook his head and held a small bottle up to the light. A brown-glass medical vial, of the sort Jack had become too familiar with over the last few years, wide-mouthed and stoppered with a lump of soft lead and a wax seal. A neatly hand-lettered label was pasted crookedly across it. Jack squinted, trying to read, but it was covered with Japanese characters. Only at the very bottom someone had written in a shaky hand.

FUSARIUM APERIAX SPOROTRICHELLIA
FUSAX 687

Jack turned to Leonard. "What is it?"

Leonard hesitated. Then, "It's an experimental drug," he said. "Dr. Hanada calls it Fusax. The 687 is a batch number—it's the most recent one."

"Dr. *who*?" Jack shook his head. "Leonard—what the hell *is* this?"

Leonard smoothed his leather kilt against the top of

his thighs, fiddled with a loop of gold chain dangling from a sleeve. Finally he began.

"I have a client, a CEO at Zeising, who collects birds. Apparently there was a sighting a few months ago of a Himalayan griffon. Of course they're supposed to be extinct, like everything else, but you'd be surprised what turns up.

"Anyway, my client arranged for me to go to Gyantse. Private jet, fake visas—the usual shit. Only when I got there the guide who'd been arranged for me had mysteriously disappeared—I never found out what happened—and I was stranded for two weeks in Lhasa. Just as well, since I needed the extra time to acclimate, so I wouldn't get altitude sickness. I spent most of my time at Nechung Monastery. The monks weren't crazy about having me at first, but eventually we came to an—understanding—and they allowed me to live there for several days.

"It was the griffon that did it. Sky burials, you know. In Tibet they chop you up and put the pieces on a mountaintop for the vultures, unless you're a lama, in which case you're cremated or buried. I—"

Jack sighed, "I remember." Five years earlier, Leonard's customarily graphic *Cemetery of the 84 Mahasiddhas* had caused some problems at Sundance. With a grim expression, Jack held up the vial of Fusax. "*Leonard. What* does this have to—"

"—I told them about the griffon," Leonard went on coolly. "They consider it sacred there in Nechung. It's a holdover from the Bon faith. Very rarely, holy men are given sky burial; if the griffon comes to the funeral, it's considered a sign that the dead man has been accepted into the highest level of existence in the afterlife, and will not be reborn. Griffons oversee the passage between this world and the world of the dead. Really, it's just a vulture—a very beautiful vulture.

"One night, a monk came to my room. He spoke a little English, and he understood that I didn't want to hunt the griffon, or to kill it—they'd seen all my equipment, helped me hide it, as a matter of fact, in case the PSB came looking for me. He told me that there was a place I should visit, another monastery on an island in the sacred lake of Yandrok-tso. He said I might see the griffon there; but he also said there was a man I should meet. A monk. Someone who had been waiting many years for me to come."

Leonard fell silent, his dark gaze fixed upon the window. Jack grew increasingly uneasy. In motion Leonard possessed a certain predictability; sitting still he filled Jack with alarm. He tried hard to think of something to say that would disarm the moment—like, who in their right mind would have been waiting for *Leonard*?—but any answer to this question was too ominous to contemplate.

"So I went to Pelgye Kieria," Leonard went on. "That was the name of the island, and the monastery. An amazing place, Jack! Only seven monks are left there, from this sect that goes back to Ghenghis Khan. They say they protect the door between the worlds. They protect us from Brag-srin-mo, the demon of the cliff. Beneath Pelgye Kieria is the secret gate to her heart, which leads to the underworld. That's what the monks believe, anyway. . . .

"I was at Pelgye Kieria for three days, before I learned that there was a Japanese monk there with them. Quite an elderly man—the others were relatively young, I mean in their forties or fifties—but this monk was old, and very frail. He didn't take his meals with the rest, and no one at Pelgye Kieria mentioned him to me, even though I told them that the monks at Nechung had sent me there specifically to meet someone.

"I tell you, Jackie, the whole place gave me the fucking creeps, and by then I was pretty goddamn sick of yak butter and *tsampa*. They wouldn't let me take any pictures inside the monastery, so I spent all my time out on the rocks, looking for the Himalayan griffon.

"Without any luck, as it turned out; for all I know they *are* extinct. By the third day I figured I'd just about shot my wad at Pelgye Kieria. I was outside taking pictures of the cliffs, trying to think of some way to get back to shore, when this very old man came up and started talking to me.

"He had his head shaved, and he was wearing the same robes and everything as the rest of them. So I probably wouldn't have figured out that he was Japanese and not Tibetan: he just looked like another incredibly ancient wizened monk. But he spoke *English*—I just about swallowed my gum when he started talking to me—and he said that he had heard I was looking for him. I told him about the monk at Nechung; he just nodded, like he knew all about it. But when I asked what *he* was doing there, he just shook his head and said 'Nga lam khag lag song. Ha ko ma song?'

"That means 'I'm lost,'" Leonard explained, smiling wryly. "One of the few bits of Tibetan I *do* know. 'I am lost: do you understand?' I thought he was joking, and so I laughed.

"His name was Keisuke Hanada. *Doctor* Keisuke Hanada; he was careful to tell me that. He had heard that an American photographer had somehow managed to enter the country, looking for the griffon, and had visited Nechung and shown interest in the paintings of the demons there. He thought I was a newspaper reporter; he very much wanted to talk to me.

"He told me that he'd come to the monastery in 1946, right after the war. I don't know how or why they admitted him; he was pretty evasive about answering any questions. He described himself as *samsara*—'wandering on'—you know, that whole Buddhist thing of being trapped between here and various afterlives. He'd had virtually no contact with the outside world since right after the war, and the other monks at Pelgye Kieria pretty much left him alone. I guess if you were to look at it from our perspective, he was there to make atonement, to ease his guilt. But guilt's a pretty Western concept—I don't think that's how Dr. Hanada would have put it.

"He invited me to his room, and—and showed me what he had in there. He said the time had come for him to tell someone the truth about his life. He wanted to tell an American. It was—very important to him, that he talk to an American. . . ."

Jack looked up, surprised at the hesitancy in Leonard's voice. But his friend only stared at the window, then continued.

"His room was your typical Tibetan monk's cell. But he had set up this sort of—laboratory—in it. Not exactly state-of-the-art, either. He'd brought his own equipment with him fifty years ago, and since then he's just sort of jury-rigged everything with—well, you can imagine the kind of shit you'd find in a Tibetan monastery, right? No electricity whatsoever. We're talking Dr. Caligari here, Jackie. And he had a bunch of other stuff—photos and documentation, field notes—though he didn't show me those on that particular visit.

"But it was a real working lab, and he'd been working in it, for all those years. He—he showed me. And he told me this—story. This very long, almost unbelievable, story. For two days, he told me—oh, everything! It would take me a week to do it justice."

Leonard turned. There was something in his expression that Jack had never seen before. A look of *abundance*, of satiety. It would have been captivating in anyone else. Seeing it on Leonard's merry death's-mask of a face, Jack shuddered. When Leonard spoke again, his voice was a hoarse whisper.

"Have you ever seen someone look tortured? I don't mean depressed, or sad, Jackie, but really tortured. *Tormented*. There's this expression they get—it's like they're looking beyond, like they're seeing the other side of something. . . . When I did that series in Nairobi, after the femicides—I saw it there. Or remember that poem we learned in freshman English? 'And then I saw his face/Like a devil's sick of sin'—remember? Well, *that* was what Dr. Hanada looked like.

"He's a kind of *saint*, Jack. I mean a real, live saint, like Mother Teresa, or—well, I don't know. Thomas Merton, maybe? The Dalai Lama? I mean, I've *met* the Dalai Lama, Jack, and it wasn't like this.

"Because Dr. Hanada—he had *done* things. Like Merton, you know? He hadn't just been in this monastery his whole life, he'd had this whole other life, this—Christ, you wouldn't have believed it, Jackie. *I* didn't believe it, at first—I thought he was just some crazy senile old man.

"But he had the photographs. And he had that lab. He's been there for over fifty years now. . . ."

Jack shivered, watching his old lover's face trapped somewhere between horror and ecstasy, seeing out there in the ragged sky something Jack could not comprehend.

". . . fifty years . . ."

But Leonard had always seen it. The end of the century, the end of the world: Leonard had always known what was coming. In high school, the two of them on summer nights would sneak into the Episcopal church and in the myrrhy darkness they would fuck breathless, nearly hysterical at their adolescent daring. Afterward Jack would lie exhausted across the front pew, his T-shirt pulled up to cool himself, bare feet pressed against the smooth wood. Leonard would sit at the church's old pipe organ, and play and sing. He knew only one song. He played it over and over again, hands pounding the worn keys and feet stomping the treadles, shouting in his scorched voice until Jack's hair stood on end—

"How do you think it feels?"

He sang himself hoarse, his face growing red and damp as he hunched over the keyboard. Above him the organ's reading light glowed in the darkness, and dust motes spun like flies. To Jack the words sounded like prophecy, a threat of terrible vengeance to be wrought on that small town with the woods pressing close around it like another, greater night.

"How do you think it feels?
And when do you think it stops?"

Whatever secret horrors fed Leonard's vision, Jack had always believed his friend wanted nothing more than this: to make everyone else see what he saw: corpses rotting in a suburban bedroom, the husks of butterflies drained by spiders, naked men trussed like cattle in darkened basements.

And now we know, thought Jack. His gaze fell upon his friend's ravaged face, the death's-heads tattooed and branded and scarified across his wiry arms and the arc of glowing chips above his left eye. Nothing was left of the smooth-skinned boy Jack had loved except his eyes, which had never been boyish at all. The rest Leonard himself had smelted away, leaving bones and scars and unruly pockets of flesh; the only things that had ever interested him, anyway.

"Fifty years," whispered Leonard. "You know what he was like? Have you ever seen a picture of Padmasambhava?"

Jack made a face. "Not in Yonkers. Not recently."

"Really? Well, here, look—" Leonard rummaged in a knapsack until he found a battered leather wallet, opened it, and flipped through its contents. "*This* guy," he said, holding up a little rectangle like a trading card, its lurid colors somewhat tempered by a fine crosshatching of tears and folds. "Padmasambhava. He's a Tibetan magician, this legendary yogi. Anyway, that's who Dr. Hanada looks like."

Jack took the picture. It showed a demonic-looking figure with madly rolling eyes standing on one leg. In his left hand he clutched a staff almost twice his height, impaled with human skulls.

"Right," said Jack. Very deliberately he placed first the picture and then the vial of Fusax into Leonard's hand. "You know, I don't think I want to hear any more about any of this, Leonard. Thank you all the same. And I'm pretty tired, so maybe we could see about getting together some other—"

"It's the cure, Jack."

Jack gaped at him. His friend stared back, his expression withdrawn, almost hostile. Without a glance, Leonard dropped the picture of Padmasambhava. It wafted across the floor and beneath the bed.

"The cure." Leonard held up the vial so that light from the window flowed over it, sparking its contents with flecks of gold and green. "A miracle, Jackie."

Rage swelled inside Jack, pushing aside exhaustion and fear and even curiosity. *"What?"*

"You heard me, Jackie." Leonard's eyes glittered. His mouth stretched into a grin as broad as it was merciless. "All that other stuff they've been giving to us all these years? It's *bullshit*, sweetheart. *Bullshit*—

"*This* is it. This is the cure. For AIDS, for petra virus, all of it. This is what's going to change fucking human history. *Fusax*."

For a long moment Jack just stared at him: the corona of light around Leonard's hair, the little bottle in his hand like a bright grenade.

Then, "You fucking son of a bitch," said Jack.

And he decked him.

"*Hey—!*"

Leonard crashed to the floor. Through the blood pounding in his ears, Jack heard the crack of his friend's skull against wood and felt his heart start joyously, as though a lover had called his name.

"*What the fuck?*" Leonard flung his arms protectively across his face, the bottle rolling toward the wall. "WHAT THE—"

Jack ignored him. He walked over to where the vial had come to rest against the leg of his father's old desk. He picked up the bottle and eyed it warily.

FUSARIUM APERIAX SPOROTRICHELLIA
FUSAX 687

He pondered the indecipherable Japanese characters above the Latin name. But of course they had nothing to tell *him*, good old dependable Jackie-boy. Mysterious doctors never shared their secrets with him, and the only demon Jack had ever known sprawled on the floor behind him, moaning and cursing.

". . . fucking *nuts*, Jackie, you know that? Fucking . . ."

Jack continued to stare at the vial, giving it this last

chance to redeem itself. At last he turned, facing the window with its rippling wands of carnival light, and with all his strength hurled the bottle from him.

"JACKIE! *NO*—"

He had expected it to shatter against the pane. Instead the vial shot right through the glass, leaving a surprisingly small neat opening, like a bullet hole. Jack walked over and examined it.

"*Wow.*" He wasn't *quite* foolish enough to stick his finger through. Instead he crouched down and eyeballed it, shaking his head in wonderment at a hole the size of an old-fashioned silver dollar. There was no radius of cracks, no broken glass. Just that perfect bull's-eye. "I was *sure* it would break."

Behind him Leonard stumbled to his feet and limped to the window. Jack flinched, but the other man seemed not even to notice him. Leonard put his hands upon the glass and pressed his face close, his breath fogging the pane as he peered at the lawn below. A bruise was already darkening his left cheek. "I can't believe you did that."

"Me neither." Jack glanced at him warily, but his friend only stared outside. His dark eyes were filled with tears.

"Oh, shit." Jack's bravado melted into remorse— he'd only seen Leonard cry once before, at Rachel Gardino's funeral. "Leonard, I'm—oh, Jeez, Leonard . . ."

"I can't *believe* it. I was only trying to—trying to—"

Jack shook his head. "You'd better go," he said hoarsely. His knuckles throbbed from where he'd struck Leonard. He felt like he was going to burst into tears himself. "Okay? I just think you'd better go."

Leonard nodded. His hands still rested upon the windowpane, the small hole framed between them. Suddenly he turned.

"I know why you did that." His tone was calm; he rubbed his bruised face almost lovingly. "*Jackie*. You really need to get over it. You'd be a lot better off if you learned how to deal with your feelings for me, you know that? All that rage? It'll kill you, Jackie-boy. But this—"

He gazed out the window, to where the lawn with its fringe of sickly daffodils shimmered beneath the golden sky. "—*this*," he repeated, his voice starting to shake. "You may really have fucked up this time, Jackie."

Jack just stared. Was Leonard *threatening* him? But then Leonard laid his hand upon Jack's shoulder.

"I have to leave now," he said. "And I'll be gone for a while. I'll call you when I get back."

Leonard's grip tightened, his fingers digging through Jack's robe until they fastened on a cord of muscle. Jack writhed and let out a small moan.

"*Ow*—"

"You *better* 'Ow.'" The placebit in his front tooth sent out a ruby flare. "Pissing off Padmasambhava like that."

With a disdainful smile he let go of his friend. Jack fell back against the bed, his face contorted with pain. With one last glance out the window Leonard picked up his bags, then headed for the door. In the hallway he stopped.

"I'm not angry, you know, Jackie." He hoisted a bag over his shoulder, bones and mirrors clattering. "Believe it or not. I really *do* understand—"

He cast Jack a sly look, then, grinning, stood on one tiptoe and began to recite.

> *Prince, when I took your goblet tall*
> *And smashed it with inebriate care,*
> *I knew not how from Rome and Gaul*
> *You gained it; I was unaware*

> *It stood by Charlemagne's guest chair,*
> *And served St. Peter at High Mass.*
> *I'm sorry if the thing was rare;*
> *I like the noise of breaking glass.*

He grinned wolfishly. "Watch your back, Jackie-boy—"

And with a soft clatter upon the stairs he was gone.

It took Jack forever to fall asleep that night. His fever was back, his hand ached, he felt guilty and ashamed and generally overstimulated. An hour-long search of the grass beneath his window had failed to turn up anything except for a few rusted malt liquor cans and an IZE ampoule. He didn't find so much as a shard of glass. When evening fell he had Mrs. Iverson bring dinner to his room, canned beef bouillon and Uneeda Biscuits and a glass of tepid water. Exhausted, he fell into bed before nine o'clock, and proceeded to toss and turn until eleven-thirty, marking the hours by the chiming of Lazyland's clocks. He finally resorted to his grandfather's remedy and crept downstairs to warm some milk on the Coleman stove, adding a shot of Irish whiskey from his grandmother's precious hoard. By the time he'd mounted the stairs again to the top floor, he was yawning and feeling pleasantly high. He sank back into bed and soon was breathing deeply.

Just before midnight he awoke. A sound had broken his sleep. A familiar sound, beloved though only half-heard, so that for a few moments as he lay drowsily beneath the heaped quilts and down comforter, Jack felt utterly at peace. He was just drifting off to sleep once more when he heard it again. And froze.

It was a tread upon the stairs: a slow, purposeful,

step. Jack could hear the creaking of the wide oaken floorboards, the softer echo of feet upon the second-floor landing below him. Two more steps and silence; then a nearly inaudible *click*. Jack held his breath. The footsteps resumed. He tracked them as they went from the landing into the next room, the one that had been his aunt Mary Anne's when she was a girl, before she disappeared. He could not hear what went on in there, but he knew, he knew. His heart was pounding so hard it was a wonder he could hear anything at all, and he almost laughed aloud, crazily: he no longer had any doubt but that he was losing his mind. Because this was how it had always been when he was a child, this was how it was supposed to be.

He was hearing silence at midnight, when all the clocks should be alive. The preternaturally loud ticking of the grandmother clock outside the linen closet had been stilled, and the gentle *nick-nick* of the old Dutch regulator. There was no loud clatter from the captain's clocks in the living room; no hum from the little ladder-back clock with the white mouse that climbed until it struck one. Only that slippered tread, stopping here and there like a nurse checking for fevers; and after each pause Lazyland grew more still, its burden of silence increased as one by one the clocks were stopped.

"No," Jack whispered, as the footsteps moved from Mary Anne's room. *"No."*

In the great house beneath him his grandfather was walking. Room to room, floor to floor, always aware of midnight looming before him, when if they were not silenced, all the clocks would strike at once. Pausing a dozen times or more upon each landing to gently open countless glass faces, then to lay a finger upon the hands to halt them. As he had always done when Jack or any of the grandchildren stayed over, quieting each clock in turn, so that the song of all those chimes and gongs would not awaken them.

It was the last sound Jack had heard every night at Lazyland, when he would awaken to that patient tread. Lying in bed confused by twilight sleep, hoping to catch a glimpse of his grandfather as the old man mounted the last steps to the top floor, where the old nursery clock on its oaken library table gently ticked off the hours. In all those years Jack had never once seen his grandfather on his errand; only awakened each morning to the smells of coffee and bacon and cigarette smoke drifting up from the kitchen, sunlight falling in neat yellow squares upon the weathered floor, and a triumphant cascade of chimes echoing through the house as all the clocks struck seven.

Now Jack lay rigid in bed. He could hear the steps move from his uncle Peter's old room into Aunt Susan's, the room where Mrs. Iverson now slept. There the thick oriental carpet muffled all noise. But after a minute the tread sounded once more. It moved into the tiny corner room, that held only a cobbler's bench on which sat a cottage clock. *Snap* as the casing was opened; *snick* as it closed again. Creak of the door pushed shut. The footsteps hesitated at the bottom of the stairs, then began their final ascent.

Jack listened spellbound. His dread was gone. Instead he felt anaesthetized, almost giddy; because surely this was what it was like to die? Didn't loved ones sometimes arrive to take you to the other side? A thought lodged like a stone at the bottom of his consciousness told him that this was just a dream—he had often dreamed of his grandfather in the years since his death—and yet that did nothing to mute his exhilaration. He tried to sit up, but his arms and legs were paralyzed. This, too, happened in dreams, you tried to move and could not, struggled in vain to open eyes weighted with stones and earth; but he only fought harder, writhing frantically beneath the covers. The footsteps came more slowly now—it was a long haul up all those steps—but Jack was ready, his heart thundered, and his breath came faster and faster, he was almost gasping with joy. He would see him, finally, all those fruitless nights of waiting up would be redeemed; all those mornings waking to find that it was just a dream, Grandfather was really dead and the world not as it had been when Jackie Finnegan was a boy.

And now he heard the solid thump of Grandfather's foot upon the landing, then another as the old man pushed himself forward, one hand lingering upon the banister to keep his balance. The door to Jack's room flew open. A breath of cool air wafted inside, followed by a close warm smell, cigarette smoke and Jameson's, the scent of starch on a white cotton shirt. Jack opened his mouth to cry aloud but gaped within a sudden airless void, the scents of tobacco and whiskey sucked away.

In the doorway a figure loomed. He was cast of light as a shadow is drawn of darkness, light everywhere, so that he seemed to be aflame. Jack recognized the unruly crest of white hair above a broad high brow, the proud beaked nose and the eyes behind wire-rimmed glasses, icy blue, deep-set. His grandfather's mouth opened as though to speak. A roaring filled Jack's ears: he could hear nothing. His grandfather only smiled and stepped into the room. Jack strove to rise but all strength was gone from him. He lay limp abed like a sick child, staring.

"Jackie."

His grandfather's voice sounded within his head; that deep voice, with its slight smoker's rasp. He thought he would swoon as the old man drew near the bed. Upon Jack's brow was the touch of a hand, cool and dry as paper. A blurred shadow moved before his eyes. He gazed up and saw what, as a sleeping child, he had always missed: his grandfather standing there with tears in his eyes, gazing down upon him.

"Jackie."

Something brushed his cheek, like a moth or leaf blowing past. The voice came again, a whisper of familiar words: what his grandfather had always said in farewell, when Jack left Lazyland to return to his own home.

"Jackie-boy. Be well."

Be well . . .

Like rushing water, air filled his lungs again. Jack choked and gasped, found himself sitting bolt upright in bed, sweat-soaked, the damp covers tumbling to the floor. About him the room swam with gold and emerald. Greenish sunlight streamed onto the floor from the window with its small neat bull's-eye below the muntin. From downstairs echoed the clamor of the old grandfather clock striking seven.

"Jesus." Jack dragged a hand across his brow. He was trembling fiercely. "Another fucking dream."

It was only when he stood shakily, tugging his pajama sleeve from beneath his pillow, that he saw in the downy hollow where his head had lain a small parcel wrapped in tissue.

Be well . . .

His heart began to thump, but slowly now, as he picked up the parcel and unraveled the thin paper, letting it fall to the floor. When he was done he turned to the window and raised his hand, so that sunlight nicked what he held. A small glass bottle stoppered with lead and wax, and the label:

FUSARIUM APERIAX SPOROTRICHELLIA
FUSAX 687

CHAPTER FIVE

Iconography

T heir second day in Boston, after their very last tour performance, Trip woke and thought his room was on fire.

They were staying at a church-owned hostel near Cambridge. The building felt pleasantly outdated. The rooms were spare but many-windowed, the obsolete unfiltered arches facing southeast across the Charles River. Trip's bedside cabinet held furled copies of *Guideposts*, *The Screwtape Letters*, a Dorothy Sayers mystery, an Isabel Allende novel, a tiny book of Meditations. The only television was in the common room downstairs, beneath a framed photograph of the president. Another photo showed the president and a hostel prefect at the inaugural ball held by the Christian Majority Alliance/United We Stand For Freedom. The television, when it worked, was tuned to JC–1, so that now and then Trip heard his own voice echoing from downstairs. The entire house had an agreeably antiseptic smell, not the cloying sweetness of Viconix but the old-fashioned scents of pine deodorizer and lemon and ammonia. Trip's bed was narrow, the coverings clean and cool and white. It all made him think of the single summer he had gone to camp down in Union, Maine, before his father died. The night after his performance he lay in bed with his eyes closed and tried to project himself back to Alford Lake, with loons wailing instead of sirens, water lapping softly at Old Town canoes and Sunfish.

It didn't work. Instead a dream of burning desert sand edged Trip into wakefulness. He blinked, staring confusedly at the tiny room. Suddenly he sat bolt upright.

"What the—!!"

Flaming columns rose from floor to ceiling. They flickered from crimson to gold to the lambent white of an empty IT disc. With a cry Trip started for the door, stumbling on his blankets; then stopped.

The room was filled not with flames but light. The high-arched windows were so brilliant he had to shade his eyes. Even the floor glowed, the plain pine burnished to molten bronze. From the corridor he could hear excited voices.

"What is it?" Trip asked breathlessly as he opened the door. "What happened?"

"Nothing." Jerry Disney leaned against the wall and yawned, running a hand across his shaven forehead. He was standing with one of the hostel's prefects, a grey-haired woman still in her bathrobe. "The glimmering. Sunspots or whatever it does. Everything's down again. Go back to bed." He turned and shuffled down the hall to his room.

"Robert's checking on his shortwave." The prefect was more excited than Jerry, her face rose pink in the shifting light. "I mean, it's four A.M., and it looks like broad daylight! Isn't this terrible? Last month we were without electricity for almost a *week*. Did you all get that?"

Trip shook his head. "We were in Dallas. But I heard about it."

"Were you supposed to leave today?"

"Tonight, I think."

"Well, don't bother packing. I'll let you know if Robert patches into any news."

They were stranded for a week. Power was disrupted across the entire northern hemisphere, knocking out computer networks, satellite links, airports from Greenland to Norfolk. The oceanic system of telecom cables was already weakened by an increase in volcanic activity since the Ross Ice Shelf disaster. Now the increased demands for power crippled it still further. Communications were scrambled worldwide. A record number of air crashes occurred, as the shift in the magnetic field played havoc with automatic flight systems. There were riots on the floor of the New York Stock Exchange. In Durham, New Hampshire, seventeen people died in the city hospital when emergency generators failed. Outbreaks of *e. coli* bacteria left dozens of children dead; in Boston, the National Guard had to assist the Red Cross in getting potable water to the South End.

Word of the extent of the disaster gradually filtered into the hostel in Cambridge, where they made do with camping equipment left over from happier times. Coleman stoves and lanterns, wool blankets and water purification kits for what they could hand-carry from the green and viscous Charles. Except for a few group forays to the river, Lucius Chappell made the tour members stay inside—he was terrified of riots.

"Scared shitless of Negroes and *fellahin*," sniffed Jerry Disney. He looked over at Trip and grinned slyly. "Probably thinks *you'll* just book."

By Thursday rudimentary power was restored in some places. At the hostel they still ate by candlelight, working their way steadily through canned soups, canned beans, freeze-dried pasta dinners. Now the only television station they could pick up was an equal-access cable hookup from MIT, staffed mostly by wild-eyed cranks who could be glimpsed inhaling bluish powder on-camera.

"Boil water, avoid brownouts, stay indoors, don't run that A/C, folks," a girl said, giggling as she read from a torn page. She glanced at a bearded young man beside her who was shouting into a cellular phone. "A/C. What's that?"

"Air-conditioning," he replied.

"Jesus, air-conditioning!" She twirled a plastic Frank Sinatra mask, knocking over a bottle of diet soda and registering more alarm than she had while reporting a fire downtown that had killed six people. "*Shit!* That was my LAST ONE—"

Through it all, Trip seldom ventured from his room. He slept with a towel over his eyes, to shield them from the glowing crimson ribbons streaming down through the windows day and night. His dreams were troubled, though he could seldom remember them. He wanted to dream of Alford Lake. He wanted to dream of the blond girl. He never did, but he thought about her constantly, masturbating even though it left him feeling more depleted and depressed than ever. When they left Stamford, he'd crammed a small canvas bag with lilac blossoms. The flowers had since crumbled into brown fragments, but they retained a sweet faint smell. Hour after hour he lay in bed, pressing handfuls of perfumed dust against his face as he tried to summon up the girl's wan image, her twilight eyes. He refused meals and company, pleading sickness; but John Drinkwater at least wasn't fooled.

"You want to talk?" he asked once, standing in Trip's doorway and staring worriedly at the pale figure hunched beneath the blankets.

"No. Tired, that's all." Trip thought of his mother, saying the same thing over and over in the months following his father's suicide. When she finally got out of bed it was to go to Roque Beach and the whirlpool at

Hell Head. "I think maybe I need some time off from touring."

John gave a short laugh. "Well, you're getting it. But Peggy said she thinks she can get a doctor to come by tomorrow, someone with the church—"

"I'm *fine*. I told you, I'm just tired—"

John stared at him measuringly with his calm brown eyes. "Well, I hope so. God forbid you got something from that guy at the airport—"

"You don't get petra virus that way. Look—"

"Forget it." John turned to go. "But if you *want* to talk to someone—well, you don't have to talk to *me*. There's Peggy, or Robert. And the minister's coming by tonight. Just keep it in mind, okay?"

Trip forced a smile. "Okay." When John left he burrowed deeper into his bed, his legs and chest and groin matted with dead lilacs.

By the weekend, a few airports were open, accommodating those passengers (and airline crews) willing to risk traveling. Jerry and the other band members were impatient to leave. Even Trip was ready. But John Drinkwater refused.

"You guys crazy? It's going to be a madhouse at Logan, might as well wait a few days until things ease up. We're just going home, so relax, okay? Pretend you're on retreat."

"More like freaking house arrest," Jerry muttered, and for once Trip nodded in agreement.

The next morning Trip got a phone call. On his private number; it woke him, and he had to dig through mounds of sheets until he found his phone.

"Yeah?" he said guardedly.

"Trip, Nellie Candry—"

A flash of panic: she knew! the girl had told her—

"—how you kids doing up there?" Her cheerful

voice sounded impossibly small and far away, a lady-bug's voice.

"Uh—we're fine. I mean, the same as everyone, I guess." He moved around the room in hopes of improving the reception and stopped at the window, frowning. "How'd you find me?"

"Remember? You gave me the number. At the hotel that night—"

"I mean how'd you find me *here*. We haven't been able to talk to anyone—"

Her laughter tinkled from the phone. "Sweetie! I'm GFI—we talk to *Elvis!* We *never* shut down! But listen—you're in Cambridge, right? By MIT?"

"Uh, yeah," Trip said warily. "I think."

"Well, I need you to go there. I've set something up for you—they have a studio, they're like the only people who've managed to stay up all week. Did Ray Venuto get in touch with you?"

"Who?"

"Our contracts lawyer. He was supposed to fax you—"

"No. I mean, it's a mess up here. Hardly anyone's been able to call in or out."

Pause. Then, "Well, okay, that's okay. I still think we can swing this. We've got Legal behind us, in case there's any question. But probably you shouldn't talk this up yet, 'cause it's just gonna be you. I mean they don't want the rest of the band, not this time. Capische? I want *you* to go to MIT, Trip: just you. The studio's at the Atkinson Center, I have no idea where that is, but I'm sure some-body can get you there—"

Trip stared bewildered out the window. "What? When?"

"This afternoon."

"But I don't understand. I mean, I can't do a recording without a band. Plus there's no power up here, not for stuff like that—"

"Believe me, sweetie, the world could end and MIT would not lose power. They siphon off the grid: as long as *someone's* got power, somewhere, they're okay. And it's not a video. It's an IT studio. Since you haven't actually signed the contracts yet we'll call it an independent demo, just in case anyone gives us a hard time later—"

Trip shook his head, a little desperately. "But—"

"But they won't! I *promise* you they won't." Nellie's voice faded into static. Relief flooded him, but after a moment she was back, her tone lower now, conspiratorial.

"Listen, Trip—the truth is I ran into Leonard Thrope the other day, down at Hellgate. I told him you were signing on, and he got real excited, I mean I haven't seen him so psyched up about something for a while. I told him I wanted you to do an IT and he told me about the studio at MIT, he's friends with some guy there and he wants to shoot you, Trip! An icon and some stills, I mean, can you believe it? Leonard fucking *Thrope*!"

Trip bit his thumb. "Who's Leonard Thrope?"

"What, they keep you guys under a news blackout?" Nellie laughed, but then her voice grew thoughtful. "Actually, Leonard Thrope is probably not your basic Xian poster boy. He's a very, *very* famous photographer—he founded the mori school, you've heard of that, right?"

Trip grimaced. "He's that guy who makes movies of dead people?"

"*Mors Ultima*. Yeah, that was Leonard. But he does other stuff, too, fashion shoots, a lot of stuff for private patrons. He's on Radium all the time, you *must* have seen his stuff—"

"I know who he is."

Trip angled so that he could look down to where a tiny red electric car inched its way along the street. Ladybug voices, ladybug cars. "Look, Nellie—I don't know, this guy is kind of weird, isn't he? I mean, maybe this isn't the sort of thing I should be doing, 'cause like I know for a fact that Peter Paul Joseph would have a heart attack if he—"

Nellie sighed. "We should be so lucky. Listen, Trip, I'm not going to pressure you. And maybe you need to think some more about all of this. Mustard Seed's been good to you. Your sales are solid, you got a nice little fan base. Maybe you should stay there, maybe we should talk again in a couple months, you know? Maybe in a year GFI buys out your whole fucking company and all our problems are solved."

Her voice grew faint and staticky. A shaft of fear ran through him—he had no number for the blond girl, no address, nothing to bind her to him save this little voice chirping in his head, distinctly less cheerful than it had been a few minutes ago.

". . . so we'll just—"

"No!" He shoved the phone against his ear so hard it hurt. "No, it's okay, I'll do it, I'll do it. But you got to tell me how to find this place—"

She told him. "And listen, sweetie, don't *worry*, it'll be great, you are going to be so *happy* you did this. Leonard's a sweetheart, all that other stuff is mostly just PR, you know that, right? Go on now, I'm gonna call Ray and tell him you're—"

Her voice crackled out. Trip shook the receiver. Silence. He shrugged and stuck the phone in his pocket, went to dig a wristwatch from a pile of dirty clothes. Nellie had told him one o'clock. It was 11:30, which meant people would be gathering soon for lunch. If he left now, someone would be bound to come looking for him. But if he stuck around for lunch and then tried to sneak out, he might not have time to find the MIT campus, let alone some mysterious basement studio. He decided to leave.

He pulled his worn pea coat over his old fisherman's sweater and walked hurriedly downstairs and out the back door. He met no one, though John Drinkwater's deep voice boomed from the living room, and silhouetted in the kitchen window he glimpsed Peggy's silver head, bent over the sink.

Finding the MIT campus didn't take as long as he'd feared. Once there he saw students everywhere. Black-clad, intense-looking young men and women, and more Asians than Trip had ever seen in his life, carrying books and backpacks and looking as though it would take much more than an East Coast blackout to disrupt their studies. Trip wondered if classes had even been canceled. Probably not, he decided, watching two patrician-looking blond girls with blinking placebits in their eyebrows hunched over a palmtop. They glanced up at him and smiled absently, then went back to their work. Trip watched them with a mixture of wistfulness and disdain. His own college career had been brief: just those two semesters at Olive Mount Bible College in Bangor, where he'd gotten a music scholarship. His grades were terrible. He read at a sixth-grade level. Even simple algebra and the most basic computing skills were remote as astrophysics. But he had a remarkable memory: he could quote Scripture and even Shakespeare if only he could be made to understand the words on the screen in front of him, or if someone were to read them aloud.

He could, fortunately, read the words MAS-SACHUSETTS INSTITUTE OF TECHNOLOGY on a metal sign glazed with ice. Good thing, since otherwise he might have walked right off campus, thinking he was in just another youth ghetto. He stopped in front of the sign, shivering in the lurid orange glow of midday. He was too embarrassed to ask a student for directions. They all looked so *expensive*. Dressed in faded black, or wrapped in cardboard and rags like the *fellahin*, they would betray themselves by smiling, showing even white teeth and glinting placebits. Except for the cranks, whose eyes within shrouds of spun acrylic were uniformly silver-grey; what hair they had was glossy and flecked with light. Like Trip himself, few of the students wore masks—this, along with The Last Generation's continued sexual and pharmacological indulgences, was a constant source of head-shaking and hand-wringing for parents. Trip watched them hurry into buildings, dousing cigarettes, the girls laughing and shaking back their fine black hair, the cranks huddling together to share a spoon. Overhead the sky shimmered from green to gold to blue. He felt awkward and out of place, no longer the nascent Xian supernova but trailer trash from Moody's Island. For a miserable quarter hour he wandered around, before getting up the courage to stop an older man in a worn black overcoat.

"'Scuse me, I'm looking for the divit lab?"

The man shrugged. He pointed at a very thin middle-aged woman with a shaved head and a bright red faux-mink coat. "Sorry. Ask Sonya there, she's in computer dialectics—"

Trip crossed to her. "Uh—excuse me—"

The woman looked at him curiously. A transparent silken web covered her vividly lipsticked mouth.

"Are you one of my students?" Her scalp had been neatly incised with paragraphs of text, not tattooed but scarified black lines fine as drypoint. On her right temple scowled Ignatz Mouse, a word balloon hovering above his mouth.

THOSE WERE SOME MIGHTY
GOOD OLD DAYS IN
COCONINO COUNTY,
OH WHY DID THEY HAVE TO END?

Trip shivered in his pea coat, wondering how her poor bald head could bear the cold. *The word made flesh.* He shuddered and looked away.

"N-no," he said. "I mean, I don't think so. But—"

She smiled, a glister of white beneath the silken web. "That's okay. You just looked familiar, that's all. You want the Bloembergen Lab—"

Trip shook his head. "She said divit. I mean the lady who sent me, she said the divit lab, or something like that."

"That's Bloembergen. DVI-IT technologies, they call it divit. Come on. I'm heading that way, I'll make sure you don't get lost."

He walked beside her. The wind sent eddies of dust and grit flying up into their faces. The woman coughed, tugged a heavy woolen scarf from the collar of her coat, and swept it across her face.

"Doesn't that get cold?" Trip asked. The icy wind made him shudder. "Your head like that?"

She glanced at him, her almond-shaped eyes glinting with amusement. "This?" She patted her scalp, and Ignatz winked at him. "No. Feel it—central heating."

He gave her a dubious look. "Go ahead," she urged, stopping on the sidewalk. "Colar implants. You've never seen them?"

She lowered her head. Tentatively Trip let his hand trace the edges of a scarified paragraph. The raised flesh felt distinctly warm and slightly rubbery, like a lure worm. As his fingers moved across the words thin music sounded very softly, a *glissando* of piano and fluttering drumbeats. From the back of her neck a voice whispered.

Think twice before causing
Just anything to be.

Trip snatched his hand away. The woman laughed. "Morton Feldman. Isn't that neat? I treated myself when I got tenure. Okay, here's your stop—the lab's downstairs, I think there's a sign, but you basically just keep turning right. See you later."

Inside the building was softly lit by bursts of gold falling from the windows. There were no guards, no electric lights. The security checkpoint had been deactivated; beside the magnetic arch a hand-lettered sign read SORRY FOR THE INCONVENIENCE, with Japanese characters penciled beneath. A few students sat in a hallway eating and listening to music percolating from a colorful spinning top. Trip found the stairs and went down slowly, his hand sliding along the cool metal rail. He felt tired and anxious and completely unprepared to do a recording session of any kind. The basement was numbingly cold. A few emergency panel-lights cast a faint grey glow, so that he could see where cockroaches skittered across the floor. All of the rooms he passed seemed abandoned, heaped with metal chairs and desks and the gunmetal grey bulk of old computer monitors. Finally he reached a black metal door emblazoned with the words

**BLOEMBERGEN LABORATORY:
DIRECT-VOICE INTERACTION/
INTERTEXT RECORDING
STUDENTS: PLEASE BE PREPARED
TO SHOW YOUR PASS!**

Under this someone had taped a piece of paper
scrawled with magic marker.

**PRIVATE RECORDING SESSION.
SORRY. NO ADMITTANCE.**
T. Marlowe please knock!

He knocked. No one came. He listened but could
hear nothing, had his knuckles raised to knock again
when the door cracked open.

"Yee-es?" a voice drawled.

Before Trip could say anything someone grabbed his
hand and yanked him inside. The door slammed shut.

"Trip Marlowe! You made it!" A slight black-clad
man much shorter than Trip whirled him into the room,
yelling, "Great, this is great! Sammy, get your shit
together, we got a go here. Look, boys: *Trip Marlowe.*"

Trip shoved his hands into his pockets. He glanced
around helplessly, embarrassed by the man's mocking
tone, the bored expressions of the two technicians who
slouched in swivel chairs beside a bank of recording
equipment, pointedly ignoring him. They were watching television; it showed the GFI experimental dirigible
fleet at rest on an airfield, then abruptly cut away to a
scene of flames, the tiny cartoonish Blue Antelope logo
in the corner of the screen.

"I guess this is the right place?" Trip asked, hoping it
wasn't.

"Oh, ab-so-po-*lutely*," the man replied. He clamped a hand on Trip's shoulder and steered him toward the far end of the room, where white crosshatched screens rose in front of a lethal-seeming array of still cameras, vidcams, halogen lights, and what appeared to be sophisticated types of surgical equipment. There was an indefinable but suspicious smell of smoke. "Nellie said you'd be here, but things have been so fucked up, I was supposed to be in Mirbat for another oil spill—like, where do *they* get the oil?—but of course our little atmospheric challenge changed all *that*. I was marooned for *two days*! Then, of course, the only place I was cleared to land was Logan. I had to leave the troupe back in the city. A total wipeout, but then, thank God, YOU were here—"

The man let go of Trip's shoulder and gazed at him appraisingly. After a moment, "Leonard Thrope," he announced.

"Uh—Trip," said Trip in a stunned tone. "Marlowe."

"Please." Leonard gestured at an empty chair standing forlornly amidst all that glittering paraphernalia. "I'll just be a moment."

Trip sat. Leonard strode to a pile of bags and began pulling bottles out of a knapsack. Without a glance at labels or contents he opened them, ingesting their contents in a seemingly arbitrary fashion.

"*Not* what you think," he reassured Trip. "Selenium, pantothenic acid, astragalus, this is some kind of blood purifier. Vitamin K. Spirulina. Saquinavar." He replaced everything except a tiny lacquered snuffbox. "*This* of course is Persian Cat," he added matter-of-factly, and took a few discreet sniffs. "Want some?"

Trip shook his head, horrified and dazzled. "N-no. Thanks." If all the preachers he had ever known had been able to get together and create, from scratch, their own unqualified, indubious, and absurdly outfitted vision of the abyss, this would be it. Leonard Thrope moved with the savage authority of a very small dog approaching an unwary child. His tangled grey-streaked hair was long and braided with glass beads. What little of Leonard's flesh Trip could see—hands, face, a scabby bit of ankle—was covered with an intricate web of flowers, cuneiform characters, and crude sexual graffiti. When he moved, flashes of virent green and yellow appeared through rents in his clothes, like trapped fireflies.

Leonard tilted his head, curled his fingers around the proffered snuffbox. "Right," he said. "Probably better you don't," and tossed it into a bag. "Okay. Let's roll 'em."

He walked lightly back to where Trip sat and took him by the hand. Involuntarily Trip shrank from him. He expected something dry and scabrous; a crudely illustrated church pamphlet featuring Eve and a boa constrictor leapt unbidden to his mind. Instead Leonard's hand was muscular and smooth, his lingering touch feather-light as he eased him from the chair.

"Hey," he said gently. He looked into Trip's eyes, brushing a wisp of blond hair from his forehead and letting his hand rest for a moment on the boy's cheek. "It's okay. Really, I don't bite. I forgot, you've probably had kind of a sheltered life, huh? You Xian kids. But this'll be fine, it'll go really well, and when we're done GFI will sell every other act they own to buy this disc. So just try to relax and enjoy it—"

As he talked he steered Trip through the maze of recording equipment until the boy stood in front of the white screens. "You've never done this before, right?"

Trip shook his head.

"Good. It's better that way. Not so self-conscious."

Leonard hunched behind a tripod and adjusted a series of lenses. One of the technicians switched off the TV; they both pulled their chairs closer to the monitors and began playing with keyboards and dials. "What we do is, we get some footage of you, dancing or whatever. Picking your nose. I mean, you can lie there asleep if you want to, it doesn't matter to them. Later it all gets jacked up on computer. They just want something to work with. Get your essence, right?

"That's for the IT stuff. Me, I want to take some pictures."

Trip glanced at the technicians. "You just want me to stand here?" he asked doubtfully.

"Whatever," one of the young men said.

"*I* don't." Leonard's hazel eyes glittered. "Pure white light: that's what *I* want. Wait . . ."

He reached for a leather satchel plastered with Orgone holograms and shiny new Blue Antelope decals. "Music, you'd probably like that, right? Here—"

Leonard tossed something at one of the technicians. A moment later a haze of feedback filled the room.

> *"Dearly Beloved,*
> *We are gathered here today to get through this*
> *thing called LIFE . . ."*

Trip cleared his throat, took a few practice steps in front of the screen. "You're a photographer, huh?" he asked, trying to sound casual.

Leonard disappeared behind a huge black lens. "Sociocultural pathologist, actually."

Trip stared blankly. "Photography's dead," Leonard went on. There was a series of soft clicks, a faint humming from one of the more dangerous-looking tripods. "*Everything's* dead. The world needs an undertaker. So:

Atlantis sinks, Pompeii burns—I'm *there*. I'm doing some stuff for Blue Antelope now. You ought to know *them*, right? All you little Xian apocalypse nuts. Portfolio called Vanishing Act. Last month I got this thing in Ruwenzori. Dwarf otter-shrew, gorgeous. I've got some proofs here, check 'em out—"

He pushed aside the camera and grabbed yet another bag, pulled out a folder and handed it to Trip. Clear plastic sleeves held rough-edged Cibachrome prints of a small lithe brown animal emerging from a stream. Its most distinguishing feature was a bristling mass of whiskers around a bulbous nose.

Leonard peered over his shoulder and sighed. "*Micropotamogale ruwenzorii.* Beautiful, isn't it?"

Trip glanced up to see if he was joking. "It looks like a rat," he said.

"It's not. See its nose?" Leonard's finger stabbed at a print. "It works like a hydrofoil, sniffs out little crabs and things in the water. This is the last one, probably— that's why I was there. Blue Antelope's filed a lawsuit— there's a big fight going on, whether it should be put in a lab so they can save its genoprint or just leave it there. In case another one shows up."

He laughed sharply and turned to the next photo, showing a fan-shaped array of bones with shreds of flesh between them, like a desiccated leaf. "That's a horseshoe bat. Or was. *Rhinolophus ruwenzori.* Another interesting nose. I was a little late for that one. Fortunately I have a patron who prefers them that way. Dead, I mean. *Really* the last of their kind."

Trip grimaced. "But they're so ugly." He looked up and saw Leonard staring at him, his green-flecked eyes narrowed.

"No, darling," Leonard said in a very soft voice. Carefully he put aside the portfolio, then took Trip's chin in his hand and gently pulled him forward, until he was only inches from Leonard's face. Trip swallowed. He glanced out of the corner of his eyes to see if the technicians were watching, but they only stared raptly at their monitors. Leonard's fingers traced the outline of the cross branded upon his forehead, then his jaw, lingering on the soft hollow of his cheeks, the outer corner of one eye.

"You've got it all wrong, Trip," he murmured. "They're not ugly. They're the most beautiful things in the world. But you and I—"

His fingers tightened. The nails dug into Trip's flesh until the boy cried out, trying vainly to twist away. "—you and I, Trip? *We're dirt.*"

Trip could feel his jawbone shift beneath Leonard's grip, his teeth grinding together like misplaced gears. "*Just dirt,*" Leonard repeated. His tone was dreamy, almost wistful. Trip flailed helplessly, until Leonard wrenched his hand away.

"*Caput mortuum,*" he whispered. For an instant his gaze rested upon the portfolio. Then he turned and strode back to the waiting cameras. Trip caught his breath, gasping.

". . . *electric word, Life,*" rippled from the speakers. "*But I'm here to tell you there's something better—*

"*The Afterworld . . .*"

One of the technicians glanced over his shoulder with a questioning look. Trip got to his feet and started for the door, head throbbing with pain and rage.

"What? Did I hurt you?" Leonard called after him.

Trip stopped. "*Yes,*" he spit, rubbing his chin.

Leonard stared at him, slowly smiled. "Good," he said, raising a camera to his face. "Now get the fuck over here, and let's do our job."

Trip hesitated. "Come on, Trip, don't be an asshole,"

called Leonard. "Meter's running. Don't blow it, okay?"

He did the shoot. The afternoon passed in a haze of heat and burning dust from the halogen lamps. The constant click and whir of recording equipment was like the buzz of locusts Trip remembered from his childhood. He felt dizzy, not a little sick. His jaw ached, and his head. But oddly enough the pain seemed to spur him in front of the camera. After a few stiff minutes he moved antically through the small studio, neatly avoiding bundled cables and the miniature Himalayas formed by Leonard's bags. A technician replaced the music with something atonal and clamorous, that faded into somber gongs and chanting, the high-pitched singing of frogs set to the hollow boom of *djembe* drums.

Trip recognized the frog part. It had been a surprise dance hit a year ago, a melancholy amphibian *chant du cygne* recorded in a remote part of Quebec, where there were still a few spring peepers left. Their wistful music gave way once again to gongs. Trip began to move more artfully, recalling the graceful hands of the Javanese dancer on television.

"I will give you the morning star," he sang, his voice rising in counterpoint to the gamelan. *"I will bring you the end of the end. The end of the end . . ."*

He pulled his shirt off, running his hands across his sweat-streaked chest, toying with the cross on its gold chain. He shut his eyes and thought of the blond girl suspended above him on a bed strewn with lilacs, her fine hair tangled in his mouth, her eyes. He danced and sang, songs from his album, new songs he had only thought of and never written down, songs he hadn't sung since he was on a ramshackle school bus crossing the Kennebec. Finally, after hours had passed and the room was littered with cameras like spent ammunition, Leonard Thrope announced, "Okay. That's enough."

Trip sank onto his haunches. He was breathing hard, but he felt exhilarated, better than he had felt in days; since before he met the blond girl. "Okay," he said, panting, and grinned.

For some minutes he sat there, wiping his face with his shirt and listening to the blood thrum in his ears. Leonard rewound film into canisters and plugged some of the tapes and discs into a monitor, scanning them before shoving them into a leather carryall. A technician tossed Trip some bottled water.

"That was cool," the technician said, unsmiling, his plasmer lenses slate blue in the reflected light of his monitor. It was the first time he had spoken all afternoon. "You want to see what I've done so far?"

Trip rose, but the technician motioned him back. "No, stay there—"

One hand glided across the keyboard. The other slowly turned a small projecting lens. Out of nowhere a figure appeared, crouching on the floor beside the singer. Trip gasped. The figure stood and began to sing. The technician smiled, very faintly.

"I possess the keys of hell and death, I will give you the morning star . . ."

It was Trip himself, of course. But not the Xian Trip, with his haunted eyes and the cross hanging from a gold chain about his neck. Instead the analogue was that of an Indonesian Baris dancer, barefoot and wearing a sort of brocade loincloth stiff with gold and crimson beads. Its hair was lost beneath a dizzyingly ornate headdress that rose pagodalike from its skull. The face was Trip's, but no longer human: it had become a mask the color of new leaves, through which Trip's blue eyes glowed. The figure moved as Trip had, but impossibly fast. As it spun and pirouetted, gold flecked the air, and little flames licked at its heels.

Trip stared, aghast. "How—how—"

"Wait, I'll give you some music." The technician reached for the keyboard again. The monotonous tones of a gamelan rang out, the same four notes repeated in time with the figure's singing. "It's an icon—we just scan your image, right? And then—"

"No!" Trip glanced around for Leonard, but the photographer sat cross-legged on the floor, scribbling on film canisters. "I know how it works! I mean, how'd you *know*," he said agitatedly, gesturing at his demonic shadow. "To make it look like *that*."

The technician shrugged. "Stock footage. Just pulled it out of some file. I dunno, the music I guess, it reminded me of something. But this isn't *final*—"

His tone indicated that Trip was an idiot for thinking so. "—we're just fooling around here. The master'll go to New York; they'll dub it in their studio. This is just the playback."

He turned and switched the sound off, began conferring with his mate at the console. Trip sank back onto the floor. Above him his phantom double silently whirled and crouched within its golden cloud. An analogue; an icon.

"Pretty intense, huh?"

Trip didn't look up when he heard Leonard behind him. "I've seen them before," he said sullenly. In fact he had only seen an IT recording once before, in Dallas, when during a few unchaperoned hours Jerry dragged him to a skin show in Deep Ellum.

"I meant watching yourself." Leonard scraped the stool across the floor and perched on it. "*I* think it's kind of a trip—"

He laughed. "—*Trip*. I do it whenever I can," he added confidingly. His eyes were fixed on the singer's shining twin, but then he gave Trip a sideways look. "It makes for a pretty amazing fuck."

Trip blinked, felt himself blushing. "Not a *fuck*, exactly," Leonard went on in a lower voice, "I mean, with an icon there's nothing actually *there*; but—"

His hand moved. Trip froze, terrified that Leonard was going to touch him, but instead Leonard began to slowly stroke the inside of his own upper thigh, smoothing the stiff folds in his cracked leather trousers and probing a small rent near his groin. His gaze was fixed on Trip's *doppelgänger*, its beautiful blank masked face, its arms drawing arabesques in the glittering air.

"It's really beautiful," Leonard breathed, his tone for once without mockery. A small ridiculous anger fought through Trip's unease.

I'm *really beautiful*! he thought, glaring at the icon and then at the man beside him. "That mask looks stupid," he lied, feeling like an ill-behaved child.

"Oh, I don't think so," Leonard replied softly, his voice catching. Trip tried to force himself not to look but failed: when he glanced over he saw the outline of Leonard's swollen cock, a small sheen of smooth red skin showing through the rip in the leather. "People are so *obsessed* with masks now, I think the mask is what *makes* it—"

Leonard let his breath out in a shuddering sigh. Without warning he stood. He crossed the room, walking right through Trip's double, and crouched beside one of his leather carryalls. Trip closed his eyes.

Go, he ordered himself. *They have the recording, what the hell are you still doing here, GO!*—

He jumped when someone touched his shoulder.

"Here." It was Leonard, hand outstretched. In his palm he held two brilliant emerald green capsules, cone-shaped and with a moist sheen like a frog's skin. "One's for you."

"Wh-what is it?" Trip stammered. But he knew what it was.

"IZE." Leonard lowered himself beside him. "It heightens the whole IT experience—oh for Christ's sake, don't look at me like that!"

"I'm not taking it," Trip said.

Leonard gave an exasperated sigh. "Look, it's practically legal, approval is pending from the fucking FDA, okay? It'll just—*relax* you—"

"I'm not—"

"Look, Trip—you know that everyone who sees this disc is going to be on IZE, right? I mean, who do you think this stuff is *for*? Don't you think you should have *some* fucking idea of what your audience is seeing? Jesus!" Leonard shook his head. "You think this is like Reefer Fucking Madness, right? Well, it's *not*—it just relaxes the inhibitors in your brain. So you, like, register the IT stuff as *real*, get it? You're watching *Macbeth* or something, but you no longer have this perceptual curtain drawn between you and what you're seeing—you're *part* of it."

"No," Trip repeated, but weakly this time. "Look, I better go . . ."

"Wait." Leonard grabbed him. "Millions of people are going to see your disc—*hundreds* of millions. And this is just a demo, Trip—Agrippa's going to want you to do more. A *lot* more. You owe it to them, at least, to have some vague fucking idea of just what it is you're doing. By the time your single's out, these are going to be like aspirin—"

He raised his palm, so that Trip could see the ampoules: each emerald cone as long as the first joint of his little finger, with a tiny needlelike projection emerging from the cone's apex. "It doesn't make you *high* or anything," Leonard explained. Behind him Trip's analogue froze, then began moving backwards, faster and faster, until it was a golden blur of legs and hands. "It just increases the amount of calcium entering some of your nerve terminals—calcium, right? *Not* a scary drug—and it boosts the production of gamma-aminobutyric acid, this neurotransmitter that inhibits anxiety and—stuff. And, well, then it helps create these new neural pathways within the various areas of the visual cortex. You get your visual stimuli coming in through the retina, processed through all these neuro-cellular layers of the visual cortex; but then the stimuli sort of get rerouted into *other* parts of the brain, like the limbic system. All the inhibitory mechanisms that would normally tell you that this is just like, a *video*, are overruled. So you get this incredible emotional response to what you're seeing. It's like the reverse of this weird thing called blindsight—people who are totally blind, but they can still process visual information because parts of their brain respond to stimuli, even though they're not aware of it."

Leonard's voice grew softer. When Trip looked up he saw that the photographer's expression was rapt and without guile. "I mean, it's really very *beautiful*, how it works—"

"How do *you* know so much about it?" Trip demanded, but his tone was more curious than hostile.

Leonard shrugged. "Just part of the job." He smiled, the crimson implant in his tooth glowing. "Look, I told you—it's not going to make you high or anything like that, you'll be disappointed if you're expecting some kind of teenage head-rush. It's just going to help you integrate better with what you're watching. Like when you're hypnotized—you're not going to do anything you wouldn't ordinarily do."

Leonard leaned back on his heels, his proffered hand still holding the IZE cones. Trip swallowed, his throat dry. He thought of the blond girl in the planetarium, kneeling with her head bowed between his legs, of her slim body sliding fishlike through his hands; and wondered if there *was* anything he wouldn't ordinarily do. "I better not," he said at last.

"It doesn't even hurt. Look—"

Leonard pinched one of the cones between thumb and forefinger, held it upside down so that the tip rested against the inner crook of his elbow. Gently he pushed the ampoule against the chiaroscuro of tattoos and raised scars, then squeezed it. Within the cone there was a phosphorescence flash. A smell like a spent firecracker filled Trip's nostrils. After a second Leonard pulled the ampoule away and tossed it onto the floor. Trip's brightly spinning icon raised up on tiptoe above it.

"See?" Leonard murmured. The icon winked out. "Now you—"

He took Trip's hand and pulled his arm straight. Trip grew rigid. Before he could protest there was a prick at his inner arm, like a mosquito bite. He started to cry out, then gasped as warmth suffused his entire body, a rush that started at his gut and spread down through his groin, up through his torso. Terrific heat spread across his face, he could feel his skin flushing, but there was no pain, only an almost unbearably heightened awareness of every atom of his being. He could feel each hair upon his body stiffening, and the prickle of pores opening and closing across his cheeks. His hands and feet tingled as though he had thrust them into a swarm of stinging ants, and he realized that he was actually sensing the blood swimming through his extremities, the countless explosive bursts of neurons firing—*really* feeling them, as though he was an ocean and all the complex systems of his body myriad creatures passing through him in electric waves. He shuddered. The sensation was like a symphony, spangled lights flickering everywhere and warmth flooding down the front of his skull until it centered upon his eyes. He blinked, sending glowing orange pinwheels reeling across his field of vision, and mouthed the words *Holy cow*.

"It'll calm down." Leonard's soothing voice came to him with its own explosive accompaniment, thunderous booms and an array of twinkling fish. "The initial rush provokes mild synesthesia, it goes away . . ."

It did, almost immediately. Trip felt an intense burst of regret. His eyes welled with tears as the waves of sensation condensed into a sort of mental strobing, an intermittent, seemingly random pulse of emotions—sorrow, rage, lust, dismay—that gradually subsided, until he found himself sitting cross-legged on the floor and staring fixedly at the air before him.

"Feel better?" Leonard settled beside him, slowly, as though trying to avoid frightening a skittish colt. "The first time is a little intense . . ."

Trip nodded: *yes*. He perched on the edge of his stool, his hands gripping his knees, his eyes wide and staring.

But not with fear. Rather, he had never felt his attention so incredibly, intensely *focused*: on the bright dust motes moving in the air, each so sharply limned it was like watching tiny crabs scuttling against dark sand; on the bitter sneezy smell of dust burning on the halogen bulbs; on the sound of Leonard's breathing, the faint wheeze when he inhaled and the almost imperceptible hum of the placebit in his front tooth.

"All right then," he heard Leonard murmur. Trip started to glance aside at him. Before he could the air exploded with light and sound. Trip stumbled to his feet, knocking the stool to the floor. Momentarily he was blinded by his own heightened sentience: unable to dis-

tinguish between his hand fluttering before his eyes and
Leonard's grinning face, between a sweet high chiming
sound and the trilling of blood in his skull. Sparks of
gold and scarlet filled the air, like the afterglow of fireworks. He blinked, slowly lowering his hand from his
eyes, and gazed enraptured.

In front of Trip, near enough that he could have
embraced it if he wanted, his jeweled shadow stood
poised on one foot, head cocked as its blue eyes
burned into the singer's. The mask was gone, and the
towering golden crown. The face that stared adoringly
at him was Trip's own: Trip's strong narrow jaw shaved
of blond stubble, the cleft in his chin more pronounced, the scar left by a childhood fall on broken
glass smoothed away. Light danced about its face and
settled into the hollows of its cheeks. Trip's mouth
parted as he tentatively reached to stroke the straight
long hair that fell across the icon's brow. As he did, the
icon raised its hand, its astonished expression mirroring Trip's own. Their fingers met in the glittering air, a
shimmer of flesh and flame; but Trip's hand closed on
nothing. His heart jolted with disappointment, but
when he lifted his head, his face was still there gazing
at him with wide mad electric blue eyes. The tip of a
crimson tongue flicked across its lips, left them gleaming like the moist curve of an apple. He could see the
rayed petals of its irises, its skin smooth and
unmarred by pores or scars but with a sheen like
sweat. Overwhelmed, a little frightened, Trip took a
deep breath and sank to the floor. The icon didn't
move. Its eyes remained fixed on Trip, its hands
extended imploringly.

Trip sucked in air, his heart pounding dangerously
fast. Maybe this hadn't been such a good idea. From
where he sat he had a rather intimidating view of his

double: it was naked, and it had an erection. The body mirrored Trip's own, its slender torso plucked of the few stray hairs that always embarrassed Trip because there weren't more of them. Its legs were smooth and muscular, and its arms. Its cock seemed no larger or smaller than Trip's own, which was somehow disconcerting, as was the fact that as he stared at it, Trip found himself growing hard. But he couldn't look away. His heart fluttered as it had when he'd been with the blond girl. His breath came in shallow gasps; he felt the same swooping vertiginous sensation as of flying or falling, the same insane realization that somehow this was his life, this was happening, this was *real*—

"Hey." It spoke to him, and he shuddered. His own tentative voice, the inflection questioning, half-fearful; shy. He shut his eyes and took a deep breath; opened them: he was still there. "You okay?"

Trip nodded, too fast. The motion made him dizzy. The icon extended its hand and touched his cheek. Trip's shudder became a low moan, but he didn't move away, just sat there as the shining boy in front of him leaned forward and cupped Trip's face in his hands. "Don't be afraid . . ."

Something in its voice slashed through Trip's fear. A slight warbling in its tone, the barest hint of an echo that gave the voice a faintly mechanical quality. But it was enough to remind Trip that what was before him was neither mirror nor memory but only his own borrowed *mien*. It was enough, momentarily, to break the spell.

"N-no." Trip's voice cracked. Somehow that made him feel better, made him feel more sure of himself, more sure that he *was* himself; because surely the icon's voice wouldn't break? He remembered that Leonard Thrope had given him a drug, remembered that he was in a room, and there were other people there, even if he couldn't see them. He rocked back onto his heels and looked around, saw only jagged rays of light and darkness, a faintly glowing blue square. In front of him the icon crouched, pantherwise, blond hair falling in a bright wave across one piercing eye.

"'Thou art beside thyself; much learning doth make thee mad,'" it recited. "'Thou hast created all things, and for Thy pleasure they are and were created.'"

Trip's tongue cleaved to the roof of his mouth. He tried to whisper *No,* but the word died in his throat.

"'For in Thee we live, and move, and have our being; as certain also of your own poets have said, For we are also his offspring.'"

Something warm brushed against his knee. Trip looked down and saw the icon's hand there, its long pale fingers and the pronounced bone of its wrist like a bird lighting upon the dark fabric of his jeans. As he stared the hand began to move, sliding along the inside of his thigh until it reached his groin. He felt another hand stroking the taut fabric, watched now in detached disbelief as the icon's head, with its glittering sheaf of hair, nudged between his legs, its hands gently pulling them apart so that it could rub its cheek against his swollen crotch, moaning. Trip moved his own hands to his breast and crossed them there, gasping when he heard the soft *shirr* of his zipper and felt his shorts being tugged down, the clouded warmth of its hair spilling onto his exposed cock. He squeezed his eyes shut, but it was no good: he could see it still, his own face as in a mirror, lips parted and sudden heat, its tongue flicking at his balls and then a shaft of molten pleasure as its mouth closed around him. With a groan he tried to push himself up from the floor and away from it, but it was too late, its hands slid behind him, shoving his jeans down farther as it grabbed his ass and pulled him roughly forward. A tick of pain: a tooth nicked his glans and Trip shook his head, maddened, his eyes wide and black in the spent light. He tried kicking out, but there was nothing for his foot to connect with; only that ragged whorl of golden hair between his legs, the broken silhouette of a boy kneeling, like the dreamy pattern of wind-tossed leaves. Its fingers splayed across his ass, rough-edged nails and fingertips stroking the tender declivity of his anus and then probing there, so quick and hard that tears flashed from Trip's eyes as he abruptly came, a searing jolt that sent him arching backward as his double sucked greedily at his cock. Its hands tightened, slid upward, tracing the long line from hip to ribs and then falling away from him like ice from a tree limb. Trip lay upon the floor on his back, the pulse of his cock ebbing and the roar in his head dying away, his eyes open and staring numbly at the ceiling. Dust moved there, myriad galaxies trapped in the closed basement. There was the smell of semen, and smoke.

"*Well* now. I guess this just proves that the Lord really *does* work in mysterious ways."

Trip sat up, blinking, his breath still coming in small painful bursts. The IZE's wild glory had faded, and with it the room's harlequin array. Instead he saw only the dark regiment of cameras and recording equipment and raised screens, now empty and lightless, and the shadowy figures of the two technicians beside their monitors. His jeans and underwear hung to just above his knees. He had a glimpse of someone's wrist bent across the fold of his waistband, a shimmer of luminous green as the wrist drew back and left a trail of grey smoke.

"But you know, I must be going," said Leonard Thrope, and got to his feet.

Trip stared at him. He felt as though he had been clubbed: his ears rang and there was a sharp knocking pain in his skull, blood throbbing and his own tiny voice saying *no, no no.* Leonard shook his hair back from his face. He pulled his trousers tight about his waist and zipped them, his eyes still fixed on Trip. A shining seam spilled down one pant leg; absently Leonard let his hand fall across it, rubbing until it disappeared into cracked black leather. *"Experimentum crucis,"* he said, eyes glittering. He dropped his cigarette, left it burning as he stooped and swung one of the leather camera bags over his shoulder. He started across the room, stopped beside one of the technicians and picked up a computer disc. He pocketed it, then took another object, a flattened silvery cube slightly smaller than the computer disc: the IT recording.

"I'll send someone for my things." This to the technicians. They nodded, each raising a hand in farewell as he strode toward the door. "Oh, and Trip—"

His gaze flitted across the boy's face. Leonard smiled, not unkindly. "—it's been a slice. Believe me— this thing is going to *make* you." The ruby placebit winked as he turned and left, the door shutting softly behind him.

For a moment Trip just stood there, hands hanging limply at his sides. His head felt as though it was going to explode. Dimly he could hear the soft whir and tick of computer equipment, one technician asking his colleague a question. Someone had switched a halogen lamp back on, so that dust motes were ignited in a vivid parody of the IZE's light show. Bright jots swirled, congealed into the mask of a grinning blue-eyed demon, blond hair aflame. Its mouth opened, showing a slit of scarlet and pearl, as Trip's own reedy tenor pronounced,

"Fear is the main source of superstition, and one of the

main sources of cruelty. To conquer fear is the beginning of wisdom."

With a cry he raised his arm before his face, blotting out his double, then turned and stumbled for the door. The room behind him was silent as he fled weeping down the deserted corridor.

He did not return to the hostel. Could not return, knowing that door was closed to him forever as surely as if John Drinkwater had slammed it in his face. He staggered through the building lobby, nearly empty now save for a few students huddled with their palmtops beneath a window. They looked up as Trip hurried past, his eyes blank as paper, his mouth working noiselessly.

"Kata tataki," one student murmured. *A tap on the shoulder*: that is, bad news.

"No—*katoshi*!" another said—*Death from overwork*— and they all laughed.

Outside the streets were empty, the sky a raging glory of green-shot violet. The frigid wind tore at Trip as he stumbled along, but it wasn't until he had gone a good five or six blocks that he remembered he had left his pea coat at the studio. The realization was almost a relief, the way terrible news is a relief—*your mother is dead, your father is dead, and now you are going to freeze to death*. He lurched down an abandoned alley where a fine sifting of snow covered dead leaves and broken glass. He walked and walked and walked, until the city fell behind him, with its bonfires and makeshift generators spun from old cars and photovoltaic cells, its windows aglow with candlelight and the sound of arguing voices falling into the street like hail. He walked until he was breathless with cold; until the sky curdled into dawn, milky yellow streaked with lavender and green, and the distant roar of the city's single electric train echoed from Back Bay; until the last small stars, brave and ever faint, trickled into the pulsing core of gold and emerald that was the sun. He walked until he could walk no more; for two days, with a ride now and then from someone in an electric car or eighteen-wheeler racing toward the Canadian border. He walked and sometimes he slept, and sometimes even ate, food from a kindly woman who said he reminded him of her daughter and bread scavenged from a Dumpster in Kittery. He walked until his feet bled inside his old Converse sneakers, until the rusted bridge that spanned the bay between Lockport and Moody's Island appeared before him, until he reached the ruins of his grandmother's Half-Moon trailer off Slab City Road. He walked until he reached Hell Head, and then he lay down to die.

CHAPTER SIX

The Golden Family

J ack started taking the Fusax. After all, he'd spent
the last twenty-five years jumping off bridges
because Leonard Thrope told him to: why stop
now? He had nothing to lose except his life, and that
was pretty much in hock to the virus anyway. So he took
the dropper from one of Emma's vials of organic skullcap, sterilized it in boiling water, and proceeded to play
home pharmacy. He had no way of knowing what the
proper dosage would be, and no way of getting in touch
with the mysterious Dr. Hanada to ask. But if this bottle
was all there was, Jack figured he'd better make it last.

The bottle was difficult to open. The wax had hardened, and he had to chip at it with a nutpick, then prise
free the lead seal. When he was done there was a little
pile of broken wax and a disarmingly small glass vial on
the nightstand in front of him.

"Well," he said aloud, peering suspiciously into the
opening. "'Drink me.'"

Whatever was inside had a very faint, alcoholic
smell, like one of Emma's tinctures. A slightly grassy
odor, redolent of tansy or goldenrod. Jack sniffed it curiously—he had thought it would smell bad, but the scent
was pleasantly innocuous. He glanced at the glass of
water he'd set on his nightstand. He'd planned on
putting the Fusax in there and sipping it slowly and
mindfully, the way Emma told him herbal remedies
should be ingested. Instead he found himself taking the

dropper and, almost before he knew what he was doing, squeezing a few drops of the fluid beneath his tongue.

He felt a slight burning sensation from the volatile spirits, again not unpleasant; and that was all. He sat on the edge of his bed for a full hour, watching the hands of the old captain's clock sweep from 5:00 A.M. to 6:00. Nothing happened. This was mostly a relief; Jack's previous experiences with putting things Leonard gave him into his mouth had been unfortunate. But he felt disappointed, too—which was absurd, even the most miraculous of cures wouldn't work within the first hour. Finally, when he could hear his grandmother and Ms. Iverson moving around downstairs, he found a tiny cork to replace the lead stopper and put the vial into the drawer alongside his other medication. Then he got dressed and went down for breakfast.

March trudged into April and the wettest spring on record. At first the rain was almost welcome. Although the storms couldn't hide the glimmering completely, the heavy clouds did mute the spectral disturbances, so that some days, for an hour or even an entire afternoon, you could almost forget the shattered sky was there.

In the west, heavy weather took a more bizarre turn. An unrelenting series of fronts hung above the plains and farmlands, a squall line that stretched from Texas north to the Dakotas. Storms broke constantly, but in the phenomenon known as *virga*, the rain evaporated before it hit the ground. Immense scythes of lightning raked sky and drought-ridden prairie, starting fires that burned until there was nothing left for them to feed upon. In the wake of the thunderstorms, the mesocyclones spawned scud clouds and funnel clouds and tornadoes, land spouts and, upon the Great Lakes and

Mississippi River, waterspouts that swallowed pleasure
boats and freight barges. Some of the tornadoes were
tracked spinning clockwise, all but unheard of in the
northern hemisphere. As the deadly fronts moved east
and the twisters collapsed, they left mounds of debris,
the remains of houses and livestock, planted fields and
shopping malls. In Kansas a church filled with refugees
was flattened, killing more than three hundred people.
Afterward the church marquee was photographed in the
branches of a scrub oak tree seven miles away.

I SAW A NEW HEAVEN AND A NEW EARTH FOR THE FIRST HEAVEN AND THE FIRST EARTH WERE PASSED AWAY

Across North America crops failed. In the cities, the
first soft footsteps of famine could be heard, and there
were rumors of cultists who claimed to see a shimmering green brilliance hanging about the bodies of those
who would die within twenty-four hours.

By the time the storms reached the Atlantic Coast,
they had dissipated to warm rain and a steady wind.
From his room at Lazyland Jack could watch the fronts
moving from the Palisades across the Hudson, passing
overhead to break at sea like so many vast leaden waves.
At night the usual array of flickering bonfires was gone,
as were the tents that marked the *fellahin* encampments.
Instead, through the tattered scrim of trees Jack could
see figures moving inside the ruined mansions that
flanked Lazyland. At night he smelled the caustic scent
of burning plywood, and heard staccato bursts of music
from the smoke-blackened remains of the maharani's
carriage house. And sometimes he glimpsed the squatters themselves, all but naked despite the spring chill,
their long hair matted as they stood in the shattered

windows and stared defiantly across the filth-strewn lawn at Jack; and once he heard a baby crying.

It all infuriated him.

How can they live like that, he thought. Until one day, returning home exhausted and empty-handed from yet another futile trek up to Getty Square in search of food, it struck him—

We all live like that, now. The *fellahin* were just better at it than he was.

Still, inside Lazyland all was relatively warm and bright. The house was heated by an ancient coal furnace. In January, Jack had had the coal cellar filled; there was enough fuel to see them through to the next winter. When there was electricity, television reception became such a game of chance that most nights they didn't bother—the risk of seeing something horrible outweighed even Jack's considerable hunger for news. When the phone lines worked, there were obscene faxes from Leonard to break the monotony, and the usual trickle of calls regarding submissions for *The Gaudy Book*. Jack's network of loyal editors and writers continued in their doomed efforts at triage, arranging for articles to appear on-line, for popular artists to have their holographic or recorded likenesses on the magazine's cover in a futile effort to boost sales. He never wondered if *The Gaudy Book* was worth it. It was not, certainly not from any financial standpoint, and as a cause of stress in his own life he would certainly be better off without the dying magazine. But he was haunted by the image of his father and grandfather, who had never doubted that *The Gaudy Book* would greet the new millennium.

He spent nearly the entire month of April indoors, except when he walked out to his office in the carriage house. Then the smell of rotting vegetation choked him, and the scent of damp earth that belonged not here but a thousand miles to the west. For the last four weeks he had been taking the Fusax religiously, half a dropperful every morning, on an empty stomach. The little bottle was about a quarter empty.

And he was feeling better: no doubt about it, he was feeling better. His brush with pneumonia had left him weak, with a ghastly cough. At the hospital they'd given him antibiotics, which Jack took religiously until they ran out. The cough, however, had lingered, as did his general malaise and the too-familiar checkpoints of fever, diarrhea, loss of appetite.

Now the cough was gone. The diarrhea was gone, and the fevers. He still had little appetite, but there was no nausea and no weight loss that Jack could measure. Instead he began to wake each day with the sort of joy he had not felt in over twenty years, a rapturous delight over the simple act of opening his eyes and finding the world there to pry open, like the door to some enchanted place. There was no rational reason for this feeling, he knew that. It must be the Fusax.

It's working, he thought.

He felt exhilarated, almost exultant; almost he would have gladly made the pilgrimage to Saint Joseph's AIDS Clinic, just to see their faces when they read his numbers.

"It's working," he whispered to himself one morning, staring at his reflection in the bathroom mirror. His skin was no longer dried and flaking. When he stuck his tongue out, there was no telltale curd presaging thrush. His eyes were clear; the dreadful ache he had carried within his chest like a stone was gone. Only a faint dizziness worried him occasionally, and the fact that sometimes he saw blurred shapes at the corners of his eyes, like those fireworks he would produce in bed at night when he was bored, knuckling his closed eyes to see spurts of green and red and orange. When he bounded downstairs into the entry room, his grandmother looked up from her chair in alarm.

"Jack?"

Grinning he kissed her, leaving a damp smudge on her powdered cheek. "Any calls?"

Keeley gestured dismissively at the huge mahogany table. "Oh, I don't know. Someone might have called, but I didn't answer; I was in the kitchen, and Larena is taking her nap . . ."

Jack nodded cheerfully and started for the door, stopped when he remembered he'd left some correspondence in his room. "Fine. Oops—gotta get something, then I'll be in the carriage house." He glanced back at her. "Do you need anything, Grandmother?"

She adjusted her gold-topped cane, her gnarled fingers closing around the gryphon's beak that formed its capital. "No, dear. You go do your work. I'm glad you're feeling better."

He hurried back upstairs. Light streaked through the clerestory windows, bathing the stair runners in pale green and butter yellow, so that one could almost imagine true spring outside, instead of the glimmering's spurious April sky. Midway to the third floor Jack paused, to reach up and chuck the moth-eaten caribou head beneath its chin.

"Ha," he said, loping up the last few steps. "Hooray for Dr. Hanada."

By the time he got to his room he was out of breath. He reached for the drawer in his nightstand, removed the little bottle of Fusax and cradled it in his palm, then held it up to the light. Within its glass cell the liquid swayed and sparked. For several minutes he sat there staring at it. Then he slipped it back into the drawer, behind his stash of ibuprofen and inhalers and the Mass card for his grandfather. He found the forgotten stack of letters and went downstairs again. In the mudroom he grabbed his raincoat, a tea-colored Burberry that had been his grandfather's, and headed for the carriage house.

Outside, rain slanted down in bright columns, green and gold and silver. On the cracked blacktop, the droplets left a muddy brownish residue that never had the chance to dry: the remains of topsoil stolen from the Great Plains. Wind sent heavy clouds scudding across the sky, their dark bellies splintered with red. Jack walked quickly down the drive, kicking at stunted pine cones and broken twigs as the wind plucked at his neck. To his left, behind the driveway's turnaround, Lazyland's once-grand lawns and neglected garden glowed a faint poisonous green. The first spring flowers were a flattened grey mat. New leaves torn from trees had blown against the chain-link fences that separated Lazyland from its neighbors. High up in one of the ancient tulip poplars a crow perched, tilting its head as Jack hurried by. When he reached the carriage house the bird raised its wings and let loose a hoarse rattling cry, like the sound of stones plummeting down a well, then shuffled its feathers back into place and resumed its glowering watch.

"Aw, stuff it," called Jack. He paused to wipe rain from the brass door plaque his father had installed forty years before—

THE GAUDY BOOK
OFFICES & ACCOUNTS

—then slipped in the key, jimmying the recalcitrant lock until it gave way, and went inside.

The carriage house itself was large enough to qualify as one of those shingle-style "cottages" built by wealthy rusticators in New England a hundred years before. There was an apartment upstairs where Jack's great-grandmother had lived, and which until recently had been rented out to a series of increasingly unreliable tenants. Rows of clerestory windows framed discrete bits of sky. The far wall held a huge picture window overlooking the Hudson, but Jack had drawn its louvered shutters. His eyes had been paining him these last weeks, so there were no lamps lit. Only the spectral glitter that fell from the narrow clerestories and a single dimly glowing computer screen.

The weird light suited the offices of *The Gaudy Book*, trapped as it was between two eras, like a moth pressed in glass. There were old overstuffed armchairs, their chintz worn by authorial bottoms, and scoliotic bookshelves warped by decades' worth of *The Gaudy Book* and its rivals—*The New Yorker*, the *Yellow Book*, *Spy*, *Harper's*, *Punch*. The walls were covered with framed and unframed works by Dave McKean, Edward Steichen, Leonard Thrope, Charles Addams. A Windsor chair held curling prints by Leonard and some of the other mori artists, photos that Jack lacked the nerve either to look at or throw away. There were computers, monitors, printers, CD players, fax and vox and transix and his father's ancient Magnavox Hi-Fi. The same sixth-grade picture of his aunt Mary Anne Finnegan hung in a dim corner. Jack's office pharmacopoeia occupied a shelf between tattered dictionaries and *The Elements of Style*. Tubes of AZT, tamoxifen, Elsat; vials of echinacea and goldenseal from Emma; inhalers and huge bottles of vitamins, a small bag of sensimilla. There was the mummified corpse of a cat, also from Leonard. A silver frame held a society-page photo of Jack, wearing his customary Ur-Wasp garb of chinos and blue-striped oxford-cloth shirt, blond hair falling across his broad forehead, his teeth bared in an uneasy grin. He looked much younger than his forty years; much younger than he did this moment, for all that the picture had been taken only a few years before. Jack stared at all of it, and the windows shuttered against the world, and sighed.

"*Now* what?"

The day before, he had spent an hour on the phone with the company that handled printing of *The Gaudy Book*. The printer was going under, effective April 30—just eleven days away (their distributor had long since folded). This wasn't exactly news, with the cost of paper what it was; not to mention the cost of transportation, when it could be arranged; not to mention *The Gaudy Book*'s microscopic subscription base. Along with his largesse, Leonard's momentary interest in *The Gaudy Book* had disappeared, and with it the readers he had tantalized. Still, Jack had vainly hoped for another miracle. The glimmering might be stopped—they were working on it, a multinational concern was going to set up sky stations from which to repair the ozone layer. People might start reading again.

And I'm Marie of Roumania, thought Jack. He stood by the door, his good humor dampened. After a moment he crossed to where the floor was covered with cartons containing the most recent issue of *The Gaudy Book*. The last issue, it seemed; the boxes had been sitting there for several months now. The cover displayed the familiar eidolon—half Cupid, half death mask, an impudent retort to Eustace Tilly's supercilious gaze—and the familiar scroll of words with their *passementerie* border.

THE GAUDY BOOK
A CODEX FOR THE CENTURY
ISSUED QUARTERLY
SPRING 1999

The century referred to was not the present one. Across the cover's lower edge trailed the magazine's motto, from Juvenal—

Aude aliquid brevibus/Gyaris et carcere dignum,/Si vis esse aliquis.

Dare to do something worthy of imprisonment, if you mean to be of consequence. During one of his unexpected visits, Leonard had suggested the Latin would best be changed to reflect the changing times.

"*Fidelis ad urnam scribendi*, that might be a nice epitaph."

Jack scowled. "And what does *that* mean?"

"'Faithful to the memory of the written word.'"

And Leonard triumphantly tossed the last issue to the floor.

The magazine still lay where Leonard had dropped it. Jack picked it up and stared sadly at the thick glossy cover. Tiny holograms winked up at him, hinting at what lay within, and there was the musky scent of a popular new cologne called Myrra. He flipped through the pages, past advertisements for Broadway musicals and vintage Bentleys, embalming parlors and dance recordings and IT portraiture, fabulously expensive and quite popular amongst the wealthy. Amidst all the enticing ads articles appeared like nutritious bits of grain in a bowl of sugar and colored fluff. Trip glanced at a few of these, wondering vaguely if the checks he'd mailed to various writers had reached their destinations and cleared.

"I'm too old for this," he said aloud.

He flipped past the Chutes & Ladders section, with its desperate efforts to salvage some gossipy dignity from the detritus of the city, glanced at a few cartoons. The lead story was about the international success of a Xian crossover artist named Trip Marlowe. Its headline flickered crimson and gold—

STORMING HELL!

—while a musical chip played the opening chords of Marlowe's most recent hit, complete with gamelan and what sounded like a woman's dying screams. With a shudder Jack let the magazine fall back atop one of the flimsy cardboard boxes. He had half turned to go to his desk, when the front door began to shake.

"Hello?" someone called from outside.

Jack stiffened. "Who is it?"

The door shook more violently. Jack had a flash of what lay behind it: wasted *fellahin* in glittering rags, sawed-off assault rifles; anorexic cranks with filed teeth and hybrid mastiffs. His hands went cold as he glanced helplessly around the room. With a groan the door bulged inward, then abruptly swung open.

"Mister John Finnegan?"

Just outside the door, rainbow light swept across a wedge of broken blacktop stitched with leggy chick-weed and rust-colored grass. Beyond it Jack could see the extravagant bulk of Lazyland shimmering like a mirage. It was a moment before he made out the figure standing in the doorway, like Jack blinking in the spectral afternoon glare.

"Mr. John Finnegan?" A Japanese accent, but with crisp Etonian diction. "You are Mr. John Finnegan? Editor in chief of *The Gaudy Book*?"

"Uh—yes?" Jack shaded his eyes and squinted.

It was a man. Perhaps twenty-five and a head shorter than Jack, with delicate Asian features and very beautiful soft black eyes. He wore a zoot suit of green-and-orange-plaid velveteen, ornamented with amulet bottles holding the dyed skeletons of infant rats and mice, floating blue and pink in their chemical baths. A stylish rubber satchel was slung over his shoulder. Jack glimpsed an insignia, another fabulous skeletal animal, kirin or gryphon, surmounted by Japanese characters. In its claws the gryphon grasped a pyramid, beams streaming sunwise from its apex. The young man's hands were clasped in front of him. His long black hair was glazed into a fabulous spreading pompadour that added several inches to his height and seemed to provide the same kind of UV protection a hat would. Jack, embarrassed, found himself thinking of the curl of Hokusai's *Under the Wave at Kanagawa*. His visitor seemed to have anticipated this, and bowing ever so slightly gave him a smile that held within it everything of forgiveness and generosity and even amusement.

"Mr. Finnegan. Good morning. You received my telephone message?"

Jack shook his head. "No," he began, then sighed. "Don't tell me. Leonard sent you—"

The man frowned, puzzled.

"Leonard Thrope," Jack went on. "He's a friend. A very *bad* friend," he added darkly. "Did he—"

"Yes. Mr. Thrope. He—"

"I *am* sorry. But we don't—I mean I don't, the magazine does not, we don't have visitors. To the office. No interviews, submissions by mail only—"

"Please." The young man opened his hands in a suppliant gesture. "I am not a—"

An imperceptible pause, as though steeling himself to pronounce the next word. Then,

"—a *writer*."

The man took a step forward, so that his foot rested upon the threshold.

"May I?" he asked, tilting his head and peering up through that absurd pompadour.

Oh why the fuck not, thought Jack bitterly. "Of course—please. Come in."

His visitor stepped inside. Jack pulled the door shut after him. The room filled with the same musky fragrance that had risen from the pages of *The Gaudy Book*, and for an awful moment Jack had the ridiculous fear that he had been cornered by a perfume salesman. Then the man smiled, a disarmingly childlike smile that showed off two dimples in his cherubic face. With his dark eyes and smooth skin he reminded Jack of Leonard in his youth. Despite himself, he smiled wanly back.

"Larry Muso," the man said by way of introduction. His brow furrowed. "You *are* John Finnegan?"

"Yes—but Jack—please, everyone calls me Jack." He ran a hand through his hair. "Um—so. Larry. What can I do for you?"

Larry Muso smiled again. "No—what can *I* do for *you*—"

He shrugged off the rubber satchel. Jack's heart sank. *Oh God. He* is *a salesman.* He watched as Larry Muso opened the bag and pulled out a small parcel.

"For you," his guest said.

Jack took a step backwards, his heart beating too fast. *A letter bomb? Delivered by suicide courier?* He shook his head, refusing the package—they'd finally caught that guy in New Rochelle, but who knew how many others might be around here?

But the young man only stepped forward and slid the package into Jack's hands. The only way he could have refused it was by dropping it. Even faced with the possibility of receiving a bomb, Jack Finnegan was too polite to do *that*.

"It is a gift." Larry Muso stepped back, still smiling, and dipped his head. "For you . . ."

Jack stared at the rectangular parcel, carefully wrapped in a square of cotton, green and yellow and indigo, patterned like fish scales. He drew it to his face, smelled Myrra and that exotically pleasant, slightly musty scent he associated with Oriental groceries— wasabi powder, tamarind, sandalwood incense.

"Please," urged Larry Muso. "Open it."

He did. Slowly, untying the raffia ribbons and unfolding the thick fabric until he found it, nestled within the fragrant cloth like a gold ingot.

A book; a very *old* book. Its cover looked like watered silk, crocus-colored and remarkably unfaded, with an Art Nouveau pattern of acanthus, stippled with gold, and in the center the title in raised gold letters.

"Wow." Jack laughed. "I don't believe it. . . "

"For your collection," said Larry Muso.

Jack opened the book gingerly. The frontispiece showed a Beardsley-esque line drawing of a grotesque mask and the date 1895, opposite the title page.

THE KING IN YELLOW
BY ROBERT W. CHAMBERS

"The King in Yellow," whispered Jack. "A *first*. This is incredible . . ." Very carefully he turned the pages, stopped and read.

> Now that the Government has determined to establish a Lethal Chamber in every city, town, and village in the country, it remains to be seen whether or not that class of human creatures from whose desponding ranks new victims of self-destruction fall daily will accept the relief thus provided. There a painless death awaits him who can no longer bear the sorrows of life. If death is welcome let him seek it there.

He closed the book and looked up. Larry Muso was beaming, stray light striking the tip of his pompadour so that he looked like a burning candle.

"It is very beautiful, isn't it, Mr. Finnegan? The first edition, you see. Eighteen ninety-five."

Jack shook his head. "But—" He started to explain that it had been his grandfather, not him, who collected books, then stopped. "But I don't understand. Who *are* you?"

His visitor slipped a hand inside his velveteen jacket, withdrew a card case embossed with a hologram of the same logo that appeared on his satchel. He opened it and presented Jack with an illurium business card. The iridescent metal was etched with Japanese characters and a skeletal winged creature with grasping claws. When Jack tilted the card, English letters flickered beneath the Japanese. There was the nearly imperceptible sound of bells. A woman's voice whispered the words as Jack read.

"*Gorita-Folham-Izod: The Golden Family.*"

"*Altyn Urik,*" Larry Muso offered. "That is our name in the archaic tongue of the Mongol people." With a soft *click* he snapped the card case shut and replaced it inside his jacket. "It means 'The Golden Family.'"

Jack raised an eyebrow. "And *that* means . . . ?"

"My employer. We are a joint Japanese-American-Mongolian corporate enterprise, engaged in mining and other industrial operations, but also incorporating your ALTCOM and the entire NOREX Telecommunications Group. We are based in Dalandzagad, and of course the Pyramid here is our American headquarters, but our work extends very far, far beyond these places."

Jack nodded weakly and stared at his visitor with growing despair. He knew all about GFI, of course; but obviously this guy wasn't from GFI. Some kind of terrorist, then? He had some vague sense that things were unsettled in Mongolia, but then they were unsettled everywhere. In the wake of the glimmering strange alliances had sprung up across the globe, most especially in those places heretofore ignored because of their very isolation. Places like central Canada and Siberia and Mongolia, now besieged with investors and developers fleeing the flooded coasts, the diseased cities and ruined farmlands.

"The Golden Family has many interests!" Larry Muso said brightly, as though he had read Jack's mind. "But today I am here on other business—"

He turned and for the first time seemed to take in the room around him: swaybacked bookshelves, outdated computers, and all. He breathed in sharply, and Jack watched, bemused, as a beatific expression spread across Larry Muso's face. After a moment he looked back at his host.

"You have such beautiful things." Larry Muso's eyes were moist; his voice soft, almost chastened. "They told me you had very beautiful things, but—to *see* them, that is a different matter. You see, I studied library engineering, at Oxford—that is why I was chosen to come here. *That*—"

He tipped his head in the direction of the book in Jack's hand, still shrouded by its cloth wrappings. "I myself selected that for you, Mr.—I mean Jack—because like yourself I love beautiful things. Like yourself, *we*— The Golden Family—love beautiful things."

Jack nodded. "I see." He felt more at ease, now that it appeared he was not going to be murdered by an exploding antiquarian volume. "Um—well then. Won't you have a seat?"

Larry Muso followed him to a small sitting area composed of a wicker table and three very old unsprung wicker chairs, their more dangerous parts covered with faded chintz pillows. He settled in one gingerly, turning to stare into the carriage house's shadowy corners.

"I'm sorry I can't offer you anything," Jack continued. "But we really don't receive people here. When my grandfather was alive, the magazine's offices were in the city—"

"Gramercy Park."

"Yes, that's right." Jack tried not to look annoyed. "But needless to say we can't afford offices there anymore—"

Larry Muso frowned. "But that, too, was your family's home? Am I correct?"

"Well, yes, but—we sold that place years ago." For a long moment Jack stared at the book in his lap, his fingers tracing the raised gold letters, the smooth ribbony feel of the silk cover. His grandmother would adore it, of course; might not ever forgive him for letting it go.

So Jack wouldn't tell her. With a sigh he wrapped the copy of *The King in Yellow* back in its cotton covering and placed it on the table. "Look, Mr. Muso—"

"Larry—"

"*Mr. Muso,*" Jack repeated firmly. "I don't mean to be rude, but this is a bad time for me, okay? A bad time for *The Gaudy Book*—" He stared pointedly at the rows of cartons by the door. "*That* is probably our last issue, right *there*—"

"Yes!" Larry Muso exclaimed. "*That* is why I am here! *The Gaudy Book*! We want to buy *The Gaudy Book*!"

Jack's dismay curdled into anger. Pushy Japanese subscribers! This was *worse* than a terrorist.

"I'm sorry." He started to his feet, no longer caring how rude he sounded. "This is our *editorial* office. We don't handle *subscriptions* from here, we *never* handled subscriptions from here, the only reason *those* magazines are here at all is because, as I just told you, we're going under, the printer folded, the distributor folded, and now presumably *we* are going to—"

Larry Muso waved his hands excitedly. "Yes, I know! I am here representing The Golden Family, and we would like to *buy The Gaudy Book*—the magazine enterprise itself—as an investment. A corporate investment. An *aesthetic* investment," he went on quickly, "an *artistic* investment. You, of course, would retain all artistic control, Mr.—Jack—because we have the greatest respect for you, for your entire family, and the contributions you have made to literature. To literature in English," he amended, and paused to pull a large silk handkerchief from his pocket.

Jack stared at him dumbfounded. Larry Muso gave him another of those childlike smiles.

He's kind of cute, Jack found himself thinking; *in a Japanese Elvis kind of way.*

"You understand this?" Larry touched one corner of the handkerchief to his cheek, a gesture at once so subtle and affected that Jack wondered if it was some sort of coded message. *Permit my multinational corporation to purchase your failing periodical, and I will be your love slave.* "We believe in protecting the few beautiful things left in this world, while we can. Your magazine would be very precious to us. And we would, of course, seek to preserve it as a commercial property . . ."

Jack thought of Leonard, of his records of human and animal extinction purchased by collectors in Manhattan and Vancouver and Bloemfontein. He sank back into his chair. "Have you—have you ever actually *read The Gaudy Book*?"

Larry Muso pursed his lips, finally shook his head. "Myself, personally? No. But Mr. Tatsumi, our CEO—*he* reads it. He used to travel a great deal. He said that *The Gaudy Book* was the only thing he could read on an airplane."

Jack tried to figure out if this could possibly be a compliment. "Well," he said at last, "does he still travel much?"

"Oh no. He has not left the desert in two years."

"Probably behind in his reading, then," Jack said, and was rewarded with a smile.

He straightened, putting on his best Face the Trustees expression, and stared pointedly at *The King in Yellow* on the table. "I'm afraid I can't accept this."

Larry Muso looked puzzled. "Why not?"

"Because I'm not in a position to do business with you. *The Gaudy Book* is no longer a going concern. We're suspending publication—"

"I know, Mr. Finnegan." Suddenly Larry Muso's voice sounded less conciliatory; more the voice of a man determined to do business, swiftly and with no interference. Surprised, Jack looked up and saw the other man draw a tiny palmtop from his pocket. "In the first quarter of this year, you showed a loss of— nearly two million dollars," Larry Muso said thoughtfully. He frowned, tapped once more at the keyboard. "Last year, your friend Leonard Thrope made the magazine the beneficiary of a modest grant—"

"A *loan*," Jack said hotly, but he knew he was losing.

"—which enabled you to produce the current spring issue." Larry Muso tilted his head in the direction of the cartons by the wall. "Now you are unable to afford the cost of shipping those to your few remaining subscribers. If—"

"Did Leonard put you up to this?" Jack broke in angrily. "Because—"

"*If* you would let me finish, Mr. Finnegan," Larry

Muso went on, "I would be able to tell you that yes, Mr. Thrope has been in touch with us. We have mutual—friends."

In another oddly poised gesture he opened his hand. His fingers spread delicately, like the fronds of some feeding sea animal. *"Friend,"* he corrected himself. His soft black eyes gazed searchingly into Jack's. "Another collector."

Jack made a grim little face. "I see."

"I hope you do. You must understand, Mr. Tatsumi is not just a collector. He is a collector of *Americana*. But very eclectic. Mr. Thrope has helped him with many items. An Edward Hopper, some Winslow Homer. Notebooks of Sylvia Plath and Ariza Davis. A drawing by Jeffrey Dahmer. He owns Judy Garland's dress from *The Wizard of Oz*. Many letters of Thomas Jefferson—Mr. Tatsumi is very fond of Thomas Jefferson."

"As was Mr. Dahmer," muttered Jack.

Larry Muso did not hear him. "As I mentioned, Mr. Tatsumi enjoys reading *The Gaudy Book*. And he is not insensitive to your plight—"

"Which he heard about from Leonard."

"Which he heard about from Leonard. And so, I am here to deliver a proposal to you—"

As abruptly as it had appeared, the glossy black palmtop disappeared back into his voluminous jacket, and Larry Muso slid a sleek metal folder onto the table beside *The King in Yellow*.

PROSPECTUS FOR PURCHASE OF
THE GAUDY BOOK
19 APRIL 1999
GORITA-FOLHAM-IZOD
THE GOLDEN FAMILY INTERNATIONAL
AN UNLIMITED PARTNERSHIP

In the center of the portfolio, the silvery holographic image of a skeletal gryphon reared and grasped within its claws a spinning orb.

"I see," said Jack. He stared at the portfolio, fingers tightening on the arms of his chair, then picked it up. Despite the metal cover it felt light as tissue. When he opened it, the same faint bells chimed, the same breathy female voice whispered *The Golden Family Welcomes You.* He flipped through the pages, incomprehensible sets of numbers for the most part, with here and there the small square IT image of an athletic-looking blond man in a conservative dark suit, poised to deliver instructive commentary to arbitrage-impaired readers.

Like me, thought Jack, and felt himself blushing. He cleared his throat again, tapping the prospectus against his hand. "Well, okay. I'll have our attorneys take a look at it."

Larry Muso tilted his head, eyes downcast. "Mr. Thrope suggested that perhaps you use *his* attorney, rather than Mr. Gardino."

"Tell Mr. Thrope I'll keep my own goddamn counsel." To Jack's horror he felt tears pricking at his eyes. He tossed the prospectus onto the table and stood, too quickly, so that he felt a surge of dizziness and had to steady himself against his chair. "Thank you, Mr. Muso—I have some things to do now—"

Larry Muso jumped to his feet. His knees knocked against the table, sending the prospectus sliding onto the floor. At once he stooped to retrieve it; Jack did the same. The two of them nearly collided, Larry straightening with the portfolio in his hand, his pompadour grazing Jack's cheek as he stepped awkwardly backward. At the touch of his hair Jack shivered, felt an involuntary *frisson* at how soft it was. Not hard and lacquered at all, but warm and silky and fragrant with that expensive perfume. For an instant he imagined them somewhere else; not in bed but sitting side by side in some forever lost and ordinary place, a bookstore perhaps, an espresso bar, knees touching as they turned the pages of a magazine. *The Gaudy Book*, of course: the special anniversary double issue. The image overwhelmed him, he could smell new glossy paper and scalded milk and feel a hand resting upon his . . .

Then the vision was gone. He blinked, seeing again those odd whorls of light at the corners of his eyes, and drew back, trying to cover his confusion. When he looked up he saw Larry Muso staring at him: his cheeks were spotted each with a single bright red dot, as though they had been jabbed with an accusing finger.

"Excuse me," Larry Muso said in a low voice. He dropped the portfolio onto the table, where it clattered and whispered to itself.

"I'm sorry." Jack shook his head. "I—I didn't mean to be rude—"

"No, no—" Larry smiled, a false bright flash. "It is your decision, of course. Only we were under the impression that the magazine's demise was—imminent. Perhaps we misunderstood . . . ?"

Jack made a bitter face. "No, you understood perfectly. God forbid Leonard should ever miss a death-watch." Larry stared at him, his expression still frozen in that mask of benign agreement, but his dark eyes held a flicker of unease. "I just—well, even if I *did* want to sell the magazine, there's the matter of choosing a successor—another editor."

The unease melted into another conciliatory smile. "Mr. Tatsumi would like *you* to continue as editor."

"But I don't *want* to be editor anymore. I'm sick," Jack said, and no longer cared if the bitterness leached into his voice. "I have AIDS. I've spent my whole fucking life on this magazine. I'm ready to give it up. Can you give *that* message to Mr. Tatsumi?"

He had thought it might be gratifying to insult his visitor. Instead, Jack immediately felt awful. Larry Muso stared at him with such pity and embarrassment that Jack found himself reassuring *him*.

"Look, Mr. Muso, maybe I could help you find someone to replace me, someone who—"

"But your family—the magazine has been in your *family*—"

Jack shrugged. "Well, yes, but it was always just a sideline to the department stores. And it's been a hundred years. I mean, we've had a good long run—"

"I think—I am *certain* that Mr. Tatsumi wants the magazine intact." Larry Muso shook his head; his pompadour waggled furiously. "It is part of the entire aesthetic of the purchase. We will have to discuss this, I think."

Jack sighed. He cast a quick look at the prospectus on the table. "Maybe," he said, trying to imbue the word with menace. "But right now I really have to get back to work. So—"

He beckoned at the door and waited for the Japanese man to leave. Instead Larry Muso stared at him, no longer with pity but with an oddly frank sort of interest, neither sexual nor businesslike; as though Jack were wearing some highly unusual item of clothing. After a moment he said, "What are you doing for it?"

Jack frowned. "Some phone calls—I have a few—"

"No, no—for your disease. What treatment are you undergoing?"

"That's none of your fucking business." This time Jack felt no rush of remorse. His face tightened with anger as he shouted, "I said, GET—"

"Because you are looking very well," Larry Muso

went on. He stepped around Jack, still giving him that appraising stare. "There are some unusual drugs, we have several major pharmaceutical holdings, and I was just—"

"—*OUT!*"

Larry Muso's shoes tapped softly across the floor. Jack stormed after him, but at the door Muso stopped and made him a slightly mocking half bow.

"That was inexcusably rude. Please forgive me." His eyes narrowed, and for a moment Jack thought Muso was going to burst out laughing. But he only regarded Jack with mild disinterest. "But I should warn you, Mr. Finnegan—The Golden Family is quite serious about acquiring your magazine. I volunteered to make this inquiry, out of respect for what Leonard Thrope told me of your work, and because I thought it would be more—palatable—than introducing you to our attorneys so early in the negotiation process. But the attorneys will come . . ."

Absently he fingered one of the little bottle-amulets hanging from his waistcoat. "There is a word we use, Mr. Finnegan—*nemawashi*. It is a business term, but the word is derived from gardening. It is what one does when planting a tree. To cut the roots, to wrest the plant from the earth too quickly, is to kill it. The roots wither, the tree will die. A wise gardener will pluck and prune carefully over several weeks, so that the tree can adjust to its new life."

Larry Muso's eyes gazed directly into Jack's. "These are dangerous but very interesting times for investors, Mr. Finnegan. That is why The Golden Family is launching a sky station from the Mongolian desert. That is why we have very exceptional gardeners."

With a flourish he smoothed the front of his velvet

frock coat, bowed again, and crossed to the door. Jack could only watch, chastened and amazed, as the slender figure strode vigorously back up the rain-streaked drive, until it was lost to sight.

"Well, shit," he said after some minutes had passed. He turned and walked back to the wicker table, sank into a chair, and picked up first *The King in Yellow*, and then The Golden Family's prospectus. The novel he gazed at longingly and set aside. The prospectus earned more resigned attention. He weighed it carefully in his palm, wondering what, exactly, the metallic cover was made of—the material felt smooth and taut, but also supple, like the skin of an underripe fruit. Tentatively he pressed it with a finger, and was rewarded with a slight dimpling in the material.

"*Another product of The Golden Family, GFI International,*" breathed the portfolio. "*Manufactured entirely in the Nippo-Altai Commonwealth.*"

"What's it made of?" demanded Jack, half-fearful that he would get a reply; but the portfolio was silent. He opened it and turned to the first page, activating the icon there by pressing it with his finger.

"*John Finnegan! We welcome you,*" spoke a clear brisk voice. "*Within these pages you will see the future that The Golden Family has to offer you and* The Gaudy Book—" A chiming sound, followed by a sort of throaty *boom*, as of a huge gong being struck. "*The Golden Family is a privately owned corporation formed by the merger of four major international corporations from the United States, the European Union, Mongolia, and Japan. In 1987. . .*"

The voice was silenced as he turned the next page. Rows of numbers here, interspersed with small but luminously beautiful photographs: trees, mountains, a welder smiling behind a mask as golden sparks fell about her head. He pressed another icon.

*". . . assets in excess of forty-seven billion dollars annu-
ally, chiefly from holdings in . . ."*

The next page brought a molten sunset over
Mongolia's Flaming Cliffs, the sound of tinkling herd-
bells and chanting.

*"In 1995, GFI completed the acquisition of a 75 percent
working interest in the Saraagalt Basin, Mongolia. GFI now
owns 100 percent of two contract areas in the Saraagalt Basin
in the Gobi Desert, totaling 7.32 million acres. Historically,
Mongolia has not had access to its mineral and natural gas
deposits. Consulting geologist and engineering firms hired by
GFI determined that vast untapped stores of minerals and fossil fuels beneath the Gobi could in future . . ."*

Jack shook his head in a sort of desultory amazement. *The sky is falling and they're still buying up mineral
rights*, he thought. He turned to the center of the
prospectus, where a double-page spread showed a sky
pulsing with color: purple, green, indigo, gamboge yellow, crimson. Stars showed very faintly through violet
flames. In the foreground a shining silver dirigible
towed some sort of platform, a huge golden grid with
batlike wings. Behind it trailed the true stars in the *real*
sky, glittering constellations like so many diamond
brooches tossed upon a jeweler's velvet table. As he
read the captions beneath the picture, the same earnest
voice intoned,

*"In late 1999 The Golden Family will set in place the first
SunTerminus™ skystage. Designed and produced by an international team of the world's foremost research scientists and
aerospace engineers, SunTerminus™ is the most innovative
system ever designed to offset the dangerous effects of ozone
depletion in the earth's atmosphere. Unlike conventional satel-
lites, which have been crippled by recent atmospheric disturbances, the worldwide network of SunTerminus™ stages will
be set aloft by GFI's Lighter-Than-Air (LTA) fleet of Fouga™*

Dirigibles, each one capable of towing a five-ton payload. Once in place, SunTerminus™ will be the newest, most reliable telecommunications network on earth, providing broadcast and communications services for a wide range of bandwidths. Because of their lower placement in the earth's atmosphere, the stages will be unaffected by terrestrial catastrophes, and GFI's unique and highly specialized security system will prevent any risk of terrorist attack.

"At the same time as the telecommunications system is introduced, The Golden Family will launch its remarkable Fouga™/SunTerminus™ configuration known as the Solar Universal Nucleo-Radial Array (or SUNRA™). By first polarizing particulates and toxins in the earth's atmosphere, SUNRA™ can then 'attract' unwanted compounds much as a magnet attracts iron filings, and so take the first step toward repairing the ozone layer . . ."

"Yeah, yeah, save the ozone. Very nice," muttered Jack. "But what about *me?*" He turned the prospectus's last few pages, and finally found there what he was looking for.

"The Golden Family International, henceforth known as GFI, lets it be known that of this date, April 19, 1999, it has made to John Chanvers Finnegan II, editor in chief and owner of the periodical known as The Gaudy Book, *an offer in the amount of $3,000,000 for purchase of said periodical. GFI would then become sole proprietors of . . ."*

He closed the prospectus. Around him the room was silent, save for the tapping of rain at the windows.

"Three million dollars," he whispered. It was more money than the family—*his* family—had possessed in over twenty years. Illness and bad investments had shorn Jack's father's share of the Finnegan fortune. The bulk of his grandfather's money had, of course, gone to Keeley; but it had long since been squandered on Lazyland's upkeep, as well as gifts to various Finnegan children and great-grandchildren. *Three million dollars . . .*

But what was that worth, nowadays? He could hear Leonard's mocking voice—*"Three million bucks'll buy you a latté in Uzbekistan!"*

But GFI was certainly solvent, at least right now. One of the world's biggest corporations, after Disney and Matsushita; he could be fairly certain that the check wouldn't bounce. He would use the money on the house; put in a stairlift for Grandmother and Mrs. Iverson, repair the damage left by ice dams and flooding. He could afford some of the medications he had stopped taking, if he could find a source for them. He could stop pretending to save his family's dying literary legacy, and retire—his brothers had been telling him to do that ever since he became ill. He could travel.

He could buy time.

"Jesus," he said aloud. He tapped the prospectus gently against his chin, and smiled. "Well—"

Quickly he turned and crossed to his battered desk, fished around until he found the telephone beneath a snowy heap of unpaid bills. He grinned triumphantly when he heard a dial tone, then punched in Jule Gardino's number.

"—I guess I need a lawyer."

CHAPTER SEVEN

Death by Water

He went home to die. It took him two days from Boston, and by the time he got there he was so sick and exhausted he might as well be dead already. Innocent that he was, Trip didn't know that IZE was more addictive than crack or heroin: that it had been deliberately manufactured so that the brain's receptors for the drug, once activated, would continue to crave it, even after a single dosage. He felt nauseated and almost frantic with anxiety; his head ached, and in the corners of his eyes he saw faint flickerings that mirrored the sky overhead.

Now Roque Beach stretched before him, glittering in the thin greenish sunlight. Maine was one of those places where rich people fled when the world fell apart. The small population base meant there were fewer viral outbreaks (though more militias), fewer attempts to impose quarantines and environmental interdictions—although the atmospheric effects of the glimmering were, if anything, intensified in the northern latitude. And not even the end of the world could temper the Maine winter. But Moody's Island was too raw and remote to attract refugees from the Hamptons. Only people like Trip Marlowe called it home. And only a Marlowe would return to Hell Head to die.

He staggered to the huge rocky outcropping that overlooked the whirlpool and stared down into its vast turning eye. Expecting perhaps to see something there—his father's white battered face staring up at him as from the bottom of a cliff; his mother with her long hair aswarm with tiny crabs. Instead there was only the churning water, marbled black and green, the peeping cry of storm petrels as they fluttered above the smoother surface of waves farther down the shore.

That morning he had Roque Beach to himself. It was early April, but on Moody's Island winter still held court. The sky was icy blue laced with silver. Underfoot the stones were greasy. More than once Trip nearly fell, his sneakers sliding into shallow declivities filled with kelp and mussels and water the color of lager. His feet grew numb as he stumbled down the shoreline, periwinkles crunching like acorns beneath his heels. Sea spray and sweat coursed in a little rivulet down his back; his flannel shirt grew stiff with rime. Stones went flying as he walked, and he swore at them, a whispered monotone chant, all the words he'd never been able to say aloud, all the words he'd never even been able to *think*—

"Shit fuck piss shit piss fuck fuck fuck."

Overhead the sky darkened from pale green to metallic indigo, shot with threads of glowing white like lightning. The brilliance made his eyes ache; moaning softly, he drew a hand across them. He stumbled across the beach, blinking painfully. He'd always been thin; now he looked emaciated, his eyes sunken and the corners of his mouth crosshatched with sores. He jammed his hands into his pockets, shivering, pulled up the frozen collar of his shirt, and stared out across Grand Manan Channel, across the steely Atlantic to where a lone lobster boat plied the unsettled waters.

He had lost all track of time. He'd thought it was early when he stumbled onto the beach, but with the sun lost within lurid clouds there was no way of knowing what hour it was. The ominous sky made him think that a storm was blowing, but such portents were all but meaningless now. Fireflies no longer flew low before a rain, but clustered close upon screen windows at mid-day, blinking madly. Locusts brought not fine weather but sudden snows; spiders undid their webs and hid, storms or no. Jellyfish and crabs washed up on shore in the millions, and loons flew out to sea in the middle of lashing rains. Everywhere the natural order had been betrayed by the skies: you could fly from Newark to New Delhi and back again (if your navigational systems worked, if you had fuel enough, and money), and never see sunset, never see dawn; never see the sun nor true night at all, but only the shifting spectacle of the world falling apart.

Not that it mattered anymore to Trip Marlowe.

He turned from staring out to sea and carefully stepped down onto the long ledge of stone that stuck out over Hell Head like the plank on a pirate ship. A heavy beard of bladder wrack scrunched and popped underfoot. Acorn barnacles tore at the soles of his sneakers. When he stooped, he saw that some of them held their feathery *cirri* aloft, fooled by the whirlpool's heavy spray into thinking they were still underwater.

"Good-bye then," he whispered, his finger brushing against the barnacle's open mouth. Immediately the *cirri* retracted. The shell snapped shut. Trip stood.

From across the open water came an icy wind. In the distance the lobster boat appeared to stand still, buf-feted by waves. A nor'easter blowing up, his grand-mother would have said. What would she have thought of a storm that lasted six weeks, of the sight of the Mississippi delta spreading across the Midwest like a red stain? What would she have thought of her grandson fucking a young girl in a planetarium, then taking a drug that made it possible for him to have sex with his own double while a perverted homosexual watched?

His stomach clenched. He shut his eyes tightly for a moment, fighting tears, then opened them. He took a few steps toward the edge of the narrow outcropping, his feet seeking familiar pockets in the stone hidden by rockweed. He could hear the grinding roar of the whirlpool, magnified by the rising gale. His clothes were soaked through with spray, his hair stiff where it jabbed into his neck. The insides of his ears ached, from the cold and wind; the gold cross felt like a brand upon his chest.

A sharp cry made him look up. Too quickly; he almost lost his balance, flailing as he sank into a half crouch, until he felt steady. When he stood again he saw a cormorant, perhaps ten yards off, futilely beating its great wings as it sought to head inshore. The shifting wind sent it keeling down and up, its long neck arcing and the yellow patch of its chin seeming to glow in the weird light. Its wicked beak opened, and Trip shuddered as it cried out: a desperate keening sound, abruptly cut off as a sudden downdraft caught the bird and, without warning, it spun end over end and plummeted into the whirlpool.

"*Ohhh.*"

Trip moaned, his fingers tightening into fists. The bird struck the water headfirst, the sound of its impact lost amidst the thunderous vortex. One wing splayed across the surface of the water; the rest of it he glimpsed as an inky shadow beneath mottled foam. For several moments it spun, caught in the curved lip of the whirlpool's perimeter. Trip glimpsed the pale-flecked feathers of its throat, its bright staring eye already dulled and insensate. Its wings spread across the water like the shattered ribs of a Chinese fan. Then it fell into the center of the vortex. There was a froth of bloody spume, a prickling of stray feathers like the spines of a porcupine; and it was gone.

On the ledge Trip stood and gazed into the black water. It seemed there should be something to show that a creature had just died there, but of course there was nothing, not even a feather. All about him the wind wailed and sent grey sheets lashing above the waves. He could no longer feel his fingers where they clutched his shirt; could no longer hear anything except that numbing roar of wind and water. Rage built in him, thinking of the cormorant: that something that strong and wild could so quickly be lost, and unmourned. He was shaking from the cold but still he stood there, still he gazed into that mindless tormented eye, until finally he began to sing.

It was an old song, something his grandmother would sing to him when she returned from one of her beano nights, her breath warm with beer and cigarettes. He'd relished the way her reedy voice would quaver, whooping drunkenly on the chorus as she sat in front of the trailer in her bottom-sprung lawn chair, swatting at blackflies and tossing spent cigarettes onto the dirt.

> *Oh it's such a sad old feeling*
> *All the fields are soft and green*
> *It's memories that I'm stealing*
> *But you're innocent when you dream,*
> *Oh you're innocent when you dream.*

The words fell slowly from Trip's raw throat. When his mouth opened he could taste the wind, its rich salt broth of decay, of fish and rotting kelp. It was a familiar taste, a familiar scent. A storm smell, that would send women running out to pull laundry from the line, and the men to the 52 Variety, where they'd smoke and swear about the ravaged ground-fisheries, the boats that no longer plied the bay.

A storm. His hands trembled as he tried to shade his eyes. They felt tender, and he imagined this was what it was like when you had surgery, those first moments after the bandages were removed, and even in a darkened room you blinked painfully. Weird blobs and jots of color swam across his field of vision, like what he had seen once, looking at the sun through a torn piece of Mylar balloon—flares leaping from a black corona, wriggling shapes like paramecia swimming across the bit of stretched material. Only there was something oddly purposeful about these shapes; as though they had some existence independent of him and his ruined eyes.

He shook his head and stared into the boiling pit below him. For an instant a single black quill perched on a viridian coil of seawater, then disappeared. He could see his breath form in the heavy vaporous air above the whirlpool. When he sang the sound was harsh and bloodless as a gannet's cry.

The gale ripped across the water and sent grey eddies racing beneath the ledge. Trip's shirt flapped open. The buttons were gone, and it snapped in the wind, so that his chest was exposed. Spray stung where he'd clawed himself, half-mad with the agony of withdrawal, long shallow fissures still open and unhealed. Trip grunted and doubled over, but that only made it hurt more. He started pulling off his shirt, the fabric disintegrating into clots of thread as he tore it from him. Shouting in pain he threw the shirt into the air, hugging himself as he waited for it to plummet into the spume of black and green.

It didn't fall. Instead a sudden gust tore across the channel, dragging with it a frigid curtain of rain. For an instant the shirt twisted like a snagged line. Then it rose,

ragged arms trailing like wings, and blew end over end
out to sea.

Trip watched in amazement. The wind shifted and
the shirt with it, so that for an instant he could imagine himself there above the violent water with his arms
outspread, skimming like a stone. The wretched fabric
bellied out, cuffs flapping, until another gust whipped
it into the greening air and off it sailed. An odd fleeting
sorrow tempered Trip's astonishment as he watched it
go, a brave bright speck growing smaller and smaller
until at last it disappeared into the heart of the
approaching storm. He murmured aloud in disappointment.

"*Ohhh.*"

The poor little shirt.

Unexpectedly he laughed. Salt stung his lips and
tongue as the wind drove the breath back down his
throat. The whirlpool's roar grew deafening as the gale
tore at the circling waves and Trip swayed, his sneakers
sliding across a jellied mass of kelp. He couldn't hear his
own voice, only feel the words tearing at his throat as he
screamed into the storm.

> *We're running through the graveyard*
> *And we laughed, my friends and I . . .*

Spray lanced his bare flesh but he no longer felt it.
He could see nothing but a slanting blur of green and
grey. His nostrils filled with water, but still he sang,
beating his arms against the air. A string of kelp heavy
as a leather knout lashed his ankles. Glancing down
Trip saw blood welling through his sneakers. He
blinked, for a moment fancied he could see another
cormorant hovering in the air before him, its crimson
eyes ablaze. As he stared the bird banked into the gale

and disappeared. Trip's entire body shuddered. Any moment he would fly apart just as the first cormorant had done, his body shearing into pieces like rotted cloth.

He smiled at the thought. He felt exhilarated, almost exalted, by the storm; by the thought that minutes from now he would be dead. He inched from the rubbery bed of sea wrack to the cleaved stone at the very tip of the protruding ledge. The stone slit through his sneaker and cut into his bare foot. A cluster of barnacles sliced his heel, and he shouted in anguish, then caught his breath and forced himself to go on.

A few inches of ravaged granite was all that held him there above the maelstrom. But he was not afraid, he had never been so unafraid. It was *all* a storm now, all the earth overtaken by tempest, and he was part of it, as much so as the yellow foam curding about his bloody foot, as much as the streaming rain and boiling sky. Somewhere a flying shirt dipped and sank beneath an indigo wave; somewhere little crabs nibbled and fetched at the milky shreds of a cormorant's flesh. For one last moment Trip stood there upon the ledge, blinking as he gazed upon the ruptured world, Grand Manan Channel and the black bulk of Hell Head and the raging whirlpool.

Poor little Trip, he thought. And he was gone.

PART TWO

Everyone's Invited

CHAPTER EIGHT

The Lady of Situations

Through some miracle of coincidence—he would not have been surprised to learn that The Golden Family was behind it—when Jack lifted the telephone there was a dial tone. Not only that, he was able to complete a call to Jule Gardino and leave a flustered message on the answering machine. It had been months since he'd put a call through this easily.

"Julie! Uh, it's Jack . . . Listen, I need to talk to you, about some business. I mean lawyer-type business. I mean I'd like to talk to you anyway, of course. So call me if and when you can. Oh, and tell Emma hi. Hi, Emma! Bye . . ."

He set the phone down. Suddenly he felt exhausted, and experienced a familiar *frisson* of anxiety. Had he taken all his medications that morning? Was it time to begin the next round of his remaining pills and inhalants and herbal tinctures, or had he already missed something? He looked around for a working timepiece, saw only ornate horological confections with hands set at odd hours. Twenty past seven, five past noon, or was it midnight? With a sigh he decided it was time to go back in. He gathered a few things—the GFI prospectus, *The King in Yellow*, a manuscript from a man who wrote passionately about rocks—thinking morosely how once again he had gotten no work done. Then he returned to the main house.

It was later than he had imagined, well past noon. Mrs. Iverson had made lunch, tinned sardines on stale

crispbread with a drizzle of the olive oil left by Leonard
at Christmas. Jack ate quickly and absently and alone,
preoccupied with thoughts of corporate largesse and
also with the lingering image of Larry Muso's dark eyes
and soft, ivory-colored skin. His grandmother had lain
down for a nap. This seemed like such a good idea that
when he finished lunch he did the same, first checking
his arsenal of pills to make sure he hadn't missed any.
He squeezed a dropperful of Fusax onto his tongue,
then placed The Golden Family's prospectus on his
nightstand. He heard the faint tinkling of chimes,
breathy words rising from a hidden voice chip. The
comforter, when he pulled it over his clothes, felt warm,
with that pleasant heft he recalled from childhood ill-
nesses: blankets so heavy they pinned him to the bed.
He yawned and pummeled his pillow. He was looking
forward to thinking about Larry Muso's offer, to imagining what three million dollars might buy. Perhaps even
some time with Larry Muso himself? But within minutes
he was sound asleep, while outside the relentless April
rain tapped cold against the windows.

He woke not knowing how long he had slept, or what
time of day it was. He rubbed his eyes and sat up, feeling groggy and out of sorts. Jack had never liked naps;
to him they implied a sort of slovenliness, mental and
physical, a relinquishment of adult responsibilities on a
par with other moral declensions such as hangovers,
weight problems, heroin addiction. He stood; the comforter fell to the floor, revealing that he was still in chinos and frayed cable-knit sweater. It had been daytime,
then, when he lay down. Another moment and he
recalled his morning in the carriage house, the gentle
cant of Larry Muso's sloe eyes and the small triumph of

a telephone call successfully placed to Jule. With a yawn he crossed to the window.

Outside the lawn stretched grey beneath a seething sky. Rain-fed streams and brooklets crisscrossed the matted grass, culminating in a broad boggy stretch at the bottom of the garden, where a few stolid birch trees rose bravely from the mulch. Earlier that week he had seen figures moving down there, well within the boundaries of the estate. There was a security fence, of course, but it was an electrical fence, all but useless now. At night he could glimpse fires through the broken windows of the fallen houses adjoining Lazyland; he tried to take that for a good omen, since it meant the encamped *fellahin* were content to remain within their own broken homes and leave his alone. He leaned against the windowsill, so that his forehead rested against cool glass, and stared out at the flickering sky.

How long has it been since I've seen the stars? One year? Two?

Jack's breath left a fog on the glass, and he rubbed at it, frowning as he touched the little bull's-eye left by the Fusax bottle.

Could you see the stars in Mongolia, or Japan? Was there anyplace left where you could see them at all?

Certainly not here, where the gaily clouded sky had given itself over to a perpetual carnival of night, with no clear cold atoms to hint that there was a world, any world, beyond this one. All the broken lands below him cast back to the heavens that same unquiet light, fires raging in empty towers, the waters of New York Harbor burning where freighters had released their cargoes, glowing traceries of fuselage left by jets that had failed in transit. Lightning streamed across the sky and lit upon the Palisades, crimson and violet, so that for an instant he saw fireworks bursting there as upon a summer night long ago. A wash of corrosive orange swept across the cliffs and was gone. At the bottom of the garden something pale humped through the bushes. From the darkness came a howl, a dog's, Jack thought, but then the sound fractured into screaming laughter.

But it could as easily be dogs as men: they sound the same now . . .

Horror choked him, the taste of bile in his throat as poisonous as the rain gnawing at Lazyland's ruined lawns. Horror not of the grinning refugees who filled the stands of dying trees but of what came next, when pestilence and famine claimed them all.

We know what we are, but know not what we may be.

The awful laughter rose, louder and louder. Above the lawn billowed a sheet of brownish mist, smoke borne from some unseen fire. The wind beat against the house, and the smell of smoke seeped through the walls, thick with the reek of burning plywood, foam insulation, paint fumes. He gagged and covered his mouth; the wind gusted and as quickly as it had come the smoke was gone. Around and behind and beneath him he could feel the house moving, shuddering as the wind beat about its eaves. On the window in front of him, where his finger had smudged the damp glass, he saw a darkness like fine fur: some new kind of spore or fungus, already hungrily seizing upon the warmth and dead tissue left by his touch. He felt the dull pulse of blood inside his veins, and knew it not for his own life but the mindless tremor of nature. He shook his head numbly, with a soft shock saw that he had all unconscious leaned against the window again, both hands pressed against the cool smooth surface. When he reared back the imprints of his fingers began to blacken upon the glass as though charred by an invisible flame. But it was not ash left there in his wake but innumerable threads of living matter: he could smell them now, a whiff of foul gas as rises from the open grave. With a cry he stepped back from the window but there was no escaping it, it was all around him now if invisible, like a shroud being woven by a tireless army.

And as though it were spoken to him by the sky itself he knew what it was he saw, knew that he had gone to sleep in one world but woken to the wasteland. He wept then, hands battering at the glass until something splintered, dug into his palm, and there was blood then to worry about as well, blood to worry about again. He wept, but his weeping brought no peace or sense of freedom; not even exhaustion that might lure sleep. Only the certitude that comes with suffering, the knowledge unasked for, unwanted, that he was dying and the world with him: not just the world within him but that without; and nowhere on earth would a one survive to shrive or mourn its passing.

Later he came to, lying on the floor beneath the window. He had been dreaming of Leonard, of the two of them resting in the shadow of an abandoned farmhouse in Via Ardeatina. Leonard's hand upon his breast, his own hand on Leonard's cock; feeling him harden beneath his fingers. He gasped awake, flooded with desire and an aching sorrow that grew immeasurable, unbearable, as he took in the room around him and remembered: he was forty-two years old, he was ill, Leonard had fled him long ago.

On the floor dust bore his footprints as though in powdery sand. The cries of the *fellahin* had faded. A dull purplish sheen hid the sky. A somber radiance on the eastern horizon made Jack think it must be dawn. But when he found his watch, a Cartier hermetic timepiece with radium numerals, it said 10:15. The little brass carriage clock within its glass globe was chiming two. He stood, shivering, and gazed at a dark imprint on the window: nothing horrible there, only the normal amount of dirt and grit and grease. He frowned, looked at his hands for traces of blood, a scar: nothing. The wind blessedly had died away. Even more remarkable, the rain had stopped. Jack decided it must have been this that woke him, the unaccustomed silence after so many weeks of storm.

But the air felt dank and chill. There was a cloyingness to it, a weirdly palpable sense of *vitality*. With a shudder Jack turned and started for his bed.

That was when he heard her. Even from the first instant he knew it was a girl. A high, shaking sound of sobbing, faint but clear, and rising from somewhere just below the morning balcony. It made him think of his sister at play long ago, hiding in the hydrangea bush and crying because he was taking too long to find her. He stopped beside the bed and looked back at the window. He waited, expecting the sound to fall into silence or else flame into one of those unnerving screams. Instead it continued no louder or softer than before, frail and piteous.

"What the hell," Jack whispered. He rubbed his eyes. Exhaustion tore at him, but he walked back to the window, wrenched it open, and leaned outside to scan the half-lit garden below. For a moment the crying stopped. He could imagine whoever was there looking up and seeing him, a tall white wraith commanding this battered ship. The crying began again, as miserable as before. He searched the rounded humps and shadows of half-dead shrubs and fallen statuary, seeing nothing. But the thought of someone down there gazing frightened, at *him*, was too much for Jack to bear. He went to his night table and pulled out his inhaler, took two quick breaths, and hurried downstairs.

From the kitchen floated a warm acrid smell—the dried dandelion roots Mrs. Iverson was using to eke out the last of their hoard of coffee. He passed swiftly and quietly through the foyer and into the mudroom, holding the great oaken door so that it shut without a sound. He pulled on boots and his grandfather's ancient raincoat and went outside.

The cold assailed him, and the near silence. The air was so still that he could hear the thrum of a single car echoing from far away, solid and portentous as the tolling of a church bell. He listened raptly as it drove off; then the sound of weeping stirred him again. He fastened the raincoat's single remaining button and strode down toward the garden.

It took him only minutes to find her. He had thought—hoped, actually—that whoever it was would have fled by the time he got outside, or at least fallen silent. Instead as he passed from crumbled tarmac to the rank squelching lawn the cries grew louder and more desperate. Jack shook his head, dismayed and also somewhat embarrassed.

"Hey," he called softly. His voice cracked, and he stopped, clearing his throat and tasting the bitter aftertaste of his inhalant. "It's okay. I'm not—I won't hurt you."

The weeping ceased, then with a hoarse cry resumed, so close that Jack took a nervous sideways step. He looked about at the sodden limbs of juniper and ilex, streaked black and faintly shimmering in the purplish light. Water pooled about his boots, releasing a thick rank smell as of spoiled mushrooms. He shoved his hands into his pockets and was just starting for the yew hedge when he saw her. His mouth went dry, and he stumbled to a halt.

It was the child he had seen in his vision, the child who had led the procession of hornéd men. The same white face and windblown hair, the same wide empty eyes, the same thin mouth opened now to weep rather than blow upon a flute. But even as he stared aghast the child shuddered and turned, so that Jack saw it was not a child but a girl of fourteen or fifteen, so emaciated and frail she looked younger. Her cheeks were hollowed, touched with violet where the light struck them, her sunken eyes a vivid troubling blue. She crouched in the leaf-strewn declivity beneath a hydrangea bush, her fingers curled about a handful of moldering leaves and her lips drawn back so that he could see her teeth, very white above gums that were almost black. She wore some kind of cheap raincoat, the plastic ripped and gummed with filth. Beneath it Jack could glimpse filthy white pants and shapeless shirt, ripped down the middle so that her small breasts were exposed. As she stared at him she made a hissing sound, like a cornered snake.

"Hey," whispered Jack, and backed away from her. Suddenly he felt frightened and incredibly stupid: was he *crazy* coming out here like this? The girl watched him with eyes empty of anything but raw fear. If he extended a hand to her, he was certain she would bite, and he knew what that bite would bring: plague, pestilence, cholera, death.

But then, inexplicably and without thinking, Jack *did* reach for her; watched with a sort of amazed horror as his own hand moved before him, palm up as he would approach a strange dog. The girl's gaze wavered between his face and his hand, as though weighing which held the greater threat. Then with a low cry she lifted her head and stared unblinking into his eyes. He stared back and saw there hatred, dreadful hunger, and an unassailable fear; but mostly fear.

And it was that which touched him. And so he knelt before her, awkwardly pulling at his raincoat as he murmured, "It's okay, I won't hurt you, come here, come here . . ."

The coat billowed about her shoulders and she clutched it, still not taking her eyes from his. He reached clumsily to straighten it about her but it was like cloaking a bare scaffold: he could feel nothing but emptiness and the dead stalks of hydrangea. He moved his hands ineffectually for a minute or two and then drew back, forcing a smile.

"There. Are you better now? Warmer?"

The girl looked up at him, her lusterless hair like dead grass. For a moment she seemed not to understand, but finally she nodded.

"Thank you," she whispered. She had a vaguely European accent.

"You're welcome," said Jack, and immediately felt like an idiot. He cleared his throat again and stood. Cold enveloped him like another garment; he gazed down at the girl, torn between his desire to hurry back inside and the burgeoning awareness that, having started something, he couldn't leave it unfinished.

"Shit," he said miserably. In front of him the girl began to weep again, silently, tears fine as needles streaking her gaunt face. Not just the act of cloaking her but the coat itself had given something of humanity back to her. For a cruel moment Jack cursed himself for not going out in his pajamas; but then he ran a hand across his damp brow and shook his head.

"Come on, then." He sighed, his tone resigned and impatient. "I can't leave you out here to die on the fucking *lawn*."

Once again he stretched his hand toward her. The girl crouched back against the barren shrub, then with a shiver stood on unsteady feet. She ignored his hand and stumbled forward, walking slowly at first, then faster and faster, passing from grass to broken tarmac as she hurried up the drive. Jack followed, very very slowly—he was hoping she would break into a run and flee Lazyland. But when he reached the top of the drive she was waiting for him, clutching his grandfather's raincoat around her narrow shoulders.

"Right." Jack's resignation burned into soft despair. "The front door." He gestured at the house. "Don't worry, I'm coming."

She waited until he had passed her, still staring with those twilight eyes. Then she followed, taking care to keep a safe distance between them. This made Jack so angry he wanted to shout. Instead he hurried on, drawing a nasty satisfaction from watching her stumble as she tried to catch up.

"Here—" He bounded up the two broad steps onto the porch. He had thought—hoped—she might hang back, but the girl darted forward so quickly she bumped against him as he fumbled with the locks. He glanced down and had a glimpse of her feral gaze, half-hidden behind her matted hair. She smelled like rotting leaves. He scarcely had time to remove the key before she shoved against the door and tumbled into the dim mudroom, gasping.

"Now listen," Jack said as he pulled the outer door shut. "My grandmother lives here, she's very old and frail, and I don't want you—*bugging* her."

The girl stared at him as though he had barked like a dog. Jack blushed and elbowed past her toward the inner door, calling out softly.

"Grandmother? Grandmother, there's someone here, don't—"

He stopped, biting his lip in dismay, and glanced

back at the girl. *I must be fucking crazy.* What was he
thinking, telling her about his grandmother? Some
insane little bitch planning to rob them in their sleep, or
just waiting to signal her cronies to break into Lazyland
and kill them all . . .

Why didn't I see that? He stood in the open doorway,
trying to summon the will to turn and shove the girl
back outside, when his grandmother appeared at the
foot of the stairs.

"Yes, Jackie?"

The girl made a low mewling sound, then with sur-
prising strength pushed past him and into the main
entry.

"Grandmother," she whispered. Her grim little face
contorted. Jack edged forward protectively, fearful she
was going to strike the old woman. Instead the girl
looked up at Keeley, ran a hand self-consciously through
her filthy hair, and smiled.

"Well." Keeley's hands tightened on her gold-topped
walking stick. "Is this a—friend? Of Leonard's?"

"Umm, well, no—" Before he could go on, the girl
stepped forward, letting the Burberry fall from her
shoulders. Jack lunged to catch it, praying his grandmother wouldn't notice her husband's coat put to such
use.

She didn't. She was staring at the girl with a soft
marveling expression that smoothed the wrinkles from
her cheeks and made her look—well, not *young*, but
certainly not a hundred years old. Very slowly a smile
broke across her face.

"*Lunantishee,*" she said; Jack recognized the Irish
intonation but not the word. "*A cailin a vic O!* What are
you doing *here*?"

The girl's smile faded. She glanced over her shoulder
at Jack, her blue eyes frightened. Jack forced himself to

smile reassuringly—for Keeley's sake, not the girl's. "She was outside in the cold, I just thought we might let her in to dry off, and then—"

"Of course," said Keeley. She continued to gaze at the girl, but the wonder drained from her faded blue eyes; whatever she saw now, it was not the *lunantishee*. "Bring her in there, she can sit by the stove"— she raised her walking stick and motioned toward the kitchen—"I'll have Larena find something for her to wear. Go on now—" This to the girl, in the same brisk tone she'd used on generations of animals and children. "Go on."

The girl clutched at her torn clothes, then, staring resolutely at her feet, walked down the dark hallway toward the kitchen. With an apologetic sound Jack turned to his grandmother, but Keeley was already standing at the foot of the regal staircase, thumping her walking stick.

"Larena! Larena dear—"

With a sigh Jack headed for the huge kitchen, the most modern room in the great shaky pile that was Lazyland. His grandfather had renovated it shortly before his death in the early 1970s, as a gift for Keeley; all the original woodwork had been replaced with shiny blond cabinets and turquoise Naugahyde. As a teenager Jack had loved the kitchen, proof positive of the Finnegans' continued stature in the world. Across the river, the Sparkle-Glo factory may have shut down, but here upon the hill Thanksgiving turkeys were roasted, Yorkshire puddings baked, and Irish Mist poured beneath fluorescent lights so brilliant they cast no shadows.

Now the kitchen was a catafalque. The fluorescent bulbs had long since flickered out. The electric range was covered with ancient outdoor gear dredged up from one of Lazyland's sub-basements: a blackened Coleman stove and tiny white gas—driven heater that boiled water and scorched rice. The refrigerator was unplugged, the occult pantry with its folding doors and lazy Susans sadly underutilized. At the far end, a shadowy doorway opened onto the lace-drawn formal dining room. Still, with the vivid light falling through its many windows, the kitchen was the brightest room in the house, and Larena Iverson kept it scrupulously clean.

Certainly the ragged girl was impressed. Jack found her standing beside the stool where younger cousins had been wont to take their afternoon cocoa, her expression somewhere between suspicion and awe.

"This your *house*?" She began to cough.

"Yes," said Jack. "I mean, my family's," he added, trying to evoke a vast hidden clan that dealt speedily and fatally with all intruders. "Look, we're pretty busy right now, maybe I can find you a towel or something, you can dry off, and then you'd better—"

Behind him there was a soft wheeze and the pad of slippered feet. "Oh, poor thing! Look at you, soaked to the skin, what was your mother thinking?"

Mrs. Iverson struggled across the room, burdened with heavy wintry-looking clothes and a large pink appliquéd bath towel. The girl looked up, confused. "Mother?"

"Wait till I have a word with her," Mrs. Iverson went on. "Look at you, a skinny wretch, what were you think-ing, get into the bathroom now! Right this *minute*—"

The housekeeper extended her laden arms and began herding the girl back toward the dark corridor. A moment later Jack heard the bathroom door creak shut, the gasp and blast of water surging up through the recalcitrant pipes. Mrs. Iverson's voice rose and fell, and after a minute or two he heard the girl laughing.

"Great," he muttered, and crossed over to the stove. A thermos held what was left of the morning's brew. He poured himself a mug, grimacing as he picked out bits of dandelion root and grounds, and stared unhappily out the window. The kitchen telephone sat on a shelf there beside a ragged copy of the Yonkers telephone book. He thought of picking up the receiver to see if there would be a dial tone today, checking in the Yellow Pages for whatever defunct agency had once dealt with circumstances like this. Child Welfare? New Hope for Women? Emma would know what to do. He could call her, arrange for Jule to hydroplane down the Saw Mill River Parkway and take the girl to an appropriate shelter somewhere.

Oh please! He could just hear Leonard's derisive laughter. *Shelter? Where's your sense of Christian duty, Jackie-boy? Throw her back to the wolves!*

Oh, fuck off, thought Jack, and reached for the receiver. He'd long ago stopped trying to find any sort of pattern in when the phones would work, just as he had stopped trying to find a reason for the power outages. *It's just the Way We Live Now!* Leonard would cry gleefully, and hum a bit of an old AT&T jingle; but more than the outages themselves it was the constant uncertainty that maddened Jack.

Because if you *knew* there would be no electricity for, say, the next fifty years, you could Just Make Do. Remember the Depression? Remember Sarajevo? Some people live like this all the time!

But when the power popped back on at 3 A.M, there was always the same insane rush for lights and a hot shower, the cappuccino maker, the computer and the television and the VCR. It made no difference that this just made it all worse. Jack himself knew that when he heard the telltale bleat from Lazyland's carbon-monoxide detector, the sudden soft click of the VCR or faint music rising from a forgotten radio, he would find Mrs. Iverson struggling downstairs to do battle with the washing machine and his grandmother rolling pie crust in the kitchen, even as Jack made a beeline for the stereo.

Jule told him that in the city it was even worse. Brokers and traders camping out on the floor of the Exchange, so as not to miss that instant when its black and cavernous reaches suddenly burst into light and life; the very wealthy pouring from their luxury towers and commandeering hansoms for impromptu parties and lightning visits to restaurants, nightclubs, galleries that opened only by electric light. People addicted to the new interactive drugs rushed to the electric avenues where they could sate themselves. Musicians and club kids filled streets and warehouses and tunnels, and for a little while life began to take on some of its old contours: trains running, businesses operating, people complaining about jobs and missed flights instead of the search for bottled water and fresh produce.

But sooner or later it would all come crashing down again. And an entire secondary industry had sprung up around *that*—people who made it their business to handicap whether or not the NYSE would be open on a particular day, or when the datalink from the Tokyo Exchange would kick in with its daily offerings. Jule— who had many friends, if not clients, and occasionally still ventured into the city with them—told of watching a beautifully dressed young woman decapitate a black rooster on the floor of the Exchange, while her partner collected international currency and more useful offerings—chocolate, coffee, a small strand of black pearls— from a surging crowd of commodities brokers.

So it was with mild trepidation that Jack lifted the

telephone from its cradle. And yes, there was a dial tone and the familiar recording that warned of delays.

"... *constantly working to improve our service to our customers* ..."

"*All right, dear!*" He started, replacing the handset as Mrs. Iverson's shrill voice heralded the opening of the bathroom door. "*Let's go stand in front of the fire and get warm—*"

Jack listened to the soft parade of footsteps going from hall to entryway. Finally he started after them. *Was* there a fire today? He certainly hadn't made one. But when he got to the living room he found the girl crouched in front of the blazing hearth, wearing clothes that were much too big for her.

"*What* was her mother thinking?" Mrs. Iverson demanded of Jack. "Make sure she stays warm while I take care of *those*—" Her eyes narrowed, fixing on the pathetic mound of tattered cloth she'd dropped back in the hallway. "We should call the doctor, too," she added vaguely, and toddled off.

At the word *doctor* the girl shot Jack an alarmed look.

"Don't worry. There's no doctor. Not unless we bundle you off to the hospital." He crossed his arms, trying to strike a pose between beneficence and menace. The girl looked so puzzled that he gave up and sank into an armchair. "Oh, screw it. So what's your name?"

The fire's crackling all but drowned her reply. "Marz."

"'Scuse me?"

"Marz. Marz Candry."

"Marcie?"

"*No.* It's short for Marzana—Mary, in Polish. Just call me Marz, okay?"

"Polish, huh?" That would account for the accent,

also the starved-refugee look. He shut his eyes, opened them to focus on the figure hunched at his feet. Her pale hair had been combed slick against her skull. Where the firelight touched her cheeks it left dimpled imprints of gold and black. A faint warm scent of wet wool hung in the room, pleasant and slightly doggy, and the sweet incense of burning fruitwood. "Mary, that was my aunt's name. Mary Anne. I never knew her, really," he added, as though she had asked. "She disappeared when I was a kid."

He drew himself up in the chair, leaned forward to gaze at her more intently. "As a matter of fact, those are some of her clothes, I think."

He pointed at the heathery pink sweater that billowed across the girl's chest, the voluminous folds of a red dirndl skirt that spread about her like a pool of melting wax. "Let me see, move over here . . ."

The girl looked at him suspiciously as he took her by one shoulder and gently pulled her around. He tugged at the sweater until it grew taut as a tent flap in front of her, smiling when he found what he was looking for: a ragged web of black thread, the remains of an embroidered monogram.

"Mary Anne Finnegan. See?" He traced the raveling edges and shook his head. "No one knows what happened to her. She ran away to California in the sixties and never came back. A couple of people told me some character in *The Electric Kool-Aid Acid Test* was actually her. Probably she just OD'ed somewhere. But weird, huh?"

The girl scrunched deeper into her woolen tent. *"What?"*

Jack bit his lip. "Oh, never mind. So are you, uh—what? A runaway? Or something?"

"Something." Her tone was coldly disdainful. Jack waited for her to go on, but she only inched closer to the fire, strands of lank hair falling across her cheeks. He fought an urge to demand a better reply, instead sank back into the armchair. He was rewarded with an exaggerated sigh as the girl extended her bare toes onto the hearth.

"Nice and warm at least," Jack suggested. She ignored him.

No good deed goes unpunished, he thought.

"Mmmm . . ."

The girl yawned, moving so that tiger shadows streaked her face. Watching her, Jack wondered how he could have ever mistaken her for the child from his dream. She was obviously older, and obviously female, despite being all but hidden by that mass of wool. There was a piquant, almost hungry sharpness about her features: hollow cheeks and small pinched nose, black slit of a mouth that opened on small white teeth; straggling corn-silk hair. No jewelry save a simple gold ring. There was nothing remotely pretty about her, save those deep-set slanted eyes, so deep a blue as to be almost purple in the flickering light. Jack felt a surge of annoyance. Even now, crouched safely on the hearth with a faint steam rising from her wet hair, she twitched and glanced suspiciously over her shoulder, as though willing him to leave.

". . . upstairs then."

Keeley's voice sounded from the entry room. There was the hollow thump of her walking stick. A moment later she appeared in the doorway.

"Now, dear." Jack looked up obediently, but his grandmother was staring at the girl. "Larena said she found you some clothes? Let me see if they fit."

The girl glanced up but didn't move. "Stand *up*," commanded Keeley, stepping into the burnished circle of firelight. "I want to see, she said they were too big."

The girl got to her feet. The sweater's sleeves dangled almost to her calves. Keeley shook her head.

"We'll have to do better than *that*," she said flatly. "Did Larena get you something to eat?"

The girl shrugged. "No."

"Larena!" Keeley turned and pounded her walking stick on the floor. "*Larena—*"

From upstairs came a shrill reply.

"Larena will make you something." Keeley swung back around. She reached to tug at the sweater and scowled. "Why ever did she give you *that*? Mary Anne would have made three of you."

For a long moment Keeley regarded her with icy blue eyes, her gnarled hands tight around the handle of her walking stick. When Larena entered, she turned away.

"Larena dear, see if there's any of that soup left."

"Well." Jack stood awkwardly in the middle of the room. "I guess I'll check the furnace."

He waited a moment, in case anyone might ask him to stay. No one did. He headed downstairs, stopping in the basement bathroom to get a surgical mask from the box Emma had given him. Then he went to the coal cellar, a room the size of a big closet, and started shoveling chunks of anthracite into the furnace.

It took forty-three shovelsful and the better part of an hour. Once he could have done it in fifteen minutes. Now the effort exhausted him. His arms ached, and his back. After a few minutes he had to pause between loads, turning his face from the rising cloud of black dust to cough and hoping the mask would magically protect him. He thought numbly of the vial of Fusax on his nightstand. Had it been only yesterday that he felt so much better? He coughed, imagining the girl upstairs: a stranger's mouth to feed, a stranger's body soaking up warmth while Jack struggled in the mansion's bowels like some medieval lackey.

Finally he was done. Sweating, he dropped the heavy shovel with its splintering wooden handle and trudged back upstairs.

He found his grandmother alone in the living room, sitting in her high-backed wing chair with a tumbler of whiskey on the table beside her. No lamps had been lit. The fire had burned down to a glowing heap of embers. The room was dusted in shadow as though with a layer of ash. Hot air rose from the floor's elaborate brass registers, and the harsh scent of anthracite overpowered the last sweet remnants of applewood and Keeley's perfume.

"How was the furnace, dear? Did it bother your lungs?"

Jack removed his mask and stuffed it in a pocket. He jabbed ineffectually at the embers with a poker, then settled into a chair. "Fine. No trouble this time."

"Is there enough coal?"

"Plenty. And it will be spring, soon . . ."

His voice died as he gazed at the somber square of window behind his grandmother, whorled with the pulsing greens and purples of an early sunset. "Well, it will be *May*, anyhow."

His grandmother nodded slowly and reached for her glass. "Your father was so set on taking that furnace out, back when he put those solar panels in. I don't remember now how James talked him out of it."

Jack shook his head, stifling a yawn. "He didn't. I remember. It would have cost too much to remove it, so they decided to just leave it."

"Lucky thing," murmured Keeley. She tugged at the mohair shawl draped across the back of her chair.

"Where's the girl?" Jack wondered.

"Larena put her to bed in Mary Anne's room. Where did you say you met her?"

Jack gave a sharp laugh. "I *met* her in the backyard. Under the hydrangeas."

"Under the hydrangeas! How did she get in?"

"I don't know. I didn't think to ask her—she just looked so miserable—"

"Of course, of course."

"I'll call someone tomorrow." Jack held his hands out, seeking a warm spot in the air. "Emma will know somebody."

"Have you talked to them? How are they?"

Jack nodded. "A week or so ago. They've been busy—well, Emma's been busy at the hospital, and I guess Jule's got a few clients in the city. I think it's hard for them right now—there's not a lot of work for him . . ." His voice trailed off.

"Well, doctors are always busier than lawyers," Keeley said loyally. She loved Jule, who had lived at Lazyland while attending law school at Fordham twenty years before. "People are always getting sick. Especially now." She sighed and set her tumbler back onto the side table. "Did they say when they could come visit?"

"Maybe before too long, if the rain keeps off," Jack lied. "Emma used all her time off to come take care of me. Every time I talk to them, they want us to move up there with them—"

Keeley shook her head determinedly. "Too far away."

"I know. They just worry, that's all."

"Well, I hope they can find her parents."

Jack stared at her. "Her parents?" It was a moment

before he realized she was talking about the girl. "Oh! Right—"

"Though she said she lived with someone in the city," Keeley went on absently. "I think she was lying. Who would raise a child in the city?"

They sat in silence for several minutes. Then, Jack asked, "What was that Irish word you used before, Grandmother? Like 'banshee'—?"

Keeley shut her eyes and tilted her head, as though listening to faraway music; after a moment answered.

"*Lunantishee*, you mean? That's what your grandfather used to call me," she murmured, stroking the fringe of her shawl. "They were fairies of some kind, I don't remember. Pretty girls. That's all I meant," she ended, and she looked up at him. "Why don't you go check on her on your way upstairs, dear. Thank you."

He was being dismissed. Jack stared at his hands, after a moment nodded. "All right. Maybe I'll try calling Emma tonight—the phone was up a little while ago."

"Very good, dear."

He stood and stretched, for a minute remained in the middle of the room and stared out the west-facing window. Beyond the black-and-violet-edged line of the Palisades a molten glow lingered, sending ruddy flourishes across the rain-swollen Hudson. Jack felt the strange blurry sensation that overcame him sometimes, when some bright fleck of his childhood surfaced and the terrible weight of the poisoned sky momentarily lifted. Almost he could imagine the sun bulging red upon the western horizon; almost he could see the first stars showing through, and the glitter of electric lights in distant skyscrapers. A spark of gold leapt across the darkness and Jack's heart with it, as upon its promontory overlooking the Hudson the skeletal arches of the Sparkle-Glo factory blazed with sunset.

And then it was gone. A blast of wind shook the window as a rain squall swept through, bringing with it sheets of coruscating yellow and acid blue. On the horizon the sun disappeared, swallowed by brilliant gouts of green. Day had ended, but there was no night, only a tumult of hail against glass. With a stab of dread Jack was brought back to a darkened room thick with the smell of burning coal.

"Good night," he whispered. He kissed his grandmother's cheek and fled.

On the second-floor landing his grandmother had left a candle burning within a cracked glass mantle. Outside the wind banged and hooted at the eaves. There was the creak of a shutter that had gotten loose, the tired exhalation from a hot-air register. Jack shivered and debated going straight up to bed, but then he heard a small sound from the bedroom that had been his aunt Mary Anne's. He crossed to the open door and peered inside. A hurricane lamp cast its glow across the huge old four-poster. He could barely make out a lump beneath the spread.

"Knock knock." He rapped softly at the door. "Can I come in?"

Silence. Then, "Okay," a muffled voice replied.

He entered, feeling distinctly uncomfortable: he was a man, alone in a dimly lit bedroom with a teenage girl. "Uhumm." He paused and cleared his throat. "Are you—how are you feeling?"

The bed loomed before him, an eighteenth-century cherry four-poster complete with white chenille spread and canopy of once-sumptuous, now somewhat Miss Havershamish, Belgian lace. An alpine array of pillows marched across its head; at its foot a down comforter waited like an immense nougat to be devoured at need. Somewhere in between was the girl. He could hear her breathing, uneven and noisy, and even smell his grand-mother's imported lavender soap.

But it was another minute before he could pinpoint her: a bulge beneath the worn chenille, neither long nor wide enough to form a decent bolster, with a faint feathering of silver showing where her hair tufted up from beneath the blankets. Another moment and he could make out her pinched face, her slanted eyes staring at him with a ferocity that might have been fear or just fatigue.

"I feel like *shit*," she snapped.

A spasm of coughing shook the bed. *Rather overwrought*, Jack thought with clinical unkindness. He waited until the coughing subsided, then drew closer.

"I'm sorry," he said, immediately aware of how unsorry he sounded. He asked in a gentler voice, "Can I get you anything?"

"*No.*"

This time the voice sounded distinctly like a sob, neither overwrought nor duplicitous but merely miserable. It would have been nice if the sound had torn at Jack's heart, but in fact it annoyed him—*everything* about this girl annoyed him—and that in turn made him feel guilty, which made him sigh.

"I'm sorry," he repeated. Idly he traced a raised diamond on the bedspread, trying hard not to stare at the sharp little face an arm's length away. "Can't I get you something? Some milk maybe?"

"I *hate* milk."

"Oh. Well, um, that's good, because there isn't any. But—are you hungry? Did Mrs. Iverson get you anything to eat?"

A small shudder beneath the blankets. "Some soup. And some crackers." The shudder extended into a snaky sort of motion that ended with the girl suddenly sitting up, the bedspread pooling around her like cream. "Actually, do you like have a Coke or something?"

"Actually, no." He paused to see if the girl would smile. She didn't. "I think there's some tea, chamomile tea? No? Okay, let's see, there might be—"

With a dramatic sigh the girl flopped back against the pillows. She pulled the covers up to her chin, burrowing down until she all but disappeared, save for her burning eyes. "Oh *forget* it."

Jack took in her fierce wedge of face, that elegantly accented voice so inflated with childish annoyance: the butterfly that stamped. Unexpectedly he laughed.

"What?" she demanded.

Jack shook his head, moving aside the hurricane lamp so he could lean against the nightstand. "Nothing. Just, I think it's customary under these circumstances to say 'Thank you.'"

"*What?* Oh." The face shrank still deeper into the bed, like a currant in bread dough. "*Thank you.*"

Jack ignored the ungrateful tone. "You're welcome." He toyed with the shade of an old electric lamp, clicked the switch experimentally a few times before turning back to her. "Marzana Candry. Is that your real name?"

"I already told you."

"I mean your real last name. It doesn't sound Polish."

Hostile silence. He could see her eyes glittering. After a moment she hissed, "*Yes.*"

"Marzana Candry." At her baleful look Jack corrected himself. "*Marz* Candry. Where are you from, Marz? Where in Poland?"

Silence.

"Let's try again: where were you before you came *here*? New York? New Jersey?" Her eyes squeezed shut. "Connecticut? Long Island?"

Still nothing. Jack's momentary good humor vanished. He thought of going through all fifty states, viciously, and then starting on individual cities, but before he could the girl said, "My parents are fucking dead, okay? And I'll fucking kill myself before I go back to Poland, and I'll never tell you where I came from so forget it, okay? *Okay?*" she ended in a near shriek.

"Okay," Jack agreed, startled.

"The only reason I even *came* to your stupid house was by *mistake*. I was—I was with my friends and we got, like separated, okay? And I got lost, it was night and raining and I didn't know *where* the fuck I was going and if I did I wouldn't have come *here* to your stupid fucking house, all right?"

Jack nodded. He looked beyond her at the wide dormer window, its panes slashed with blue and gold. Out there, somewhere . . .

"Your friends. *Fellahin?*" Immediately he was embarrassed at how stupid he sounded: like his father calling Leonard a hophead.

The girl snorted and rolled her eyes. "What, you get that from the *web?* Some subway hippie Scientologist? *Fuck* that. They were my *family*. We were living down by the river and the fucking cops blew us out."

"Oh. What happened to the rest? Your friends?"

"I dunno. Wasted, I guess. Who cares? *You* care?" She fixed him with a defiant stare. "Huh?"

Jack stared back, after a moment shrugged. "No. I guess I don't actually give a fuck."

That shut up her up. An odd look played across her face, something between amusement and anger. She sat up, tossing her head so that a sheaf of fine hair hid her eyes, and made a small gesture with one hand.

"So what is this?" she asked, a little hesitantly. "A museum?"

Jack laughed. "A museum? Yeah. And I'm the mummy."

The girl frowned. "Really—is it a museum?"

"No—it's my house—my grandmother's house, actually. My family's."

Her eyes widened. "You *live* here?"

"Sure. If you can call this living," he added. "Why?"

The girl shook her head. "It's just so . . ."

Her voice trailed off. She clutched the blankets to her thin chest, while above her the bed's canopy stirred in a draft. Jack looked around and tried to see it all as she must. The worn expanse of oriental carpet, its threadbare pathways trodden by generations of bare feet; the marble fireplace with its carved wooden screen and dried hydrangeas; the monolithic old Victorian furniture, caparisoned with doilies and antimacassars and bits of velvet patchwork. A Chatty Cathy doll that had been his aunt's, wearing faded blue dungarees and dusty yellow T-shirt; a Marymount College mug filled with pens and eyebrow pencils; a corner where a brass incense burner and peeling plastic daisy decals were all that remained of a shrine to The Turtles.

"It doesn't look like *my* house," Marz said at last, very softly.

Several minutes passed. Outside the wind tore at the dormer window. A soft clitter marked where a mouse made its way somewhere within the walls. Shadows washed across the floor, scattering the carpet with dark roseates. An odd sort of peace came over Jack: how long had it been since he'd sat in this room? As a child he'd slept here, as he'd slept everywhere in Lazyland. But this room had always held an unspoken sadness after his aunt had run away. He had been ten at the time, Mary Anne an ancient seventeen. When she had left Yonkers, hitchhiking cross-country to disappear in the winter after the Summer of Love, she had been scarcely older than the sullen girl before him.

"It is so beautiful here Mom & Dad, I wish you could see it . . ."

For the first time he was overwhelmed by the thought of what a terrible grief his family must have gone through, his father and grandparents and uncles; a long slow tide of grief, creeping inexorably over them all as the months went by and there came no more cheesy postcards of the Golden Gate Bridge, no more collect calls; nothing.

And he had never known, really; sensed it only as a child senses death, as an inexplicable absence that has less to do with the disappearance of the dead themselves than with the empty places left in those who mourn, the empty places left in the house itself. He had never known what shouts and sobs must have filled the sunny rooms when he was playing elsewhere. As an adult with his own numberless dead to mourn, he had never thought to ask his grandmother what it had been like to lose her child.

"Mmmmm . . ."

He looked up to see the girl yawning, her defiant expression softened by weariness. Jack moved the hurricane lantern back to its accustomed place, and made an awkward little bow.

"I guess I'll say good night, then." He waited for the girl to say something, but she only stared resolutely at the ceiling. "All right. Good night."

At the door he paused, turning to cast a final look into the room. The girl lay in the enormous old bed like a shipwrecked child in a battered lifeboat. In the chimney the wind roared and sent a flurry of ashes into the room. A profound uneasiness pierced Jack, to gaze into that familiar place and see a stranger there. He closed the door and hurried upstairs to his own room.

CHAPTER NINE

What the Storm Said

Spring came late to Mars Hill. Even before the glimmering, the season had always been a long slow sputtering fuse: ice-out on the lakes in late March or early April, followed by the first few sparks of green amidst lichen-covered stones and the sloping shoulders of the Camden Hills ten miles to the south. What most people recognized as *spring* didn't come to Maine until the end of May, or even June. And of course the chimerical weather of the last two years had changed even that.

This spring, ice-out didn't occur until the morning of April 19. Martin knew when he saw the first loons flying overhead, making their way inland from the bay to Swan Lake. Somehow the loons always knew, and would arrive at their summer homes within an hour of the final thaw. Martin Dionysos (né Schuster) stood on the porch of his tumbledown cottage, the hairs on his neck prickling as he watched them arrow overhead, the air rent by their wailing.

"Oh, welcome," he whispered. Tears sprang to his eyes and he let them come, weak and shivery with gratitude—it had not been so very long ago that he had been terrified he would never be able to cry again, just as he had been certain the loons would not return, or the peepers in the marsh abutting the eastern slope of Mars Hill. But while there was nothing that could keep the broken sky at bay, or the terrible weather, enough magic resided still in the spare bones of this place that Martin could lie awake at night in his worn cannonball bed, haunted by the song of frogs. Now he clutched the decrepit porch railing and watched the loons fly past.

"There they go." From a neighboring cottage wafted the voice of old Mrs. Grose, one of the three year-round residents at the crumbling spiritualist community. "'Magic birds.'"

Martin smiled. "'Magic birds.'" That was what the Abenaki Indians had named them. "I guess spring'll be here someday, too."

Even from his own porch Martin could hear Mrs. Grose sigh.

"Perhaps," she said in her accented voice, hugging her L.L. Bean windbreaker tight around her ample chest. At her feet wheezed her ancient pug. Martin's son, Jason, and Jason's wife Moony had once figured that the pug must be well over two hundred in dog years. Even Jason resisted the temptation to try and calculate Mrs. Grose's age. "But spring isn't really spring anymore, is it? My primroses, they were so sickly last year. And the lupines . . ."

Her voice died as she turned, staring down past the other toy Victorians nestled on the hillside to where Penobscot Bay sparkled blue and gold and violet in the early-morning light. Martin felt his initial burst of joy ebb as he followed her gaze.

"I know." He stared down at the first blades of dandelions thrusting through the earth, a pallid brownish yellow. "Mine too . . ."

Last spring, after years of watching his friends and lovers die, Martin himself had finally succumbed to his illness. At Jason's urging, he'd left his apartment in San Francisco and moved back to Mars Hill for good. The virus had gone into remission almost immediately. But his weakness remained, the damage done to his lungs by pneumonia, lesions on his arms and calves that even

Mars Hill's singular magic could not heal. And the ceaseless gnawing at his heart that was grief for not just lovers and friends but for an entire world that had been destroyed: books that would never be written, songs never sung, children never born, tracts of the heart and soul that would remain unmapped. Martin himself *terra incognita*, the undiscovered country; because who was left now to love him? He had Mrs. Grose for company, of course. And his son Jason and his wife, Moony, came up from Woods Hole as often as they could, but flights to Maine were all but nonexistent unless you chartered a plane, and Jason couldn't afford that.

So Martin spent his days indoors, priming canvases with his failing reserves of linseed oil and turpentine, or scouring the beach for usable things: driftwood, salt-sodden telephone poles, plastic milk cartons, beer bottles. The bleak loneliness of the Maine winter left him depleted and depressed. He did no painting. The stretched canvases were left standing about the cottage like so many blank windows and doors, and they filled it with their strong resiny scent. His on-line columns for *Queer* faded to bi- and then trimonthly, not because of the lack of power (fitful, but you could usually count on at least one day in the week to bring electricity) but because he had lost all heart. This caused webwide speculation as to whether he was still alive. Martin of course knew more people now who were dead than not, and spent mordant hours in bed devising new addresses for himself: timormort@acadia.com. He moved the photograph of his dead lover John deMartino from the bedside table, because some nights it seemed to speak to him. He read the same lines of poetry over and over again, as though tracing the lineaments of his lover's cheek—

so many,
I had not thought death had undone so many.

We who were living are now dying
With a little patience . . .

Within his veins he could no longer sense his own blood stirring. Martin could not die yet, but he was not healed. Days and nights on end he waited at a window overlooking the wasteland, eyes seared by what lay before him, wounded sky and stranded dolphins rotting upon the beach; he stood and waited for death to come.

"Open!"
To whom? Who are you?
"I would fain come into thy heart to thee."
'Tis a small space you crave!
"How, shall I scarce find lodging-room? If I press in
    and enter, thou needst not rue it! I will tell thee
    of wondrous things—"

He was, he knew, losing his mind. At night he lay awake and heard people moving softly in the room about him. They whispered, and he could hear his name amidst other words only half-understood, and he recognized the voices. His father was there; his first lover and many others; and once he knew the corrosive chime of laughter from his old nemesis, Leonard Thrope. He had not heard that Leonard had died, but was not surprised at the thought; nor by the twinge of sorrow that accompanied it.

But mostly he heard John. The voices, of course, must be the first stages of HIV dementia—or cryptococcal meningitis, or toxoplasma encephalitis, or CNS lymphoma, or progressive multi-focal leukoencephalopathy; neurosyphilis or cytomegalovirus encephalitis or the half dozen other kinds of madness that came with the territory where Martin spent his days. He knew there was no Good Death awaiting him; yet somehow he had not expected *this*. One night the whisperings grew so intrusive—scrape of bat wings against the window, giggling cold breath against his forehead—that he took a very deep breath and opened his eyes, determined to prove to *them*, at least, that there was nothing there.

Only there was: an entire roomful of phantoms, all familiar faces as at a spectral cocktail party, chatting and moving their hands quite animatedly. The one nearest to him—it was John—turned and with a smile opened his mouth to greet him. Martin screamed. His entire body spasmed with such horror that he shat the bed. He did not repeat the experiment. He took to swallowing tranquilizers at night and slept with a pillow over his head.

So it was with more than the usual green-starved longing that Martin awaited spring that year. One by one he'd cast off the few remaining ties that bound him to the rest of the world—lovers and friends, telephone, television, radio, car, even computer—surprised at how easy it had become, and how commonplace, to take up all the antediluvian burdens this Hotspur century had thrown aside. Chopping and carrying firewood, retrofitting an old hand pump for the kitchen; getting used to the sheen of ice on the interior walls and windows of his poorly insulated cottage. Mrs. Grose's canned zucchini and wax beans (the only things that grew reliably anymore, though they hardly flourished), a hot bath once a week. He'd offset the expense of wax candles by gathering stunted bayberries in the fall, and cursed himself for not installing solar panels years ago, as John had urged him. Now, of course, it was too late.

"Tired?"

From his porch Martin smiled wanly at Mrs. Grose. "A little," he confessed. No use lying to a centenarian psychic. "I was thinking I might walk down to the beach."

Mrs. Grose cocked her head, still staring across the bay to the ragged bulk of Dark Harbor, the small shadowy humps of Mount Desert and Blue Hill. "That was some storm we had, eh?" At her feet the little pug gasped, as though at a bad memory. "I thought the roof would blow away!"

"I'm surprised it didn't," said Martin.

They stood in silence for some minutes, watching the uneasy sky. "Well, I guess I'll go down and see what the storm washed up," Martin said at last. He lifted his hands from the porch rail, paint chips cascading around his feet.

"Dinner tonight?" Mrs. Grose called after him. "Diana's supposed to come and bring us a chicken."

"Then I'll be there."

He bent to pick up the canvas bag he took with him on his sea walks. Then, waving, he stepped from the porch and started downhill to the pier, past the sign so faded now that its letters were imprinted only in his memory.

MARS HILL
SPIRITUALIST COMMUNITY
FOUNDED 1883

Drifts of matted leaves clung to the base of the signpost, but not so many as there had been, once. Martin glanced down at the few sickly daffodils thrusting through the mulch, and winced. Moony had always said she hated spring at Mars Hill: "It's so *hopeless*!" To which Mrs. Grose had patiently explained that there was *always* hope—spring always came, followed by that sudden brilliant burst of northern summer that you never were quite prepared for, no matter how many times you'd seen it. But when Martin had last seen Moony a few weeks earlier, she'd avoided any mention of spring, avoided her annual rants against mud season and snow in May and the necessity of fires in cranky woodstoves that aggravated her asthma. At the time he and Jason had laughed about it (though not within Moony's hearing). Now Moony's unaccustomed silence seemed ominous.

She knows something, Martin thought as he trudged down the pitted gravel road to the beach. *She knows and she's not telling.*

Overhead the sky gleamed a soft metallic grey, more pewter than silver, streaked on the horizon with undulating bands of violet and green. Seagulls called plaintively, trailing in the wake of a solitary lobster boat puttering out to Dark Harbor. The air had a harsh metallic scent, hard to pinpoint but unmistakable. Jason was a marine biologist, and he believed the massive die-offs of krill and other plankton were changing the chemical content of the ocean. In the water a few cormorants bobbed, their heads snaking suddenly beneath the surface. Beside the rickety building that served as the summer community's storage shed, Martin's sailboat stood raised on concrete blocks. WENDAMEEN was painted on its bow in plain block letters. Martin looked at the boat and sighed, quickly turned and walked the last few yards to the beach.

Here, at last, things looked pretty much as they always had. No sand, just rocks everywhere, smooth and rounded by aeons of pounding waves. Braids of kelp and bladder wrack, stony hollows filled with periwinkles and goose barnacles; every now and then the fractured puzzle of a broken sea urchin's shell, the astral shadow of a starfish or sand dollar. If you stared at your feet as you walked along the shore, you might almost imagine the world was as it had been, as it should be. But a glance at the bruised sky, the reflected glare of purple and gold on somber waves put the lie to that.

The gravel path petered out beside a shriveled stand of rugosa roses. For a few minutes Martin stood and watched the lobster boat disappear into the glowing horizon, hands jammed into the pockets of his windbreaker. In the storm's aftermath the day was calm and almost windless. But the air had a nasty bite: there was no hint of warmth or snowmelt, none of the vernal promise that usually followed a spring nor'easter. Martin frowned and thought of returning to his cottage, but that would mean facing a sink full of dirty dishes and a recalcitrant hand pump. He began to walk once more.

He kept his head down. Now and then the wind would bring a strong scent of the sea untainted by that poisonous stench of dying krill. He picked up three flattened Budweiser cans and a single brown bottle, origin unknown, and shoved them into his canvas sack to be traded later at the Beach Store for credit. Spray stung the back of his neck. He walked slowly, hoping for a find that would match his best days of beachcombing. A twenty-dollar bill, all but worthless now, prized for its novelty value; a diamond engagement ring, hocked for food; the Bakelite casing of an old radio, miraculously intact save for its plundered electronics.

Nothing so exciting today. A broken skate's purse, many broken razor clams. The nubbin of a brick, too small to bother adding to his salvage walkway. Ubiquitous and seemingly innumerable petrified rubber bands that had once kept luncheon lobsters from pinching hungry picnickers. A dead gull lay upon a bed of kelp, feathers matted, small black crabs spoiling at its breast. A few yards farther on a gang of its fellows squawked and beat their wings just above the beach. Martin lifted his head, surprised because he had not smelled the salt-rot of beached whale or dolphin that almost daily drew white skeins of gannets and shearwaters, petrels and the lovely white fulmars that almost alone of birds possessed a sense of smell that helped them find the dead.

But the dolphin was there, its pale grey body barely glimpsed beneath the moving shroud of seabirds. Martin's step quickened. He always checked on the stranded animals, to report to Jason at the Woods Hole lab: another sad and terrible task, pressing his hands upon their sides only to feel the great proud hearts fall silent, the splendid envoys turned into grey slabs of stinking meat that protein-starved locals sometimes butchered right there on the beach, fighting off the greedy seabirds with sticks.

This time, though, it was different. This time it was not a dolphin, but a body.

"Oh, fuck," whispered Martin.

He began to run. Shouting and waving his arms so that the birds screamed and lifted higher into the bright air, until they banked and fled. He reached the body, sliding on the dank stones and falling into a crouch beside it. He flinched, his breath catching in his throat. *"No—"*

It was a young man; a boy, really. He was naked save for a torn pair of pants twisted around his legs and an ornate cross hanging from a chain around his neck. His skin had turned the color of the sea, greyish green and darkly blotched with bruises, pinked crescents where fish had nibbled but all bloodless as a sponge. Seaweeds wrapped about him, long ropelike strands of kelp and maidenhair and knotted wrack. His right hand lay upon his breast, broken at the wrist so that it curved outward at an impossible angle. When Martin moved it oh so gently he saw black grit under the fingernails, a cloudy white scum that was soft flesh. On the third finger a gold ring glinted dully. His hair was so thick with dulse and laver it looked red, but beneath the weed Martin could see a frayed blond mat heavy with sand. His face was scraped raw, a cusp of exposed cheekbone so startlingly white it was like a wedge of mother-of-pearl. A tiny fish louse had embedded itself upon one swollen eyelid. With a grunt of disgust Martin pulled the parasite loose and flung it into the sea. The eyelid fluttered open and revealed a blue iris in a crimson bed. It stared at Martin, insensible as a stone.

But alive: he was alive.

"Shit!" Martin cried out, and fell backward onto the rocks. He shook so hard he had to hug himself, hard, to calm down. Almost immediately he leaned forward again and placed a hand upon the boy's chest.

Yes. Alive, though less a heartbeat than a faint pressure, like another finger there beneath the cold rind of skin.

He had no time to think, to worry about moving the boy and so finishing the sea's job of killing him. He knelt and took him in his arms, gasping not because the boy was heavy—he felt like nothing so much as a sodden bundle of cloth—but because he, Martin, was so much weaker now than he had been even a month before. With a groan he stood, then turned and stumbled up the rocky headland to his cottage.

He laid the boy upon his own bed, taking care first to put an old wool blanket beneath him. Then he rushed to boil water on the big kitchen woodstove, gathered towels and antibiotic ointment, latex gloves and iso-propyl alcohol. There was no point in trying to phone for help. Even if the phone were working, no ambulance would come. The hospital in Belfast was too far away and too poorly equipped now to do much more than offer the reassurance of watching its few doctors com-plain about the lack of money, medicine, staff.

He cleansed him as best he could, scraping off sand and salt, shreds of seaweed and torn skin. He inhaled sharply at the raw flesh of the boy's chest. What at first appeared as a blackened hole in the mid-dle of his forehead proved instead to be some kind of cross-shaped scarification. Still, despite his wounds, there was no odor of decay; his flesh, though battered, seemed free of infection. Martin set the broken wrist as best he could, splinting it with the wood he used for frames and an old coat hanger. Finally, he swabbed the cuts with antibiotic gel. The broken skin stirred like small mouths beneath his gloved fingers.

Throughout the boy remained unconscious. *Young man*, Martin corrected himself. His face was too badly bruised to get a sense of how young, but his hair where it had not been torn from his scalp was long and blond, his musculature lithe. Martin glanced down at his own arms, gaunt and stippled with lesions. He pulled a sheet lightly over the boy's exposed body, checked the room's woodstove to make sure it was warm enough. He removed his gloves and took them into the kitchen, to boil and save them. Then he stepped onto the front porch.

Outside the light had shifted, from violet to pale lavender. The sea was calm, the silhouette of Dark Harbor shell pink and seeming to tremble in the unset-tled air. Gulls flew above the island like sparks, flickering from indigo to gold as they rode the wind. Martin's heart ached to look upon it all, so unspeakably lovely and strange that it preempted any effort to capture it on canvas.

Or anywhere else, it seemed. When he left San Francisco, the most common topic at parties and funerals was of how hard it was now to write, to paint, to compose or sing or dance. Common chatter on-line dealt with the futility of even trying. Only Leonard Thrope and his cohort of mori artists seemed able to endure what the world had become, and profit from it. Martin thought of Redon's print for *La Tentation de Saint-Antoine*, a shrouded skeleton reaching for a naked young woman.

"Death: I am the one who will make a serious woman of you; come, let us embrace."

He was determined to find another way of seeing. When he first returned to Mars Hill, Martin had sat outside with notebooks and drawing paper, canvas and palette knife. All for nought. The glimmering transfixed the eye even while it froze the heart: he could stand and stare at the sky for hours, awed and terrified, then go back indoors and face his empty canvases not with disappointment but mere relief, that they offered a still point, a void that he could safely contemplate, an abyss that did not defy comprehension. After a few weeks he gave up. What need was left in the world for art? Nature had taken up its own knife and was scouring the page; they had all become the canvas. He turned and went back inside.

In the bedroom the young man was still unconscious. But it seemed now that he slept. His breathing had become stronger and more even. At his sides his arms lay still, the crude splint a broken wing edging off of the bed. His face was tilted slightly to one side, and through the bruises something of the boy himself now showed, a face more sweet than handsome. His ghastly pallor had eased into a nearly luminous albescence. Not the whiteness of bone or any flesh that Martin had ever seen but an eerie, almost iridescent overlay through which could be glimpsed all that lay beneath: shimmer of blood, spleen, ligaments, the heart's chambers opening and closing like a conch's. Martin felt a pang of amazed fear. Who *was* this boy? and what had saved him?

He pushed the unsettling thought away, tried to focus only on the idea that this young man washed up on the shoals was very strange.

And, he thought, pulling up his old Windsor chair and sinking into it to spend the afternoon at the boy's bedside, this boy—whoever he was, *wherever* he was, poised between death and waking, black ocean and Mars Hill—was quite the most beautiful thing he had ever seen.

He got up several times over the next few hours, to feed the woodstove and check on the boy. In late afternoon Mrs. Grose knocked on the front door, to remind him of dinner that night.

"Roast chicken," she beamed. At her feet the pug yawned hungrily. "A nice *fat* one—"

"I can't come." Martin slipped out onto the porch and shut the door behind him. "Something—I've got something to do."

Mrs. Grose's eyes widened. "Are you sick? You should not be outside so much—"

"No, no, I'm not sick." He hesitated. No way to keep a secret at Mars Hill. Probably no way to keep a secret from Mrs. Grose, anywhere. "Listen—can I tell you tomorrow? It's—it's important, but I think I need to be by myself this evening."

Mrs. Grose regarded him with her wise tortoise-shell eyes. After a moment she nodded. "Of course, darling. I will even save some chicken for you." She retreated heavily down the steps, at the bottom turned, clutching her windbreaker to her bosom. "Be careful, Martin."

"I will." When she was out of sight he returned to his room to stand watch.

He woke next morning, surprised by how well he had slept in his chair—no nightmares, no furtive whisperings. He stood, yawning, and stepped over to the bed.

The boy was still asleep. Carefully Martin drew the sheet down, to check on his myriad cuts. They seemed no worse, at least, than before. The unblemished skin around them still had that pearly sheen, but now Martin was more inclined to think that had to do with the antibiotic gel. He found his gloves and applied some more, took a clean washcloth from the basin he'd set up and moistened the boy's lips, then went to get more water. When he turned back to the bed, the boy was staring at him.

"Owff—!" Martin dropped the washcloth. Hastily he retrieved it and hurried to the bedside. "Are you all right? Are you—"

He bit his lip. The boy looked like death: how could he be all right? Beneath its gloss of ointment his face was battered and swollen. He blinked, his bloodshot eyes mere slits beneath sunburned lids. He seemed to comprehend nothing around him.

Very tentatively Martin extended his hand, halted himself so that it hung trembling a few inches above the boy's head. "My—my name is Martin," he said softly. "I found you. On the beach, you'd washed up. Can you tell me what happened? Can you tell me your name?"

The boy said nothing. He closed his eyes. Martin lowered his hand until it rested upon the boy's brow. Beneath his gloved fingers the boy's hair felt friable as dried kelp. Martin wished he could remove the gloves, but dared not. He cleared his throat, then asked again. "Can you tell me your name? Do you—do you remember what happened?"

The boy's head moved. His eyes remained closed, his mouth opened to croak a single word.

"Trip."

"A trip." Martin nodded eagerly. He lifted his head to gaze out the window at the bay, sanguine sunrise behind Dark Harbor. "On a boat? In the storm? Do you remember where you were going?" Gently he touched the third finger of the boy's right hand, where the gold ring winked. "Do you have a family? Is there someone I can call?"

The boy tried to speak, was overcome by coughing. Martin gasped. "God, I'm sorry! Wait, wait—"

He ran to the kitchen and found a plastic cup with lid and straw, relic of John's last illness. He filled it with water and returned to the bedroom. "Here—just sip it, okay, don't try to drink too much—"

He slid the straw between the boy's lips and waited as he sucked at it, fruitlessly at first, then greedily as he tasted water. "Not too much!" cried Martin, but he smiled. "Better?"

The boy nodded, his head scarcely moving. He looked around, but the effort was too much. A moment later he was asleep again.

Martin spent the morning watching him. Whenever the boy stirred, he plied him with water, heavily laced with electrolyte solution and honey. Hours passed; the older man sat in his chair, looking in vain for some sign of recovery. A wash of crimson to the boy's translucent flesh; murmured words; even an anguished moan. Anything that might tether him to that room.

But the boy hardly moved. His breathing was not labored. He barely seemed to breathe at all. Once Martin rose and stood above him, his heart straining with fear as he stared until his eyes ached, trying vainly to see the boy's chest move. He was afraid to probe for a pulse, the boy's arms and neck were so badly lacerated. He finally resorted to clumsily holding a large gilt-framed mirror above the boy's mouth. And yes, a faint fog appeared at last, so little breath, it seemed not enough to keep a mouse alive. Martin sighed with relief. The boy's chest rose and fell, the cross stirring slightly where it lay upon his breast. For the first time Martin could hear the sigh of air leaving him, a soft wheezing in his lungs. A jab at Martin's heart: almost surely the boy had inhaled water: he could be developing pneumonia. Martin fetched the plastic bin that held eight years' harvest of medications and hurriedly rifled it, tossing aside morphine syringes, inhalers, empty bottles of AZT and erythromycin and crixivan. At the very bottom, buried beneath wads of sterile gauze and hospital-size tubes of antibiotic ointment, there was a package of penicillin ampoules. Martin squinted at the label.

5-BBS-Lot 609 Exp. 10/97

It had expired over a year ago. He removed one of the ampoules and held it up to the light, searching for something that might indicate decay: matter floating in the plastic bubble, discoloration. It looked fine. Meaningless, he knew, and probably the drug was useless now; but in the back of his head he was thinking, *If it's less potent, maybe there's less chance of him dying from a reaction to it.*

And answering himself, *If it's less potent, there's less chance of its helping him.*

He would chance it: in his ears the sound of John retching up his lungs, his lover's voice flayed to nothing by PCP. He picked up the bin and brought it to the night table.

For several minutes he stood staring down at the wasted body within its nest of blankets. At last he took a deep breath and began searching for a spot to inject the drug. He found a place above the crook of the young man's elbow where the skin was raw but unbroken. The antiseptic smell of ointment mingled with that of seawater as carefully he straightened the arm, stroking the pale turquoise tendril of a vein, then jabbed the ampoule against it.

He had not expected the boy to react. But he did, jerking his arm from Martin's hand and gasping. Martin looked up, frightened, and saw the boy's eyes fly open, his mouth agape. He coughed, then gagged, choking as Martin grabbed his shoulders and tried to restrain him as he lurched up in the bed.

"Wait!" Martin cried. "Please, don't—"

He pushed him against the mattress, frantically trying to stuff pillows behind his back. A nurse's voice shouted in his head: *Keep him upright, they choke on their own sputum.* Horrified, he watched as the boy wrenched away from him, arms and legs moving convulsively as he thrashed at the edge of the bed, as though trying to stand. Without warning he coughed again, violently. A gout of water poured from his mouth. Martin stumbled backward. Slowly the boy raised his head and stared at him with burning eyes.

"Where is she?"

Martin raised his hands, stammering. "Who?"

"The girl—the dead girl—" The boy's voice was like something dragged across stones. "Is she here?"

"I only found you—on the beach, outside—" Martin looked desperately at the window on the far side of the room, then forced himself to ask as calmly as he could, "Can you remember anything? Were you on a boat? In the storm? Were there others with you?"

"They're everywhere." His pupils were swollen, his eyes wide and staring, though it was not Martin he saw. "They came through the holes—can you find her? Can you find her?"

His voice became a shriek, babbling strings of nonsense. His head shook back and forth, frantically, as he staggered to his feet. Martin seized him in time to keep him from falling, wrestled him back into bed and pinioned him there. His skin was slick and soft beneath Martin's hands, like fallen petals; too late Martin realized he had forgotten to put his gloves on. His mind raced through the accustomed checklist of his failing body: scabbed fingernails, bleeding gums, a lesion on his thigh—

". . . see them? *see them*?"

—but too late, too late now. Grunting Martin reached with one hand for the night table, knocking aside water bottle and candlesticks, the closed plastic disposal tub with its biohazard warning. The penicillin went flying before his fingers closed about what he wanted: a Ziploc plastic bag filled with morphine syringes. Without looking, relying on long nightmare habit fueled by fear, he tugged one free, turned, and plunged it against the boy's neck. The boy continued to struggle as Martin pulled the needle loose and tossed it heedlessly onto the floor.

". . . *where* . . ."

Martin gazed in pity and revulsion at where the young man's flesh bore fresh abrasions; at his maddened blue eyes and frantic hands. But after several minutes the boy was quieter. His eyes grew calm, as though some invisible hand had wiped them clear; his body in Martin's hands grew still, no longer rigid with dread. He even smiled, the same soft silly smile Martin knew from tending dying friends. For the first time, his gaze focused on the older man. The smile became a grin, grotesque in his beautifully ruinous face.

"Who are you?" he asked.

"I'm Martin Dionysos." Martin leaned forward, resisting an urge to lay his hand upon the boy's brow. "I found you on the beach. Yesterday. You were—I thought you were dead, at first. Do you remember what happened to you? Did your boat sink? Can you tell me your name?"

The boy shook his head. "I jumped. I was scared. The bay." He looked down at his chest, plucked feebly at his breastbone. "I jumped." His gaze moved distractedly across the room.

Like a child, thought Martin. Once again he prodded, gently. "Your name? I want to help you—"

That silly grin. "Don't you know? I'm not changing it."

With a sigh Martin turned away. From the medicine bin he took an unopened pair of latex gloves, morbid luxury, and pulled them on. Glancing back at the boy he saw that his eyes had closed. He looked peaceful; Martin knew he was only stoned. He stood and was at the door when the voice came behind him, almost a whisper but laughing, too; he sensed the smile and looked back to see it there.

"Trip." The boy's eyes remained closed. He raised a hand like a bruised iris. "My name is Trip Marlowe." And slept.

*   *   *

Days passed. Then weeks. You wouldn't know it from
the sky or shrouded sun that skulked across it; but
Martin could gauge a sort of summer blooming as the
boy's wounds healed. First his broken skin; then his broken wrist. *What next?* wondered Martin, who spent a lot
of time staring at that gold ring on the third finger of the
boy's right hand. "The nameless finger," his Swedish
grandmother would have called it. To Martin it was
infinitely something. He and John had been married by
a Universalist minister, exchanging rings that they wore
on their right hands. Martin still bore his. So did John,
in a San Francisco cemetery two thousand miles away.

"Are you married, Trip? Do you have a girlfriend, or
a boyfriend—I could try to contact them—"

Trip said nothing.

"The ring," urged Martin softly. "Where did the ring
come from?"

For the first time Trip stared down at it, with dull
surprise, then shook his head. "I don't know," he
murmured. "She had one, too . . ."

Okay, thought Martin, fighting an unreasonable disappointment. A girlfriend, then, or wife. "Okay."

There were no more tussles with morphine, but the
sweet smile stayed. Martin wondered if he had suffered
brain damage in the wake of his accident, or even if he
had been simpleminded to begin with. Mrs. Grose had
been consulted, and the Graffams, about any foundering
boats. And yes, a trawler had gone down in the storm,
off the Libby Islands. There was a light there, but it had
been unmanned for years; the Graffams knew only that
pieces of the trawler had washed up at Bucks Head. No
one knew who had died, or how many. The boat had
shipped from Cutler, and that was very far away, now. In

an old telephone book Martin found only two Marlowes, both in Liberty. He had no listings for anything farther down east than Bar Harbor, and there were no Marlowes there at all.

He was relieved.

Mornings he would prepare breakfast. Oatmeal and raw milk and Grade B maple syrup, dark as old motor oil and with an ineffably sweet, scorched taste. Sometimes eggs from their neighbor Diana, their shells tea-colored, pale yellow, the soft blue-green of a vein too near the surface of the skin. Martin and Trip would sit in near silence at the kitchen table, Trip wearing a loose worn flannel shirt and pajama pants that had belonged to John. Too big by far for his slight frame, but Martin was fearful of fabric catching against the flesh not quite healed, and it was not warm enough to go shirtless. While Trip spooned oatmeal or liquescent yolk Martin would try to engage him in conversation. Where was he from? Where had he grown up?

But Trip never replied. He would talk, uninspired musings on the weather, the eggs, how he had slept; but he would not answer questions, or ask them. At first Martin thought this, too, a manifestation of whatever disaster had befallen him. But as the weeks went by and he came to map the boy as once he had mapped canvas, he started to recognize a certain look that Trip had. Or rather, the absence of a look: a shuttering of his eyes, a retreat that Martin could observe as certainly as he could mark a falling leaf. The boy was not amnesiac, not as simple as Martin suspected. He was reticent, skittish, purposefully shy. He was in hiding.

After breakfast, water heated for washing the dishes and everything tidied up, they would walk to the beach. Trip was stronger, now. He could have walked by himself, and though he never said anything, he seemed to welcome Martin's company. He did not like to be left alone in the bungalow; he did not like to be alone. Nights, sleeping on the futon couch in the living room, Martin would often be awakened by the boy's cries. He would go to him, murmuring until Trip fell asleep once more. The boy claimed not to recall his nightmares. Only once, Martin letting his fingertips graze Trip's healed wrist, feeling a fissure in the bone that surely had not been there before: the boy looked at him and said, "She was already dead."

Martin nodded, waiting for him to go on; but the boy withdrew his hand and said no more.

"The rest must have drowned," Martin explained to Mrs. Grose one evening, surrounded by flickering candles in her cozy living room. "He said they went through the holes. He keeps saying something about a dead girl . . ."

Mrs. Grose sipped her brandy thoughtfully. "His sweetheart, you think?"

"I guess." Martin stared into his glass. "He wears a wedding ring, but it's on this finger—like mine." He turned his hand, so that candlelight slid across the thick gold band. "And some kind of Maltese cross. She must have drowned."

"Perhaps." In her lap the pug snorted, and she stroked his head. "Have you tried to find his family?"

Martin shrugged, uncomfortable. "Yes. But how can I? He won't say anything, I mean he won't tell me where he's from, who they are . . ."

Outside, in the endless shifting twilight, branches tapped against the windows, overgrown lilacs that Mrs. Grose was afraid to prune lest they never grow back. The pug yawned, a curl of pink tongue in its laughing mouth. Mrs. Grose shifted on the couch, cradling her brandy against her chest. "Why are you keeping him, Martin?"

He started to respond testily, but stopped. A candle sputtered, flame leaping, then went out. After a moment he said, "Where could he go? If he left here—"

"He is not like you, Martin," she said gently. "He does not have a disease. He seems strong enough, strong in the body. It would be cruel to keep him here, Martin."

Martin ran a hand through his long greying hair. He whispered, "I know. I know. But where could he go?"

"It doesn't matter. Not to us. I know it's hard, Martin. It's because you saved him—"

"I didn't—"

"He would have died there, if not for you." She stood, the pug tumbling from her lap with an affronted groan, and crossed the room to lay a hand upon his shoulder. "You saved him, Martin. And for some reason he's still alive. But he has to go . . ."

"Reason?" The face Martin lifted to her was raw with despair. "What reason can there be? What?"

Mrs. Grose sighed. She stared past him, to where the lilacs scratched at the panes. "I do not know. Maybe none," she said, and stooped to pick up the gasping pug. "But you must act as though there is one, anyway. Good night, my dear—"

She lowered her head to kiss him, leaving a breath of brandy and Sen-Sen upon his cheek. Her tortoiseshell eyes seemed bleary, not with that vague distant expression Martin knew so well but with something strange and disturbing. Genuine weariness, the detached surrender of great age to a well-earned sleep, or more.

"Adele? Are you all right? Do you feel bad?" His voice was unsteady: he had never asked her that.

"Just tired," she replied, and began to walk heavily toward her room. "Just tired. That's all."

He went the next day to the beach alone. Trip seemed content to sit in the living room, gazing at the expensive array of compact stereo and video equipment that had been John's.

"Sometimes it works." Martin picked up a remote and tentatively pressed a few buttons. "But not today, I guess. I'll be back in a while. Okay?"

Trip nodded without looking up. "Okay."

The wind was from the north that morning, bearing with it the acrid scent of burning. He had heard there were fires along the border in Canada, started by renegade environmentalists: the kind of vague rumors passed among the denizens of the Beach Store more freely than currency. But certainly there was fire somewhere—the air's accustomed scintillation cloaked in a thick yellowish haze that stung the eyes and throat and nearly made Martin turn back.

But he did not, and by the time he reached the shore the wind had shifted again, and the smoke slowly dispersed, leaving only a dank foul smell. His eyes moved restlessly across the ground as he walked, longing to find something familiar, yearning for it as Martin had never dreamed possible. Fallen white-pine branches pressed into the mud, their green fans mimicking gingkoes; ferns; new growth beneath the sickly mulch of leaves and yellowing birch bark. Everywhere he looked he saw a world robbed of color save for a lurid yellow burst of lichen upon an oak tree, the mauve carpet of wintergreen leaves, and copper-green scraping of tamaracks against the sky. Brazen sky, guilty sky, with its stolen shades like rippling pennons, grass-green, luminous orange, periwinkle blue. It sickened him, and he hurried on.

Alongside the decrepit boathouse the *Wendameen* sat up on blocks, its faded tarp flapping. Gaps in the plastic covering showed where the wooden hull needed to be scraped and repainted, seams that needed to be filled, floats replaced. Martin looked away, thinking how long it had been since he worked on the boat—a year? two? It wouldn't be worth salvaging if he didn't get to it soon. He knew he never would.

From high up in a scraggly red oak a woodpecker clattered. The smell of the sea cut through what remained of smoke. Martin kicked along the beach, miserable but without the accustomed baggage of things that he *knew* made him miserable. He was not thinking of John, he was not thinking of dead friends, he was not thinking of lesions or tumors or T cells piling themselves into a caravan and driving off a cliff. He was thinking of Trip Marlowe and the way his long hair fell across his cheek, leaving it half in shadow; of the small protuberant knob in the wrist Martin had set, badly, which was like a stone under the skin. He was thinking of Trip's eyes, winking blue like a gas jet turned too low; and somewhere behind that he was thinking of Adele Grose's eyes as well, how last night they had seemed less vivid, once-bright marbles gone opaque from too much use.

It would be cruel to keep him here, Martin . . .

His foot struck savagely at a stone. *But I'm not keeping him!* he thought.

But you are, you are . . . the gulls answered. He stooped and grabbed a rock, hurled it ferociously at the sky. The birds dived as it plummeted into the red-streaked sea. He could feel rage building inside him like a fever, even as he turned and headed back to the cottage. He shoved the door open with such force that it slammed against the inside wall. Trip looked up from where he sat on the couch, idly turning the pages of a magazine.

"Trip." Martin stood in the middle of the room, panting a little. "Do you need to go somewhere? I mean away from here—do you want to go?"

The boy gazed at him with calm blue eyes. "New York," he said after a moment.

"New *York*?"

Trip nodded. "She—I think that's where she is. That's where I met her. New York," he said softly.

"New York." Martin sank onto the couch beside him, smoothing back his windblown hair and shaking his head. "You mean Manhattan? You were in New York City?"

"Just a few days."

He waited, but Trip said nothing else; just stared at the magazine in his lap. Finally Martin said, "New York. You're sure? That's where you want to go?"

The boy lifted his face. "Yes," he whispered.

Martin stared at him. After a moment he reached and gently pushed a lank strand of hair from Trip's eyes.

"Then I'll take you," he said. His gaze passed beyond the boy, to the window that looked down upon the rocky beach where a twenty-six-foot gaff cutter was raised on wooden sawhorses and concrete blocks. He leaned forward, and for just an instant hugged the boy's spare frame to his own, before he felt Trip flinch and start away. "Don't worry. I'll take you—wherever you want to go."

CHAPTER TEN

Heart and Soul

At Lazyland, spring staggered into a sullen summer. The daffodils bloomed, rust-streaked, their inner horns twisted into fantastic shapes, and gave off a scent like lilies. From the tulip poplars a heavy fragrant pollen fell, staining Lazyland's cracked drive acid green and orange. The sky shivered in its Stygian dance; some mornings, stars appeared amongst the clouds, and sun dogs chased them above the swollen Hudson.

When news reached Lazyland it was so corybantic as to seem a mishandled communiqué from another century: plague vaccines that caused mass hallucinations; children awaiting spaceships upon the Golden Gate Bridge; Disney World seized by tattooed militia wearing animal masks, who took orders from a teenage girl in combat uniform and a Blue Antelope T-shirt. Only of course this could be nothing *but* Today's News, fractured as it was and endlessly divisible, the militias and strange millennial cults begetting their own plagues, their own viruses, electronic and corporeal; their own rites and rhythms of destruction, their own precarious groynes and parapets thrown up against what was immanent, and imminent.

. . . the end of the end, the end of the end . . .

Jack would stand upon the mansion's grand old porch, surrounded by ancient wicker furniture and his grandfather's telescopes, and stare across the river to where the ruined Sparkle-Glo factory glowed upon the

Palisades, black and gold and crimson in the night. In the carriage house the fax machine would now and then stir, like a restless sleeper, then spew forth press releases detailing myriad magnanimous ventures spearheaded by The Golden Family. Snow leopard DNA encoded on the head of a pin, test launches of the dirigible fleet that would tow SUNRA to its place in the poisoned sky. The archival purchase, for $3.3 million U.S., of the historic American literary magazine *The Gaudy Book*. During these electrical intermissions the answering machine would blink and beep, and Leonard's voice would hail Jack from London or Voronezh or the Waterton Glacier. Mrs. Iverson would do laundry and make toast. From somewhere within Lazyland a radio cried out with more strange bulletins. Fragments of pop music and *Götterdämerung*; the advertising slogan for GFI's new global network: Only Connect. Umpty-ump covers of "1999," and a new song that got extraordinary airplay, considering the broken bandwidths one had to gyre through these days—

> *I possess the keys of hell and death,*
> *I will give you the morning star:*
> *The end of the end, the end of the end . . .*

—while on his own shaky parapet Jack kept watch, listening as he fingered the vial of Fusax in his pocket, holding it up to the light to measure its diminished contents and praying that it might, somehow, be enough. He heard the *fellahin* laughing in Untermeyer Park, marked the progress of a dirigible, not so much sausage- as eye-shaped, moving slowly through the clouds. He looked at his hands, the bones seeming almost to protrude through his skin. He was losing weight. His sight was strained as well; bright shapes flitted at the corner of his eyes, and sometimes he heard voices that did not arise from radios or rooms within the house.

But at the same time it was as though some new and more subtle sense filled him, even as his old ones faltered. He felt the century 'round him hurtling harum-scarum toward its end: an infortuitous concourse of atoms, a runaway train slamming into the roundhouse with everything it contained slingshot skyward: quarks, drag queens, *The King and I*, Einstein, Telstar, Hitler, mustard gas, Thomas Mann, Jerry Mahoney, Victor Frankl, IBM and AT&T and GFI. He felt his blood quicken, hearing footsteps in the parlor, unseen musicians tuning up for the grand finale.

And, finally, one afternoon he entered the carriage house to find an inelegantly worded fax scrolled onto the floor: yet another missive from GFI. SUNRA was to be set aloft six months hence, on the evening of December 31, from GFI's pyramid in Times Square. Gala celebration, many celebrities, at especial request of Yukio Tatsumi the presence of your company is desired. At the very bottom of the coiling strip of paper there was a scrawled addendum to the corporation's formal invitation.

FYI: New Year's Eve, 1999: This Offer Will Not be Repeated. Will I see you there? RSVP, Regrets Only. With very warm regards, Larry Muso.

The next morning, Jack went downstairs as usual. He found the blond girl in the kitchen, also as usual, eating stale Cheerios with his grandmother and Mrs. Iverson. More of his aunt Mary Anne's clothes had been found for her, a pair of soft brown corduroy bell-bottom trousers, too long and cuffed around her ankles, and a bright red plaid flannel shirt. Her hair had not been combed; it stuck out around her head in a ragged white halo, and once again Jack marveled at his grandmother's self-control during these last few months, that she hadn't attacked the girl with a brush and scissors. Otherwise, Marz seemed alarmingly well behaved. She murmured "hello" to Jack as he poured himself some of the brown bitter liquid that passed for coffee these days, and said "thank you" when Mrs. Iverson handed her a napkin.

Still, her presence at the table never failed to unsettle Jack. He poked desultorily at his Cheerios with a spoon, pouring a thin stream of powdered milk dissolved in water into the center. He forced himself to eat, imagining Jule and Emma at their breakfast table sixty miles to the north, with the remains of whatever frugal harvest they'd taken from Emma's garden, dried apples and cherries, blueberries and black walnuts. It was an image that usually fortified him. But this morning it only made him sad, seeing Marz in the chair where Jule and Emma's young daughter Rachel had once perched. He finished his Cheerios quickly and excused himself, setting the empty bowl in the sink. There was electricity today: he let hot water dribble from the tap into his bowl, inhaling the steam as though it were perfume.

"I'm going out to work," he said.

At the table three heads turned.

"Will you be busy, dear?" His grandmother sipped at her ersatz coffee in its Limoges china cup. "Have you found another printer?"

His fingers tightened on the edge of the sink. "No, I haven't found another printer." Larry Muso's face stared calmly up at him from the rippling surface of his cereal bowl. "I—I have to try to send some faxes. While the power's on."

"Of course, darling," his grandmother said sweetly. He looked back and saw her smiling as Marz shoveled Cheerios into her mouth. "Will you be going to the city today?"

"The *city*? No, Grandmother—I don't go to the city anymore. Remember?"

"Of course, dear. I thought your grandfather said he had a meeting this afternoon, that's all."

God, she's drifting! Jack turned away and his heart constricted; but why shouldn't she drift? In six months she would be one hundred years old, her wizened body still remarkably strong but how long could, or should, that last? She had been a widow for twenty-five years, she had lost one child to God knows what, drugs or suicide or murder, and two others to more ordinary circumstances. She had outlived all her friends; should she outlive the century, too?

"It's all right, Grandmother," he murmured, crossing the kitchen to kiss her cheek. "I'll be in for lunch . . ."

In the carriage house he turned on everything— lamps, radio, television, fax, answering machine, computers, electric typewriter, stereo. Even with the volume turned down on the TV and radio, the office hummed and rustled as though he'd smashed open a wasps' nest. He could feel the electrical currents surging through the room, and watched as dust motes circled purposefully above the compact fluorescent bulbs, insectlike. He sat at his desk and held his hands above the keyboard, fingers spread. They tingled as though he'd been stung by nettles. As he typed a reply to GFI's faxed invitation he could see his fingertips turning fiery red beneath pallid half-moon nails.

If circumstances permit I will be happy to attend GFI's New Year's celebration. However, transportation from here can be difficult . . .

He faxed off the reply, for good measure also sent an electronic response to the address on Larry Muso's postscript. Faster than he would have thought possible, an icon on his monitor began flashing to signal that a message had arrived.

FROM: muso.shugenja@Pelgye.gfi.com

Jack! So glad to hear from you! Don't worry about transport, lodging, all will be attended to on this end. Julie Braxton-Kotani from Special Events will have a courier be in touch with you by midsummer, to arrange security clearances et&, I anticipate no difficulties. I am on special assignment til Sept/Oct at the earliest but VERY MUCH want to see you again! All best & warm Wishes, Larry M. P.S. Mr. Tatsumi says that he enjoyed the last issue of The Gaudy Book. Please let us know when we can expect the next one.

Later in July it snowed in New York. Environmental terrorists seized the George Washington Bridge and closed it off to traffic, erecting makeshift shelters and hanging an immense banner painted with a cerulean antelope across the Washington Heights end. The strike forces marshaled by city and federal government were destroyed by napalm guns Blue Antelope had obtained from the sympathetic interim governments of Madagascar, New Zealand, and Kalimantan, as well as by ecologically noninvasive nerve gas smuggled in from the group's Icelandic mission. News of other attacks by the Xian radicals filtered through the net to reach Jack at Lazyland: logging operations brought to a halt in the Pacific Northwest and Brazilian rain forest; the flooded ancient temples at Ayutthaya in Thailand captured by armed Buddhists who joined forces with the Christian environmental extremists. Pope Gregory XVII's weekly message from St. Paul's was interrupted by students wearing animal masks. In North America and Japan, outlaw electronic and video broadcasts by Blue Antelope spokesman Lucius Chappell made outraged claims that multinational corporations including GFI, TRW, Matsushita-Krupp and Gibson/Skorax were involved in a global conspiracy to release newly developed neurological toxins into the water supplies of First and Third World countries. The wife of Yukio Tatsumi, CEO of multinational giant Gorita-Folham-Izod, was found dead in their Paris apartment, an apparent suicide. Friends said she had been despondent for some time. The wildfires that had consumed Houston roared their way into Galveston Bay and on into the Gulf of Mexico, igniting offshore drilling platforms like Catherine wheels. The poisonous chemicals released into the clouds caused spectacular effects that could be seen as far away as Tampico and New Orleans.

At Lazyland, of course, life teetered on. Jack had several messages from lawyers representing both The Golden Family and the interests of *The Gaudy Book*—the latter, despite all Jack's protests, arranged by Leonard Thrope. It appeared that the sale would proceed without any difficulties; by year's end, little Jackie Finnegan would be a relatively wealthy man. The realization caused him neither great happiness nor distress, but rather a vague sense of well-being, and gratitude that he would be able to provide better for his ancient grandmother. Keeley and Jack's brothers had to approve the sale, which they did. Jack had already spoken to Jule Gardino about changing his will once the sale was complete: upon his death, the estate would be divided amongst his siblings and their children, with a generous allotment given to the Hiram Halle Memorial Library in the small town where Jack had grown up, and provisions made for Keeley, if she should outlive him. Provisions also had to be made for someone to take over the helm of *The Gaudy Book* itself—Jack was serious about no longer wanting to be responsible for managing an outdated literary quarterly, even one that would continue under the benison of a zillion-dollar multinational corporation. *Especially* one that would continue under a multinational corporation.

But qualified prospective candidates were few. Articles about the magazine's sale had appeared on all the major financial sites, sparking inquiries from a number of corporate leaders and venture capitalists with literary ambitions, as well as from an incarcerated former director of corporate finance who had written a best-selling autobiography. There was also a witty letter and set of *vitae* from a professor of American Popular Food Culture at Tokyo University, and several annoying foot couriers sent by an agent representing the author of *Lovemaking Secrets of Chianghis Khan*. Jack left most of these unread on his computer or his desk, and found himself experiencing bursts of happiness whenever the electricity failed.

The truth was, he was more preoccupied with the dwindling level of his vial of Fusax than any of these other life changes. Or rather, in the curious fact that while the Fusax seemed to dwindle and dwindle and dwindle, the bottle never quite emptied. He was only taking a few drops a day now, under the tongue. Even so he was certain that any day there would be nothing left in the vial.

But there always was. Not much, surely not enough to last more than a few days, a week at most; but then the weeks became one month, and another, and then it was summer, or what passed for summer with its fractal sky, its scintillant air that shone like gaudy night but smelled like burning petroleum.

And still, when he held up the brown bottle he saw splintered brilliance inside and the tiniest swash of liquid, as though he held one of those miniature environments sold at expensive department stores, a few precious milliliters of seawater and algae and endangered krill. Whatever it was he *did* hold was no less beautiful and strange, and he wondered always at what changed tides shifted within him now, what had been replenished or transubstantiated within the cloud of moving particles that formed his immune system. Could it be alive, somehow, and breeding? He felt better, he thought; perhaps he had never felt better. Though he was troubled almost nightly (and sometimes daily) by strange dreams; though his sight bothered him; though he could see in his grandmother's eyes and Mrs. Iverson's, as well as in his own reflection, that he was losing weight at an alarming pace. But he never felt nauseated or feverish, as he had before. He had no more problems with his breathing. His dry skin cleared up. So did the violent cluster headaches that had plagued him intermittently since childhood. He showed no symptoms of thrush. If anything, he was most acutely aware of an increasingly heightened sensual consciousness: being able to hear a yellowed leaf falling from the tulip poplar; noticing from across the kitchen table a fleck of bright green in Marz's left iris; waking from a preternaturally alert sleep to smell carnations, and then searching the decrepit garden for forty minutes before he found a single frayed dianthus blossom that, when he drew it to his face, breathed the same sweet peppery scent. When one evening his grandmother suggested he visit the clinic at Saint Joseph's he shook his head.

"I feel okay," he said, and having pronounced the

words savored them with faint surprise. "I really *do* think I'm okay."

Keeley stared at him. "You don't *look* very well, dear. You look thin. Are you still taking all your medicine?"

"Yes," he lied. It had been over a year since he'd been able to get all his prescriptions filled at the pharmacy in Getty Square. "But I *feel* really, really good. And I'm strong—I mean, I'm not as tired as I was, I don't feel sick all the time . . ."

Something is working, he wanted to say; *something has changed.* He crossed the living room to hug her. "Don't worry, Grandmother."

"But I do." She sighed and shut her eyes. "I'm so tired, Jackie. And you shouldn't be sick. It's not the way it should be, Jackie."

He smiled wistfully and let his cheek rest against hers, groaning when he felt tears there. "Oh—don't cry, don't cry . . ."

"It's *not*—" Her voice broke, not with sorrow but the same unforgiving rage she had shown when her husband died. "*Where* are they now, where is all the good of it, where *are* they . . . ?"

She began to shake, and he held her close as she wept and railed, knowing that whoever it was she blamed—priests, angels, family, doctors, the beautiful unfaithful *sidhe*—they had left him long ago.

On the 27th of July, a courier in black helmet and the red-and-gold livery of GFI puttered down Hudson Terrace on a silver solaped. She parked and chained it to the fence, climbed over the security gate, and strolled down Lazyland's winding drive, singing to herself. Jack watched her from the living-room window, biting his lip. His grandmother and Mrs. Iverson and Marz were all napping upstairs. When the doorbell rang he flinched, then walked silently into the foyer.

"John Finnegan?" Beneath a hazy violet sky the courier's retinal implants glowed silvery blue.

"That would be me," Jack admitted.

"Do you have some identification?" Before Jack could snap an unpleasant retort she explained, "I'm from GFI—" and simultaneously flashed an ID badge and held up her palm so he could see a gryphon tattooed there beneath numbers and the name *Luralay Pearlstein*.

"Yeah, just hold on," he muttered, locking her outside while he went to find his wallet. When he got back she was sitting on the porch in the lotus position, silvery eyes wide-open and staring at the sky. The skin on her face and hands had the chrome yellow taint of the *acaraspora* lichen ingested for its UV-repelling properties by those who had to work outdoors. Jack stared down at her, nonplussed. Then he said, "Okay. Here it is—"

She looked carefully at the driver's license he handed her. "It's expired."

"Yes, it has." A nasty edge crept into his voice. "That's because it's impossible to get gas anymore on the North American continent, and because I no longer have a car, and also because I have nowhere to fucking *go*."

The courier returned his license. "You should join one of those religious cooperatives," she said mildly. "*They* don't seem to have any problem. Okay, this looks fine." She yanked at her shoulder pack and pulled out a large envelope printed with peacock feathers, held it out to him, and declaimed, "This is your official invitation to GFI's gala New Year's Celebration and SUNRA launching, to be held at the Golden Pyramid on Friday, December 31."

He took the envelope, and she went on in a slightly less officious tone. "*That* is only your invitation. It won't get you onto the field. For *that*, you need *this*—"

She held up a small black object, the size and shape of a VCR remote but with a rounded end like an old-fashioned telephone receiver. Blinking red lights chased themselves in a circle across the plastic as she explained. "I can give you a preliminary clearance code now, so that all you need to do at the gate is have them do a retinal and DNA scan—"

Jack laughed incredulously. The courier gave him a sheepish look and shrugged. "Hey, what can I say? Better living through modern chemistry. But if I don't do this today, you'll have to get down to the Pyramid and go through the exact same shit. Only *there* you'll have to stand in line."

Jack shook his head. "Isn't that giving a *courier* an awful lot of power? What if I was lying or something? All you did was check an expired driver's license!"

The young woman smiled wryly. "Well, it *looks* like you, doesn't it? Plus—"

She lifted her helmet, so that he could see a slender black tube running just beneath the skin at her temple and disappearing at her hairline. "—see? I'm wired. My beta waves and pulse show anything weird, they scalp me. *Bing*-o! No more Luralay! But they have good health insurance, so give me a fucking break and let me scan you, okay?"

"Uh, yeah. Okay." Jack frowned. "Are you telling me they—"

"Shhh—if I think about it too much, they get a hot reading. Now, just hold your hand up—no, right hand—it doesn't hurt, kinda feels like holding a vibrator or something—"

Her gloved hand took his and held it outspread

while she fitted the scanner against his palm. There was buzzing, a dull stinging sensation. Immediately she drew her hand back, removed a disposable sheath from the end of the scanner, stuffed that into a tiny biohazard container, and slid the scanner back into her pack. "Okay, that's all! The entry chip won't be activated until December 31—that's New Year's Eve, at 12:01 A.M. It'll last exactly thirty-four hours. Then you turn into a pumpkin." She grinned and gave him a mock salute. "Merry Christmas, Mr. Finnegan! Don't lose that envelope—it's got all the instructions and stuff, in case nobody's able to get in touch with you between now and then. Ciao—"

She turned and strode back up the drive, arms swinging. Halfway to the gate she began to sing again.

Jack stared after her, then looked down at his palm. There was nothing there whatsoever that he could see. No marks, no scars, not the faintest imprint of anything at all. He heard the courier's bike firing up as he went back inside and locked the door after him.

The house was still, save for the perfunctory drip of snowmelt still falling from the gutters. Lavender light glazed the windows. In the air hung a stale smell of that morning's burned toast, scorched over the Coleman stove's peripatetic flame—there had been no electricity for eleven days. Jack walked into the study and settled into the oxblood leather chair by the window. It was a reclining chair, and it had been his grandfather's; even now Jack felt too small by far as it tilted backward. He took a silver letter opener from the side table and deftly slit the gorgeously patterned envelope. And as though it had been a real peacock served at Trimalchio's feast, a small explosion of glitter and green smoke filled the air. Jack yelped in surprise and nearly dropped the envelope, before realizing this was just part of the entertainment package. The smoke faded, leaving a tropical scent; the glitter turned out to be more permanent, evading all of Mrs. Iverson's later efforts to remove it from the oriental rug and Grandfather Finnegan's chair. Jack looked up, embarrassed, half-fearful that he would see Marz smirking at him from the doorway.

But no, he was still alone, except for the oversize and very beautiful piece of paper he held in his hand. Tissue-thin, it had the watery sheen of fine silk and was patterned with lovely, shifting designs: golden zeppelins, a medieval sun, samurai in armor, a velvety black sky covered with glowing constellations, and the grasping skeletal gryphon that was GFI's corporate logo: what at first he thought were extraordinary watermarks, but which instead seemed to be more tricks from GFI's fanciful technological inventory. He spent several minutes just staring at the page, turning it so that it caught the light in different ways to display different patterns. Letters appeared, now Roman, now Japanese characters, now Arabic and Cyrillic. Between his fingers the paper seemed to move of its own, as though he grasped a moth by its wings. Faint bell-like music played, the same song he'd been hearing off and on for months now:

> I will give you the morning star:
> The end of the end, the end of the end . . .

Finally, "Jesus Fuck," he said, and shaking his head he began to decipher the invitation.

FAR AWAY, IN A GOLDEN PYRAMID, LIVE 6 OR 7 SHAMANS.
BY USING SORCEROUS SCIENCE
THEY CHANGE THE MOST EVERYDAY JOURNEY
INTO A MILLENNIAL MYSTERY TRIP. IF YOU COME ALONG,

THE SHAMANS WILL
TRANSPORT YOU TO A BRAND NEW WORLD!
MAYBE YOU'VE BEEN ON A MILLENNIAL MYSTERY TRIP
WITHOUT EVEN KNOWING IT.
ARE YOU WILLING TO JOIN US?
LET'S GO!

He laughed and read on.

ON FRIDAY, DECEMBER 31, 1999,
HUMANKIND WILL ENTER A NEW MILLENNIUM:
A NEW ERA, A NEW DAWN!
THE GOLDEN FAMILY OF
GORITA-FOLHAM-IZOD
INVITES YOU, JOHN "JACK" FINNEGAN,
TO BE THERE AT THE GOLDEN PYRAMID WHEN
SUNRA™ IS LAUNCHED
AND THE FUTURE BEGINS . . .

There followed a lengthy list of attending international celebrities, musical entertainments, fashion models, sports and religious figures and CEOs from across the globe, as well as both units of the Ringling Brothers Barnum & Bailey Circus (incorporating Cirque du Soleil, the Moscow Circus, and the Mongolian Entertainers Alliance). The only persons who it appeared would *not* be at the Pyramid on New Year's Eve were the Pope, the Dalai Lama, and John "Jack" Finnegan, if he chose not to go.

Only, of course, it appeared that he *had* decided to go. He closed his eyes and pressed the invitation against his forehead. Larry Muso's sloe eyes shimmered in front of him; he felt again that brisk electricity when their hands had touched, a scent of chypre . . .

VERY MUCH want to see you again! All best & warm Wishes, Larry M.

He shook his head: Larry M, at least, might well get his warm wish. For another minute Jack sat there, then opened his eyes and reached for a volume on the library table in which to place the invitation for safe-keeping. *The Crock of Gold*—his grandfather's favorite book. Jack's childhood had been filled with the sound of Keeley's voice reading it aloud to her husband, her soft brogue burnishing the tale so that Jack himself had never been able to read the book all the way through: the words seemed chained to the page. Now he opened it at random, practicing casual stichomancy as he read.

> *The Philosopher lit his pipe.*
>
> *"We live as long as we are let," said he, "and we get the health we deserve. Your salutation embodies a reflection on death which is not philosophic. We must acquiesce in all logical progressions. The merging of oppositions is completion. Life runs to death as to its goal, and we should go towards that next stage of experience either carelessly as to what must be, or with a good, honest curiosity as to what may be."*
>
> *"There's not much fun in being dead, sir," said Meehawl.*
>
> *"How do you know?" said the Philosopher.*
>
> *"I know well enough," replied Meehawl.*

"Right," murmured Jack. He closed the book around the invitation, set it back upon the table, and stood to go. As he did so his hand passed through a shaft of light falling from the wide window behind his grandfather's chair. Emerald brilliance glanced off his palm, elvers sliding quicksilver through his fingers, then darting off into the darkened room. But bright enough to catch his eye; bright enough to ignite within the whorled and crosshatched flesh the ghostly holographic image of a gryphon rampant, clasping a pyramid within its claws.

A week later, Mrs. Iverson told him the blond girl was pregnant.

"*WHAT?*"

"She is. She won't talk about it, but it won't go away. She *has* to eat better." The housekeeper scowled and funneled powdered milk into a plastic jug. "Can you imagine? That tiny thing—"

"Are you sure? How can she—"

"She is. She says she was with a boy in March. She won't say who, not that it would do any good."

"But her family! There must be someone—"

Mrs. Iverson turned scolding blue eyes on him. "But there's *not*. She's been with us all this while, she won't say who she belongs to, she won't go back—we'll have to care for her, Jack. And the baby; and barely enough as it is." She sighed. "But I guess you'll be getting your million dollars soon enough. We'll just keep our fingers crossed, that's all."

She filled the jug with water and shook it into an unappetizing white froth. Jack leaned against the stove and gazed despairingly at the ceiling.

"I don't *believe* it! Does Keeley know? She hasn't even seen a doctor! I mean, this is just *medieval*—we'll be boiling water and tearing up fucking bedsheets—"

"Oh, *hush* your language, Jack." Mrs. Iverson glared. "Babies get born all the time without your help. If she needs a doctor, we'll bring her to Saint Joseph's."

"But folic acid—you're supposed to *take* things—"

Mrs. Iverson rolled her eyes. "What would *you* know from taking things for babies? You and your friends . . . That poor little girl, all this time and she didn't even know. *I* think she *pretended* not to know. Your grandmother saw her in the bath Sunday and called me in. Poor little girl—just a stick with a big belly. But you could feel it kicking. She'll be all right."

"*March . . .*" Jack did the math in his head: almost five months. "I had no idea," he said softly.

"Of course you didn't. You wouldn't be a one to know about girls." There was an edge to Mrs. Iverson's voice, and he flushed. "But just as well, everything considered; she doesn't need any more trouble with boys." With a sigh the housekeeper turned to go. "But it would be nice if you'd go and talk to her sometimes, Jack. She likes you—"

"She *does?*" Barely less astonished than by news of her parturience.

"—and she's lonely. Ah God, that poor girl . . ."

She went upstairs, leaving Jack to shake his head. He went out onto the porch and leaned on the balcony above a scraggy patch of blue hydrangeas blighted brown and yellowy green.

A fucking baby! It *was* medieval. Worse than that—crudely archaic, like one of those awful engravings from the time of the Black Death, crazy-eyed monks, strangers turning up like stray animals to drop their young on the floor. He ran his hands through thinning hair, too long, when had he cut it last? Over a year. He must look medieval, himself. *We* all *must.*

Though the Philistines may jostle,
you will rank as an apostle in the high aesthetic band,

If you walk down Piccadilly with a
poppy or a lily in your medieval hand!

Suddenly he began to laugh, very hard and for once without rancor. Thinking how impossible, how ridiculously apocalyptic this all would have seemed, just three years ago: the sky in flames, coyotes in the South Bronx, oceans rising and burning. People fondling old issues of *Vanity Fair* and *Vogue* as though they were rare Victorian pornography. Daffodils coming up yellow and blooming black. The world dismantling Lazyland as though it were a shipwreck, plucking at the water supply and electricity, plundering floorboards, foundation giving way because somewhere down the long slope to the Hudson a tree had fallen; because somewhere within the basement beneath a broken window another tree was starting to grow. Because we forgot to buy end-of-the-world insurance. Because we forgot other things.

And still the flowers bloom, he thought wonderingly, gazing down at the hydrangeas. A brave sickly show, all their charms gone; sad vegetable lover here. But *blooming*. See?

He let his hands fall, and barely grazed the wilted flowers with his fingertips. The heavily clustered blossoms felt damp and cankered, like moldering fungi. He wrinkled his nose, trying to find their scent in heavy air that smelled of burning; leaned farther down, until he could cup them beneath his palms. To his shock, the corrupted flower head *moved* beneath his hand. With a small cry he reared back, clutching at the rotten balustrade, after a moment cautiously looked down again.

The entire bush was aswarm with numberless insects. How had he not seen them? He blinked. They came into focus, myriad ruddy beads like spilled paint, each no bigger than a ladybug. But they weren't ladybugs; their carapaces were true red untinged by orange, and they had no spots. What they did have was very

large, beautiful golden eyes. Not the kind of eyes that
beetles had, insofar as Jack knew; more like a wasp's, or
fly's, casting vitreous sparks of gold and blue. Something
about their movement fascinated him, and after a few
minutes he realized what it was: they were not swarming mindlessly as he had always assumed bugs did, but
in a very particular circular pattern, stemming from the
center of each hydrangea blossom and then swirling
slowly outward, as though they were creating the pattern of the flower rather than merely treading upon it. It
was like watching waves on a beach, a random motion
propelled by some greater thing, and Jack actually
glanced up at the flame-colored sky, half-expecting to
see the Insect God there choreographing the waltz.

But no, no Insect God today. He looked back down
upon the dance. It had not slowed or quickened, it had
not changed; but it seemed now that its symmetry had
within it a certain stillness; that the shifting pattern of
legs and wings and eyes, pistil, petals, stem all formed a
single image, unmoving, perhaps unmovable. He leaned
over the parapet, drawing close enough to catch the
frank green scent of the hydrangeas.

And saw that the pattern the insects had formed
upon each flower head was an eye: at once fluid and
motionless, lidless and shuttered: myriad crystalline
eyes, and each solitary beetle a facet therein. He would
have shouted, but it was too lovely; fallen, but the balcony caught him. And he could not push down a throb
of nausea, to see all those living things put to one purpose—

And what the fuck was *that*?

"What are you *doing*?" The words came out
unbidden. And suddenly it was as though he had
swept his arms through the heavy blossoms rather
than spoken to them: for all at once the insects

erupted into a great bright blizzard of wings. There was an acrid smell, a memory-flash from childhood that ladybugs smelled like this; then insects everywhere, not a horror but a glorious cloud, and alive, he had never known before how *alive* things were. His breath came out in a loud gasp of astonished laughter. He stumbled backward as they flew around him, his arms outspread and head thrown back so that he felt the tremble of their thousand wings against his skin, wings and little legs everywhere, as focused in their intent as the hand of a lover. Like a lover he responded, not with arousal but with a sense of transport, of enchantment, as startled by this shock of joy as he was by the shimmering brood. They moved around him in skeins like falling water, blinking red and gold. And for a minute Jack spun there with them, even as they lifted up and around him, the center of that soft live storm. For an instant he could see himself as something else must: the vital eye's bright mutable nucleus, part of the world's strange change; its aperture.

Then they were gone, dispersed into the sky like a waterspout. Jack stood alone on the ramshackle porch, dazed and breathless. He could hear though not see an airship thrumming somewhere above the river, and a bird chirping sleepily. The air was warm, so he stripped off his shirt; and saw that there were numberless welts upon his arms and hands, as well as on the small uneven V where his shirt had been unbuttoned. The welts were painless, though he felt the very faintest tingling when he touched one. And they were on his face, too: he drew his hand across his cheek and felt more small raised bumps, a whisper of sensation. A series of small alarms rang off in his skull—hives! shingles! anaphylactic shock!—but before he could go inside to raid the medicine chest the welts began to fade, like a blush.

He touched his chest and upper arms wonderingly, and felt the same breath, as of the tiniest electrical shock.

But the welts were gone. He started to pull his shirt back on, then stopped. The insects had touched it, he could smell their acrid odor upon the fabric. Perhaps it would be dangerous to wear?

But with their scent came the rush of memory: that prescient eye and himself within it, all as real as the sagging floor beneath him. What little Jack knew of magic or science, he knew they faded, sure as love and paint.

He would wear the shirt, for a while.

It was not long after this that Emma and Jule came to dinner. They did not come *for* dinner—the phones were down at Lazyland and they'd been unable to call—but there had been fuel deliveries in the northern part of the county, Jule's battered Range Rover had a full tank of gas and several full ten-gallon containers in the back of the car, and Emma had earned four days off from her work at the hospital, by virtue of having been on duty when the survivors of a train derailment at Chappaqua were brought in.

"Round the clock for seventy-two hours, almost," she told Jack and Keeley and Mrs. Iverson over tea in the living room. "Christ, I haven't gone without sleep like that since—since my residency." She looked down at her teacup and smiled wistfully; Jack knew she had started to say *since Rachel was killed*.

"I don't know how you go on, dear," said Keeley from her chair. "James could go without sleep, but I never could—"

"Me neither." Jule grabbed his wife's hand and squeezed it, then reached for his glass. He had brought several bottles of Jack Daniel's ("Comes from the same fuckers who drive the gas trucks," he'd explained cheerfully to Jack, "your one-stop fuel shop!") and one was set on the table in front of him beside an untouched teacup. "I don't get eight hours of sleep, I'm a chocolate mess."

Keeley laughed in delight. "Oh darling, I'm *so* glad you came!" Of all Jack's friends, Jule had won her heart thirty years before, when he had shoveled her new forest green Mustang out from under two feet of snow during the 1969 blizzard. Even after Jack's family moved from Yonkers, Jule continued to visit Keeley, riding the blue crosstown bus to North Broadway and walking the last half mile to Lazyland. From the beginning they had been an odd sight, the unruly giant from the Italian neighborhood in Tuckahoe and the aging Irish beauty who doted on him as she never had on her own boys. After James Finnegan's death, it was the teenage Jule who fixed things at Lazyland, replacing washers and fuses and lightbulbs, calling the men who mowed the lawn, arranging for the house to be painted when its grey shingles began to peel and crack. Keeley would feed him roast beef and popovers and apple pie, then send him back to the bus stop with a Wanamaker shopping bag full of Snickerdoodles. Later, during summers off from rooming together at Georgetown, he and Jack took over Lazyland's top floor. Keeley would decorously ignore the occasional waft of marijuana smoke that made its way downstairs, the sound of footsteps at 4 A.M. as some furtive guest made his or her way outside.

". . . really, we were just talking about you! Jule, do you remember . . ."

On the couch Jule held his big hands carefully in his lap, cupping his highball glass like a votive candle. Now and then he leaned over to touch Emma's hair, or pat her knee, or to adjust Keeley's shawl. "Mmm, no," he boomed, "but my ears must've been burning. Go on, go on—"

Jack smiled sadly at his friend's genteel *déshabillé*. Buttons missing from the stained cashmere overcoat, expensive Italian shoes scuffed and cracked, the lapels of his Donna Karan jacket frayed: all part of Jule's slow-motion decline since his daughter's death. Emma had lost herself in her work; Jule merely got lost. He was a big man, six-foot-three, burly and elegant as a gangland lawyer, with curly black hair dramatically shot with white and the woeful brown eyes of a cartoon hound. Even in his present unkempt state he managed to retain the illusion of civility, as though he had been broadsided on his way to the Winter Cotillion.

"That sonofabitch! I *wondered* what happened to him!" Jule roared with laughter, some joke that Jack had missed (again). At his side Emma dimpled, shaking her fuzzy blond curls even as she cast a wary glance at Jule's glass, and then at Jack.

"Mmm, he *was* kind of a head case," she began, but her glance had drawn Jule's: he downed his whiskey and poured another. Emma said nothing, only stared at Jack, her blue eyes beseeching.

Jack turned to his friend with a huge fake grin. "Uh hey, Jule—you wanna help me with something?" He slapped his knees and motioned at the door behind them. "I got to fill the coal bin, *you* could do it in about three—"

Jule opened his mouth to boom some reply, then stopped, whiskey poised in midair before him as he stared out into the entry room. Emma raised her eyebrows, Doctor Duck meeting a new patient.

"Umm—hello?" she suggested. "More company?"

Jack turned to see Marz standing in the doorway.

Struwwelpeter hair combed for once, and wearing a pink shetland sweater and shapeless grey plaid uniform skirt. But with white bony bare legs, and bare feet. She really *did* look like a refugee.

"Ah—who's *that*?" said Jule *sotto voce*. "Kate Moss's cadaver double?"

Jack frowned. "That is our houseguest. Marzana."

"Marzana? What the fuck kind of name—"

"*Jule*," warned Emma.

"Mary Anne," said Keeley with a sweet smile.

"Hi," said Marz. "I'm going to take a nap. Okay?" She grinned shyly, hands hidden in her sleeves, and turned to go upstairs.

"Let me help her," cried Mrs. Iverson, and followed.

Jule stared after them. When they were out of sight, he raised an eyebrow at Jack. "So tell me—did Fagin kick her out for not finishing dinner? Or what?"

"No, Jule. She's a runaway."

"A runaway? What the fuck she doing *here*?"

"Jack found her," explained Keeley, looking pained at his language. "In the garden . . ."

"What, under a cabbage leaf?" Jule ignored a sharp poke from Emma and stared wonderingly at his friend. "Jackie?"

Jack sighed. "She was in the garden. She was crying—I mean, Christ, Jule, she's just a kid—"

"*How long?*"

Jack hesitated. "Two months, I guess. Maybe three."

"Three *months*?" exploded Jule. "Jackie, you—"

"She's pregnant," said Keeley. Her teacup trembled in front of her mouth; an amber drop slid down her chin. "I'm *so* glad you came, Emma—she hasn't seen a doctor—"

"Pregnant?" Emma tilted her head, gazing at the empty doorway. "Oh! Wow. Well. This is quite a lot for you all to be handling here, Keeley. Jack. And for three months . . . I didn't think it was that long since we talked." She shot Jack an accusing look. "But you've *spoken* to Julie, Jack. About the magazine—why didn't you tell us?"

Keeley closed her eyes and sipped her tea.

"The time wasn't right, it wasn't something I could just bring up. When it was—well, the phones," said Jack defensively. "I wanted to call, I mean I *tried* to call—you know what it's like."

"But you're sure she's pregnant? She's been tested? She's been tested for everything?"

Jack yelled in exasperation. "Of course not! She hasn't been tested for *anything*! I don't even know who she *is*—"

"She sounds foreign," brooded Jule.

Keeley opened her yes, set her teacup on the side table. "She's Polish. Marzana is Polish for Mary Anne."

Jule and Emma exchanged another look, then turned to Jack. "Her name is *Marzana*," he said emphatically.

In her chair Keeley sighed, loudly. The Queen was weary of bickering courtiers. "I'm tired. Emma, could you help me upstairs?"

"Oh I'm sorry, Keeley, of course, of course—" Emma bustled from the couch and helped Keeley to her feet, put the walking stick in her hand, and carefully guided her from the room.

"You can stay for dinner?" Keeley's voice was plaintive.

"Of course—we brought food, Jule will bring it in. You're not to do a *thing*, Keeley, I *forbid* it. But if it's all right, we thought we'd stay over tonight—"

"Oh, darling." Keeley stopped, catching her breath, and looked up at Emma with full eyes. "We would love that."

"Great!" Emma straightened. Her voice took on the brisk cheerfulness of the doctor on duty. "All right! Up we go."

When they were gone Jule refilled his glass, spilling whiskey on the table. Annoyed, Jack wiped it up with his sleeve.

"Be careful, will you? You'll ruin the finish—"

Jule snorted, leaning back so that the couch creaked beneath his weight. He cradled his glass in one hand, the Jack Daniel's in the other. "Jackie, Jackie," he rumbled, "you fucking idiot. Some cracked-out kid—"

Jack stood and grabbed the bottle. He poured a shot into his teacup and gulped it, did another, slid onto the couch, and glared at his friend. "I was *going* to call Emma. To ask what I should do with her."

"What, like feed her?"

"No, you asshole. Like tell me whether I should call the Child Welfare League or whoever the fuck it is you call about things like this."

"Have you tried the police?"

"No. I told you, I haven't told anyone. The phones are too screwed up." Which wasn't always true, of course. Jack hesitated, trying to remember exactly why he hadn't called anyone. "But I mean, Keeley just took her over. You think I should call the police?"

Jule shrugged and knocked back his drink. "Was she breaking into the house or anything like that?"

"No. She was *here*, though. I mean she was on our land, so she was technically trespassing, I guess."

"Well, these days you're not gonna get a big response to a call about some kid trespassing, Jackie," said Jule dryly. "My suggestion would be that you give her a nice meal—if you can get her to eat it, she looks like she's pumping ice or some such shit—and send her packing before she causes trouble."

"That's *exactly* what I thought," Jack broke in, "but Keeley is doing the whole stray-cat thing—"

"Yeah? Well, then, maybe *you* should go the whole nine yards and do the whole stray-cat thing and like, *dispose* of her. Don't give me that look, I don't think you should *kill* her! I just mean *take* her somewhere, drop her off, and let her go back to wherever she crawled from. Capische?"

"I know, I know." Jack nodded unhappily. "But she's pregnant—"

"And the sooner the better"— Jule pounded the sofa, so that the picture behind him shifted on the wall—"I mean, weeping Christ on a stick, Jackie, what're you *thinking*? A kid like that, alone here with you and all these old ladies? Sometimes I think you have no common sense."

"But she's *pregnant*."

Jule's bleary eyes suddenly focused on his friend. He looked aghast. "Jesus, Jackie—not by *you*? Okay, okay—I just thought, you know—it happens." He started to laugh. "That'd be right up there with the Immaculate Conception, huh, Jackie? Kinda skinny for my taste."

Jack grinned ruefully. "She's not a bad kid. I mean, she's actually incredibly *quiet*."

"Does she help out? With Grandmother and Mrs. Iverson?"

"I guess. I don't know *what* she does, really. I think maybe she sleeps a lot. I haven't—I haven't spent much time with her. Alone, I mean. But no, she's no trouble. And Keeley and Larena, they just seem to love her. I guess because she's a girl." Jack gave a broken laugh. "*I* didn't even know she was pregnant."

Jule nodded. "Well, I can see that. I mean, *I* wouldn't've known, she's so skinny." He leaned back on the couch, balancing his glass on one great knee. "A girl. Yeah, girls are different."

His tone grew wistful, and Jack looked up, fearful of what he might see on his friend's face. But Jule seemed peaceful. After a moment he tipped his head, smiling, and asked, "But how are *you*, Jackie? You look pretty good—"

"Good, good, I feel—"

"—but you look skinny." Jule's red face folded into worry. "You getting enough to eat here? I mean, all of you soaking wet weigh five pounds—you getting enough to eat?"

"Of course we are. The grocery at Delmonico's still delivers, every couple of weeks. We do okay. And—"

"Delmonico's!" Jule grinned dreamily. "God. They still have that caponata? You don't get *shit* where we are. I mean, the movie people can get it flown in, sometimes, but the rest of us, stores and stuff—if you can even get there, they don't got shit for food. But Emma grows everything, anyway . . ."

They talked for a long time. As evening came, the room a swirl of lavender and yellow, Emma brought them food—cumin-scented rice, tiny bitter eggplant, last year's dried apples—then left. It had been a year, at least, since they'd had the luxury of time, a night together without the long treacherous drive back north for Jule, without Jack having to worry about whether his friend would make it home in one piece—Jule drank heavily since Rachel's death, there was nothing else to be said about it—and no assurance that Jule would be able to call to let him know that he'd gotten there safely. And it had been much longer than a year since they'd really talked, unfettered by business or the need to break bad news, or to console—could it have been since Jack's fortieth birthday?

"Yeah, you gotta watch those birthdays, Jackie," said Jule. "Fuckin' A, Jackie Finnegan turns forty, and the world comes to an end!" He roared, wiping his eyes; then abruptly was weeping, crying as though he would never stop.

"Oh Jule—" Jack reached for him on the narrow couch, sending a glass ratcheting to the floor. The first bottle of Jack Daniel's was long empty, a second only half-full. "Don't cry, Julie," he stammered, not yet aware he was weeping himself. "Oh please don't cry—"

Jule raised a hand, begging silence. His big ugly face crumpled in upon itself like a broken box. He grabbed his friend and pulled him close, shuddering as he cried out.

"Oh Jackie Jackie, why's it all happening? Why? Why—" that big arm shaking as it hugged Jackie close, and the two of them huddled in the endless shifting twilight, their own fragile landscape: mountain and bent willow, little Jackie and big Jule, together at the end of all things, as they had never thought to be.

Jack rose late the next day (he guessed it was late), went into the bathroom and threw up (at least *this* time he knew why he was throwing up), poured water from an old china pitcher to wash his face and clean the sink. He walked downstairs, very very slowly, clutching at the banister, passing the blond girl's bedroom and noting his grandmother in there with her, the two of them going through old clothes on the four-poster. The grand-mother clock greeted him with its customary *sushing,* the immense weighted pendulum sweeping back and forth, back and forth, as though endlessly pushing something from sight. When he finally got all the way downstairs he sank into one of the blackened Stickley chairs to catch his breath and stared up at the huge grandfather clock's intricate face. Placid three-quarter moon peeking out from behind a beaming sun, dials showing high tide, low tide, the stars, the seasons, everything it seemed that could be calibrated by chime rods and winding drums, brass bobs, and golden slaves. Was there a dial in there for Jackie Finnegan? For Jule? A clatter from down the hall drove him from his chair, moving wearily across the frayed Chinese carpet to the kitchen.

"Good morning, Jackie," said Emma, smiling beside a window she had filled with mason jars full of dried beans, pasta, different-colored lentils. "You look like you spent the night with my husband."

"I did," whispered Jack, falling into another chair. "Remind me never to do it again."

Emma laughed. Her eyes betrayed something else. Not anger or annoyance; a kind of habitual assessment as she gazed at Jack holding his head in his hands. He raised his eyes to her and saw there what she did: he looked sick. He wasn't getting better. She was a doctor. She thought he was dying.

"Well." Her lips pursed, and she returned his look, complicitous: *we understand each other*. "Jackie, I want to look at you later. Okay?"

He nodded, and, too quickly, Emma turned away, to place another jar upon the sill. Then Mrs. Iverson came in, shaking her head and frowning at Jack's hungover appearance.

"Some people *never learn*," she announced in her quavering voice. "At least Leonard isn't here."

She poured him coffee with real milk in it, more of Emma's bounty, and Emma gave him some bread she'd baked herself, a little stale but rich with molasses and sunflower seeds.

"How come you can do this and we can't?" Jack asked, sick and misty-eyed with gratitude. "Grow all this stuff. Bake . . ."

Emma bustled around the room, swiping fiercely at countertops, checking cabinets, collecting spent jars and bags and replacing them with what she'd brought: tea, flour, powdered milk, dried fruit.

"Because this is what women *do*," she answered, mouth a little prim: Doctor Duck does not approve of strong drink. "Get food. Make sure everybody has enough to eat—"

"Perform brain surgery?"

Emma nodded. "—perform brain surgery. Ugh, is this *oatmeal*?" She glanced accusingly at Jack, who only shrugged. "*Jack*. The world doesn't come to an end just because the phones are dead—"

"Emma, we haven't had power for ages. And before that—"

"Neither have we. It doesn't matter." She dumped the oatmeal into a bowl of things destined for compost, handed it to Mrs. Iverson as the housekeeper left the room. "Jule Gardino, taking the fucking luxury of killing himself with alcohol—"

Her voice shook, he was shocked to see how angry she was, jars rattling as she shoved them in the cupboard. "—it doesn't all come screeching to a goddamn fucking *halt*," she finished, face pale with fury.

"You mean the world doesn't come to an end, just because the world is coming to an end."

Jack turned to see Jule filling the doorway. He was unshaven, his hair mussed; otherwise, he seemed unaffected by the night's bout.

Emma took a long breath, turned to a window, exhaled. "Oh, Julie. Please spare me."

"You know what your problem—"

"I'm going upstairs." Emma shoved her hands into the pockets of her cardigan and crossed the room. She paused to kiss first the top of Jack's head, then stood on tiptoe to kiss Jule's chin. He twisted in the doorway to let her go by, his hand touching her ass as he winked at Jack. In the hall she turned and stared back at them.

"You know he's killing himself?" she said to Jack, as though they were alone in the room. "You know he's going to kill himself, one of these days?" Then disappeared down the corridor.

"Yeah, but not today," Jule said cheerfully. "I'm not scheduled for today."

He walked across the kitchen and poured himself some coffee from the thermos, went to the cupboard where liquor was kept and rummaged there until he found a bottle of Irish Mist. Jack watched silently as he poured some into his mug, then came back to sit at the table.

"Morning, Jackster. You look like shit."

"Yeah, no lie." The smell of whiskey floated up to him, and he turned away. "Christ, Jule, get that away from me before I puke."

"You know what you're problem is, Jackie? *Pacing*. You don't pace yourself. It's like the marathon—"

"I am *not* fucking interested in running a Jack Daniel's marathon, especially with *you*. Okay?"

Jule whooped derisively. "The Kip Keino of booze! Whoa baby, I'm breaking records here, Jackie!"

"Oh, shut up." Jack shook his head. "Jesus Christ. This is like that time the door fell on me."

Jule laughed, remembering: a disassembled, three-hundred-pound fire door leaning against a wall at Georgetown, suddenly falling; Jack pleated beneath it like a rug, so drunk he was completely unharmed. "Yeah! You got nine lives, Jackie."

Jack gave him a wry look. "Well, I'm probably running down to the last one."

Jule furrowed his brow, took a long sip of his spiked coffee. "You feeling bad, Jackie?" he asked softly.

"I don't know. I mean, no. I actually feel better than I did a few months ago, when I was in the hospital." He traced the rim of his coffee cup, seeing how the bones of his hand stuck out, like a bat's vestigial fingers. "But no one believes me."

"I believe you," said Jule in a low voice. "I've seen some things lately, made me think differently about all this—"

He waved his hand, vaguely indicating the deteriorating house around them, the world. "Not anything I can really share with you right now—Emma doesn't like me talking about it." His big broad face took on an absurdly furtive look, the cartoon hound trying to hide something under the rug. "But I'll tell you about it at some point, Jackie. I think you know what I'm talking about."

Jack looked up into his friend's dark fervid eyes, already showing a fine glister of drink. "Right, Jackie? Right?"

"Uh, sure." Jack took a nervous sip of his coffee. He had no *idea* what Jule was talking about. Some bizarre reverse Twelve-Step program? Countermarch across grief and alcohol like Chuck Berry going backward across a stage, drinking himself back to sanity and health? "You hungry, Julie? There's some bread—"

"Nah. Maybe in a little bit. Got to wake up first—"

He returned to the cabinet and poured some more Irish Mist into his mug. Jack watched him, suddenly undone by his own sorrow, and anger, the smell of Irish whiskey. "Look," he said, standing (too fast, he had to grab the back of his chair to keep from keeling over), "Julie, I feel pretty lousy. I think I'm going to try and lie down again for a while, see if I can sleep. You're going to be here all day, right?"

Jule stared thoughtfully out the window. "I think so. Maybe tonight, too, if that's okay with you all. Unless the Allied High Commander's changed her mind."

"Okay. So in an hour or two, okay, I'll be back down—"

Jule turned to him, eyes far too cheery-bright. "Sure, Jackie, sure. We'll talk, later."

He slept, though badly. Dreams of Leonard, Jack's formerly derailed system of arousal now, oddly, back in place. Lowering his head between Leonard's thighs, his hands parting Leonard's muscular legs, taking Leonard's cock in his mouth and tasting him, spoiled sweetness like a fruit left too long in the sun. Then Jack himself coming, the first time in absolute ages like that, from a dream: arcing himself awake, hand between his own legs, groaning.

"Ah, *fuck*." Orgasm blindsided into a skull-jarring headache; he fumbled at his nightstand until he found the precautionary water glass he'd set there earlier. *Leonard, why am I dreaming about LEONARD?*

Though the real question, of course, was *Why haven't I ever* stopped *dreaming about Leonard*? Something he should have taken up with his therapist, back when New York had therapists instead of soothsayers on the stock exchange.

Too late now.

He lay there for a while, not really thinking about anything; just trying to will away his headache, a dreadful underlying tiredness that, he was beginning to sense, had too little to do with too much Jack Daniel's. After fifteen minutes he sat up, painfully, and pulled open the drawer of his nightstand. Took out the vial of Fusax, placed a half dropperful beneath his tongue. He had just replaced the bottle when there was a knock at his bedroom door.

"Jack? It's Emma. May I come in?"

"Sure," he croaked, and swung his legs over the side of the bed. He smiled gamely as she entered, wearing a faded denim jumper and cotton paisley blouse, her tousled curls held back by a child's flowered headband, and carrying a big canvas bag.

She's wearing Rachel's headband, he thought, the smile shocked away.

"Feeling a little better? You shouldn't try to keep up with Jule, you know—"

"I wasn't, I wasn't—"

"—you should leave that to the professionals." More bitterness there. "When was the last time you saw a doctor, Jackie?"

He thought back: the hospital, early spring. "A month," he lied. "Maybe two."

"Where? Those assholes at Saint Joseph's?"

He stared at the floor, mumbled something about another clinic.

Emma looked unimpressed. "What are your numbers these days? When was the last time you got them?"

He bit his lip, looked up at her. "I don't know, Emma. I mean, I don't remember."

"When you were in the hospital they were pretty lousy, Jackie." She sighed, sitting beside him on the bed with the canvas bag at her feet. "I'm not going to fuck with you, Jack. Right now, to me, you look pretty bad—"

"I'm just thin, Emma. I don't feel—"

"Even before last night: you just don't look healthy to me. So. I want to check you out. Okay?"

She pulled on latex gloves and mask, took his temperature, blood pressure, pulse. Felt his joints and examined him for lesions, scabs that hadn't healed, damp spots in the crook of knee or elbow. Stethoscope to his chest and back, first warming it with her gloved hand, then checking for the telltale sough of fluid in his lungs, his heart stirred too fast or slow by evil humors. Jack sat through it all with troubled patience: something medieval in this, or Victorian: the earnest much-loved doctor armed with ear trumpet and little else, certainly nothing that could shout above the din of invisibles swarming, replicating inside him. Jack watched her in a despairing silence, Dorothy Gale to the Wizard: *I don't think there's anything in that black bag for me.*

Away with the stethoscope, out with the ophthalmoscope to peer into his eyes, then change the instrument's black avian head to examine ears and throat and nostrils.

"Huh." Emma drew back from him, frowning.

"What?" demanded Jack.

Off with the laryngoscope and back to the eyes again. "I don't know," she said after a moment. She looked puzzled. "Have you had thrush?"

"No." Spark of panic. "Do I now?"

"No. I mean, I don't think so. But there's something weird in there. Like a growth—"

"A *growth*?" Panic pulsed into nausea. "What *kind* of growth—"

"I don't know. Here—" She slid a tongue depressor from a sterile packet, and something like a very long Q-Tip, what they used for throat cultures. "Say 'Ah,' I want to scrape some of it . . ."

He said, 'Ah,' gagging a little. *Growths. Fungus.*

"Huh." Emma's eyes widened as she turned to hold first the wooden depressor and then the culture probe to the light. "This is very strange."

"*WHAT?*" he cried, past all patience now.

"Well, look—there's definitely something going on in there. See?" She held the tongue depressor so he could see what was on it, a thin film of something granular, faintly greenish—not a sickly mucousy green, but crystalline, like dyed salt. The same thing adhered to the Q-Tip.

"What is it?" he whispered.

Emma shook her head, eyebrows raised. "I have no idea. I've never seen anything like it. Or heard of anything like it." She stared at him, wonderingly. "It appears to be in your eyes, too, Jack. Are you having trouble seeing? Blurred vision, anything like that?"

"Uh, well—well, yes, maybe a little." He gazed at the cultures in her hands. "Jesus, Emma, what is it? Is it a fungus?"

"No. It's definitely *not* a fungus. Not thrush. A fungal infection doesn't look like this. I don't know *what* looks like this. And your temperature isn't elevated, for whatever that's worth, and there doesn't seem to be anything in your lungs.

"Actually, you *do* seem sort of okay—I don't see any lesions, or anything like that. But you have obviously lost quite a bit of weight, which isn't so great. Any nausea?"

"Not really. Just—I don't feel all that hungry. I feel kind of speedy, actually, most of the time. And my dreams are weird . . . ."

He thought of the Fusax, inches from his elbow in the nightstand drawer. He nodded, slowly, his mouth opening to tell her—

"Huh." She fixed him with an odd look. "Jule has weird dreams, too. Has he told you?"

Mouth snapped shut. Then, "No."

She bent beside her canvas bag, withdrew two plastic Ziploc bags. Deposited the cultures, one in each, then scribbled something on the labels. "I'm going to have these checked out. It's very strange, these crystals—they almost look like uric acid does, when you get dehydrated."

"What could it be?" Thinking of all the horrific things the world had given humanity these last few years: viruses from rain forests and newly exposed meteorites, mass amphibian die-outs and now a new disease, courtesy of Leonard Thrope.

She cocked her head. "I don't know. Did you ever see *The Andromeda Strain*?"

He gaped, feeling himself grow hot with anger; then started to laugh—horrified, almost delirious.

"I'm sorry!" She swept him into a hug, kissing the top of his head, cradling his head with latex hands. "Oh God, Jack, I didn't mean that—"

"It's okay," he gasped, his entire body shaking. "It's okay—"

"—it's just so strange, you read all the time about these weird new things. But some of them are *good*, Jackie—you know? I mean, at least in theory, this could be good," she added somewhat dubiously. "I'll run it by the lab, have some other people look at it. Are you doing anything different? Some weird therapy?"

Again, the Fusax in the drawer. He decided, flatly, to say nothing. "No."

"Huh. Okay, then." She peeled off the gloves and slid them into a biohazard container. "Well. You feel up to eating, after all this?"

He laughed again, more easily. "Oh, sure, Emma! This is like, a real stimulant to the appetite—"

"Not right now. Maybe a little while?" She leaned down to kiss him, slung the canvas bag over her shoulder. "I'll have Julie come get you."

He watched her, heart spilling. There were deep

lines around her eyes; her skin looked grey and listless. "You look tired, too, Emma," he said after a moment. "You never get a break, do you?"

She smiled sadly. "No. But that's okay. I've been overdoing it, probably. I've felt for a while now like I'm coming down with something. Occupational hazard," she added with a grimace.

At the door she stopped. "Oh—I forgot. I looked at Mary Anne—"

"*Marzana,*" he said, weakly.

"Whatever. She's definitely pregnant. But she seems okay, as far as I can see. I gave her some vitamins. I brought some for you, too—can you make sure she takes them?"

"Sure, Emma. Anything you say."

"All right. I'll see you later." And she went down-stairs.

They left early the next morning, rush-hour-traffic time, back when there had been traffic. Emma very small behind the wheel of the Range Rover, with all its weird protective encrustations—barbed wire, kryptonite locks, chains. Jule beside her, looking, at last, defeated by drink and fatigue. Jack had gone to bed early the night before, leaving his friend by himself in the living room with a bottle, Keeley's *millefleurs* spread across the table in front of him. When Jack had come down for break-fast Jule was there still, planed awkwardly into the couch. His big hand curled, conchlike, several inches above the floor, where one of the heavy glass paper-weights lay broken in two, a crystal heart revealing splintered chambers.

Now Jack watched as Emma started the car. He'd already filled the tank for her, hefting the heavy red plastic gas can and spilling some on the drive—one didn't need television or radio to hear horror stories about people who ran out of gas on the Hutch, or the Saw Mill, or the Cross Bronx Expressway—and then replacing the container in the back of the Range Rover amidst coils of barbed wire and unknown, slightly threatening-looking objects covered with tarpaulins.

"Well," said Emma, cracking her window and speaking from behind a stainless-steel veil. "I guess we're off."

Jack nodded and made himself smile, though it hurt, it hurt. "Yeah. Drive carefully, guys."

Beside him Keeley sniffed. Instinctively he put his arm around her, looked down and saw her smile, painful as his, her worn blue eyes filled with tears. He wanted to pull her close but felt a shaft of anxiety: her shoulders seemed thin and insubstantial as balsa wood, he might break something.

"You take care of your grandma now, you hear?" bellowed Jule, sausage fingers thrusting beside Emma's head. Jack nodded, assuming Jule spoke to him. But at that moment the blond girl stepped down from the porch where she had been standing with Mrs. Iverson.

"I will. Don't worry," she called. Her accented voice was sweet and high and cold, like a bird's. "Don't worry."

She hugged Keeley tightly to her slender frame, and Keeley smiled, detaching from Jack. Jack stared at them, flushing. Surprised, stunned even, to suddenly realize how physically alike they were: the same fragile build and finely etched bone structure, lovely long fingers and slender wrists, large eyes and thin mouths; the same thin bright hair, Marzana's corona inclined to sun, Keeley's to moon.

The car's engine roared. "Good-bye!" cried Mrs. Iverson from the steps. She blew her nose loudly. "Be careful, don't stop anywhere!"

"Good-bye!" called Emma, smiling. "We'll call, *call us*, Jackie! Take your vitamins!"

"Good-bye!" shouted Jule, and everyone else, watching the car nose up the twisting drive. "Good-bye!"

Jack's throat tight, hurting now too, and his eyes.

Good-bye, good-bye.

CHAPTER ELEVEN

The Wendameen *Responds*

It was high summer at Mars Hill; at least, as close to summer as the world would get. Heat without true warmth, UV rays but no sun splattering the rocky beach; birches and rugosa roses furred with yellow-green, leaves stunted but growing nonetheless, bravely; barely. Lobster boats and trawlers puttering out, still, to fish the Grand Banks, but no fish. Martin tossing awake at night on the couch, suffused with longing, raging with it; a yearning that sucked at the very marrow of his bones: love but no lover. Knowing always that the boy was in the next room, in Martin's own bed, John's bed, breathing deeply and imperturbably as waves moved upon the shingle. Two things that don't change, even at the end of the world—sound of the sea and straight boys sleeping soundly in other rooms.

Some nights, Martin could bear it, as he had all the greater sorrows of his life. Breathing through this as he had breathed through John's death, and others: focusing on the air in his lungs, hear it come and go; another tide. But now even this was harder, breathing. He had to use his inhalers more often, every three or four hours day and night, gasping as he sucked at first one little plastic tube and then the next, the minutes between albuterol and prednisone taking on the weight of granite in his chest, waiting for the steroids to kick in, the permeable walls of mast cells to thicken. He was in danger of coming down with pneumonia—his precarious emotional state made him vulnerable, as it always had, to illness.

Arguments with John that would within twelve hours escalate into strep throat, a vast secret army hidden within that waited only for such carelessness as this to attack with fevers, blisters, white spots in the mouth.

Men have died from time to time, and worms have eaten them, but not for love.

But yes; yes, for love.

This could kill me, thought Martin Dionysos in the night, as he had, oh, perhaps a hundred thousand times before. Watching as some beautiful club kid thrashed around on the dance floor wearing a water bottle taped to his thigh and not much else. Dappled light spilling from mirror balls or lasers, or summer sun or stars. Eyes changing color, and hair; only desire remains the same.

He thought of a song John had loved, dancing to it even at the end; the two of them swaying in bed together and singing along with the tape player.

> *When I'm alone I hear and feel you*
> *I wish that I could reach right out and touch you*
> *Starry eyes . . .*

Martin groaned, buried his face in his pillow even as he thrust against the couch (too hard, too soft, finding a space between the cushions: just right), cock straining against his hand and all of him exploding too quickly as he came. He gasped, moaning softly and still moving, imagining the boy there beneath him, silent, his blue eyes seeing something inside of Martin that had not been warped or left wanting by illness, by the horror of standing on a curve of shoreline and watching as it was eaten away by the storm, watching as everyone he ever loved slowly drowned.

And yet, desire flickered, even as black water lapped

at his feet. He felt like a broken clock, innards unsprung, heart uncoiled, gears rusting; but the alarm still works, shrieking and clamoring until the hand reaches out to silence it. Thinking of the boy in the next room, who would not die, probably; might even be here later, maybe, after Martin himself was gone.

> *Starry eyes*
> *Forever shall be mine.*

He slept.

And hours later, started awake. The room was not dark, but filled with the strange moving colors that sometimes came after midnight, like moths drawn to the cottage windows. Velvety blue and violet and a shimmering white. To lie there was to watch their wings stir, and wait for sleep to fall again. Someone had spoken his name. Martin blinked and stared at the doorway, wondering if it had been the boy? But no—he was dazed with sleep, most certainly Trip had not stirred. He never did.

But still, someone had spoken—

"*Martin.*"

Even before he turned he knew who would be there.

"*John.*"

The name was ice on his tongue.

He stood in front of the window, gazing outside. He was naked, as thin as when he had died; but somehow he no longer seemed emaciated. Light streamed over him, that strange milky white, and seemed to clothe him, filling the hollows of ribs and throat, his sunken cheeks and pitted eyes. A long moment passed, in which the figure continued to stare up at the sky, and Martin's dread grew—the only thing worse than a ghost would be a ghost that *ignored* you. But then the figure stirred, and turned.

"Martin," he whispered, smiling.

The smile undid Martin: it was so much John, it was what he had never thought to see again in all eternity. He began to sob, desperately wiping the tears from his eyes so that he could see him, so that he would miss none of it.

"Is it difficult, Martin?" The figure crossed the room to stand beside the bed. Pityingly, and yet there was something remote in its gaze, too. Martin gasped, trying to silence his weeping, then shuddered, thinking absurdly of Ebeneezer Scrooge and a voice intoning *They seek to interfere for good in human matters, but have lost the power forever*. "Martin?" the figure asked again. "Is it so very hard?"

Martin looked up, saw that within the hollow of its eyes something flickered that was not an eye. Hastily he lowered his gaze, to the figure's hands.

"It is—very hard," he said at last. He swallowed and forced himself to raise his head. "And you, John—is it—is it—"

The figure stared down at him, and for a moment the misty white light seemed to fall away, so that Martin was not looking upon a glowing creature but only a man, a man who stood in shadow. John tilted his head. His face grew gentle, and he stretched out his hand, as though to touch Martin's brow. But Martin felt nothing, not cold nor warmth nor even the faintest breath of movement. And he saw, too, that the hand cast no shadow.

"It's not so hard for us," said John, gently. "Because we remember, it's not so hard as it is for you—"

"You remember?" Martin seized on the words, crazily. "You *do* remember?"

"Oh, sure," answered John, nodding the way he always did, then grinning. "We remember. I remember—"

The grin spread as he opened his mouth, a glimpse there of more darkness, roots of teeth exposed like pilings. "*I remember you—*'"

He was singing, one of John's dopey old songs in John's sweet off-key voice, so clear and pure it made Martin's head ring.

> *There were three ravens sat on a tree,*
> *They were as black as they might be.*
> *The one of them said to his make,*
> *"Where shall we our breakfast take?"*

Martin began to cry again, out of love and terror, staring up into that light-struck face and laughing, too, in spite of it all; because he had always *hated* that song.

> *Down there came a fallow doe*
> *As great with young as she might go.*
> *And laid her down beside his head*
> *So that the maid knew her love was dead.*
> *She buried him before the prime,*
> *She was dead herself before evensong time.*
> *God send every gentleman*
> *Such hounds, such hawks, such a leman . . .*

The song ended. There was silence; then John's voice whispered, "Go with him. You won't lose your way, Martin. I'll find you . . ."

His words hung in the air, notes settling like dust into Martin's skin. He was weeping so hard now he couldn't see, had to close his eyes and clutch himself to keep from exploding into grief. When he opened them again the room was empty. The light had clouded from white to amber, lavender to indigo. A thin wind stirred across his skin. He sat up, mouth dry, fumbled for the bedside clock and saw that it was 5:00 A.M.

He put the clock down, blinking wearily, then for the first time saw an object in the middle of the floor. A small wooden box, its corners rounded from being handled over the years. With a cry Martin stumbled from bed. His bare feet skidded across the floor until he abruptly dropped to his knees, picked up the box, and cradled it in his hands—

"Oh John, John—"

—then opened the lid, his trembling fingers feeling the worn velvet within and what it protected, cool hard metal forming the apex of a triangle and the sharper edges of the mirror and glass filters, a slip of pale green paper with a message written in peacock ink. Martin lifted his head and raised his voice in disbelief.

"—*GOD!* John, how—"

He had lost it, it had been lost for, oh, five years now, since right before John's last illness, he had looked everywhere for it, here and in the house in San Francisco and in the *Wendameen*; because he had wanted to bury it with John, the present he had given Martin when they bought the boat for their seventeenth anniversary.

"—oh, John."

A sextant, glittering now in his hands, bronze tipped with amethyst where the light struck it, the little mirror sending out sparks as he tilted it this way and that, then clutched it to his chest and sobbed as though his heart would break.

For you, dearest Martin, for seventeen years
and a hundred more—
So you will always find your way.

After some minutes he got up, unsteadily, still clasping the sextant to his breast, and went into the room with the boy. Martin watched him breathe, Trip's chest rising and falling like a leaf stirred by a very soft wind. His yellow hair falling across his brow, spreading over the pillow like pollen; his face half-turned so that Martin could see his mouth barely parted like a child's, bit of a tooth behind his lower lip. Restless light played across his cheeks, indigo and orange, touched the cross on his breast so that it glowed. Martin moved closer, until he stood beside the bed, the boy outstretched behind him, the topography of desire. The light changed and Martin blinked, found that one hand hovered above the boy's face, near enough that Trip's breath pooled against his palm, near enough that his warmth was like burning. Martin closed his eyes, hard; fought down his arousal and took a step backward. Opened his eyes again, the boy still there, and desire: no, truly, it does not go away, they do not go away. His gaze shifted to the flickering square of window, the *Wendameen*'s curve upon its rough scaffold.

New York, Trip had said. *I think that's where she is. That's where I met her. New York*. Slowly Martin drew the sextant upward to his face, until he held it cupped beneath his chin. His stare remained fixed on the *Wendameen*.

We will go away, together.

The next day he began work on the boat in earnest. First clambering up the ladder and climbing down into the cockpit and then the companionway, to check the seams between planking. Looking for spots where the boards had shrunk and the light came through, replacing cotton caulking and running seam compound into the gaps. The boat had been up on jack stands for over two years now, but it had not dried out as badly as he had feared. He worked by the light of one of the *Wendameen's* kerosene lanterns, and lost himself in it as he had not done in ages; not in painting, not in anything. There, belowdecks, with the oily familiar smells of kerosene and salt and Callahan's Wax and the warm golden glow of varnished wood, all was just as it had always been, as it should be. It was exhausting, but somehow it enlivened him, too, because he could lose himself, lose the world around him. After three days he was sorry to turn to other work, but by then it had all come back to him, the hours and days of labor needed to keep a boat alive, and the cries of gulls above the bay.

He moved the ladder, climbed down, and walked around beneath, so that he could see to the hull and begin the task of repainting the entire boat. The *Wendameen* had a copper-sheathed bottom, which protected it from worms and rot; but it all still had to be scraped and sanded and primed. He spent hours in Mars Hill's old boathouse, scavenging half-empty cans of primer, scraping rust from tools and cleaning brushes with the turpentine he used for his paintings. Then came days of scraping, hands and fingers aching inside the heavy suede gloves, paint scales covering the ground beneath like gull droppings. Prising out a rotten plank and replacing it, the slow process of planing, honey-colored curls of wood and the smell of shellac in the salt air. Then fitting the new boards between the old, like setting a falsely bright new tooth. Then sanding it all, again and again, by hand, the widening gyre beneath his palm growing smoother and smoother still, until it was like milk, like silk, like skin. There is a love of wood as of other things that do not answer to our touch; entranced and exhausted, heedless of the fever that had begun to tear at him, Martin shaped the *Wendameen* into a boy.

When it came time to paint the exterior, Trip came down to help.

"I can do that," he said, cocking his head like a bird. "I used to help my uncle." A few yards away high tide lapped at the gravel. Trip bent and picked up a flat stone, expertly skipped it across a wave.

"Can you." Martin looked down from the ladder and smiled through his exhaustion. It was the first time the boy had spoken, without prompting, of something in his past. So: an uncle, then, and a boat. "Well, there's another ladder in the boathouse. Do you think you can get it by yourself? If you need help, just holler."

Trip dragged the ladder out. He looked a little better these last few weeks, not so thin, his hair growing out. Not great, but better, like someone fighting a long illness; like Martin himself. Though the odd translucence of Trip's skin remained; in the endless sunset he was sometimes hard to see, another trick of the light. He hauled up the rusted cans of paint and more ratty brushes and set to. Martin explained the color scheme: white hull and topside, magenta boot stripe, bulwark two shades of grey, like the breast and wings of a shearwater. Trip listened distractedly. He ran his finger along a seam and frowned, then gently freed a pine needle that had gotten mired in damp paint. Martin watched him, heart so full he felt dizzy. Trip with the intense scowl of a child laboring at something: paint, brushes, wood.

It took them two weeks. Every evening they had to set the cracked blue tarps on a wooden frame above the boat, in case of rain. Geese flew overhead, honking. There was the nightly confusion of phoebes and chickadees in the white pines by the boathouse, trying to decide if it was really time to roost. One afternoon

Martin walked up to the Beach Store, more exhausted than he could have imagined possible by the additional effort, and asked Doug to bring by a case of beer if and when they got some in. A few days later beer arrived. After that, Martin and Trip would sit on the ladders and each have two, sometimes talking, usually not. Watching amethyst-colored lightning play over the bay, the occasional passing of a white green-trimmed lobster boat; once the huge silhouette of a Russian factory ship, merging into the darkness of Blue Hill far away. In the extreme humidity it took a long time for the paint to dry, several days between coats, so they started on the interior. Cleaning out the bulkheads. Putting bunk cushions on deck to air, and the sails, all smelling of mildew but, happily, undamaged. Checking out the engine. Martin cannibalized furniture and machinery in the boathouse and cottage for screws, nails, shims. He collected unopened and nearly empty pints of oil, carefully cleaned old filters because there were no new ones, and finally went to the big old plastic gas tanks he had stored the diesel in over two years before.

"Shit," he said. "Water." So there was the task of getting water out of the fuel, and then filling the tank, and starting the engine in a cloud of foul smoke while Trip cheered, and then praying that when the time came, the engine would remember what it had to do.

"This is a beautiful boat, Martin," said Trip one afternoon. The *Wendameen* was almost ready, as ready as boats get, and they were having lunch in her shadow, eating fresh sweet mealy tomatoes from Diana's garden. Martin swallowed them all, even the rough nub where the stem had been. Trip fastidiously ate around the soft core as though it were an apple. He leaned happily against a jack stand, flushed and pearled with sweat, his blond hair capped by a red bandanna that had been John's, every inch of him speckled with white and red paint. His face was sunburned, which worried Martin a great deal; but Trip shrugged it off. "A *really* beautiful boat. You took good care of it."

"Not really."

"*Someone* did. Some cunnin', this boat." Trip's voice roughened easily into the broad northern accent, and he grinned. "Ayah. She'll do, Martin. She'll do."

Martin laughed. "She'll have to do pretty goddamn good, if we're going to get to New York before hurricane season."

Trip tossed his head back, staring at the sky. His eyes flashed a deeper blue, and for an instant Martin saw him lying on the beach, weeds snarled upon his breast, eyelids parting to reveal that same distant flame. "I never been sailing. Just once, over to Jonesport, when I was a kid. I threw up."

Martin smiled. "Yeah, well. I've thrown up, too." He gazed at Trip, his brow furrowing. "You sure you want to do this, Trip? I mean are you sure you're up to it? We could—we could wait a little while."

But it would not be a little while. It was September now: it would be eight or nine months of waiting out the long Maine winter, almost another year. The boy here for that long . . . Martin's heart pounded at the thought.

Trip shook his head. "Might as well go now," he said cheerfully; but Martin could hear what was underneath the brightness. *He wants to go. He knows and he wants to go . . .*

"Right," Martin said, finishing another tomato. He grimaced, his stomach thrashed inside him like a snake—that was what happened when he ate, these days—and thought how Trip never wondered how *he* was; never commented on how Martin looked flushed, pretended not to notice when he was sick in the middle of the night, said nothing when they stripped off their shirts to race into the cold water of the bay and Martin stood there, ribs like the fingers of an immense hand pushing out from within his chest.

He's afraid, thought Martin. But also perhaps he was being polite, the way Mainers were when they were uncomfortable, or embarrassed, or just plain shy. Talking to you with eyes averted, you right there beside them and them focusing on you several feet away in front of the woodstove. *Ayah, that boy Trip. Some cunnin'.*

"Well," Martin said, wiping his hands on filthy paint-spattered khakis. "Let's get going, then."

That night he got the charts out, and the Coast Guard light list, and the Coast Pilots showing the Atlantic from Eastport to Cape Cod, Cape Cod southeast to King's Point.

All hopelessly out-of-date—the most recent one read 1988—but there was nothing to be done, except maybe visit the Graffams and see if they had anything to offer in the way of charts and advice. They piled the charts on the scarred dining-room table, and the faded pilots, stiff and cumbersome from age and water. Trip was enthralled, and spent an hour exclaiming over the chart that showed Moody's Island, but Martin was puzzling over something else.

"What is it?" Trip finally asked, almost knocking a glass of water on Eel Head.

"Hmmm? Oh, well . . ." Martin sighed and leaned back so that the front of his Windsor chair lifted from the floor. "Well, I'm just wondering, how are we going to get the boat into the water?"

Trip gaped, eyes wide. "Holy cow! I never even thought—how *are* we going to get it into the water?"

Martin stared thoughtfully at the pile of charts. "Well, in the olden days we could've just gotten Allen Drinkwater to come over with a flatbed and a lift, or someone from Belfast with a big hydraulic trailer."

"Do they still do that?"

Martin laughed. "I doubt it. There's no gas for the trucks, for one. Plus we could never afford it, even if there *was* gas."

Trip looked stricken. "But then—what are we going to do?"

"Well, in the *really* olden days, to launch a boat you'd have to build a launching ways. Like a wooden ramp, down to the water. And you'd have to build a wooden cradle around the boat, and then you'd let it go, so it'd go down onto the skids and kind of slide into the water at high tide."

"*Jeez.*" Trip's expression went from stricken to sheer disbelief. "It *slides* into the water?"

Martin shook his head. His chair bumped back down on all four legs. "No, really—we saw it once, at the Rockport Apprenticeshop. They were launching a Friendship sloop they'd built for someone. You make this long ramp, and you grease the boards up. They used vegetables—"

"*Vegetables?*"

"I swear to God." Martin laughed even harder at the memory. "They used lard, and vegetables—pumpkins, squash. All those zucchini you never want to eat. And some Shell gear lube, but we don't have enough of that. You build the ways at a gentle enough slope, the boat can pretty much launch itself. They had about a hundred people there, apprentices and people watching, and if it started moving too fast, they threw sand on the skids, to slow it down."

"A *hundred people*!? But—"

"But you could do it," Martin said softly, thought-fully, staring beyond Trip to the window that framed the *Wendameen*, resplendent in its new paint beneath a glowering sky, "if you had crowbars, and were really, really careful, and took it slow, and if the ways was done right—you could do it, I think, with two."

And that's how they did it; though first they had to build the launching ways. Mrs. Grose, of course, came to watch (she had been there all along, on her decrepit porch with her pug, occasionally wandering over into the *Wendameen*'s shadow to offer advice on avoiding paint drips, and foul weather), and Doug from the Beach Store and a few of his cronies, who donated some more beer and valuable scrap lumber. The rest of the wood came from warped boards and planks and plywood stored beneath the boathouse, augmented by birch trees that Martin had Trip take down, Martin himself being too weak to handle an ax. One of the Graffams even heard about Martin's plan, and dropped by one windy morning to inspect the ways.

"Not too bad, there," he pronounced, ducking his head to light a hand-rolled cigarette, "but you're going to have t'weight that cradle, else it ain't going to fall away when you get her into the water."

"I hadn't thought of that," Martin said glumly, and Dick Graffam's look told him that's about what *he* would've expected, someone from away trying to launch a twenty-six-foot gaff cutter in hurricane season and sail down to New York City.

So then Martin had to figure out what to weight the cradle with. Lead is what you'd use, if you had it; but who had lead in their summer bungalow? He kicked around for most of the morning after Graffam left, bad-tempered and almost shaking with fatigue. A raw wind was blowing from the southwest, a tropical storm brewing somewhere, probably. Martin swore and paced down the beach, the hood of his anorak flapping back from his face so that the spray stung his cheeks. The sheer lunacy of his plan had all been there in Graffam's look. It was the first week of October, the butt end of the season even for experienced sailors, of which Martin was not one. In the best of times, you wouldn't get underway this late.

And this was, in every possible way that Martin could imagine, *not* the best of times. But it was done, the boat was done, and the launching ways would be completed soon. He slid his hand into the pocket of his anorak, felt the smooth wooden box that he carried always, now. A voice stirred in his head like a breeze from a warmer place.

"Go with him. You won't lose your way, Martin. I'll find you . . ."

His hand tightened around the sextant's box, and he looked out to sea with something like dread. Something like resignation, and relief. Knowing, for the first time, and with absolute certainty, that he would not be coming back.

CHAPTER TWELVE

The Pyramid Meets the Eye

The power had been down for almost a month, autumn skidding into winter, October so fast Jack would have missed it, save for Marzana's swelling stomach. November now an uneasily ending dream of lurid yellow skies, bare trees and smell of burning and a harsh northeast wind that whistled without cease and tore the shingles from Lazyland's gables. He felt well these days, thin but strong, untroubled by coughs or fevers, though his eyesight did blur sometimes, there was always that sense of things half-seen, motes of living matter swimming across his cornea. He received a courier-delivered postcard and a book from Emma, telling him that she had sent the odd samples off to several labs for identification. One sample had been lost, but she hoped to hear about the other, someday, soon, Love &tc., Dr. Duck. That had been in early October; he had no news since from either Emma or Jule. Whatever the peculiar granular encrustations had been, they seemed to clear up by November. He checked his throat and eyes obsessively, several times a day, scraping at the inside of his mouth so much he had a raw spot there that took a while to heal. But it did heal, and the crystalline matter did disappear. One day it was just gone and never recurred. Jack chalked it up to the extra vitamins Emma had left, and was relieved.

A stoic sort of calm claimed Lazyland as winter approached. The weather was awful, the air smoke-filled when not thick with greasy rain. Jack spent most of his time indoors, reading by lamplight in his grandfather's study, or walking around the mansion flicking electrical switches and lifting telephone receivers as apprehensively as he examined his throat and eyes. It was like an endless restless rainy afternoon, unrelieved by sun or weather reports promising a break in the clouds. One day he found a crop of tiny orange mushrooms growing along the edge of one of the silk Chinese carpets. After that he added a Fungus Alert to his list of things to watch for on his incessant rambles around the house.

He took to visiting the girl each morning, on his way downstairs, and again at night on his way to bed. Rapping very softly at the door to her room, because sometimes she slept later than he did, and it was important (his grandmother and Mrs. Iverson reminded him sternly, nightly, giving him cups of chamomile tea to carry precariously up to her bed), *VERY* Important, that an Expectant Mother get enough rest. He wondered, often, how it was babies *had* been born all these years, without him; without the entire world going on leave to take care of all those mothers. The book Emma had sent was a worn paperback guide to the oft-charted (but never quite colonized because the terrain shifted so, and so suddenly) territories of pregnancy. Jack read it at night, in bed, tracking week by week the body's journey into this terra infirma, bemused and occasionally awed by what could be found there—you can do THAT? With *THAT*? Then next morning, perched at the end of Marz's four-poster, chipped mug of ersatz coffee for him, soup bowl of oatmeal and soy powder for her, reading the pertinent sections aloud and thinking how this wasn't so strange, really, it was a little bit like traveling in Thailand or rural Italy with Leonard, learning about the monasteries the day before a visit, trying not to be grossed out by the local customs. Like, Marz's gums bled easily, because there was so much more blood now, everywhere inside her. And her hair grew longer and thicker, because of the protein supplements (also courtesy of Emma). Her pale peaked face grew rounder, and pink, though the rest of her remained thin, save of course her belly, which seemed absolutely enormous.

"Feel it?" She pulled up her flannel nightdress, grabbed his hand and put it on her stomach. "Ow, you're *cold*, Jack!"

"Sorry," he smiled. "Cold hands, warm heart; dirty feet, no sweetheart."

She laughed; that, too, was new. "Can you tell? It has the hiccups."

Her stomach distending grotesquely as the baby kicked, Jack resisting the urge to say this reminded him of that scene in *Alien*. Moving his fingers across the taut bulge until they picked up an arrhythmic tap-tap. How could it have the hiccups, when it couldn't even breathe?

Biology was amazing.

Toward the end of the month they had a Thanksgiving celebration, on what Jack was pretty sure would have been Thanksgiving Day. No turkey, but some Italian sausages he had gotten from Delmonico's in October, and saved for a special occasion. Sausage sputtering dangerously on the Coleman stove while Jack poked at them with a long-handled fork, grease flying everywhere and the occasional dramatic burst of flame. Then sitting down to dinner at the long formal dining-room table beneath the Viennese crystal chandelier, unlit but its prisms twinkling magnificently in the glow of myriad candles and Coleman lanterns. Cut-glass bowls of pickles, olives, even some canned jellied cranberry sauce.

"It's beautiful, dear," Keeley murmured, as Jack

helped her into her armchair. The four of them sat at one end of the table, with Keeley at its head. "Just beautiful."

He smiled, pondering Thanksgivings past. House abrim with cousins, priests smoking cigarettes in his grandfather's study, Captain Kangaroo in the living room broadcasting live from the Macy's parade. His brother Dennis sending an arrow through the center of a painting by a member of the Hudson River School, and never being punished for it. Cyclopean heaps of mashed potatoes and turnips and green beans, turkey the size of a shoat, whiskey glinting in crystal tumblers like chunks of topaz; and, best of all, the knowledge that this was just the beginning, the front door nudging open upon the vast sparkling treasure-house that was the Christmas season, then.

Today there were sausages, on a too-big platter. They were more highly seasoned than Marz would have liked. She did not complain, but she did grimace, like an exotic monkey with her new thick fringe of bright hair, and then proceeded to eat without stopping for a quarter hour. There was whole-wheat rotini from Emma's hoard, with dried basil, and canned tomatoes, and some nasty canned spinach which Jack had tried to save with garlic salt, which nobody ate. A gruesome-looking apple pudding from Emma's dried apples, which tasted marvelous, and which everyone did eat. Jack put a two-thirds-full bottle of Glenlivet on the table. He poured a half inch for Keeley, who sipped it slowly throughout the meal, and proceeded to drink most of the rest himself. Afterward, a little wobbly in the head, he helped Mrs. Iverson with the dishes, while Keeley and Marz retired upstairs for late-afternoon naps.

"Not like it used to be," Mrs. Iverson sighed, wiping greasy water from a plate with a linen rag. "Your grandfather . . . I think, *What* would he have thought of all this—"

She lifted her head to gaze out the kitchen window. Beyond the slope of leafless trees the Hudson was marbled black and glowing orange, like the interior of a forge. The western horizon shared this sunset aspect, and there was the occasional spatter of rain against the windowpanes, the bite of a cold draft making its way through the walls. These—along with the smells of fresh cooking, the growing stack of cleaned dishes, the smell of Scotch—made for one of those rare moments when chronology and atmospheric effects conspired to make everything seem not all that unchanged: it really *could* be Thanksgiving Day.

"He would have thought it was the end of the world," said Jack. In fact his grandfather probably wouldn't have thought that at all. But Jack did, because of the hiemal light, at once brilliant and melancholy and ominous. It reminded him of a January afternoon with Leonard, when they were both seventeen. Side by side on the floor of an empty classroom at Saint Bartholomew's, an hour or so after fucking in a closet; watching a blazing sunset fall through blackened tree limbs to ignite the windows. The sight had filled Jack with both exhilaration and dread, confused as it was with sexual fever and its aftermath, the sense of things burning, dangerously, somewhere just out of sight. Since then winter sunsets always moved him thus, a touch of terror amidst the glory. He was surprised, now, to realize he had not felt this way in some time— because there had been no real sunsets, no real winter, for over two years; and because he had grown accustomed to that soft hem of terror brushing against him daily.

". . . think I would ever live this long," Mrs. Iverson was ending with a sigh.

Jack looked up guiltily. "Oh, please don't say that."

The housekeeper shook her head and moved a stack of plates from counter to cupboard. "Doesn't matter what I say." She turned and smiled at his worried expression, placed a hand still damp with soapsuds on his. "Oh now, Jackie, don't you go looking like you just got the bad news about Santa Claus! That was a lovely meal you put together—you saw how Mary Anne ate, and your grandmother, too! You're a good boy, Jackie. Go on now, I'll finish up—"

She shooed him out of the kitchen. He went, still feeling guilty—men never seemed to stick around until every last dish was done, no matter how good their intentions—but grateful to have some time alone. Like all Thanksgivings, it had been *long*. The shadows and sense of repleteness made it feel late, but a consensus of Lazyland's clocks seemed to agree that it was only around four. He wandered through the dining room, his grandfather's study, living room, then out into the entry, feeling lost and intensely melancholy: little Jackie left alone while all the grown-ups retired elsewhere for cigarettes and more Scotch. He finally settled into the Stickley chair beneath the grandfather clock, leaned his elbows on the battered Stickley table, and stared mournfully at the telephone. He lifted the receiver. The line was dead.

"Happy fucking Thanksgiving," he said drunkenly, and dropped it back in place.

Well (he thought, with mild surprise); he was drunk, then. Notwithstanding his imbroglio with Jule some months earlier, it was very odd for Jack to be drunk. Bad for the immune system, bad for the family—how could Keeley depend on him, drunk?—bad for the household's limited supply of hooch. Bad for Jack, who had never been able to process alcohol well, and whose hangovers were more legendary than his binges. He already felt headachy, his melancholy quickly giving way to depression, the inevitable holiday fallout. He gave a loud sigh, and went upstairs.

On the second-floor landing he paused. Loud snoring came from behind the two doors shut catty-corner to each other, his grandmother's room and Marz's. Jack smiled and shook his head: so much noise from two such little people. Three, if you counted the baby. The cello-shaped grandmother clock ticked noisily but uselessly. Its hands had fallen off a year ago, and still lay upon the mahogany table where Jack had set them. From the back steps behind the linen closet he heard Mrs. Iverson exclaiming to herself, and then her heavy tread as she began to climb. He turned and hurried up the curving stairway to the third floor, taking the steps two at a time and almost noiselessly, being careful to chuck the moth-eaten caribou under the chin as he went past.

He went into his bedroom, but he didn't want to go to bed. Darkness was falling quickly through the old house, the night not spangled as it usually was but tenebrous, low heavy clouds in the west streaked with vermilion. Jack found matches and lit the heavy old square lantern. Its brass fittings reflected a reassuring glow as he went to his night table and squirted some Fusax beneath his tongue, chased it with stale water from a plastic tumbler. For several minutes he sat at the edge of the bed, watching sheaves of light ripple across the windows, black and scarlet and silvery grey. The light oppressed him, made him think of Good Friday, the altar stripped of everything save shadows and candles guttering in red glass holders. It was all like that now, he thought, disquieted; seeing the world without her makeup, the bride stripped bare, was not a pretty sight. He shivered, and held his hands close to the lantern. Wind tore at the shingles, a rattle of rain or hail swept across the roof. From somewhere down near the river echoed cachectic laughter, the explosive roaring of an engine that grew suddenly, ominously silent. Jack clenched his jaws together and forced his hands not to tremble. A sense of something terrible about to happen swept over him, certain as the rain; but what was to be done, what could be done? There was no one to call for help, no one to wake; nothing to do but ride it out.

His mother had always said, No matter how bad things are, they will look better in the morning. But now morning never came. The glimmering that bathed the globe in eternal eventide had stolen the promise of dawn. He could only take a deep breath and wait for the horror to pass.

It did, but slowly. He was not conscious of having shut his eyes, but it seemed he must have—when he blinked and focused them once more, the room had changed. The wind had died. A sharp, foul smell clung to the air, as of burned hair or feathers, a horrible smell and no draft to disperse it. And the light had shifted. It was no longer black and scarlet but a lambent glaring red, the deep lurid red of blood, the reddest red he had ever seen, and so brilliant it cast no shadows. At his fingertips the brass lamp could barely be discerned, a faint cross-hatching showing where its glass walls still held a captive flame. It was like staring at the world through an infrared lens. He gasped, jerking backward on the bed, and nearly knocked the lantern to the floor. When he grabbed at it he burned his hand.

"Oh, *fuck*—"

He stumbled to his feet, nearly blinded by the sanguinary light, found the night table and shoved the lantern there; then, clutching his hurt hand, he lurched to the window. "Fucking A," he whispered.

The sky was in flames. Not clouds that resembled flames, not the sunset archipelago with rosy shores, but *fire*, huge explosive gouts of fire stretching from horizon to horizon, roiling and expanding as though they would devour the entire sky. He watched in horror, looked down but saw nothing—no trees, no earth, not even the walls of the house beneath him. Only a vast cauldron of molten light, at once ablaze and darkly livid, and seething like some monstrous bacillus. The fervent light tore at his eyes, made them stream and burn. He turned from the window, one arm thrown across his face, and staggered to the door. He had to grope his way, he could make out nothing in the dreadful red glare. Words came to him, something he had heard or read long ago—*the cunning livery of hell*. He cried aloud, crashing against the doorframe and clutching the curved banister as he all but fell downstairs, blinded.

"Grandmother! Grandmother—"

He stumbled into Keeley's room. The heavy jacquard curtains were drawn, as always. They seemed to filter out some of the stammeled light, so that he could see the headboard of his grandmother's old Breton bed, and his startled grandmother sitting up in it, still wearing her fisherman's sweater and woolen skirt, a sleep mask pushed up over her white curls.

"Jack! What is it—"

"The fire! Are you all right—" He fell, gasping, onto the heaped comforters beside her. "Are you—"

"*Fire?*" cried Keeley. She threw her blankets aside and started to climb from the bed, slapping at Jack's hand when he tried to stop her. "Where, where—"

"Grandmother, don't! Please—"

Someone appeared in the doorway: the blond girl, disheveled in an ugly plaid tunic. She yawned and shook her head, staring at Jack curiously through sleep-slit eyes. "Fire? There's no fire. What, you have a dream or something?"

"A dream?" He shook his head. "No, I . . ."

His voice trailed off as he realized he could see her, quite plainly; and see his grandmother, and the pattern of roses on the pale wool rug, and even the ghostly vines and leaves woven into the moss- green drapery that covered the windows.

"There was a fire." He cleared his throat, then repeated himself. "Outside. There was a fire."

Marz walked into the room, bare feet padding on the thick carpet, arms crossed above her waxing belly. Her pointed little chin was defiantly outthrust as she went to the window and fiddled there for a moment until she found a heavy sateen cord. She yanked on it. The curtains rippled but did not move. Yanked again, harder this time, until with a tearing sound the drapes moved across one side of the wall, revealing half a window.

"You were *dreaming*," she said triumphantly. "*See?*"

The window framed the same view as his own did— autumnal chiaroscuro of dark trees, carriage house, sloping lawn, sluggish river. All quite visible now, untouched by any flames save a few bright brief flashes from the evening sky, silvery purple and acid green.

"No," Jack said under his breath, but the girl had already crawled into bed with Keeley, grinning.

"*I* have dreams like that, sometimes." Marz shivered, and Keeley draped a blanket over her thin shoulders. "Like I'll see the sky at night, there'll be words written up on the sky, but I can't understand them. And bridges—I have this dream, a lot, this dream about a bridge . . ."

Jack walked to the window and looked out. She was right, there were no fires. He swore softly, ran a hand across his forehead, rubbed his eyes.

Jesus fuck, it seemed so real.

"I never remember my dreams," Keeley said in her wavering voice. "Not anymore. Your father, he used to have dreams. And nightmares . . ."

Jack turned, thinking she spoke to him. But the way Keeley smiled at Marzana, the way her hand traced the headboard's carven whorls—as though another palm moved there beneath her own—told him that she spoke to the girl. That she was seeing the girl, again, as Mary Anne. *Your father* was his grandfather.

". . . one time *he* thought the hotel was on fire! He jumped up, and—"

Lightning exploded within the room. Jack cried out, and Marzana; but Keeley stared transfixed at the ceiling, where the lightning stayed, trapped within the crystal trumpets of an Art Nouveau ceiling lamp.

"The power!" shrieked Marz. *"The power's on!"*

She flung herself from the bed and raced across the room, flicking the light switch on and off. "It's on, it's on!"

"Stop!" Jack yelled. "You'll blow the bulb—"

But Marz was already gone, stampeding to her own room, where he could hear the sudden joyful blare of a radio.

"—LAST DAYS! THREE DAYS ONLY!—"

"Good Lord, what's this—oh look, Keeley darling, power's on!" Mrs. Iverson tottered onto the landing. "Good heavens, tell that girl to be *quiet*! Quick, Jack, help me bring the laundry down. Mary Anne! You help, too, bring those baby things we got out—"

They ran from floor to floor, the girl puffing and swearing as she gathered sheets and a plastic basket heaped with yellowed infant clothes, Jack loping past her with armfuls of shirts, khaki pants, mismatched socks, Keeley's warm L.L. Bean jumpers and matching turtlenecks. In the laundry room Mrs. Iverson disappeared behind piles of clothes, and the Kenmore washer gushed and groaned as cold water poured through the pipes. Marz panted back upstairs and went from room to room turning on lights, looking for radios to crank up, checking the answering machine.

"STOP!" shouted Jack from the basement. "You'll BLOW a FUSE!" Which had happened more than once; they were low on fuses, too. "MARZANA!"

When he got back to the first floor he found her in the living room, remote in hand, staring rapturously at the TV. "This is so fucking *great*," she announced, beaming. "We can, like, watch *Thanksgiving specials*."

He laughed. All his fear and horror was gone, utterly: as though it *had* been a dream. "Yeah! See if *King Kong* is on—"

He took the remote from her and began flashing through channels.

"Too fast!" Marz yelped indignantly, and grabbed it back. She rocked on her heels in excitement, squealing when the screen showed game shows, mud slides, music videos, groaning at the more numerous bursts of static where stations had been, once. "Man, this *sucks*. This is supposed to be *GUMBY* . . ."

He left her and went out to the carriage house. He booted up his computer, looked for messages there and on the answering machine and fax. There was an update on the GFI New Year's celebration, dated some weeks ago, and a letter from Leonard, photographing fish die-outs and human birth defects in someplace called Komsomolsk-na-Amure.

And there was a note from Larry Muso.

Dear Jack,

I have attempted to be in touch once or twice, offering my congratulations upon our pending acquisition of The

Gaudy Book. But my messages came back, so I will assume you are experiencing some problems there at your house Lazyland. I hope they will have improved by the time you get this.

I understand that a GFI courier tagged you this summer and that you plan to be at the Big Party. Can we get together beforehand? They are expecting a huge number of people, and in any case I am committed to attending upon our Chairman at dinner. But I would very much like to meet with you, for drinks or perhaps breakfast, depending upon how early you are able to make the transport to the Pyramid. My recommendation (I was at Woodstock III) would be that you take advantage of GFI's services and arrive as early as possible, to avoid the inevitable tie-ups that will occur as the day progresses. As communication is so difficult these days, perhaps I might suggest a meeting-spot at the gala grounds, and at your convenience you could respond if that would suit you? There will be a tent called Electric Avenue, sponsored by the AT&T/IBM joint venture, which might be of interest to you. I can arrange to be there for part of the morning (depending, of course, upon Mr. Tatsumi's plans for me), and we could enjoy a meal together, which I would like very much. If you are able to let me know of your willingness to do this, I would be very glad to oblige.

I trust that all is well with you and your grandmother, and that your house has not been affected by the severe storms in New York.

With Very Warm Regards,
Larry Muso

Jack read the message several times, surprised to feel his face growing hot as he did so. He had not thought of either Larry Muso or the Big Party for some time, and had in fact never seriously considered that he would go, despite the invisible gryphon etched onto his right palm. It all seemed just Too Much, too Dance-Band-On-The-Titanic, too Last Big Fling: too Suppose They Gave An Apocalypse And *Everybody* Came?

And how could he even consider leaving Keeley or Mrs. Iverson, not to mention Marzana, whose baby was due right about then?

I would very much like to meet with you, for drinks or perhaps breakfast . . .

But then Larry Muso's high cheekbones and darkly lustrous eyes came back to him, the feathery touch of his hair as it grazed Jack's cheek. He felt a shaft of unexpected desire; his cock stirred and he shut his eyes, lingering for a moment upon the memory of that brief meeting.

I was so fucking rude, he thought, and transposed the thought into a bit of postcoital reverie, him lying beside that slight figure, stroking that hair: *I was so fucking rude to you, why was I so rude?*

His breath caught in his throat. He opened his eyes upon the screen bright before him—it could go black at any moment, New Year's was scarcely more than a month away, he could lose it all just like that. Quickly he typed a reply—

Dear Larry,

I'd be delighted to meet you at Electric Avenue, sometime the morning of the 31st. I haven't heard anything more from GFI about transportation, so I really have no idea how or when (or even *if*) I could be there. But count me in.

Best,
Jack Finnegan

There. He read the message three or four times, ago-
nizing over whether he should say more, or less.
Feeling, too, that it was highly improbable, almost
impossible, in fact, that he would actually go through
with something so insane, leave Lazyland and attend
some corporate rout, just to meet someone he didn't
know for breakfast at the millennium.

Still, he thought—and he pressed the key that
would send the message, that *did* send the message,
assuming there was someone out there in left field to
catch it—*you never can tell.*

Afterward he checked the fax to make sure it had
enough paper. He rewound the answering machine tape,
changed a lightbulb, listened to a few minutes of a
Philip Glass CD: feeding the animals before he left them
again. He straightened a few things on the walls—his
father's law degree, one of Leonard's prints, his aunt
Mary Anne Finnegan's sixth-grade picture.

That reminded him of something. He went to a
bookshelf and found a bunch of family photo albums
from the sixties and seventies. Bleached-out pictures
from his uncle Peter's stint in Vietnam. Pictures of his
own parents' wedding, some of them nibbled by mice;
photos of Jack and his siblings, looking very Brady
Bunch in polyester stripes and solids, Twister in the rec
room. A prom picture of Jack with Denise Bartels.
Christmas trees.

But that was the wrong album. He put it back,
frowning, and withdrew another, bound in plastic with
curling daisy decals all over it. He settled onto the floor
and opened it gingerly. Most of the photos inside had
fallen out of the plastic sleeves, or never been put in
properly. Despite his care photos jumped all over him,
like the deck of cards attacking Alice. He muttered
curses and sorted them out, black-and-white Polaroids

with scalloped edges, overexposed color prints with dates carefully printed on the bottom: November 1967. December 1967. January 1968. March 1968.

They were pictures of Mary Anne in California. Mary Anne at the San Diego Zoo, wearing a floppy yellow cotton hat. Mary Anne at Big Sur. Mary Anne at the corner of Haight and Ashbury, wearing a hideous green velvet blouse and pink miniskirt, eyes hidden behind immense Day-Glo sunglasses, no doubt imagining herself the *eidos* of hippie cool but looking frighteningly young: she really hadn't been that much older than Marz.

But there was no other resemblance that Jack could see. Mary Anne was tall, with Keeley's delicate features but her father's big bones; snub-nosed, freckled, her long straight blond hair inclining to wheat rather than Marz's gossamer. He rifled through more pictures, stopping to insert some of the better ones into the perforated pages. Except for a single photo of Mary Anne with two older-looking girls in a forest, she was always alone. So who had taken the photos? Stoned strangers? Manson-Family boyfriend? He frowned, then, turning a page, came upon a cache of small color snapshots all set at the Golden Gate Bridge.

"Huh."

He laid them out upon the floor in front of him, slowly and thoughtfully, as though setting up a Tarot reading. But all the cards showed the same Significator, which in Mary Anne's case would be The Page of Cups—

A fair, pleasing, somewhat effeminate page—one impelled to render service and with whom the Querent will be connected—of studious and intent aspect, contemplates a fish rising from a cup to look at him. It is the picture of a mind taking form.

The photos showed Mary Anne posing antically with the bridge in the background, its spires rising dramatically from a golden mist. She wore a bubble-gum-pink plastic raincoat, matching rain hat, and white go-go boots, and held a bunch of purple flowers. Jack smiled: she was aping fashion spreads of the time, those silly Richard Lesterish displays of leggy models making like Egyptian wall paintings, Edie Sedgwick poised for flight atop a leather elephant. Only Mary Anne's pixie face was far too animated to pass for fashion, in spite of chalky lipstick and spidery eyelashes and an impressive pair of fishnet-clad legs. In this, too, she was unlike Marz, whose spells of sullen passivity drove Jack crazy.

And yet—and yet there *was* something there. He picked up one of the pictures and examined it closely, brow furrowed. It was a close-up of Mary Anne's face, very slightly out of focus. She pressed the flowers close against her chin, the twilight border of lilacs and grape hyacinths contrasting with her milk white skin and golden hair. Her eyes were very wide, round childlike eyes as opposed to Marz's narrow and rather sly gaze. The pupils were tiny, the irises a deep blue-violet with tiny radiating lines of yellow: one of the lilac blossoms might have fallen into her face, as into a pool.

She must have been stoned out of her mind, he thought, and felt chilled. *Who took the photos? Who was with her?*

The longer he stared at the photo, the more its unfocused quality seemed to emanate from her eyes: their gaze distant but not the least bit dreamy, and suffused with that eerie acid clarity he suddenly remembered all too well: seeing the subtle shifting patterns within one's own hands, the staggering urgency of a million cells suddenly revealed to him, the revelation that his body was a hive and had always been so.

He realized—with a shock close to pain, and fear—

that he had glimpsed that same expression on Marz's face. Not once, but often. A look as though she were seeing the multitude within him; as though she had seen a ghost.

Or been one.

"No."

He spoke aloud, and hastily began rearranging the photos in front of him, as though that might change the way he felt. A tide of unreasoning dread swept over him. It was one thing to have deliriums brought on by illness, bad dreams of his grandfather and skeletons dancing on the lawn; quite another to consider even momentarily that Lazyland was being visited by the revenant of his long-lost aunt. An old song rang through his head, one of Leonard's favorites—

Ain't you never seen a disembodied soul before?

"No," he repeated.

He glanced at the pictures one last time, then quickly put them into a little pile and stuck them back in the album. He flipped through the remaining pages, barely glancing at what was there—a few more scratched Polaroids, some photos of an empty store-front.

And then, at the very end of the album, he found a small stained envelope stuck to the back cover. It was addressed in blue ballpoint ink, in the same handwriting he recognized from the back of the photographs. But here the penmanship was definitely worse, stoned or drunken scrawl rather than that carefully looped Palmer hand.

Mr. and Mrs. James F. Finnegan
109 Hudson Terrace
Yonkers, N.Y. 10701

For a minute he just sat there holding it, a solid, terrible weight in his hand. The postmark read San Francisco, April 17, 1968. He drew the envelope to his face and inhaled, caught the faintest spicy-sweet breath of incense; then turned it over, several times, before opening it. There was no return address.

Dear Mom and Dad,
   Theres a bridge, lots of people are going over the Golden Bridge. I <u>love you love you</u> SO Much! <u>Please</u> don't <u>worry</u>.
I heard BELLS
I LOVE YOU!

Mary Anne

And beneath the signature, in uneven block letters:

There is someone here

He read it two, three, five times. Finally, heart pounding, he placed the letter and the envelope on the floor and went back through the photos, checking dates where there were any. Nothing was marked later than March 1968. He pressed one hand above his heart and shuddered, thinking back to when he had found the girl in the garden, beneath the hydrangeas. Sometime in April; it would be impossible for him to remember just when.

And when had Mary Anne disappeared? He could vaguely recall that it had been summer, he and his brothers fighting over the porch swing while strained grown-up voices spoke elsewhere, out of sight on the porch, while the scent of charcoal billowed up from the lawn. Nothing had ever been found of her, no clothes, no body washed up under the bridge, nothing. As an adult, his sister had said once at another family cookout, *she* thought Mary Anne had gone out there and gotten pregnant and killed herself, rather than face her parents. He had never asked his grandmother if there was a putative date for Mary Anne's death; never asked his father, or anyone else.

He wouldn't now, either.

He put it all away, carefully but quickly. The letter last of all, pressed between transparent plastic membranes like something on a medical slide. He replaced the album on its shelf, shut down his computer, and left. Halfway up the drive to the main house he stopped, staring up at its uncountable windows, oriels and dormers and bays and arches all glowing like stained glass in the discordant light. Behind one of them a shadow moved, up and down, up and down, as though signaling him—

There is someone here.

A few minutes later he blinked to be back inside Lazyland, the house's usual dark silence laid siege by electric bulbs, rumble-thump of washing machine and dryer, water pounding through the pipes, cheerful red lights glowing on the answering machine and coffeemaker and microwave.

And music: the television turned up so loud to accommodate a music video that Jack winced and clapped his hands to his head.

"Marz!" he shouted, striding into the living room and punching the volume control. "TURN IT DOWN!" Then, at Marz's outraged look, "Jesus Christ, it's so distorted, how can you even *hear* it?"

She glowered, which was reassuring—surely ghosts didn't slouch in the middle of the living-room floor and scowl when you turned the TV down.

"There," Jack went on, and regarded the screen with what he hoped was an acceptable level of adult interest. "Now at least you can hear what they're saying."

"It's a fucking commercial," said Marz in a venomous tone; her accent made it into *a focking commairshell*. "Who *gives* a fuck what they're saying?"

"Then you certainly don't need it turned all the way up, do you?" Jack gave her a deliberately prissy smile, which Marz ignored. "Where's Grandmother and Mrs. Iverson?"

"Kitchen." Marz leaned back against a pillow, her gaze fixed on the television.

Jack frowned. "You comfortable like that?"

Marz twiddled her hair and stared at the screen. He repeated the question.

"Huh? Oh. Yeah."

He stood there for another minute, watching her watch TV, a kaleidoscopically animated commercial for some kind of soft drink. It was amazing—miraculous, almost—how quickly the world reclaimed its commonplace aspect, if only you could turn the TV on. All the friendly backscatter that it generated, that sense of being part of something Big and Colorful and Exciting . . .

"Let's see what's on Public Television," he suggested.

"No!" Marz shrieked, and clutched the remote to her huge belly.

Jack rolled his eyes. "Just joking."

The commercial segued almost indistinguishably into the music station's corporate ID. Marz fidgeted, bumping her heels against the floor. Jack noticed that her socks did not match. When he glanced at the TV again it showed a swirling background of green and purple and gold, violently redolent of the sky outside. Across the bottom of the screen letters flowed, formed of varicolored smoke.

"Enticing magicians are performing; fear the beguiling, hypnotizing phantoms of the Kali Yuga. Enticing magicians are performing; fear the beguiling, hypnotizing phantoms of the Kali Yuga. Enticing magicians are performing . . ."

A woman's voice began repeating the words. An accented voice, eerily affectless and breathy, as though it had been generated by a computer; like one of those voices you got on the phone during the rare periods it worked, warning you to expect extensive difficulties and delays in placing your call. Very low, ominous music began to creep from the TV: gamelans and drums, a growing crescendo of guitar feedback. Within the garish whorls of color a tiny object appeared. A golden pyramid beset by rays of light and spinning like a pinwheel until it was large enough to fill the screen. Something about the image nagged at Jack's memory, but before he could place it the pyramid was gone. Instead a huge and glittering eye stared out from the television, blinked so that a tarantula fringe of lashes swept across its sky-blue iris, then wheeled back to become fixed like a gem within the face of a radiantly beautiful young man.

"Ah," gasped Jack, at the boy but also because he suddenly recognized the music. "It's that *song* . . ."

"I possess the keys of hell and death," the young man sang. *"I will give you the morning star. The end of the end. The end of the end . . ."*

He was dressed like a temple dancer, more like a woman than a man. Face ash white, lips and eyes outlined in scarlet, his blond hair all but hidden beneath a pagodalike headdress. His clothes were heavy with jewels and long fringes of brocade. Flowering vines swept quick as rain across his body as he swayed and spun, crouched and leapt across what seemed a vertiginous height. Beneath his unshod feet clouds and sea churned like dust, and the ragged peaks of mountains.

Jack watched raptly. There was something at once eerie, yet self-consciously hyperbolic, about the dancing figure which was at odds with the doomy music— *that* was merely (though gorgeously) anthemic, an irresistible pop coda to the century.

But the dancing boy—he reminded Jack of the Hindi films Leonard dragged him to when they were in Bombay in the late seventies and early eighties, bizarre epics where blue-skinned actors played gods who raped and then embraced weeping ecstatic women, only to be interrupted by waves of sari-clad Busby Berkeley chorines on acid, all singing, all dancing, all for the greater glory of the avatars of Vishnu . . .

And suddenly that, too, was oddly familiar.

". . . *fear the phantoms of the Kali Yuga* . . ."

A shiver of recognition edged up Jack's spine. He frowned, remembering a coke-fueled evening in 1983. He and Leonard and one of Bollywood's rising film stars, a golden-skinned man named Ashok Sonerwalla, sat on a terrace overlooking the Gulf of Khambhat, talking long into the night and drinking a beverage the color of Pepto-Bismol. Even now Jack recalled their conversation very clearly, because Leonard (much impressed by *My Dinner with Andre*) had videotaped the entire evening. During the months of editing that followed, Jack was forced to watch an endless loop of his intoxicated self drooling over the lovely actor.

Ashok was telling them about his current movie, something about the Kali Yuga—

"That is the cosmic period we are in now, the *Kali Yuga*," he explained in his plummy voice, and sipped his drink. "It lasts for one thousand years, and ends with a cataclysm that threatens to disrupt the divine order of the Three Worlds. There have been many, many *yugas*, of course. But this is the most evil *yuga*, this one we are in *right now*."

He tapped the glass coffee table for emphasis. "And each *yuga* has an avatar of Vishnu—this one, the Kali Yuga, has one named Kalkin. That's who *I* play. The avatars are always *very* exciting!"

Ashok laughed ingenuously, leaning across the table to gaze at Jack with wide hunted-stag eyes. "I got to play Prahlada the last time—he gets thrown into the sea with his hands and feet bound, but then Vishnu appears to him and Prahlada experiences *samadhi*—the oneness with Vishnu—and he swims back to the surface! Vishnu killed all the bad guys in that one"—Ashok giggled—"avatars cause a *lot* of trouble! But Kalkin—*me!*—he is really the avatar of the *future*, so we don't actually know what he does, except I get to kill a *lot* of people and in the end of course I finally kiss Mehnaz Sabnis! So you see the terrible disasters are worth it and divine balance is restored, after all!"

Jack's memory of that particular night was of divine balance being restored somewhere within Ashok's spacious Bhaunagar bedroom. A change in the music brought his attention back to the TV screen. He shook his head, blinking, and focused on the face of the dancing boy in close-up. High rounded cheekbones, strong jaw, cleft chin, strands of damp blond hair falling across his forehead. A distinctly occidental face—whatever it possessed of Eastern Mystery had been drawn there with makeup and computer theurgy. In the blue-white hollow of his throat a silver crucifix bobbed from a silver chain, the camera fixing for an instant upon a rapturous face that mirrored the boy's own; and that, of course, was no accident of fashion, not these days. The music pulsed and shrieked and clanged, a foment that set Jack's blood beating hard behind his temples even as he shook his head, as though to sever from himself some frightening dream.

What was it about this song, that voice, the screaming—

"No! *NO!—It's not him! IT's NOT HIM!*"

With a gasp Jack looked down, saw Marzana staggering wild-eyed to her feet as she shrieked and beat her hands against the air.

"*IT's NOT HIM! IT's NOT HIM! THEY DID SOMETHING! IT's NOT—*"

"Marzana!" Jack cried, aghast. "Marzana, what is it? *Who*—" He lunged to grab her by the shoulders. "Marzana!"

"THEY DID IT! THAT BITCH DID IT! THEY FUCK-ING—"

"*Marz!*"

Her screams gave way to hysterical crying, the girl gasping and kicking at him though her eyes never left the screen. In a panic Jack yelled at her to be quiet and tried to drag her from the room. But she was too strong for him, and so big now. With an explosive gasp she rammed her elbow into his stomach. Jack went reeling backward onto the floor, shouting in pain as the girl swept past him, stumbled to her knees, and began to wail.

"*No, oh no, he's gone, he's GONE—*"

Jack groaned and sat up, clutching his ribs. A few feet away the girl knelt with her back to him, swaying rhythmically as she moaned something he couldn't understand—it sounded like *rippp, rippp.* Onscreen the music reached its own crescendo, screeching feedback and the sound of waves and gongs, the dancer pivoting upon one foot with hands outstretched as though making an offering, or accepting one. From his eyes emerged sparks of gold and emerald that darted about him, hummingbird-like, and then shaped themselves into myriad glittering pyramids, each with a luminous corona. The pyramids arrayed themselves above the boy's head, light streaming down to envelop him until, with a final peal of gongs, he disappeared. There was a flash so blinding Jack drew his arm before his face. When he peeked at the television again it showed the same whorls of green and violet as before, with the ghostly outline of an eye peering upward through the glimmering. In the screen's lower left-hand corner black letters faded into view.

"THE END OF THE END"
STAND IN THE TEMPLE
AGRIPPA MUSIC/GFIDISC

Heart pounding, Jack leaned forward to put his arms around Marzana's shaking form. But his eyes remained fixed on the corner of the TV and the glittering corporate logo that appeared at the end of the line of block letters there—

A golden pyramid surmounted by the sun, a phantom gryphon shimmering within its rays.

PART THREE

Regrets Only

CHAPTER THIRTEEN

Into the Mystic

They made preparations for leaving.

Diana began saving vegetables for greasing the launching ways. Nothing from her garden ever went to waste—if it wasn't cooked, or baked, or dried, or canned, it was fed to the chickens or the pigs, or put into compost—but the pigs' rations were cut back, the mealy ends of potatoes and zucchini and pockmarked eggplants put into a new bin marked WENDAMEEN.

And the ways itself was completed. It stretched twenty-seven feet from shore to waterline, and then extended several more yards into the bay, where the wooden struts and pallets were anchored with lengths of automobile chain. Martin spent two days trying to figure out how to weight the cradle he'd designed for the boat. He finally pillaged his own car, a Toyota Camry, whose engine he and Trip removed and which Trip then fastened with more chain to the wooden cradle. But that didn't seem like it would be enough. So he went to Adele Grose and received permission to gut *her* car, a 1956 Cadillac that hadn't run for decades in any case. When that *still* didn't seem enough weight, he and Trip trussed the entire structure with more automotive chains and the doors from the Camry.

"It looks like it's going to take off," remarked Trip when they were done. "You think it'll do her?"

Martin privately thought the boat now resembled something from *Waterworld*. But he didn't want to jinx their enterprise, so he stayed mum. "I guess if the cradle doesn't sink, we can just hack away at it until it does," he said doubtfully, staring up at the *Wendameen*'s glossy white hull. "C'mon, let's get the rest of that gear stowed away."

He bartered with Diana for food, giving her two paintings she had long admired in exchange for jars of preserved fruit and vegetables and the promise of fresh eggs the morning of their voyage.

"But aren't you going to miss these?" Diana asked when Martin and Trip brought the two canvases over. "I mean, they were *hanging* in your place, it's not like you had them stored away somewhere . . ."

Martin shrugged. "I can always come and visit them, right?"

"Sure," Diana said absently. She was already measuring her walls for the canvases, and so didn't see Martin's stricken look.

But it was too late now. He was committed to the voyage because Trip was; and because he could no more imagine *not* taking the boy south to Manhattan than he could imagine leaving him there, forever.

Still, there was a little time left at Mars Hill. The last few days of Indian summer, blisteringly hot beneath a sky like cracked cloisonné, the beach steaming where hailstones the size of fists hammered against stone and Trip stumbled 'round gathering them, to fill an Igloo cooler for as long as the ice would last. Not long, it turned out, a day or two. Enough to keep the last four bottles of beer cold; enough for Martin to fill an ice pack to lay across his brow, fighting fever.

"*You're letting him kill you!*" his son Jason had raged. "You're going to leave me here alone—you're going to leave Moony and me and the baby—"

Yes, of course, I am, Martin thought, in bed at night watching the carnival shift of sky and sea, watching an egg-sized hailstone expire into tepid water on his bare chest. *Ashes to ashes, dust to dust/If God won't have me, the Devil must.* He ran a hand across his ribs, water trickling through his fingers to soak into the couch beneath him.

"But the world will know that I died for love," he had told his son, and with a strangled sob Jason fled down the beach.

Ah well, nothing to be done. He devoted himself to teaching Trip what he could of seamanship. On the deck of the *Wendameen*, Trip's face scrunched into that little-boy scowl of concentration as he followed Martin's nimble fingers through the labyrinth of sailor's knots: bowline, sheet bend, clove hitch, rolling hitch. Martin showed him where the harness was, in the cockpit, and warned him that in case of rough weather he was to put it on.

"Some boats have lifelines—ropes you can grab on to, if you have to. This one doesn't," Martin said, pacing from bow to stern while Trip struggled with a bowline. "So you've always got to keep your head up. You always have to have one hand for yourself and one for the boat."

Trip nodded, not really listening; and so Martin said the same things again, and again, just as he endlessly showed the boy how to thread the knots, how to secure the anchor line, how to maintain the proper tension between jibstay and jumpers and backstay. Somehow, some of it would stick, he thought, smiling as Trip bellowed with triumph and held up a length of rope: knots!

Weeks passed. Their nights were spent poring over the charts. Martin decided they would travel point to point, always within sight of shore. With no navigational aids beyond a compass and sextant (which was pretty useless, since you couldn't see the stars to steer by), and with storms a near-constant threat, it seemed the only reasonable thing to do. He showed him the sextant, its deft interlocking of mirrors, prism, filters, vernier; even took him out onto the porch to explain how it worked. How it was futile if you couldn't shoot the stars, although you could theoretically take a shot onshore, angle on three points on land, and find your way thus. The Graffams had told him that many of the old lighthouses along the coast of Maine were occupied again, since the Coast Guard no longer chased off squatters. It was rumored that some of the lights were even operational—Dick Graffam had seen one for himself, at Quoddy Head—and that a number of the old solar-powered light buoys still worked. The worst part of the journey would be getting around the ships' graveyard off Cape Cod. The Cape Cod Canal would be too dangerous, without any advance warning of freighters coming through, and so Martin plotted another course. Which would also be perilous, but he and John had sailed it before. Martin felt fairly confident that if the seas were calm, they would have little trouble.

"Let's aim for Friday," he said one night, pushing his Windsor chair away from the cluttered table.

Trip's face lit up. "To leave?"

"Well, to get the boat into the water, at least. There's no point waiting any longer." He felt a horrible stabbing at his heart: of course not, why wait? The boy wasn't going to fall in love with him, the stars weren't suddenly going to show their faces through the broken sky, the tide wasn't going to turn. "We should go now," he went on, his voice catching, "before it gets worse."

"Before *what* gets worse?" asked Trip cheerfully. "At

least it's not cold. And we've got the wind from the north, you said that's good."

Clueless, Martin marveled; *he's just so absolutely clueless*. He smiled and nodded. "I did, and it is: it's all good."

But lying alone on the couch that night—listening to Trip's even breathing in the next room, in Martin's own bed, clueless, he was so clueless—he could only sob, in rage and frustrated desire, in fury so pure and hot he could feel every hair on his body stand on end as though alight; and shout into his pillow until he was hoarse and the ticking splotched with blood—

Stop killing me.

They launched on Friday in mid-December. Morning came dawnless, as it always did, sky corrugating into emerald and cerulean and the brilliant yellow that seeps beneath a door closed to fire. On the porch Martin watched the day crack open. He had not slept, chased by fever and the knowledge that this would be the last time he'd sit here and look down Mars Hill to the bay, past decrepit cottages and leggy phlox and the *Wendameen*'s silhouette, to sparkling water and Dark Harbor on the eastern horizon. He felt beyond sorrow, oddly ebullient; buoyed by the very futility of his task. When he heard the first birds rustling in the lilacs he stood. He went inside to boil water for tea, then walked quietly into the bedroom to rouse Trip.

He slept soundly, as always. For a long time Martin stood above him, one hand on the headboard, and watched. He had always loved to do this, observe his lovers sleeping. It was like laying claim to a hidden part of them, like watching years fall away to reveal the other's pith. John had always looked childlike when sleeping, one hand curled close to his face upon the pillow, mouth parted, brow furrowed.

Trip did not. Trip, sleeping, seemed least himself. He never moved—and Martin checked, Martin would stand there for hours, memorizing the precise pattern of cheek against pillow, outflung arm, crooked knee. The boy's face had a strangely slack look, not relaxed but somehow deflated, the skin waxen and dull, lips pale, eyelids like little white shells laid across his eyes. As though some vitalizing spirit had gone. Martin frowned, thinking of all those stories where the hero's soul flees him at night, of shamans who can leave their bodies and travel to the other world, returning with magic stones, coals wrapped in leaves, miraculous cures for blindness and plague. He gazed at Trip's right hand, coiled against his breast, the gold ring there. He sighed, and gently shook Trip's shoulder.

They had a small audience for the launch—Mrs. Grose, Diana, Doug from the Beach Store. Jason had made his farewells, stiffly, during his last visit; finally collapsed into tears and let Martin hold him, weeping himself, for an hour. Martin had hoped Dick Graffam might come, but the weather was clear, no clouds that he could see; Graffam would be out fishing. It was high tide, waves lapping at pilings and gulls swooping overhead. On her jackstand the *Wendameen* gleamed cerise, reflecting the bright sky.

"You ready?" Martin clapped a hand on Trip's shoulder.

"I'm ready." Trip grinned.

"Let's do 'er, then."

Diana and Doug helped them spread rotten vegetables along the ways, cabbages and zucchini and stalks of jewelweed which spurted clear liquid when you broke them. Martin removed the wooden gate that held the boat within her cradle and, with a flourish, tossed it into a patch of withered tiger lilies. The boat creaked, its bow angling down—it looked monstrously huge up there, a terrible lion whose cage had been flung open—and began to slide forward.

"She's coming!" yelled Martin. Doug cheered. Diana waited at a safe distance with a pail of sand to throw onto the ways, to slow the boat if necessary. Martin and Trip stood to each side, armed with crowbars, but they didn't need them. As though in a dream of sailing through the sky, the *Wendameen* slid down the launching ways as Martin and Trip walked alongside, both of them gazing up and laughing for sheer wonder.

"Look at her!" yelled Trip. "Holy cow, she's gonna *do* it!"

And she did, leaving a crushed trail of green and red and brown in her wake, like the track of some immense slug: she swept down the gravel beach and into the bay. There was an awful moment when she listed to one side, and the cradle seemed to be caught. Martin gave an anguished yell and ran down the shingle, but before he could reach the water she righted herself. Trip and Doug held two of the lines, walking out onto the pier. Martin followed, so excited he could scarcely talk.

"We did it! We did it!"

Trip turned to him with shining eyes. "You did it," he said softly, and looked out to where the cradle rested in the shallows, the doors of Martin's Camry showing a faint brave yellow from beneath dark water. "You got her in the water . . ."

But they didn't leave that day; and by the next morning a storm broke. It raged for almost a week, hurricane winds, Trip and Martin frantic that the *Wendameen* would sink. She didn't; but she was damaged, so that there were more repairs to make. And another week slipped by, and another; more bad weather, and more time passing still. Until when they finally did get under way it was late in December, an insane month to be sailing; but what was to be done?

They made their farewells quickly. Everything had been loaded below, containers of water and extra foul-weather gear, lines and charts, sleeping bags and mildewed wool blankets that Mrs. Grose forced on them, just in case.

"Godspeed, Martin," she said, and held her pug to her breast. Her tortoiseshell eyes were clear but bright with tears. Looking into them Martin knew what she saw for him, but he was not afraid.

"Right," he said softly, and kissed her. Diana gave him a small mesh bag with a few onions in it. Doug produced a six-pack of Blackfly Ale. And Mrs. Grose gave him a bottle of brandy, almost full.

"It may make things easier," she said. She stood on tiptoe to kiss him, her fingers lingering against his neck. "Oh, my dearest Martin . . ."

He drew back gently, trying not to cry. When he looked down the tortoiseshell eyes were brimming; but she smiled and shook her head.

"It is not such a bad world to be leaving, Martin," she whispered, and turned away.

Martin and Trip boarded. They would motor out of the harbor, and hope for a northerly wind once they got beyond the point. Martin started the engine. Greasy black smoke rolled across the deck. On the pier everyone cheered.

"Good-bye, Martin! Good-bye!"

Martin grinned, Trip at his side in John's weather-beaten anorak. He raised his hand in farewell. The boat moved slowly, noisily out into the bay. Behind them

Mars Hill grew smaller and smaller, the waving figures on the pier no bigger than gulls. Then they were gone, and Mars Hill with them. The *Wendameen* was under way.

It took them over two weeks, dropping anchor at night to sleep within the shadow of pine trees, or offshore from sandy beaches along the Cape, or within sight of the drowned ruins of aircraft factories in Connecticut, the submarine works in Groton. Trip was seasick once, Martin often; he wished he had some Dramamine in his stores, or at least a pair of sunglasses. Above them stretched endless channels of phosphorescent green and violet and gold, with here and there a rent showing the great darkness beyond, brave wink of a star and once a nacred tooth Martin knew must be the moon. Below them the sea reflected the sky's broken face, with an underlying gesso of copper green. Martin felt they were not sailing so much as they were suspended within some vast crucible: just a matter of time before the *Wendameen* and its passengers, too, were smelted down, given back to ore and ash and bone.

They saw strange things, journeying south. A pod of whales who breached to starboard and followed them, mountains moving with great belching sighs, enameled blue and silver in the night. A creature like an immense brittle basket star, twice as large as the *Wendameen*, its central arms radiating outward like the sun before giving birth to an explosion of smaller arms, all writhing upon the surface of the sea as the omphalos turned slowly, counter-clockwise, and breathed forth a scent like apples. Rippling mats of phosphorescent plankton colored like Easter eggs, pale pink, pale green, pale blue; gulls nesting upon unmoored buoys, that rose to squawk at the boat's passage and so revealed their eggs, large as an infant's skull and pied with glowing silver.

To all of these wonders Trip seemed oblivious. If Martin pointed something out—crying aloud at a dismembered tentacle the size of a telephone pole, or marveling at a school of flying fish—Trip would only shrug, and smile.

"Didn't see that when I was out with my uncle," he said, sitting beside Martin on deck one evening and watching as a single fin, long and serrated as a fern, sliced the water near shore. "Guess they don't have them up by us."

Martin shook his head and leaned over the rail, trying to see if the fin made for shore; to see if perhaps it might clamber there on shaky new legs. "They didn't used to have them *anywhere*, Trip," he said.

And amongst all these, other things, more familiar but no less strange to see at sea. Ruins of houses, roofs floating like Dorothy's farm felled on its way to Oz, porches where terns rested and barnacles massed thick as wet concrete. Uprooted trees whose leaves had turned to bronze but had not died, had grown instead long streaming bladders and filaments that moved whiplike across the water's surface. Other boats—abandoned trawlers that sent a chill through Martin as they drifted past; battered sloops with brave patched sails and sailors who hallooed and waved but did not approach; a dinghy that appeared full of birds and clothes, and which Martin tried very hard to keep Trip from gazing into as the *Wendameen* passed it with terrible slowness, the gulls scarcely lifting their heads from worrying small heaps of bones.

Hourly they grew closer to New York. Alongshore unbroken darkness, save where fires leapt upon distant hillsides or burned within windowed towers. Snow and freezing rain that made the sails brittle as ice. The occasional terrifying surge of power through the grid, horizontal lightning that ripped through hamlets and towns and cities, erupting sometimes as flame from atop high-rises, or roaring from radio towers and airport beacons before it all collapsed once more into the endless bacchanal night, the great serpent stirring and then falling back into uneasy sleep. New Haven's breakwaters, flooded now, a channel buoy still blinking from the tip of a skeleton tower. Ships black and huge as islands, freighters or cruise ships or factory ships, that seemed immobile, unmovable, in the lavender dusk but were gone before the rippling red false dawn. It was these that unsettled Martin most; but they sailed on, past bell buoys tolling unseen beneath the remains of bridges and ferry landings. Cormorants on pilings, holding up their wings to dry. Drowned mansions. Defunct factories rising from webs of girders and shattered gantries. The art deco splendor of an amusement park, its brave promenade gone, the roller coaster's spine rising like a dream of dragons from coils of emerald water.

And Trip gazing upon it all unperturbed, unmoved. *Unknowing?* wondered Martin. But could not bring himself to ask, could not bear to think what answer he might receive: that the boy had seen it all before, that the drowned kingdoms were not new to him, or strange; that the scoured ruins of the earth Martin had loved belonged to Trip more surely than they had ever belonged to Martin, when he was whole and well and the world with him.

One night they anchored in mid-channel. After eating a makeshift meal of spongy fried potatoes and the last of Diana's rosemary they sat on deck, facing shore and watching the sky convulse above them, a slowly turning wheel of purple and indigo and a bruised deep red that was almost black. Martin had Mrs. Grose's farewell bottle of brandy beside him, and every now and then poured a jot into an enameled mug. He poured some for Trip as well. The boy didn't drink it; he balanced the cup on his lap, every now and then raising it to his face to sniff it warily. The air felt dank and viscous. It wasn't hot, but Martin still broke into a sweat, as though he were wearing clothes that were too heavy, too tight; as though he couldn't breathe.

Though maybe that was the brandy, he thought, or just fatigue. He sighed, took another sip from his mug, and winced. A strange indefinable smell hung in the air, like burning dust or gunpowder. In the distance a brilliant silvery flare leapt from a high promontory, as though something there had exploded soundlessly.

"It's getting worse, isn't it?"

He nestled the mug against his chest and glanced at Trip. "What?"

"The sky." Trip's voice was subdued. He stuck his chin out to indicate the lurid tableau above them, like a storm's inexorable staring eye. "It's not getting better. It's getting worse."

Martin looked up. He shrugged, feeling a sliver of cold where the heavy night air nosed down his shirt. "Is it? I guess I can't tell, anymore. Maybe we're just getting closer to the city—you know, more houses, more lights . . ."

"No." Trip raised the mug to his lips and took a sizable mouthful, then sputtered. "Ugh—!"

Martin laughed. "It's not *beer*. You're supposed to *savor* it—"

Trip swallowed and took a cautious sip. "Okay." He grimaced. "Mmmm. *Good*."

Martin laughed. He leaned back, gazing into the sky. "How much worse could it *get*?" he said, almost to himself. "Plus Diana was talking about those space stations they're sending up at the end of the month—I mean, joint Japanese/American technology, how can we lose?"

Trip shook his head. "I don't know," he said softly. His eyes in the infernal light seemed translucent. "It's like it really is the Rapture . . ."

"The Rapture?" Martin stared at him, not understanding; then noticed Trip's cross, the chain glinting in the hollow of his throat. "The Rapture—you mean the end of the world? You think this is the end of the world?"

Trip nodded. "The Last Days. That's what John Drinkwater used to say. My choir director," he added at Martin's quizzical look. "And my grandmother—"

He laughed bitterly, took another sip of brandy. "—she totally believed in all that stuff. If she could see me now—"

Trip raised his hand and traced the outline of the cross branded on his forehead, then shook his long hair back. "—man, if she could see me, she'd definitely think this was it. The end of the world. The end of the fucking world."

Martin listened, fearful lest the boy stop: it was the most he'd heard Trip say of himself since he'd found him on the beach at Mars Hill. Beneath them the *Wendameen* rocked gently. The boy fell silent and he waited. Finally he asked, "Is that—is that what you believe?"

Trip gazed upward. Streamers of livid gold spun from the ominous spiral, slid down to disappear behind that far-off promontory where something burned, smoke like dark thumbprints against the lurid sky. After a moment he shook his head.

"I don't know. I guess. Or no—no, maybe I don't."

He frowned. "I mean, if I really thought that, probably I wouldn't be doing this—"

He opened his hands, cradling the mug of brandy between them. "I mean, I wouldn't be letting you take me to New York," he said softly. "To look for her. If I really thought it was the end, I guess I wouldn't care."

Martin nodded, looked away so that Trip wouldn't see his expression. Because Martin *did* think it was the end—for him, at least—and somehow that didn't stop him from caring at all.

"She's your girlfriend, then? This person you're going to find in the city?"

Trip grinned wryly. "No, she's not my *girlfriend*," he said, laughing a little to soften the disdainful way he pronounced the word. "Actually, I hardly even know her."

"Was she—is she someone you knew from—uh, well, your church?"

"My church?" Trip's laughter died. He drank the rest of his brandy, then reached for the bottle and poured more into the mug. Some sloshed onto the deck, and Martin winced, resisting the urge to take it from him. "No. She wasn't exactly a church-going girl. I mean, I extremely doubt she was saved or anything like that. She was foreign, for one thing. Russia or someplace, I forget."

"But—so you want to save her?" Martin fought a faint unease, almost disgust—Fundamentalists!—that immediately gave way to guilt. "That's, um, *thoughtful*."

"No, I don't want to *save* her. I just want to—to see her again. That's all."

He turned away. His profile against the burning sky looked sharp, almost cruel, the hollows of his cheeks touched with flame, his eyes colorless. Martin's heart clenched. He tried desperately to think of something to say, something that might redeem the moment, save him from looking pathetic as he sat there staring at this boy as though *he* were the Rapture, his last best hope of sunrise.

But Trip only shook his head. "Thanks for the brandy," he said, easing himself to his feet. He stretched, looking down at Martin, and smiled; but the older man could see that it was forced. "I'll do first watch, okay?"

Martin sighed, nodding. "Okay. Thanks."

"No prob." Trip turned and walked away. Martin watched him go, fighting tears.

Clueless. He was just so fucking, totally, clueless.

The night passed with no more talk between them. Trip woke Martin to stand his watch; then, as night soured into dawn, he brought him a mug of hot tea on deck.

"Thanks," said Martin, feeling hungover and slightly ashamed. "We should be shoving off, I guess."

Unexpectedly, Trip nodded, smiled. "It's been kind of cool, hasn't it? I mean this whole thing with the boat? 'Cause like you got it all fixed up, and into the water, and—"

He spun on his bare foot, letting his arm swing out to indicate the rainbow sweep of water, the jutting headlands beyond. "—and, like, we made it! We're there!"

Martin smiled in spite of himself. "Yeah," he said, gazing into Trip's blue eyes. "We really have almost made it."

That night, they came to the East River: College Point, Rikers Island, South Brother Island. To starboard the horizon stretched green and yellow, a waste of spartina and cattails, reek of mussels and mudflats and red crabs like scorpions that nudged up against the *Wendameen's* hull upon mats of sea grass. Martin had thought, at least, that he could point out to Trip the glory that was Manhattan.

But from here the island seemed nothing but marshland. A faintly glittering haze hung above the fens, sparked here and there with blue or red. It took Martin some minutes to realize that this was the New York skyline, not so grand a thing as it had been; more a memory or fever dream of a city moored there above the restless grasses. As they drew nearer the marsh gradually gave way to decrepit waterfronts where buildings had tumbled into the channel, some frozen in mid-fall, beams and flooring and stairs like the gears of an unsprung clock hanging above the water. Pilings everywhere, black and reamed with rot, thrusting dangerously close to the little boat as it made its passage. Now and then a dinghy or barge, men and women fishing or dragging seines through the ruddy waters. And once they saw three bronze-colored dirigibles moving in formation above the river, towing something behind them. On shore people moved, the same slow dance of making and unmaking: fires, food, children, shelter: between and behind and atop broken buildings, under tarps, in cars, in houses and apartments and trees. Martin thought of Calcutta, of children living in oil drums along the canals in Djakarta—how quickly New Yorkers had caught up! The odors of their living wafted out to the *Wendameen*, so that Martin would suddenly grow faint with hunger; he had not known such hunger for months. Frying fish, chapati, garlic and onions, woodsmoke, meaty reek of unwashed clothes, excrement, incense, disinfectant, autumn leaves: he breathed it all in where he stood in the cockpit, motoring now, sure sign of journey's end; then breathed it all out again, saying good-bye.

"So where're we going to stop?" Trip hopped down into the cockpit, stooping to coil a loose line and set it alongside life jackets and anoraks and a can of baked beans licked clean. "You know someplace?"

Martin made a face. He looked at him sideways. Trip's eyes were wide and shining, his cheekbones streaked with sunburn and hair with silver-blond. He looked absurdly happy and healthy, the very picture of boat-trash in his floppy cable sweater and rolled white pants.

"Do *I* know someplace?" Martin raised an eyebrow. "You said it was about a girl you had to find. Now where would she be?"

Trip was silent. His eyes took on a detached, almost stony look as he leaned against the coaming, steadying himself as they motored between uneven rows of pilings. Martin watched him but said nothing more. They continued on, into a seemingly endless ruined landscape. *You think New York looks bad from a Greyhound bus*, thought Martin, *you think it can never get worse, but hey! Check it out—*

He almost laughed.

Refuse bumped up against the boat. From somewhere onshore echoed music, guitar chords churned by bad radio reception or shitty boom box into something almost indecipherable; but with a bright amazed burst Martin realized that he *did* know it—Sonic Youth, "The Sprawl."

And he *did* laugh, then. Because just when you think it can never, ever, possibly get anything *but* worse, someone comes up and bops you on the head with something like this, radiant guitars ringing in the wreckage of New York City, lemony afternoon light masquerading as sunshine, beautiful boy on deck—

—and suddenly for just a moment, for just that one instant, it was perfect. Even if the world was ruined, even if Martin was going to die, even if he would never know love again, never fuck again, never hear another song: if the world ended right now, it would have been perfect.

He began to cry. Aware how awful this would look to the boy, aware how awful it would feel in an hour or two, to look back and see himself like this, losing it somewhere amidst the floating garbage; but he couldn't stop.

Because it *was* beautiful. Because for that moment he had glimpsed the perfect geometry of desire, death at its apex, art and beauty and yearning bright angles below. He wiped his eyes, found a red bandanna and wiped his nose; stood and took a deep breath and felt it fall away: *The magic passes:* felt the world claim him again, for just a little longer.

The breeze left salt and a fine film of oil upon his cheek. He swiped at that, too, as the *Wendameen* nosed on through the crimson water and the music fell silent and Trip assiduously avoided looking at him. But something of the moment's radiance remained, something that Martin wouldn't let go of, not quite yet, not that easily, not without a fight. He adjusted the tiller, tossed his long grey hair back with what he hoped looked like defiance, shot Trip a manic grin; and began to sing.

It hurt, made his chest ache, and his throat; he had trouble catching his breath. Still he sang everything he could remember the words to. Not a great deal, actually. Martin had a terrible voice, there had never been much outside encouragement to learn any words. He sang "My Little Red Book" and "I Get a Kick Out of You," "Camelot" and "Yellow Submarine" and "Valentine," which had an impossible chorus;

"Santa Claus Is Coming to Town" and "Amazing Grace" and something he'd learned for his First Holy Communion and hadn't sung since. He bellowed "Coney Island Baby" and "Baby's on Fire" from where he stood on the traveler—Trip took the tiller, still not a word—tossing out the verses as though he were fishing and they were chum, let's see what rises to take this nasty bait. Rodgers and Hammerstein and old drinking songs,

> *Adieu, adieu, kind friends, adieu,*
> *I can no longer stay with you.*
> *I'll hang my harp on a weeping willow-tree*
> *And may the world go well with thee.*

He felt as though he were drunk, or tripping; felt feverish. His fingers where he touched his cheeks came away slick and hot. He had thought—hoped, maybe—that he might drive the boy away like this, such an avid unapologetic show of Baby Boom Mania, the old queer cracks at last: Rapture of the Creep.

Instead Trip in the cockpit continued to stare at the passing shoreline. Not with interest; not as though he were actually seeing it at all. Ahead of them an intricate network of docks and piers thrust out into the water, small freighters and workboats anchored amongst them. Onshore the mottled patchwork of a cobblestone street had collapsed beneath a block of eighteenth-century buildings, abattoirs that had been turned into warehouses and, when last Martin had spent any time here, artists' studios. He paused, chest a block of granite as he sucked at the fetid air, looked down into sanguine water and saw the silvery outline of a train car there, blood green, acid red, sparkling where the light touched it. He glanced back at the shore, buildings erupting from the harbor, cruciform street sign skimming a few inches above the rippling surface; looked back down and nodded, breath catching in his throat as he started to laugh.

It was not a train car at all but the Starlight Diner. He had always hated it anyway.

"What?" said Trip; the first word he had spoken in an hour. "What?"

Martin only shook his head, stumbling a little as he stepped back down into the cockpit. He was shaking. He was burning up. Maybe this hadn't been such a good idea after all. There was dust or grit in the outer corner of his eye; he ran his finger there, expecting to feel something: nothing. He blinked, raised his head, and saw it was not dust at all but the shadow of someone moving along the boom.

"Fuck," he said, shading his eyes with his hand. "Who the—"

But there was no one there; of course not, was he crazy? He started to laugh again but caught himself, turned away so as to avoid seeing Trip's expression— not accusatory, not disgusted, not grateful, not *anything*, the little fucking prick—the wind raw against his face as once again Martin began to sing, throwing another line out to the evening to see what it might catch.

> Riding on the Sloop John B
> My grandfather and me
> Around Nassau town we did roam
> Drinking all night, got into a fight
> Oh I feel so broke up, I want to go home . . .

He faltered, then lost the song, abruptly. Another sound severed it from him, cleanly and surely as though someone had cranked up a perfectly tuned PA system in the boat. Martin's mouth dropped open, and he turned in astonishment.

Trip was singing.

> *And oh, please let me go home—*
> *I want to go home*
> *I feel so sad and broke up*
> *I just want to go home . . .*

And not just singing but *seizing* the song, taking the old silly words and transforming them, so that Martin felt as though someone had shoved an icy hand down his back.

"Holy *shit*," he whispered.

Because if his voice had been a line tossed out, clumsily, Trip's was the hand that took the rod from his and plied it like a rapier through the air. His voice was clear and sweet and piercing, as pure a sound as Martin had ever heard, and *loud*—he sang like someone who had been trained to it, given to it as parents used to sell their sons to *bel canto*; born to it.

> *Oh let me go home,*
> *I want to go home—*

Martin listened, amazed and a little frightened. Was this what the boy had been hiding all these months with his self-contained silence, not a voice but A Voice?

Or—with a shiver Martin recalled the scarred luminous vistas they had seen, moon like a rabid eye, krakens and coelacanths rising from Buzzards Bay—had something *happened* to Trip, suddenly, these last few days? Unmade him as the world seemingly was being unmade, stripped like an invalid's mattress, bedclothes burned and ashes cast away; then replaced with bright new linens, vestments of silk and cloth-of-gold . . .

Let me go home
I want to go home
This is the worst trip
I've ever been on.

Trip stood, hand on the tiller, head thrown back. His voice died away into the slap of waves and gulls keening. For a long moment he stared up into the shimmering sky, gold and purple sequins stitched upon his skin. Then he lowered his face and gazed at Martin, with a look of such transcendent joy that Martin felt suddenly shy in his presence, as though he had glimpsed lovemaking through a keyhole and been caught.

"H-how," he stammered, tried to cover his embarrassment with uneasy laughter. "How did you—you can *sing . . . ?*"

Trip grinned. "Yeah. It's what I did, before. What I used to do . . ."

He glanced down at the tiller and then at Martin, a question. Without a word Martin stepped over and took it from him.

"I—you think maybe this would be somewhere you could leave me?" Trip frowned, looking at the silhouettes of broken buildings lining the shore, the silver-blue spires of skyscrapers that pinked the sky behind them. "I mean, it's like downtown, right?"

Martin looked at him, wondering if this was an attempt at irony: uh, no.

"No, this isn't exactly downtown, Trip." Martin raked damp hair from his face and sighed. "Do you have *any* idea where she might be? This woman you need to find?"

For a long moment Trip said nothing; only clenched his fists and stared at the shore. Finally he said, "No. I guess I don't. I mean I only actually saw her here once."

Martin resisted the urge to shout in frustration. He mopped his face with the bandanna, eased back until he could perch upon the edge of the coaming. A shadow passed across the floor; he glanced up but saw nothing. "Okay." He felt utterly depleted, wanted only to crawl into his bunk belowdecks and fall into blind sleep. "Okay. So you saw her once—where was that? Do you remember an address, or anything?"

Trip nodded. "That big place at Times Square—the Golden Pyramid or whatever it's called."

"The GFI Pyramid." Martin nodded, thinking, *Great, this is fucking great, I've sailed five hundred miles so this kid can look for someone he doesn't know in the middle of Times Fucking Square.* "Okay. That's a start, I guess. I guess we could find someplace to tie up and walk—"

"I—I need to go alone." The boy's voice was strained. "I mean, I know you brought me all this way, I don't mean to be like rude or something, but I—she was, I have to—"

The boat surged shoreward as Martin yanked the tiller too hard. He shot Trip a furious look, his mouth opening to argue—

But his anger gave way when he saw Trip's expression. Bleak, desperate even; and irradiated with what Martin suddenly recognized as a desire futile and intense as his own. Trip's gaze remained obdurately fixed on shore; until unexpectedly he turned. For the first time since Martin had found him upon the shingle at Mars Hill, Trip extended his hand and touched Martin's.

"Thank you," he said. There was a finality to the words, the roar of stone shearing away from a cliff face to sound unimaginable depths in the water below. "If we could maybe pull up here, somewhere—I could go."

Martin sat dumbly, waiting to see if there would be more. There was not.

"All right," he said at last. He turned away, blinking back tears; feeling old and ill and immeasurably stupid. *What* had he been expecting? Not the prince's magic kiss but more than this, certainly—a concerned hand on the shoulder, a low voice asking *Will you be all right? You look so sick, won't you tell me what it is, isn't there anything I can do?*

But Trip never spoke. A minute passed; then Martin nodded. "I'll pull up here."

He brought the boat around, steered her toward where a mound of blasted rubble, brick and stone and concrete, had fallen into the harbor, forming a sort of quay. Small dark shapes sloped along the stones. There was a putrefying smell. Martin felt a spike of mean triumph, *what a god-awful place*; then despair, and fear.

"This doesn't seem too safe, Trip." His mouth was dry. He touched the corners: they were cracked and brittle as dry leaves. "Are you sure—"

Trip nodded, then hoisted himself down the companionway ladder into the cabin. He returned a few minutes later with the knapsack Martin had packed for him. Some canned beans, dried fruit from Diana, extra clothes, sunscreen, socks. Water purification tablets that were surely past their prime. Over his arm John's anorak; John's cable-knit sweater dangling halfway to his knees. He stood awkwardly, as though trying to think of something to say; then dipped his head and stepped up on deck.

"Wait," cried Martin. He motioned for Trip to mind the engine and climbed into the cabin, coughing at the exertion. Walked unsteadily past galley and chart table until he reached his bunk, fumbling in the darkness at the pile of clothes and blankets until he found what he wanted.

"Here," he said, covering his mouth as he wheezed. "Here—"

He held them out to Trip, a wallet of worn brown cowhide and a small wooden box.

"Hey, no," Trip stammered, not all that convincingly. "I can't—"

"There's hardly any money"—Martin coughed. "—don't get excited. But there's a credit card, it should have some credit left. Not a photo one, so you might be able to use it."

Trip nodded. He shoved the wallet into his pocket, then looked at the box. "What's this?"

"The sextant." The word came out in an anguished gasp, and Martin turned away. "I—I'd like you to have it."

Trip shook his head. "But don't you need it? Can't you use it, to steer by?"

Martin's mouth broke into a smile. "I won't need it, no. You go ahead, keep it—"

He wanted to say, *To remember me by*, instead only smiled again, nodding.

"Okay." Trip stared at him. His eyes narrowed, his mouth twisted as though frowning, and for an awful instant Martin thought he was undone: Trip had seen through him, the Fundamentalist monster would stand finally revealed on deck beside the queer activist. Instead, to his shock, he realized that Trip was fighting tears.

"Okay," he repeated, thickly. He glanced away, gazing into the darkness of the cabin, then down at the sextant in his right hand. Something seemed to catch his eye. Without looking up at Martin he pulled something from his hand, then held it out to the older man.

"Here," he said, his voice too loud in the crowded space. "You can, um, have this—"

It was his ring. The plain gold band gleamed faintly in his cupped palm, throwing off glints of yellow and red.

"*Oh!*" Martin gave a stunned gasp of embarrassed

laughter. He shook his head. "Trip! I—Christ, I couldn't! I mean, that's your—isn't it from her? Your—well, who-ever?"

"Take it," Trip urged. He held the sextant close to his breast even as he nudged Martin with his other hand. "Please," he added softly. "I want you to—"

"But—"

"I don't know where it came from. I mean, she did have a ring like this, and so did her mother—but she didn't give it to me. I really don't remember how I got it."

"Well." Martin took it. The metal band was very thin and weighed almost nothing. He pinched it between two fingers, then tentatively slid it onto the pointer fin-ger of his left hand. "It fits." He fought to keep his tone light. "Thank you, Trip. Really."

"Okay." Trip looked over at him, then at the sextant, and grinned. "Wow. We really made it, huh?"

Martin smiled. "We really made it."

The boy nodded, once, then opened his knapsack and stuffed the box inside. "Okay," he said, clambering up on deck with Martin behind him. "I guess I'm off."

He stood in front of the older man, suddenly look-ing awkward and very young. Martin smiled again, thought *What the hell,* and leaned forward to hug him. He could feel Trip's shoulders tighten. After a moment he backed away.

"All right. You better go, before it gets too late—"

Martin sank into the cockpit and clasped the tiller, watching as Trip poised himself on the traveler and measured the jump he'd have to make to the stony mound below. Without a backward glance he leapt, stumbling forward a little but catching himself before he could fall.

"All right!" Trip shouted excitedly. He turned and

shaded his eyes, looked up at the *Wendameen* and waved. "Thanks, Martin! Thanks a million! Good luck—"

Martin nodded. His face hurt where tears scored his cheeks, but it no longer mattered if Trip noticed. "Good luck, Trip," he whispered, then shouted so that the boy could hear him. "Good luck—"

He revved the engine, not bothering to hold his breath or turn away from the harsh smoke that poured out; then angled the tiller so that the boat slid from the quay, her hull grating against bricks and rubbish. *I won't look back I won't look back* he thought fiercely, wiping his eyes; and for several minutes cut through the viscous waters, his eyes sternly fixed on a horizon that boiled with lurid clouds and the myriad shifting forms of distant boats.

Finally he could stand it no longer. He was far enough out now that a fresh wind began to play across the deck, tugging at furled canvas and cooling Martin's scorched face. If he squinted into the harsh light he could just make out the bright triangles of other sailboats braving the reach. He could hoist sail now, if he wanted to, make it past Staten Island and Raritan Bay and into open water. He took a deep breath, stood, and turned to gaze behind him.

In the distance the island reared, its shore a shabby tartan of decayed buildings, collapsed roads, twisted girders and makeshift landings, glass and steel towers erupting from behind the ruins like spaceships from the desert. His eyes sought desperately to find the mound where he had left Trip, but it all looked the same now, one long ragged seam—

—ah, it was too late, he had waited too long!—

—but then as in a dream Martin saw him, a bright white jot moving against black ruins, disjoined from the surrounding landscape as a gull in flight. Without meaning to Martin cried out, a wordless farewell, then formed the boy's name and shouted, madly waving—

"Trip! *Trip!*"

—and yes, the brightness halted, hovered there before the immense backdrop of the ruined city and almost Martin could imagine something leapt from it, like a flame, like a raised hand meeting his farewell.

"*Martin!*" The voice scarce heard between the wind in his ears and the hissing of waves. "*Martin, good-bye—*"

Tears burned his eyes. He blinked and dragged his sleeve across them, furiously. When he looked out again the bright spark was gone. He glanced down at his hands, twin gold slivers winking from each one. Beneath him the engine thrummed, the boat stirred restlessly as swells lifted her and the breeze plucked at the sails. She wanted to be gone; she wanted to be underway.

"It's time then," whispered Martin. "It's time.

He killed the engine and pulled himself on deck, slowly, because it hurt to move. Freed the sails and trimmed them back, ducking as wind filled them and the boom sliced through the air a handspan away. Breathless, his heart pounding, he eased into the cockpit and grasped the tiller. Ahead of him the sky coiled and uncoiled. Boats skimmed past, and seabirds. A shadow moved across the planks in front of him and this time he did not turn, this time Martin smiled and did not feel where his lips bled, he smiled and nodded without a word, recognizing the shape that streamed from the darkness there upon the back deck, the long span of arms reaching out for him and the breath that stirred the hairs on his neck. Felt his heart within him tear like a fist pounding its way out, as the tiller slipped from Martin's hand and he turned at last, heart exploding into rapture and no longer afraid, falling into the embrace that was there behind him, welcoming, John and darkness and desire all stitched at last into one, all there, all healed, all waiting; fell into it and he was light and joy, light and the end of waiting; he was nothing but nothing but light.

CHAPTER FOURTEEN

Catastrophe Theory

The power stayed on for almost three weeks, the longest stretch Jack could remember since the glimmering began. At first they all went charily from day to day, meeting at breakfast to exclaim over Mrs. Iverson's coffee cake or date muffins. There were plenty of baking supplies, since she so rarely had the chance to bake, and plenty of time to spend eating, since no one had anything else to do. After breakfast they moved into the living room—everyone except Mrs. Iverson—to sit with all the lights on, heat wafting up from the floor registers and warm smells from the kitchen, and watch morning television. Keeley dozed, occasionally woke to shake her head in dismay at goings-on in Calgary or Bangkok. On the floor Marz lay like a beached zeppelin, her lunar belly occupying a formidable portion of Jack's view of the TV screen. There were no more outbursts at music videos. Jack had not been able to get any kind of explanation out of the girl. He finally chalked it up to some bizarre Last Generation analogue of Beatlemania, and tried to convince himself that with the power restored, maybe the world had toppled back onto its axis, after all. Some evenings he found her standing in the second-floor stairwell, her swollen belly pressed against the sill, hands pressed against the glass as she stared out the window at the broken house next door. Chiaroscuro of flame and smoke and thrashing bodies, smash of bottles, raucous laughter; and the blond girl gazing hungrily as though she beheld a vision of Paradise, mouth parted, eyes foggy with tears.

I saved you from that! Jack wanted to shout when he saw her thus; but always when she heard his tread upon the floor she would turn and wobble off. Head bowed so he could not read her face behind its scrim of ashy hair, top-heavy tulip blossom snapped at the stem. *Oh God, poor thing*, he thought, aghast again at the horror of it, bringing a child into this world. But she didn't see it so; her belly bloomed even as her rail-thin legs grew hard and thick with edema and her eyes took on a distant dreaming look, as though already she were asleep after the trauma of labor; as though dreaming she saw beyond this darkness to flame and silence.

The autumn passed. One day a postman arrived, with bills and a letter from Jack's brother Dennis, postmarked eight months earlier. Lights worked, hot water came from the taps (never enough but that wasn't new), *Tristan und Isolde* thundered from his old Bose speakers. Mrs. Iverson would do the dishes, then teeter downstairs to see to the laundry, then return to start on lunch and dinner, or to bring Keeley tea and Marz some more muffins—Jack didn't eat much these days. All of them frantically tapping into the capricious current flowing through the house, as though that were the way to stave off chaos.

And perhaps it was, Jack mused as he checked the answering machine for the fourth time in an hour. There were no messages, had been no messages. The phone never rang. Power might have been restored to most of the metropolitan New York grid, but for some reason it didn't extend to the telephone system. For all he knew there would be no messages for the rest of his life, but still Jack couldn't stop fiddling with the machine, picking up the phone to see if there was a dial tone. There never was. Three, four, seven times a day he'd go out to the carriage house, peer into the fax machine's long slit mouth and check his computer for e-mail. Jack didn't like to admit it, but he was looking for Larry Muso, in all the old familiar places. Only of course with no telephone service there were no faxes, and no computer messaging. And since there had never been much Larry Muso to begin with, the search was frustrating and ultimately depressing.

Now he sank into the same wicker chair where eight months ago he had sat with The Golden Family's envoy, and picked up (not for the first time) the copy of *The King in Yellow*. Opened it at random, yet another pass at divination, and read,

THE LOVE TEST
"If it is true that you love," said Love, "then wait no
longer. Give her these jewels which would dishonor
her and so dishonor you in loving one dishonored.
If it is true that you love," said Love,
"then wait no longer."
I took the jewels and went to her, but she trod upon
them, sobbing: "Teach me to wait,—I love you!"
"Then wait, if it is true," said Love.

He waited. What choice did he have? It would not be much longer, now. Christmas was approaching, and his New Year's Eve bash in the shadow of a corporate temple. The end of the century, the end of the millennium.

The end of the Kali Yuga? he wondered, watching for the hundredth time the Stand in the Temple video on TV and that iconic singer Jack couldn't help but think of as another emissary from GFI. Trip Marlowe, his name was: Jack learned that by sitting through one of the legion of interviews, documentaries, flatulent news bulletins, and good old-fashioned commercials promoting the band.

"This is so shameless," Jack exclaimed to his grandmother in the living room. Onscreen, Trip Marlowe's talking head spoke in reverential tones of the work being done by multinational corporations to restore the environment.

"*. . . like, in the Rockies, they're trying to reestablish all these extinct species of frogs, and in some places people, like, heard the frogs singing for the first time in ten years . . .*"

"What, dear?" Keeley raised her head; she had been asleep. "I'm sorry . . ."

"Oh, nothing." Jack sprawled on the couch, disgusted equally by the singer's ingenuous blue-eyed gaze and his own lassitude, watching this crap. "It's just—I mean, *look* at this guy! It's like his entire face was reconstructed or something, he looks like he was designed by some damn corporate committee. He probably *was*," he ended viciously, and reached for the remote.

Keeley peered at the screen. "Is that what's-his-name? The one with the nose job and the face?"

"No. I mean yes, this one probably has a nose job, but it's a different nose. Jeez."

He flashed through channels, more than had been available for a year. Bombs exploding above the desert somewhere (Texas? Algeria? some Totally New and Improved wasteland which Jack had yet to hear about?), an ad for a winged Barbie that morphed into her own makeup-equipped carrying case (just in time for Christmas, Supplies Very Limited), lunchtime talk shows featuring people claiming to have spoken with deceased loved ones, a bit on CNN about the upcoming Millennial New Year's Bash being hosted by GFI Worldwide in New York City.

"Hey!" said Jack, sitting up. "That's—"

He almost said, "That's *my* party." But then remembered he had never mentioned GFI's invitation to Keeley or anyone else. "—That's *interesting*."

Keeley nodded absently. A moment later she began to snore, leaving Jack to stare nonplussed at a video montage. GFI's brazen airships in formation against an indigo sky; sturgeon slitted open so that their roe spurted onto dirty grey ice; a vault filled with ranks of champagne bottles; vintage limousines; a Japanese woman being outfitted in a stiffly embroidered kimono four times as large as she was; an aerial shot of some kind of arena or stadium, swelling out from one side of the Pyramid like a wasps' nest and covered with workers and scaffolding and construction equipment. Then the arena faded, replaced by the electronically shuffled images of some two or three hundred people Jack assumed must be famous for something. He only had time to recognize a few of them—the beloved sports figure disfigured by petra virus, a much-married millionaire Jack had thought was dead. And the ubiquitous Trip Marlowe, natch, dancing on one foot atop a Day-Glo Sphinx.

"*. . . billing it as the most fabulous bash since King Tut partied on the Nile!*" exulted the announcer. "*So—*

"*What are* you *doing New Year's Eve?*"

The segment ended and another began, this one about millenarian cults like the Montana-based Cognitive Dissidents, who were planning their own mass suicide at the stroke of midnight, December 31. There was a commercial for telephone insurance. Then a few more worried-looking people speculated about the end of the world. Jack made a rude noise. He turned the volume off, but left the TV on—he was superstitious now about turning it off—and went into the kitchen.

It was hard to believe that anything was coming to an end, except for Lazyland's supply of coffee, which was dismayingly meager. Jack gazed sadly into the cabinet: only one vacuum-sealed bag remained. Leonard was their sole link with the world of such luxuries, but Leonard had not returned to Lazyland since he'd brought the Fusax. And Jack knew better than to hope that coffee would materialize on the shelves at Delmonico's during one of his forays there for supplies.

Still, later that morning he *was* amazed to see what Delmonico's could produce. Christmas was only a week off. Mrs. Delmonico had brought out the old cardboard decorations—Santas and elves and angels, all from Finnegan's Variety Shops circa 1967—and strung up tired garlands she had been hoarding even before the glimmering began. Like some old-time general store, the venerable Yonkers grocery had begun to exhibit delicacies of the season. Oranges in wooden crates, their knurled skins more green than orange, and fist-sized pomegranates wrapped in varicolored tissue. (AND the paper could be used for wrapping presents, Mrs. Delmonico advised Jack. Wasn't it pretty?) White rabbits and evil-looking chickens dangled upside down from their feet above the butcher counter. There were boxes of strange hand-made toys, cars and boats and rocket ships carved from Popsicle sticks, sock puppets that moved Jack to tears, old Barbies whose plastic faces had been scrubbed and repainted with ballpoint ink, dressed in new hand-stitched clothes.

And one afternoon, beneath a churning claret sky, an ancient pickup truck pulled up in front of the grocery, its bed piled ten feet high with—

"Christmas trees!" exclaimed Jack. *"Wow."*

A crowd was gathering, *fellahin* who camped at Getty Square and a few wary shoppers like Jack, who carried baseball bats and wore football helmets. A *fellahin* girl, dressed in shredded garbage bags and little else, stood on tiptoe beside the truck to breathe in rapturously.

"I remember *these*!" she cried, and fell back laughing.

Jack smiled and let her pass. He moved closer himself, lifted his surgical mask, and touched the soft boughs behind their protective plastic mesh. The trees were leggy, their limbs swept into torturous angles by the webbing. He ran a finger along one slender branch. Needles rained onto the truck bed—it was covered with needles, rust-colored and greenish yellow, and twisted pine cones like arthritic fingers, and scaly bits of bark.

But then Jack closed his eyes. Immediately darkness was there, the expectant predawn hush of a house buried in snow, whispers from his brother's bed and that smell rising from the living room, the holiest scent he had even known: evergreen. To Jack that had always been Christmas. Not the toys, not the lights, not even the baby in the barn, but this: night and bitter cold, snow beneath and desolate stars above, a green tree in the wood that breathed in the darkness but breathed out spring.

"'Scuse me, 'scuse me, 'SCUSE ME, sir—"

He jolted from his dream, stood back to let the driver and his lanky teenage son open up the truck bed. They unloaded the trees—white pine, he heard the driver say, lumber trees but they were harvesting them now, they needed the money too badly—and leaned them up against the storefront, hiding the plywood and sheet metal that covered its windows. Someone asked how much the trees were. Jack sucked his breath in at the price; but then thought of the money that would be coming from the sale of *The Gaudy Book*. Any day, maybe; besides which his credit was always good at Delmonico's—a hundred years ago it had been his great-grandfather's store, old Sabe Delmonico had bought it during the Depression but the Delmonicos always considered the Finnegans part of their extended family, even now.

He bought a tree.

"Can you get that home by yourself?" Mrs. Delmonico eyed Jack dubiously, and before he could answer shouted out at the truck driver's son. "Hey! YOU! C'mere, we got a job for you—carry this nice man's tree for him, okay? Just a couple blocks. Tip him nice, Jackie, eh?"

She winked and blew Jack a kiss, then turned to survey the fragrant benison that had befallen her shop. Dunsinane had come to Getty Square.

So they brought the tree home, Jack and the boy. His name was Eben, he and his dad had driven down from New Hampshire, it took them three days.

"Truck kept breaking. We ran out of gas, then some guy tried to steal our tires, but my dad pounded him, hah!" The boy was thin but tall, exhilarated to be so far away from home. He smelled of pine resin and diesel oil. He shouldered the tree like a rifle and loped ahead of Jack, repeating over and over how he'd never been to New York and his father had promised they'd go to the city, after the trees were sold.

"My mom, she don't like that!"

Jack shook his head. "I'm with her, Eben."

At the gate to Lazyland Jack made the boy hand the tree over. "I can get it from here," he explained. He wanted to bring the tree down to the house himself. "But wait, here—"

He held out a fifty-dollar bill. It wasn't much, and for a moment he was afraid Eben would refuse to take it, or complain. But the boy only smiled, sweetly, shook his head and shoved his hands into his pockets.

"Hey, no sir, you just enjoy your tree, okay? Merry Christmas!" And he spun away up Hudson Terrace, whistling to himself.

The tree was heavier than it had looked, for all that it was downright scrawny compared to Lazyland's trees of yore. Jack dragged it down the driveway, looking back anxiously to see if he was leaving a trail of needles. Inside he was met by Keeley and Marz and Mrs. Iverson, who exclaimed and offered advice as to how to prop it up in the dining room until the old wrought-iron tree stand could be found.

"It's like Charlie Brown's tree!" Mrs. Iverson shook her head and poked the tree where it leaned against the Chippendale china cupboard, gazing disapprovingly at the needles that littered the carpet beneath.

"It's *beautiful*, dear," said Keeley. "Hush, Larena."

"Can I help decorate?" begged Marz.

So then he had to go up to the attic, rooting around in one of the odd-shaped closets under the eaves until he found the boxes there, each carton big enough to hide several children and stuffed to overflowing with Christmas: garlands, plastic holly, tangled strands of dangerous-looking lights considerably older than Jack himself, old cards that turned to dust when he touched them, waterfalls of tinsel, ancient embossed Santas with cotton-batting beards that had frightened Jack when he was small, the wrought-iron stand (hooray!) only slightly rusted, wax balls from Germany with flowers on them, numerous pine cones, ceramic and papier-mâché and cardboard Santas, elves, reindeer, trees, bells, chapels, snowmen, angels, and wreaths, as well as four statues of crippled boys and reformed cranks.

Last of all he pulled out an enormous carton that

contained box upon box of Sparkle-Glo ornaments, like the luminous lost fruits of Eden: rubies and emeralds and diamonds of blown glass, purple grapes, grinning clowns and leering dogs, churches and fish and a sailing ship with tissue-paper mast and rigging of gold filigree.

"Oh, look, *look*!" cried Marzana, sitting on the attic floor with legs akimbo, her belly awash in wrappings and ribbons and rusty pine needles. She held up an icicle of blown glass, striated silver and cobalt. "They used to sell these in Rybnik!"

Jack looked over at her and smiled. "Is that where you grew up?"

The girl watched the little dagger turn slowly in the air before her. After a moment she said, "I don't remember," her voice distant and expressionless.

Jack waited, but she said no more. "Okay," he said at last, standing and picking up one of the cartons. "I don't think you better carry any of these, all right?"

"But they're not heavy!"

"I know, but they're *big*. Here, you can carry down this, okay, that's the star for the top, just don't DROP it—"

He made five trips, pausing on each landing to catch his breath and then plunge back upward again. There was only a single naked electric bulb in the old nursery attic, which cast shadows over more of the room than it lit. Outside, night was chasing the sky in harlequin colors, black and crimson and cadmium yellow. The motley light stained the unfinished wooden floor, giving everything an expectant, slightly febrile glow. The sensation that something was going to happen filled Jack, as well; a subcutaneous anticipation of Christmas, he supposed, even a Christmas as threadbare as this one promised to be. There had been no more visits from the postman, and no word from GFI as to when he might expect the money from the sale of *The Gaudy Book*. So Christmas would pretty much consist of what he and Mrs. Iverson could cobble together from Lazyland's failing stores, or from the largesse of Mrs. Delmonico. He had put aside any notion of attending GFI's party—what could he have been thinking, with Marz ready to blow like the *Hindenburg* and no one but Jack and two ancients to attend her?

He sighed, walked to the far side of the room, and stared out the long low row of attic windows, down the black slope to the river. There was a sequined scatter of lights upon the Palisades, where for so long there had been darkness, and farther south the luminous arch of the George Washington Bridge, great red and green curves like slices of neon watermelon, nibbled black where lights had burned out on the spans. The sight should have comforted him, a return to normalcy at last. Instead it made him uneasy. It was like seeing Marzana in his aunt Mary Anne's bed that first night she appeared at Lazyland—he felt dead certain that something was very wrong, somewhere, despite this brave false show. Any moment now he would find out what it was.

He shivered and turned from the window. *What a way to think at Christmas.* Then he hefted the last carton of ornaments, switched off the attic light, and hurried downstairs to attend to the tree.

But of course the power was down again when Jule arrived unexpectedly at Lazyland, a week and a half later. It had failed the same night that Jack and Marzana and Mrs. Iverson decorated the tree in the formal dining room, with Keeley officiating from a chair. It was not exactly resplendent. Even with the lights turned off it retained its sadly etiolated quality, and drooped in the shadow of the robust Chippendale cabinet because there was no true darkness against which the glory of glass and gold and painted tin could shine. The strings of old lights (dangerously frayed and much-repaired with electrical tape) glowed bravely, the one remaining blinking light blinked a bilious green; but they were overshadowed by the vulgar show outside.

Still, they all stood and admired it. Jack made some adjustments (Marz lacked a light touch with tinsel). Keeley suggested that the crenellated spike that topped the tree could perhaps go a little more to the left, and Jack was just clambering back onto the kitchen stool when—

Eeeeep . . .

Dying wail of the CO detector, chorus of clicks from answering machine and stereo; and the gallant tree went dark.

"Nooo!" cried Marzana.

Jack shook his head. "It was these damn *lights*." He grabbed an offending strand and gave a sharp laugh. "Well, back to the drawing board . . ."

He began the search for lanterns and candles, berating himself for not making a point of retrieving them while the power was on. You couldn't find candles anymore, anywhere; or batteries, or oil lanterns. Occasionally Jack might glimpse a flashlight behind the counter at Delmonico's, bartered for food; but it would never find its way onto a shelf. The Delmonicos had family all across the city who needed light just like everyone else.

And Lazyland's supply of candles was dwindling. In a house that vast there were untold drawers that might have candle ends rolling away in them, closets with forgotten torches and automobile emergency flares; but Jack cursed his profligacy now, candles in the summer when the sky burned, lanterns at his bedside for reading . . .

In the linen closet he found an unopened box of white tapers, hidden beneath lavender-scented sheets. He tore the box's cellophane wrapping and removed four, thought for a moment and replaced one. He could find his way in the dark; *someone* had better start finding their way in the dark. Wind clawed its way through the narrow back stairwell, brought with it shrieking laughter. He turned and pressed his hands and face against the small oriel window that faced north, to where other mansions had once stood in line with Lazyland gazing down upon the Hudson.

In the last few weeks he had made a deliberate effort not to look out upon them. If he saw Marz there in her customary trance, he would continue quickly up to his own room. So he never knew whether or not electric lights ever brightened the broken windows; and he tried not to think about what kind of people were inside the ruins, starving or fighting or fucking on the floor.

Now, with spurious nightfall shadowing his home, he could not turn away; though it shamed him.

In the shattered buildings fires leapt, the broken windows gleamed as though they opened onto the inferno, molten and so much livelier than Lazyland's dull precincts. He heard music, crash of cymbals and drums; someone singing. Could they be *celebrating*? He raised his arms so that his hands touched the window's upper sill, and focused on a broad window next door. There was light within, light and music and many moving shadows. He imagined they were dancing amidst the rubble.

And suddenly it struck him, brutally, as though he had been knocked on the head: people were *living* out there in the ruins. They weren't holed up like himself or the other scared customers who could barely muster the courage to raid Delmonico's for food. They weren't killing themselves with drink and grief like Jule, or pretending nothing had changed, like Emma. Certainly they weren't bashing their heads against the wall because there were no candles left. If they were bashing their heads it was because they were *dancing*. They didn't wear masks or helmets to protect themselves from the world; they scarcely wore *clothes*. He recalled Marzana's anguished words, her first night at Lazyland—

They were my family. We were living down by the river and the fucking cops blew us out . . .

Family. The realization that something like that *could* be out there, just yards away, made Jack dizzy. He drew a deep shuddering breath and grabbed the casement, yanked the window open and from the neighboring house heard singing, a complicated contrapuntal chant, women and men and children, too.

> *I don't mind the sun sometimes,*
> *The images it shows . . .*

It was music. Even if he didn't recognize it, it was music, and had been all along. It wasn't squatters out there in the carnival darkness, crude autochthonic creatures leering at him from their gutted mansions. It was civilization.

They're adapting, he thought, and the horror he felt was not at what lay outside but at what he had kept imprisoned for over two years: heart and soul shrinking within a psychic fortress impenetrable as chiton.

But it would not be enough to save him, he saw that now, staring at the rain-streaked ground below the window, shingles flaking from the walls of Lazyland like scales from a butterfly's wing. It would not be enough to save any of them. Unbidden the last scenes of

Fantasia flashed before him, lumbering Technicolor giants on their doomed exhausted search for water, heedless of the tiny bright mammalian eyes that watched them from the shadows—

Leaning from his window out into the icy December air, Jack stared up into the cold whirling sky, eye of a storm implacable and inevitable as dawn had been, once upon a time; and heard lemurs and shrews and megazostrodons rustling in the night.

Christmas Day was muted, as it had been for several years now—Rachel Gardino had been killed by a drunken driver on Christmas Eve, and the holiday had been poisoned by that, for Jack and his family as well as for Jule and Emma. There were a few makeshift presents exchanged: some baby clothes Mrs. Iverson dredged up from the attic and cleaned, gingersnaps hard and aromatic as amber; the copy of *The King in Yellow*, which Jack presented to his Grandmother in its elaborate cloth wrapping. They ate by candlelight, not an absurd feast as Jack had prepared for Thanksgiving but bean soup and flatbread and dried fruit; then sang a few rounds of the more melancholy carols, "O Holy Night" and "It Came Upon a Midnight Clear," and went to bed early.

Four days after this quiet Christmas, very early in the morning Jack heard the familiar groaning roar of the Range Rover, more the sound of backwash from a recalcitrant small aircraft than an automobile. He groaned, slid from his bed, and trudged across the hall to look out the window. Down Hudson Terrace crept Jule's old car, dodging potholes and piles of refuse like a tipsy dowager, a loose strand of barbed wire trailing in its wake.

"Julie," Jack whispered, not at all ready for this. "Ah, fucking A."

At the head of the drive the Range Rover stopped. Jack watched as his friend emerged, an imposingly tall if unsteady figure in navy overcoat and fedora, brandishing a very large black umbrella. Jule walked over to the gate that loomed at the head of the winding drive, regarded it balefully for a moment before starting to poke at the LED readout with the tip of his umbrella. Jule had always been intimidated by the security system, all the more so since he was one of the few people granted knowledge of the secret code that granted access (Leonard had paid one of his hacker minions to break it for him). Ever since the glimmering began, when Lazyland's power came and went as casually as socialites once had, Jule's anxiety had become outright phobia: he was terrified he would be electrocuted by the gate. Jack sat, elbows propped on the sill, and observed as Jule tried unsuccessfully to gain entry.

After five minutes he couldn't stand it anymore. He shoved the window open, and yelled, "For Christ's sake, Jule! There's no power! Just get in the car and drive through!"

Jule looked up and shouted back. "But what if it comes back on?"

"It *won't* come back!"

"But what if it *does*?"

"Just DRIVE *THROUGH*."

Miming despair, Jule got back into his car, ducking beneath the fringe of barbed wire that surrounded the door. Clouds of blue exhaust engulfed the end of the drive as the car nudged at the gate, until very slowly it swung open. A minute later the Range Rover shuddered to a halt in front of the house. Jule got out, removing his fedora and mopping his head with a white handkerchief.

"Now go back up and *close* the gate," Jack yelled down. Jule shot him an angry look, then reached back into the car, emerging with his umbrella and a pair of bright yellow electrician's gloves, and plodded up the drive to shut the gate. When he finally returned to the house, Jack was standing on the front porch to greet him.

"You know, Jule, very few security gates were originally designed actually to *kill* people."

Jule shook his head. "You're wrong, Jackie, you're wrong. Somebody was just telling me about this thing he saw up at Pocantico Hills, this sort of electrified moat—"

Jack rolled his eyes and ushered Jule toward the front door. "Well, *our* system hasn't killed anyone yet. C'mon, it's fucking freezing—"

"Yeah, but you guys could actually use something like that here." Jule looked worriedly back at the Range Rover. "My car gonna be safe?"

"Yes, your car is going to be safe. What, you leave Emma at home and fall apart? Jesus, just relax for five minutes, okay?" Jack felt the old familiar sensation kick in, love and impatience and the overwhelming urge to punch his friend in the nose. "You drive up to Poughkeepsie in your sleep, go into the city and have a picnic on the fucking Major Deegan Expressway, but every time you come to *my* house you have a goddamn heart attack."

"Emma's not feeling so good these days. And electricity makes me nervous," Jule said meekly, lowering his head as he followed Jack into the foyer.

"Then you should be very, very happy, because you will find no electricity at Lazyland today."

Inside there was the soft flurry of footsteps in the hallway, the scent of Chanel Number 19; and then Jule was bending with sweet patience to hug first Keeley and then Mrs. Iverson, his unshaven jaw leaving a faint smudged impression upon their powdered cheeks.

"Jule dear! What a *surprise*!"

"I know, Grandmother, I'm sorry. I, uh, sort of unexpected, gotta do something in the city . . ."

"Of course, dear, we're just so happy to see you! How is Emma?"

"Oh, she's okay, just great—" He stared over their heads to Jack, who felt an unexpected bump of fear at his friend's haunted expression. "Uh, listen, I can't stay today, I just needed to, uh—well, I wanted to borrow Jackie."

Keeley's gaze softened. "Borrow Jackie! Why, of course you can borrow him!"

"*What?*" Jack eased himself between Jule and his grandmother. "What're you talking about, Jule?

"I, uh, got an errand in the city. I, well, I didn't want to—"

"The city." Keeley steadied herself and glanced at the old grandfather clock. "Well! Do you still go down there, Jule?"

He shrugged, uneasy. "Sometimes." He pulled at his collar, as though chilled. "Jackie?"

Jack shook his head but said nothing. He was close enough to Jule that he could smell whiskey, not just on his breath but everywhere, as though he'd doused himself with it. He had a flickering vision of Jule driving down here, the Range Rover careening through the flooded canals that had been the Merritt Parkway, a bottle tucked between Jule's legs and spilling onto his trousers. He glanced down and, yes, he could see it, a darker stain against the dark wool.

"Jule, dear, would you like some tea?" Mrs. Iverson twittered.

"No thanks, Mrs. Iverson." Jule's big hands twisted his fedora. His hazel eyes were moist with supplication. "Jackie?"

No thanks, Mr. Gardino, thought Jack. But then the chorus began shrilling in his head. *What, you jumped off all those bridges for Leonard Thrope, now you can't get into a car with your best friend?*

But he's drunk, Jack thought miserably. *He's—*

"Go ahead, dear," said Keeley. Her voice quavered slightly as she turned to Jule. "But you'll have him back by tonight?"

"God *damn* it." Jack swore furiously under his breath; as though he were still fifteen fucking years old! "I'll be back by tonight, Grandmother," he said, putting his arm around her and drawing her close. His eyes sought Jule's. "This better be good, Julie."

"Mary Anne is asleep," piped in Mrs. Iverson. She looked plaintively at Jule. "Don't you think Emma could come down to help her have the baby?"

Jule smiled. "That would be nice, huh? I know she'd like to . . ."

"Well." Keeley smiled bravely, looking from her grandson to his friend. "You'd better go, if you're going to be back by dark."

Jack stood for a moment, trying to think of some last-minute excuse. "It's just a few hours," pleaded Jule.

"Oh, all right," Jack said, crossly. "Just let me get a few things, okay?"

He went upstairs, fighting all the fears that assailed him—Jule's obvious distress and the thought of leaving his grandmother alone, not to mention the girl, for Christ's sake she could have the baby any minute!—but also feeling something he hadn't felt in years. A small burgeoning excitement: he was going to the city with his friend! They would have an adventure! He ran the last few steps to the third-floor landing, regretted it almost immediately as he began to pant. Grabbed the Fusax from his nightstand, did a quick blast from his inhaler—it was empty, he was sure of it, but prayed there might be a few bronchodilating atoms left to fight their way into his lungs— pulled his grandfather's old Burberry raincoat from the closet, and went back down. On the second floor he paused to glance into Marz's bedroom and felt a small spur of love for her leviathan form beneath the blankets, web of white-blond hair across the pillow.

"'Bye," he whispered, and shut the door.

Downstairs they made their farewells to Keeley and Mrs. Iverson.

"Drive carefully." The faintest tremor entered Keeley's voice. "You'll call if you're going to be late?"

Jack glared at Jule. "We *won't* be late."

"Of course not," Jule said gently. He leaned to kiss Keeley's forehead, and for a long moment held her tenderly. Only Jack noticed that his hands were trembling. "I promise Jackie'll be back tonight. It's just a quick trip into the city, people do it all the time."

"Do they?" Keeley murmured as she watched them go outside. "Well, be careful, boys."

"Get back in there!" shouted Jack. "Before you catch *cold*."

He had a final glimpse of Keeley's frail white face and waving hand; then the great oaken door slammed shut.

"*Now*," said Jack, following his friend to the car and fixing him with a piercing stare. "Will you tell me what the *fuck* is going on? Where's Emma?"

"I told you. She's not feeling so good," Jule said

shortly, then fiddled with his door. "And, uh, well, I got to take a little road trip, and I thought maybe you might want to come with me."

Jack gazed over the line of trees to the other ruined mansions, quiet now, woodsmoke threading from their chimneys. "Why would I want to do *that*?"

"Because you're becoming a fucking agoraphobic, that's why. I think so, and Emma thinks so—"

Jack turned to his friend in disbelief. "*Emma* thinks I should get in a car with *you*?"

"Oh for Christ's sake! You've been in a car with me a hundred thousand times—"

"Jule, you're *drunk*."

Jule looked hurt. "You used to drive with me when I was drunk."

Jack felt like screaming. Instead he said, "We were younger then. We were in school. And *that's* not even a good excuse," he added heatedly, "especially—oh, forget it. Look, Jule, why don't I try calling someone—"

"Fuck you." Jule's tone was even. He smiled affably, pulling the door open and easing his bulk into the seat. "Just get in the fucking car, Jackie. You know, Emma tried to have a, a what-you-call-it—an intervention. Because I'm an alcoholic. Ha! Like where the fuck they gonna lock me up? Her and some people we know at home, this guy from the hospital and Edgar Evans." Edgar was senior partner at Jule's old law firm. "You know what I did?"

He stopped and fixed Jack with a challenging gaze. Jack stared back, holding open the passenger door. Finally he said, "No. What did you do?"

"I belted him. Edgar. Laid him out right on the floor of the fucking kitchen. I would have hit someone else, too, but there was four of them, counting Emma, and only one of me." He leaned across the seat and stared up at Jack, his voice dropping to a whisper. "I told them, and I'll tell you, Jackie—

"I do this by choice. *By choice*. I may be an alcoholic but I have my reasons. You understand, Jackie?"

Jack swallowed, the door handle like ice beneath his palm. "I—I don't think it's that we don't understand, Jule, everyone understands—"

"You do not. You do not have the slightest fucking intimation of an idea." Jule's voice was calm. "Something's happened to me, Jackie, something very strange. Maybe someday I'll tell you about it."

He thumped the car seat and laughed. "Maybe even today. *Maybe that's why I came here to get you!*" he cried. "Ever think of that?"

"Uh, no." Jack took a deep breath and took a step backward. "Look, I'd love to go with you, Jule, but— you know, I'm thinking about this now, and I, really, *really* shouldn't leave Grandmother alone, or—"

"Don't sweat it." With amazingly fluid strength Jule grabbed Jack's arm and yanked him into the car, then pulled the door shut after him. "Here, look at this, Jackie—"

Jule patted at his pockets, grandly pulled out a small cherry red oblong. "See this here? This is Emma's. One of those beeper things, they plug into some relay somewhere so they work even when the power's down, they give 'em to all the senior doctors at Northern Westchester. I'll leave this with Grandmother. If there's any problem, she can call Emma."

Jack stared dubiously at the beeper. "And what? Emma's going to come down here with a scalpel? She's forty miles away, Jule! Plus you said she's sick—"

"I don't *know* that she's sick. She just—she doesn't look so good, that's all. Probably it's nothing." Jule shook his head. "Look, leave the beeper here, okay? Emma could at least call the police or something. Don't sweat it, Jackie, please?"

"You just told me—" Jack began angrily. But Jule had already bolted from the car and loped onto the porch to bang at the door. It cracked open and Jack could see a tiny wedge of Mrs. Iverson's face, the cherry red beeper disappearing into her hand. Before he could do anything more than gape, the car shuddered as Jule jumped back into the seat beside him.

"C'mon, Jackie-boy," he begged. "How often do I ask you to do anything? I just want some company, okay? I have a client up in Goldens Bridge, an actress, she's on *Till the End of the World*, I'm representing her in a breach of contract thing. It's the weekend, I got to deliver something to the studio, down at the Pyramid, and—well, something else, something I have to do. I thought maybe you'd like to come with me. We could talk, Jackie. It was nice, seeing you this summer. It's been a long time since we talked like that."

His tone grew wistful. Jack looked at his friend's unshaven face, glanced down and saw the glint of glass on the floor at his feet. "Well, yeah," Jack said. "But couldn't you just stay overnight here? Then we could—"

Jule shook his head. "I have this errand. I mean, one reason I agreed to it is I thought we could do this—I could pick you up, drop you off on the way back—"

His voice trailed off. He stared mournfully at the ceiling. After a moment Jack sighed.

"All right. But we *have* to be back by tonight."

"No prob." With a grin Jule turned the ignition. "*Great!* You're so great, Jackie!"

"I'm a fucking pushover, is what I am." Jack shook his head. "Let's get going. I don't want to be in the city after dark."

"You won't," cried Jule. With a groan the Range

Rover started up the drive, its barbed-wire sheath trembling like dried grass. "Isn't this *great*, Jackie?"

They were off.

Jack sat in silence, trying to breathe through his mouth, so as not to smell the nauseating odor of stale liquor, and stared outside. How utterly the world had changed! How normal it all seemed! Jule navigated the burned-out corridor of Hudson Terrace, the garish shells of mansions spray-painted with elaborate tribal designs, their filigreed verandas braided with barbed wire and broken strings of Christmas lights. Now and then they saw another vehicle, delivery vans, or automobiles creeping cautiously around potholes. Jack recognized the battered Jeep that belonged to his doctor, lurching away from the hospital.

Then they were heading south on the Saw Mill. The road was corrugated with frost heaves, the median and shoulder lined with abandoned vehicles gutted of everything; even their paint had been burned or rusted away. Some of the wrecks had been dragged back from the road to form hivelike clusters where people moved slowly and with everyday calm about their lives: tending fires, chasing children, making windbreaks out of plywood and dead trees. As the car barreled past, dogs came running up behind them, yelping triumphantly.

"Fucking leeches," muttered Jule. He swerved the Rover toward a clutch of yellow mongrels. "Someone oughta *torch* 'em."

Jack recalled the night they had decorated the Christmas tree, the air rent with incantatory voices. He said nothing, only turned to stare outside. The crimson sky gave the endless ranks of dead cars and crumbling overpasses an archaic sunset look. Jack thought of the ruined Claudian aqueduct, where he and Leonard had fucked in the dusty grass with cicadas shrilling overhead. He sighed, gazing at the ominous monoliths of Co-op City looming up from the smoke and rubble of a *fellahin* encampment.

"Thinking of Leonard?" Jule asked softly.

Jack glanced up in surprise. "How'd you know?"

"I can just tell." Jule gave him a sad smile and eased the car around a pile of burning refuse. "You have this—*noise*—you make, when you're thinking of Leonard. That son of a bitch," he added, scowling at a trio of boys throwing rocks at the passing traffic.

"Oh well," Jack said lightly, but he felt embarrassed. "You know how it is . . ."

"I *don't* know how it is, but I know how it *should* b—Jesus Christ!"

A dangerously overcrowded bus cut them off, passengers hanging from the open doors as it veered past. Jule yelled and pounded his horn, which made no sound, then turned to Jack. "You're worth ten of him, Jackie. I mean, I could understand it when you guys were kids. But carrying a torch for someone who dumped you and lives just to torment you . . ."

He shook his head. Jack glowered as they drove by the George Washington Bridge, its skeleton black against the lurid sky. Torn banners fluttered from the girders.

U.S. GOVT TO US: DIE NOW PRAY LATER!
NEED HELP? TRAINED PSYCHIC 250 FT
WASHINGTON 24 HRS
RAFAEL LLAMA MOMI

"I'm *not* carrying a fucking torch." Jack's voice rose angrily. He stared up at a defaced billboard, advertising GFI's e-service:

ONLY   DISCONNECT !!!

"It's just—I can *be* with him, you know?" Jack went on. "I can see him and get pissed at him and laugh at him and all the rest, it doesn't bother me at all. But sometimes, if I think of him—sometimes . . ."

He faltered, turning so Jule couldn't see his face. "—sometimes it's just hard. Even though it was so long ago. Because it was different then," he ended awkwardly. "Leonard was different."

"It was all different," said Jule. He pounded his useless horn again and passed the bus, his foot on the accelerator sending empty whiskey bottles rattling across the floor. "We're talking about a whole new ball game, Jackie. And *you* oughta get a new first baseman." He gave a sharp laugh and took one hand from the wheel, reached beneath the seat, and pulled out a bright pink plastic thermos with a straw sticking out of it. "Twenty years is a long time to wait to fall in love again."

Jack reddened, watching as Jule drank. "I mind my own fucking business about your drinking," he said. "So why don't you—"

"Oh, I don't know about *that*." Jule stuck the thermos between his legs. "Didn't sound like you were minding your own fucking business back at Lazyland. But listen, I didn't mean to give you a hard time. I'm sorry, Jackie." He shot Jack an abject look. "Really I am—"

"For Christsakes, Jule, keep your eyes on the *road*—"

"Ha!" Jule grinned and stomped on the gas. They roared up an exit ramp, bottles clattering to the back of the car, then down a narrow side street and onto the Harlem River Drive. Almost immediately the Rover jolted to a stop. "What shit is this?" bellowed Jule.

Traffic was at a standstill. Ragged children darted between cars, throwing themselves across the hoods to snap off windshield wipers and run away before an enraged driver could shoot at them. From overhead fell a thick rain of black ash., Jack coughed, his throat burning. His stomach knotted. Jule turned on the wipers, and they swept across the glass, leaving broad grey streaks. Then, miraculously, traffic inched forward again. The ash disappeared, as though they had driven clear of a snow squall, though a poisonous chemical reek now battled the odor of Scotch inside the car.

"Relax, Jack," said Jule as they crept along. "You'd need a bazooka to blast in here." He belted back another mouthful of whiskey, held the thermos out to Jack.

"Yeah, well, I think *that* guy has one." Jack ignored the thermos and pointed at a Cadillac wrapped with so much razor wire it was difficult to imagine where or how the driver could gain entry. "Jesus."

"These kids, they'll smash your window with a baseball bat and kill you, just for grins. Remember back when it was just washing your windows?"

"I hated that."

"*Everyone* hated it. That's why they kill us now."

Jack's gut tightened even more. He breathed in deeply, counted to eight, and slowly exhaled.

"Goddamn it, Jule," he gasped. Outside his window a girl with very black skin and filed teeth held up a broken rearview mirror. He had a glimpse of his own face, sunken cheeks and wide horrified eyes like some demonic mask. "Let's go *back*—"

"No, no, no." Ahead of them a gap suddenly opened in traffic. With an exultant cry Jule veered the car onto a side street, bouncing over a broken pile of railroad ties that had once formed part of a barricade. "See? We got through okay! Now if I can just figure out where the hell we are . . ."

Jack stared desolately out the window. "Riverside Drive?"

"Ha. Riverside Drive is the *river* now, Jackie-boy. Okay, I think this'll work—"

With a shriek of brakes the car made another turn. "Oh, *great,*" moaned Jack.

They were in an even narrower alley, slick with filth. To either side rose deserted grey buildings. Their crumbling concrete walls were smeared with graffiti: stick figures, crude faces; hands and breasts and dicks. No words, except for a warning stenciled over and over in grimy white paint.

CONDEMNED
SPECIAL ORDINANCE CITY OF NEW YORK

Only the uppermost stories had windows, tiny black squares now empty of glass. There were a few sad remnants of habitation. A towel hung out to dry into a dirty yellow stalactite; a plastic poinsettia; a child's shoe atop a pile of broken glass. Jack couldn't bear to imagine what catastrophe would have driven people from that awful place to the worse horrors of the street. He bit his lip and squeezed his eyes shut.

Oh God, just let me get home safe, home and I'll never leave again . . .

"It's terrible, isn't it?" murmured Jule. The Range Rover crawled forward, its barbed wire scraping menacingly across the broken walls. "I think this is one of those projects where the children all got that virus and died. They had to evacuate, then they ran out of money to clean it up. Nice, huh?"

Jack opened his eyes. Beside him Jule blinked several times, as though they had driven into sunlight, and went on. "It's funny. You never know just how horrible anything can be, until you have a child die. Anyone at all in the world, doesn't matter who—something like that happens, the only person can understand is someone else who lost their kid. 'The Final Club,'" he said pensively. "We all join that one, sooner or later. But *this* club is tougher to get into, Jackie. Too goddamn fucking tough."

Jule grabbed the plastic thermos again, sucked at it until a gurgle sounded: empty. He swore and tossed it behind him. As Jack watched, his friend's drunken expression hardened. His eyes grew cloudy, as though filling up with some opaque liquid. He muttered, nothing Jack could understand.

"Jule?" he asked. There was no answer.

A bottle shattered beneath the Range Rover's wheels. A few yards ahead of them the alley grew dark. A dead end; but the car kept moving. Jule's face was grey, his eyes set with the horrible calm that precedes drunken rage.

Jack glanced around furtively. *What the fuck is going on?* In the back he saw a folding snow shovel, what looked like a plastic bag full of dirt. Ghastly scenarios flashed through his mind—Jule pulling a gun on him, Emma bashed across the head with a shovel and buried somewhere in Putnam County . . .

"Uh, Jule? JULE? I *think* this is a dead end . . ."

Jule smiled mindlessly. His foot tapped the gas pedal; the car surged forward, into the shadows. Jack sat helpless beside him, hands clutching at his seat.

Oh fuck this is it—

Only instead of slamming into concrete, the Range Rover nosed resolutely into what proved to be—

—not a wall, not a building, but an immense pile of garbage, perhaps ten feet high. Plywood, broken chairs, window frames, plastic trash bags . . . slowly the car plowed through them all, wheels sliding and engine grinding, until with a heart-stopping lurch it shot out onto Lenox Avenue.

"Hey hey hey," said Jule. He reached under his seat

and withdrew another plastic bottle, this one emblazoned with a Barbie logo. He popped it open and took a
long pull. "Used to be a good Ethiopian restaurant
around here. Christ, Jack, what's the matter? You look
terrible."

Jack sank into his seat and ran a hand across his
forehead. His fingers were icy. "Listen, Jule, I really don't
feel very good. Can't you take me back?"

"No."

"Okay." Jack swallowed. His tongue felt thick,
coated with bitter dust. "How—how long is this going
to take?"

"Not long. The studio's down at the Pyramid. I'll
leave you in the car so we don't have to hassle about
parking. I'll be in and—"

Anger spiked through Jack's misery. "I am *not* waiting in this fucking car."

Jule shrugged. "Suit yourself."

They drove in silence for a long time. There was
surprisingly little traffic, considering it was the holiday
season and most driving restrictions were lifted. The
usual mess of taxis and buses; robust-looking vehicles—pickups, Jeeps, Range Rovers and Land Rovers—
commandeered by drivers wealthy enough to afford gas
and parking; astonishingly dilapidated old American
cars crowded with what appeared to be three or four
generations' worth of families from Brooklyn or Queens
or the Bronx, out for a drive, all moving slowly but
steadily toward midtown. Water was everywhere, sluic-
ing in a strong current down either side of the street
and forming whirlpools above sewer grates and spots
where manhole covers had been removed. The sky had
darkened from yellow to a tigerish orange. It made the
water look molten, the darkly silhouetted buildings like
columns of smoke. Jack watched the traffic and thought

of people fleeing Pompeii beneath the lowering cone of Vesuvius.

The Range Rover breasted through an intersection swollen with rain. To one side the road had collapsed and was now blockaded by sandbags and sawhorses. As Jack stared, a man in a bright orange kayak hove into view, his paddle cutting smoothly through blazing water as he propelled himself toward the river.

Jack shook his head, fear chased away by the sheer strangeness and perverse beauty of it all. He cracked his window, letting in a blast of cold salt air, heavily laced with exhaust. Water seeped through the floor. He drew his feet up to sit cross-legged on the damp seat and wondered if the Range Rover would be swept like the kayak to the Hudson.

"Look at that," marveled Jule. It was the first time either of them had spoken for nearly an hour. "Over there—"

A huge tree had smashed upside down against a building. Twenty feet above the washed-out sidewalk its immense root mass hung like a black cloud.

"Wow." Jack shook his head. "I didn't know there *were* still trees that big here."

"Probably there's not. Probably it came uprooted somewhere upstate and just floated down. But look behind it—"

Jack pressed his face close to the window, straining to see through the filthy glass and tangled barbed wire. After a moment he made out something caught in the limbs, ten feet from the ground. "What the *hell*?"

He made fists of his hands, fighting off another surge of fear. Above the tree trunk bobbed four skeletal faces. The water's reflected gold touched hollows where cheeks, eyes, nose had been; sent strands of light rippling across the surface like fine hair. Antlers branched from each skull like lightning. It was a full minute before Jack realized that the ghastly faces were masks, and that the stags' horns were not bloodied but wrapped round about with red ribbons.

"Aaaahhh . . ." His breath came in a long shuddering whistle. He half gasped, half laughed as the Range Rover sloshed past the macabre vision. "Jesus! That *scared* me!"

He glanced back to where the masked figures were clambering onto the tree's outer branches. One of them appeared to be attacking it with a hacksaw. Jack coughed, his mouth tasting of bile. Impulsively he turned to Jule.

"I—I had a dream like that," he said. "That's why it scared me. About these people—men, with horns like that."

Jule nodded. In the florid light his face looked almost comically inflated, like a damp red balloon. He slowed the car to take a corner, sending a jeweled arc of water against the barricaded facade of the Empire Hotel, and said, "Yeah. Rachel comes to talk to me."

"They were—" Jack stopped and stared open-mouthed at his friend. "Uh—what?" He desperately ran through any Rachels he might be expected to know, beside the obvious one. "Rachel?"

"It started about a year ago," Jule continued, his voice low but calm, as though confiding a stock tip. "When I had to go to court up in Poughkeepsie. I was just coming back, getting onto 684, and she was there"—he pointed at Jack's seat—"sitting right there. She told me I forgot to put on my turn signal."

"Oh." Jack tried to keep his tone even. "So! Uh—was it on? The turn signal?"

"Sure it was on. A little kid, what does she know from cars? But I just about had a heart attack, I can tell you."

"Uh, yeah," said Jack. He leaned forward, gazing straight ahead. Cars snaked down the street, pausing and starting up again at regular intervals; the traffic signals were working here. When he glanced aside, Jule was staring at him, his dark eyes fever-bright.

"That's why I drive around so much," he said. "She rides with me, Jackie. She talks to me."

"*Oh.*" Jack swallowed.

"She doesn't forgive me. I mean, she doesn't *blame* me, *I* wasn't driving the car that killed her. But all this shit now, my drinking, all that—she doesn't forgive me, Jackie. She doesn't forgive me."

Jack glanced up. He saw Jule's face, not slack with alcohol but somehow *hardened* by it, calcified; the lineaments like fissures in stone, his eyes dry and glittering as quartz. He quickly looked away again. "Does—have you told Emma about this?"

"Sure."

"What does she think?"

Jule shrugged. "She doesn't believe me. She thinks it's the DTs or something. Actually, what she thinks is that I haven't processed through my grief. She thinks I'm still in denial." He stared at Jack measuringly. "I mean, *you* think I'm nuts, don't you?"

Jack took in his friend's haggard unshaven face, his unruly curls and brilliant eyes, the carpet of bottles and empty thermoses covering the floor. He decided what would be nuts right now would be to get into an argument with Jule.

"I don't think you're nuts." His voice sounded so patently false he was afraid Jule would laugh or even strike him. "I think Emma's probably right—you're still grieving, or—"

A delivery van pulled in front of them. Jule beat on the silent horn. "Of *course* I'm still grieving." His voice was oddly calm, almost detached; as though Jack was the one exhibiting dubious behavior. "*You're* still grieving for that guy Eric you were in love with, aren't you?"

Jack stiffened. "Yes."

"And Peter and all those other guys who—"

"*Yes.*"

"Well, it doesn't ever really end, does it?" Jule's voice dropped. "It's like you wake up one day and they chopped off your hand. Maybe sometime it stops bleeding and scars over, but you don't grow a *new* one." He leaned closer to the windshield, frowning as he waited for a light to change. When it did the car crept forward again, and he added matter-of-factly, "I know Rachel's dead. I never said she wasn't dead, I'm not *denying* that she's dead. I just said I see her sometimes. She comes . . ."

For the first time his voice broke. Jack's heart welled as he watched his friend tighten his hold on the steering wheel. Jule blinked and shook his head. After a minute he continued.

"She comes. Right there, where you're sitting. The first couple of times it was at night—I just looked over and there she was. She'd say, 'Hi, Daddy.' I almost went off the road.

"And now she's here all the time I mean, no matter what I do, if I drink, if I don't drink: she's still there. Afterward, it always seems like maybe I was dreaming; but then she always comes back . . ."

Unexpectedly he grabbed Jack's shoulder, and Jack gasped as the car veered toward the sidewalk. But Jule only gave a harsh laugh, steering back into the line of traffic. "And she doesn't forgive me. I thought maybe if I explained things, maybe she'd understand. But it doesn't work that way. I guess they have their own itinerary. Their own way of doing things."

Jack tried to focus on something neutral, finally settling on the glove compartment. "Who?"

"The dead. Like people always think they can be summoned, with a Ouija board or a séance or whatever; but really they just do what they want to. Just like us. It's not even like they have some message. Sometimes they just want to be with us, I think."

Jack shivered uncontrollably. He recalled the sound of his grandfather's tread upon the stairs at Lazyland, the smell of cigarette smoke and Irish whiskey and his touch upon Jack's cheek, cold and feathery as snow. Before he could stop himself he blurted, "I know—I know what you mean. A few months ago I had this dream, about my grandfather. Only it wasn't really a dream. He was really *there*, and he—he gave me something."

He turned to Jule, expecting him to let loose again with that bitter laugh. Instead Jule nodded thoughtfully.

"What did he give you?"

Jack hesitated. For one moment he considered telling Jule about the Fusax. But suddenly it all seemed too bizarre. He stared out the window, depressed. Crazy as it all seemed, he *could* have told the old Jule about it, and never worried. When, at nineteen, Jack finally came storming out of the closet, Jule had only shrugged and said, "Okay by me, *kemo sabe*." At Georgetown, Jack's single, harrowing acid trip had brought Jule running from his own room, to mind-sit his friend for twelve hours in the middle of a February snowstorm. And Jule was the only person Jack had really confided in during his long disastrous affair with Leonard, and afterward when his lover Eric died.

But he was unsure of how to deal with *this* Jule. Would he go home and tell Emma? Or shame Jack into throwing it out, or bringing it to the hospital for testing? Would he even register Jack's words at all?

"It was just something I'd lost," he said at last.

"Like your *mind*?"

Jack forced a grin. "Something like that."

Around them vehicles slowed as though stuck in quicksand. They were in midtown. A few blocks to the south glittered a vast triangular complex of buildings, glass-and-steel walls shining gold and green and red like some monstrous Christmas ornament. From one side bulged a huge glass-domed arena, ovoid, still fluttering with orange construction tape and DANGER: KEEP OUT signs: the site of the millennial ball two days hence. High overhead, covering it like the motley armor of a caddis fly, an array of solar shields blinked from black to silver, turning this way and that in an urgent search for light. There were bristling antennas like the spines of some huge undersea animal. Satellite dishes and windmills vied for space with hotel and television logos, a neon sign for a restaurant named Pynchon. Across the central pyramid's surface, rippling letters splashed bright as water.

GFI WORLDWIDE

Jack gazed awestruck. Jule banged the steering wheel and laughed.

"Don't get out much, huh?"

"It's been a while." Jack smiled sheepishly. "I mean, they built that thing so fast . . . I remember when this was all live sex shows."

"Oh yeah," Jule leered. "The good old days." He stared up at the monolith with its swags of Christmas lights, his eyes narrowing. "Fucking Christmas. I hate fucking Christmas. And I hate this fucking place," he said very softly. "I really hate this place. Because they think it makes up for all that other shit, you know? They think you can walk inside and forget about everything *here*—"

He gestured fiercely at the window, the knots of barbed wire and flaming blocks of sky that could be glimpsed between the buildings. "—they think we'll just forget. Like with their fucking blimps. They think we can just pick up the pieces and start over again . . .

"But I'll tell you something, Jackie." Jule's words were like granite falling. "You can't ever start over again. Not once you've crapped in your own mess kit like we have. You don't get a fucking second chance. That's not how the world works, Jackie. That's not how it works anymore."

Jack was silent. After a minute Jule laughed; Jack half expected him to yell "Fake Out!" but he said nothing more. The Range Rover inched along, beneath a marquee whose fluid titles melted into sherbet-colored grids.

THE DANNY SHOW!
SUNSHINE SKYE LIVE!
BONITA & THE WAVETRAMPS
ION JAMIE
THE FOUR SEASONS AT
GLOBAL PYRAMID
G L O B E N E T INC.

"How can they *do* this?" Jack pointed at the shimmering edifice, the waves of people flowing in and out of revolving doors at its base. "I mean, how is it powered?"

Jule slid the car into a long line of idling taxis and limousines. He held up one hand, rubbing together the thumb and first two fingers. "*Dinero*, Jackie-boy."

"I know that! But do they have their own genera-tors? Or what?"

"Yes. *And* 'or what.' " Jule peered up at the great Pyramid. "Let's see. Solar panels, some kind of plasma grid. Windmills. A champagne-effect reflexive water-fall. Supposedly they've got their own nuclear reactor, too," he added thoughtfully.

Jack snorted. "So how come I can't make a fucking phone call?"

" 'Cause you're not on TV. You're not GFI Worldwide." At Jack's sour expression Jule laughed. "Hey, get over it! I mean, here you are *looking* at where they make *The Danny Show*! What else do you want?"

Before Jack could reply Jule gunned the motor. In front of them a lapis-colored limousine slid away from the sidewalk. The Range Rover roared into its spot. A doorman in Four Seasons livery started for the passen-ger door, but Jack waved him off.

"All right, listen," commanded Jule. He rummaged in the seat behind him until he found a leather portfolio, sat for a minute staring at his friend. His expression was intense, almost wild-eyed. But then unexpectedly he reached out and rested one hand on Jack's cheek. "You know how to drive a standard, right?"

Jack jerked away from him. "I'm *not* waiting in the—"

"*Listen*. It costs forty dollars to park here for five minutes! This'll take me thirty seconds. You wait here, anyone asks tell them you're picking up someone from *The Danny Show*. Or Sunshine Skye," he said, glancing up at the marquee. "A cop comes, just drive around the block, okay? Okay."

Jack watched as he got out of the car and strode over to the sidewalk, carrying the portfolio officiously in front of him. Before he went inside Jule turned. He was swaying slightly, and he looked immeasurably sad.

"Fuck you!" Jack said under his breath, then gave in and waved. Jule nodded and disappeared into the crowd at the entrance, and Jack turned his attention back to the scene outside. Well-dressed men and women came and went in a steady stream of overly bright colors. Lime green, candy pink, the pale, almost electric blue of a newborn puppy's skin. Glittering swathes of red and green and gold Christmas lights hung above the revolving doors. A knot of Japanese businessmen, excited gestures belying their somber clothes and retro Infoguide sunglasses that made them look like extras from *Not of This Earth*. More models in silly masks, posturing with smokeless cigarettes. A bizarrely tall, thin man like a giant insect, surrounded by people waving cordless microphones. Jack watched, trying to keep his expression blank, slightly bored; trying not to betray any anxiety as more vehicles pulled up beside him and honked.

"Shit," he muttered. He began to breathe deeply, trying to stay calm. He had no way of knowing what time it was, but at least fifteen minutes had passed, he was sure of that. He could see cars entering and leaving the public parking area with clockwork regularity. He briefly thought of parking—he wouldn't admit it to Jule, but he was dying to peek inside the world's most famous corporate complex. But he'd be damned if he'd spend his own money on this idiotic venture, and he'd be too proud to let Jule reimburse him.

"God *damn* it."

He leaned forward and starting playing with the Range Rover's entertainment system. Soft green and red lights blinked off and on. When he tried the radio he got only static, then a very long advertisement for the

Global Pyramid Four Seasons, recited by a woman with a brisk Pacific Rim accent broadcasting from the hotel. Jack shook his head and craned his neck to look up at the colorful marquee again.

THE DANNY SHOW!
BY INVITATION ONLY: THE PARTY OF THE MILLENNIUM!
STUDIO TOURS LEAVE EVERY MINUTE!

The entertainment panel had a CD and tape player. He opened the glove compartment to see what was in there, found only papers and a squashed plastic cup. There were no CDs in the backseat, either. He sighed in exasperation and glanced out the window. There seemed to be a bottleneck at one of the revolving doors. Several uniformed security guards ran down the sidewalk and began pushing their way through the growing crowd. One held a phone to his mouth and was speaking intently, his face grim.

Maybe Danny had a heart attack, thought Jack. He decided to take his chances with whatever music Jule had been listening to earlier, punched the Tape Play button, and closed his eyes. Low hissing came from the speakers.

"Damn it."

Only Jule would spend an extra three thousand dollars for a state-of-the-art music center, and then have nothing to play on it. He was reaching to stab the OFF button when the static cleared. Jule's soft voice filled the car.

"Jackie. I'm sorry this isn't Brian Eno." A pause; the sound of swallowing, something clinking against the tape recorder. "This is gonna sound really melodramatic. I'm sorry, Jackie. By the time you hear this . . ."

"No."

The voice went on, the words blurring into each other—

". . . because she's sick, she thinks I don't know but I heard her on the phone. She may have—she may have gotten it from me—"

"*Fuck!*" Jack shouted, pounding the dashboard; "*fuck, fuck!*—"

". . . can't live like this. But I—I don't want you to think it had anything to do with you, Jackie, Emma either. I know it's selfish—"

—and then Jack was out of the car and running, shoving people aside.

"*Hey! Asshole! What—*"

"Julie," he breathed, then began to shout above his roaring heart. "*JULIE!*"

There were armed guards at the revolving doors, their eyes flicking nervously across the excited mob. "Let me in!" Jack yelled desperately. "Goddammit, *I know him*! Please, let me—"

One of the guards raised her arms to block him. Just then her head mike blared, and there was an answering blast from a speaker overhead. When she looked up Jack pushed through the door and into the security checkpoint.

"—WHITE MALE, ARMED, GATE SEVENTEEN—"

More guards, dogs straining at leashes, overturned chairs and papers blown across the floor. Monitors chattered and shrieked, the high-pitched hum of head mikes soared off into static. A masked man in a black suit was shouting at several wildly gesticulating guards. Directly behind them was the glowing arc of the metal detector, and through that Jack glimpsed a milling crowd, uniforms and well-dressed women covering their mouths, people being pushed away by city police, all under a blinding sun. He moved as in a dream through the shadowy booth, slowly and with intense purpose, pushing aside a fallen chair, hearing it strike the floor with an echoing *crack*. The man in the suit turned his head, his mouth opened, but Jack heard nothing. Hands reached for him but he swept them aside, his feet sliding across newspapers as he reached the metal detector and passed through it. Then he was in the sun, blinking and shading his eyes. A few feet in front of him the crowd had formed a broad half circle, as though watching street musicians, a boy performing magic tricks. Several men and women in red-and-white uniforms knelt on the ground shouting at each other while armed guards waved back the crowd. Someone grabbed Jack and restrained him, he struck at their hands but could not pull away so stood there with the rest, staring down into the center ring.

Jule lay there on his back. His face was pale save for a circular bruise, deep red and blackish purple, that radiated from mouth to chin, up across his shattered nose to touch the pouched skin beneath his eyes. A corona of blood and what looked like black earth was etched around his head; his eyes were bright red, open, staring up into the brilliance. Medics had torn his suit open, but there was nothing to be done, even Jack could see that, blood in a long line like spittle across his chin spilling to the floor, his big hand splayed open and a policeman crouched there with a white cloth and a plastic bag, fingering a gun delicately, as though it were an orchid.

"Julie," whispered Jack. He lifted his head, his face slack, and gazed across the circle. Behind the crowd there were trees, stones, a waterfall; clouds of twinkling red and green lights. A young man comforted a slender woman in white who was shaking convulsively. A crimson arc was sprayed across the bodice of her dress. Jack shook his head, his mouth yawning open; then froze as he saw the child.

She stood within the crowd, Emma's tumbled blond curls and Jule's hazel eyes, her hands raised before her and clasped in expectation. Sun streamed onto her, so bright it made a glare of her clothes, if she even wore clothes. Jack, dumbfounded, could see only that she was smiling. As he stared she raised her head. Her eyes locked with his, Julie's eyes, wide and laughing. Her lips moved, and Jack strained to hear her voice.

"—*please*, go!"

Someone jarred him, and he stumbled, crying out. When he looked up an instant later the child was gone. Where she had been a woman with very short dark hair stood in dappled sun as though entranced, staring not at Jule's body but at a point a few feet above it in the bright air. Her features were obscured behind Noh-mask makeup. Her lips moved, and her hands. Amidst the crackle of walkie-talkies and sirens wailing in the distance Jack could hear her voice, clear and thin as falling water:

"He has come through."

Then someone grabbed him and pulled him backwards, into the security booth.

"You know this guy? You know him?" a policeman shouted.

Jack nodded, straining to look back out into the light.

"HOLD HIM!" someone screamed, and he was shoved against the wall.

They held him for questioning, first by security and then by city police, and finally brought him to another security checkpoint on the main floor, with an adjoining office that he assumed was nothing but a holding area for suspicious persons who violated GFI security. He was strip-searched and sprayed with Viconix, checked by a medic for shock and made to fill out numerous forms with GFI logos. Outside whirling red and blue lights and a deafening wail signaled the arrival of ambulances. Jack sat numbly and watched on a monitor as an emergency crew hurried in, after some minutes rushed out again, pushing a long white-draped gurney.

"His wife works in Mount Kisco," he said hoarsely, though he had no idea if anyone was even listening. "Northern Westchester Medical Center . . ."

"She's been notified." The police detective who had been questioning him turned from another monitor. She sighed, watched as a masked officer affixed a magnetic strip around Jack's wrist. "They're probably going to want to see you again, after the autopsy."

He nodded.

"Do you want anything? Something to eat?" She tilted her head, exhausted, but trying to do the right thing. On her console a tiny artificial Christmas tree listed to one side. "There's some kind of fake coffee . . ."

No.

He listened mutely as the detective and various flunkies fielded calls from hospitals, police stations, other offices within the Pyramid. The Range Rover had been impounded, presumably until Emma could take possession of it. Jack sat forgotten in a swivel chair by the wall, wondering if he, too, would have to wait for Emma to appear before he could go home. His mouth was dry; he drank tepid water from a bottle. It tasted of plastic and something harshly chemical. His stomach recoiled; he clenched his teeth, fighting nausea, a throbbing darkness that pulsed before his eyes no matter where he looked.

"You can leave now."

A shadow moved toward him. The police detective,

her face greenish from the computer monitors. He lifted his head, felt an aching weariness in neck and shoulders. Had he fallen asleep?

"Mr. Finnegan?"

"Yes?" His voice cracked. It hurt to speak.

"You can go. We located Dr. Isikoff. She—"

"Oh God."

"She's trying to make arrangements. To get down here. It will probably take her a while—she said something about a brother-in-law or a friend up there?"

He recognized the effort at kindness in her tone, but could only gaze at her in anguish. After a moment she asked, "Do you have a car?"

He shook his head.

"Do you have any friends or relatives here you could stay with? Do you want to find a hotel? No. Well. Okay, then."

She crossed to the door and remained there. After a moment he realized she was waiting for him to stand, to leave. "I'll see what I can do about arranging to get you back home. Rye, is it?"

"Yonkers," he whispered.

"Right. Yonkers. Well." She cleared her throat. Pity warred with duty in her expression. "I'm sorry. But I'll have to ask you to leave now, Mr. Finnegan. I have to finish filing my report."

He stood. He felt utterly detached from his body—hands, feet, head all untethered from the terrible shattered mass of his heart. At the doorway he stopped, that darkness rushing in, his head spinning . . .

"You can wait in the atrium." The policewoman's voice was gentle. He saw but did not feel her hand upon his arm, propelling him through the door. "I cleared it with security, they understand . . . a terrible situation. There's places to eat under the waterfall, you can sit there and wait. I'll see about getting you a ride home."

He nodded and left the office, walked down a blue-lit passage he had no memory of entering. Gradually its dimness gave way to the atrium's artificial daylight. He left the passage, walked slowly across the atrium's stone floor, staring at his feet as they crushed a thin layer of moss and lichen, very soft grass that had the look of infant hair. Tiny colored Christmas lights were strung between stands of birch trees. His breath stabbed rhythmically at his chest; he wondered vaguely if he was having a heart attack. In front of the revolving doors a small crowd still lingered, people with cameras and vidcams, security guards in GFI red and gold. But there was no sign of any medical personnel, no sign that earlier a body had lain crumpled on the grass. Outside, the ambulance had gone, and the police cars. Through the smoked-glass doors he could glimpse the same dark line of limos beaded here and there with a yellow taxi. Another gaudy knot of Bright Young Things burst in, giggling as they left the security station. From where he stood Jack could smell their perfumes, the ecclesiastical richness of myrrh and Opium overpowering the vanilla scent of Viconix.

And a briskly chemical balsam odor—he took a few more steps, stared down at the grass where Jule had fallen. It looked scorched, there was a faint blurred outline where they had poured disinfectant onto the ground. The heaviness in his chest became nausea. He turned away and half ran, half stumbled across the vast room.

He found a table on the far side of the atrium. The waterfall cascaded from several stories above him, a heavy glittering curtain with numerous small rainbows dancing where the sun pierced it. The air smelled sweetly of dirt and sun. Birds darted past him, small brown birds with red beaks, and lit upon the branches of a Japanese maple. Jack sat with hands on his knees, shut his eyes and breathed deeply, concentrating on the warmth spilling across his face, willing his mind to silence. After a few minutes he could feel his heart slow. The devastating sense of rupture fade to a preternatural calm.

It will hit me later, he thought, and opened his eyes. He raised his hands and held them before his face, stared until he was certain they did not tremble. *It will hit me later*. A waiter came and he ordered mineral water and some pepper-flavored aquavit. The liquor came in a tiny bottle shaped like a fish, prettily arranged on a cerulean glass tray with sprigs of watercress and myrtle. It was icily restorative; he ordered a second bottle, and swallowed a dropperful of Fusax as he waited.

"May I join you?"

A dark-haired woman stood on the other side of the granite block that served as a table. She wore a black dress interwoven with tattered ribbons and shreds of Mylar, very ugly, very fashionable. At first he thought she was wearing a mask, but after a moment he saw that it was makeup, chalky white foundation, red-lined eyes, birdlime mouth. He had a dim sense of recognition, after a moment recalled that she had been in the crowd surrounding Jule's body. She had been the one who cried *He has come over*. The odd words rushed at him, his head began to swim again. He moaned and covered his face with his hands.

"Here—put your head between your knees, take a deep breath—one, two—"

He felt her fingers on the nape of his neck—she had gloved hands, very warm inside their silken sheathing. "Breathe, breathe—"

He did as she said, sucking in quick gulps of air.

"Slowly, *slowly* . . ."

Her voice was low and brusque. Her touch upon his bare neck grew warmer, so much so that after a minute or two it hurt, as though someone had placed an extremely hot heating pad there.

"Okay—I'm—I'm better now," he gasped. When he started to sit up she grabbed his shoulder.

"Slow down! You'll pass out—"

At last he was upright again. She sat beside him, her hand still on his shoulder, and peered at him intently.

"Better?" He nodded. "Okay. Here, then—"

She picked up the crystal fish of aquavit and handed it to him. He sipped it gratefully, nodding thanks.

"I'm Nellie Candry," the woman said. "Christ. I saw what happened. Your friend . . ." Her gaze shifted to the Pyramid's entrance, and she brushed nervously at her hair. "Horrible. And then I saw you sitting here, you looked like you were going to pass out . . ."

She hesitated. Her gloved fingers pressed tightly along the table's rough stone edge, as though she were clinging to it. A band of shadow passed across the granite and was gone. "I work here—my office is upstairs. I thought, if you wanted to get away, have some privacy. If you needed to make some phone calls. Or just rest—I have a futon . . ."

He must have been looking at her strangely. "You can check me out with security if you want," she reassured him. "I mean, I'm a fucking vice president, okay, I'm not going to hurt you. Or maybe you just want to be left alone . . . ?"

"No." The word rang out so loudly that he winced. "I mean, no, I don't really want to be alone. I—I've been ill, this was the first time I've left my house in a long while, and—"

Her eyes grew gentle as his voice broke. "It's okay,"

she murmured. "It was—really horrible. Don't you have any friends nearby?"

He shook his head. "Not now—I used to, but . . ."

"Yeah, well, I know what *that's* like." She sighed, picked up the half-empty crystal of aquavit and tilted it toward her, peering into the fish's gullet, then put it back down. "Look. Why don't you come upstairs with me. You can have some time alone, at least—"

"But the police—they were going to find me a ride—"

"We'll call them from upstairs."

Before he knew it she was helping him to his feet. The waiter appeared, his head inclined questioningly. Nellie waved away Jack's hand as he reached for his pocket. "No—let me—"

She gave the waiter a credit card and waited as he processed it. Then she touched Jack's elbow, pointing at a softly lit alcove where elevator doors glowed blue and green.

"Come. I'll take you there."

The elevator brought them to the thirtieth floor, midway up the Pyramid's interior, then opened onto a space blazing with video monitors. Huge doors of cobalt blue glass bore a holographic logo and the words AGRIPPA MUSIC.

"This way," Nellie said, taking him by the shoulder and gently pushing him down the hall, away from the light. "We'll go to my editing room. Quieter there . . ."

He followed her down another corridor, and another, ended up in a nondescript twilit hallway lined with doors. They made little effort at conversation, besides Jack telling Nellie his name. He walked beside her, squinting to read placards: Kingston Music, First Analysis Corp., Merton Defense Systems. At a door reading Pathfinder Films she pulled out a plastic key and slid it into the wall. A grid of light exploded blue and yellow, flashed warningly as she pulled the door open and motioned him inside.

"This is it," she said.

Her office was a chilly warren of tiny odd-shaped rooms stacked floor to ceiling with silver canisters of film and black videocassettes. A few small battery-driven lights were affixed to the ceiling, their plastic housings the color of ivory. They cast a feeble sepia glow on everything, so that Jack felt as though he were in an old photograph. There was a small metal desk littered with curling brown ribbons of film, a broken light box and old-fashioned loupes, the remains of a boxed sushi lunch, a cellular telephone, some empty medicine vials. Nellie picked up the phone and rang downstairs. She gave her name and number to security and told them to notify her when someone arrived to drive John Finnegan home.

"Okay." She dropped the phone onto a pile of discs. "They're waiting for an officer who's going off duty, some guy who lives in the North Bronx. He says he'll drive you, but it'll be a few hours."

Jack nodded. "Thank you."

She shrugged and gestured toward the hall. "Can you stand okay? Here—come on, I'll give you the tour—"

More arcane objects filled the short hallway. Jack guessed they were cameras or other types of recording equipment. Leaning in a corner was some kind of tall staff. Strips of leather hung from it, and red ceramic beads. On the floor beside it lay a wooden object, a crude mask with gouged eyes and an obscenely long wooden tongue dangling from its grinning mouth. Mounted on one side was a single very large antler. Three of its points were broken off, but two very long ones remained—it must have come from an immense stag. There was a hole where the other antler had been.

"Three have been taken, but two are left," Nellie said, looking at the grotesque face with an odd smile. "Sorry about the mess." She grimaced and nudged a canvas sack stuffed with books. "This way—"

There was no other way. Four steps brought them to a miniscule bathroom with Biolet composting toilet and no provisions for running water; three more steps to a sleeping alcove taken up by a futon and a few paperback books, coffee mug, a torn T-shirt and sewing kit of the sort you used to get in middling hotel rooms. On the wall beneath a cracked plastic light box hung a small frame with a piece of plain white paper inside. Jack edged past Nellie to read what was typed there.

> Life becomes useful when you confront a
> difficulty; it provides a kind of value to your life
> to have the kind of responsibility to confront it
> and overcome it. So from that angle it is a great
> honor, a great privilege, to face these times,
> to confront them.
>
> The Dalai Lama

Beneath that was a postcard, a photograph of Albert Einstein and the printed words, "I shall never believe that God plays dice with the world: the Lord God is subtle, but malicious he is not."

Nellie laughed. "I know, I'm a Dharma bimbo! Come on—"

At the end of the hall was another small room, dark except for an illuminated monitor set into an old-fashioned editing table. Nellie edged past more film canisters, a metal cabinet holding VCRs and television sets, accordion files and manila envelopes crammed with papers and black-

and-white photographs. She pointed proudly at the glowing white screen. "My Steenbeck."

"You're a filmmaker?"

"Yeah. I know, another dying art." She ran a hand
through her close-cropped hair and gave him a wry
sideways glance, at once apologetic and defensive. "I
mean, that's not how I make my *money*—I really *am* a
VP, I'm in A&R at Agrippa. This other stuff, though—it's
like my, I dunno—"

She hesitated, chewing her lower lip. "It's like what
keeps me alive. You know? I mean, making movies,
maybe that seems—frivolous—these days. But in art
everything is frivolous. Or deadly serious."

He wondered if she were being ironic. But no. Her
expression was—well, deadly serious. Despite his misery he felt a tiny flicker of compassion. And curiosity.
There were deep fissures in her makeup; he realized she
was older than he had first thought, maybe thirty-two or
-three. Her eyes were a clear skyey blue. It wasn't until
she reached to adjust a light box that he saw the
makeup hid not just lines but scars, the gouged marks
of petra virus.

"N-no, you're right," he stammered, looking away. "I
mean, it is—can be—deadly serious." Speaking was an
incredible effort; he took a deep breath and plunged on,
as though scaling a peak that seemed impassable.
"Where—where did you study?"

She slid into a swivel chair in front of the editing
table, pulling aside the quicksilver folds of her artfully
tattered dress. "University of Chicago. I started in social
anthropology—ethnobotany. Then I went to NYU for
grad school. Knocked around for a while, finally got a
grant to make a television film about the Sami—my
mother's American, but my father's from Finland. Do
you know who they are? Laplanders, you would proba-

bly call them, aborigines. They call themselves Sami. Those who are *left*," she added. "I wanted to go on, to make more films. Only of course they do everything with computers now, so there's no audience for location films. Not to mention who goes to the fucking movies these days? So, I had some friends from school who were in a band, and I managed them for a while. They did okay, and eventually I got this job at Agrippa. Figured that was it for the movies, like, forever.

"But then, I found a patron—"

He thought she was going to name him. Instead she stopped herself, as though thinking better of it. "—a very *rich* patron. He had a project he was interested in. He'd seen my film." She laughed. "He may be the *only* fucking person who ever saw my film! He wanted to know if I would be interested in *his* project—"

She swept out her hand to indicate the anarchic mass of tapes and photos and film equipment. "All this shit? It came from him. He'd gathered all this stuff to make a documentary, but he was overcommitted, didn't have time. So he asked me if *I* would film it for him."

She paused and looked pointedly at Jack: his turn to respond. He did so haltingly. "And—of course—you did."

"No fucking way. Not at first. It was—it *is*—a horrible project. The first time he showed me some of the archival materials, I—Jesus. It was—"

Her face grew taut. She turned in the swivel chair and began to thread a strip of film into the Steenbeck. "—It was like seeing films of people at Auschwitz. Or Chelmno. Horror. It was pure horror.

"But then, you know, I got curious. I looked at the stuff he'd collected, all those photos, this old film stock. He'd already transferred a lot of it to disc or tape, so that, like, made *my* job easier. Because yeah, I took it.

And yeah, for the money; but there was more. It just—
it just became important to me. 'Cause like, sometimes
we have to do things we don't want to, I think, and
then make people look at them. Even things that people don't want to see, or read about or listen to.
Especially, maybe, those things . . ."

She gestured at the stacks of film, the sheaves of
photos and typescript. For a moment her strong-boned
profile was silhouetted against the Steenbeck. She bent
and with her right hand slowly began turning a dial.
There was a whirring sound. Across the screen images
flickered very quickly. All black-and-white, some grainy,
others sharply focused. Jack had a fleeting impression of
blurred faces, faces scarred as Nellie's own; and rooms,
and bizarre objects that might have been machinery or
aircraft or broken umbrellas. He spent several futile
moments trying to find a coherent narrative thread in
the film, before realizing that it was nothing but hundreds of still frames strung together; thousands of them.

"I had to do it." Nellie's voice grew thin, strained; like
a violin string carelessly tuned. "He knew that I would, in
the end. And he paid me really well. *Really* well. I mean,
maybe it would have been better if he hadn't—if I hadn't
taken the money. But I did. And he gave me all this"—a
wave at the editing room—"in exchange for *this*."

Abruptly the whirring stopped, and with it the
streaming images. A single black-and-white frame filled
the screen. It seemed to be some kind of glass bottle or
pickling jar, the photograph enlarged so that its contents
looked grotesquely out of scale. Nellie leaned back in
her chair so that Jack could see more clearly.

He gasped.

"Oh my God."

The jar was not out of scale. It was huge, and it held
a man. He had been bisected from head to groin. Viscera

floated in murky formaldehyde beside his upheld arms, and it was still possible to discern a grimace upon the distorted features of one side of his ruptured face. On the spongy white palm of one hand characters had been inked or tattooed; not numbers but ideograms. Above his broken skull his hair rose like ragged black flames.

Jack felt as though he had been dropped from a great height. He groaned; his heart pounded; but he could not look away. His mind raced crazily, trying to create some fathomable explanation for the photograph. There was none.

"Unit 909," said Nellie without looking at him. "Have you heard of it?"

Jack shook his head.

"A secret Japanese research project to create biological weapons during World War II. They were headquartered near Dzoraangad, in Mongolia. The Gobi Desert. Hundreds of thousands of people were killed—Chinese, Koreans, Mongolians. Some Europeans and Americans, too. They were experimenting with bubonic plague, with nerve gas and anthrax and cholera. The Geneva Convention had banned biological warfare, so the Japanese figured this must be some pretty intense shit. In 1937 they formed Unit 909. They were trying to come up with new pathogens to use against the United States in the war. They did all kinds of shit—even sent balloons across the Pacific Ocean, to drop canisters of plague-bearing fleas in the United States. Two years ago they found the remains of one of the balloons in Utah . . ."

Her hand touched the Steenbeck's controls. Once more images began to move across the screen, but slowly. This time Jack found that he could recognize them. A chamber empty save for a screaming child. Human heads floating in tall jars. White-clad surgeons standing around a table where a man sat upright, his mouth an enlarged O of pure anguish: his chest had been sawed open, and one of the doctors held something darkly shining in his gloved hand. Rows of men and women marching across a blinding white plain. Rows of lockers with Japanese characters written on them. Rows of human feet. An infant's hand with needles protruding from the fingertips. A half-inflated balloon dangling from a scaffold. Teeth.

"'The human capacity for barbarism is, seemingly, bottomless.'"

He thought Nellie had spoken. But it was her voice on a sound track, harsh and disembodied. On the Steenbeck a minute's worth of motion picture frames danced jerkily. Badly scratched black-and-white film showed the same screaming child depicted before, now glimpsed through an observation window. Pallid grey smoke began to fill the chamber; at the same time, a door swung open and a woman ran inside. Her mouth opened and closed in mute agony as she covered the child with her own body, trying to save him from the gas. In the corner of the frame a shadowy hand moved, the camera operator or one of the watching torturers.

"'We sons of pious races,'" a man's voice recited as the sequence ended and the screen went black.

> Onetime defenders of right and truth,
> Became despisers of God and man,
> Amid hellish laughter.
> Wherever I look, grasp, or seize
> There is only the impenetrable darkness.

Across the bottom of the screen letters appeared. *Night Voices in Tegel*, by Dietrich Bonhoeffer. The Steenbeck froze. The frame was filled with a white page on which words had been written in a fine, runic-looking hand.

NIGHT VOICES
UNIT 909: THE IMPENETRABLE DARKNESS
A DOCUMENTARY BY NELLIE CANDRY
PRODUCED BY LEONARD THROPE

"Leonard."

He was not aware that he had shouted until he saw her drawn face peering up beside him.

"Oh God. I'm sorry, I'm sorry, I shouldn't—"

He stumbled to his feet but she caught him, pulling him quickly toward the door. "Lie down, you should lie down—"

Get away! he wanted to shriek; but his jaw was locked. His legs, too, so that Nellie half dragged, half carried him into the room with the futon. He fought her in avid silence, feeling as though he had lost his mind; then suddenly collapsed onto the mattress. He knelt there weeping uncontrollably in the near darkness, his hands clawing at the futon's thick fabric, his breath coming in such savage bursts it was like being impaled. Finally he stopped, not from any conscious decision but because he was too exhausted to remain upright. With a soft cry he fell sideways upon the futon, and slept.

He woke to silence. A blanket had been pulled over his shoulders. He had no idea how much time had passed. Hours, maybe; he felt as though he had been very deeply asleep. The image of Jule's crumpled body glowed as though it had been branded upon his retina. For an instant he thought the suicide had been a terrible dream, confused as it was with a string of broken bodies lit as though by a failing candle.

But then he saw that the bed he lay upon was not

his own. There were papers and photographs in scattered heaps along the wall. The pillow he leaned upon was hard and smelled of sweat and stale makeup. Jule was dead, and Jack was somewhere within the GFI Pyramid, surrounded by the recorded evidence of a forgotten wartime atrocity.

"You're awake."

The woman's voice sounded very close to him. He sat up, and saw that the flickering light was not imagined. Nellie Candry knelt at the end of the futon, an ornate brass candleholder before her. In it three small candle ends burned brightly. When she picked it up to move closer to Jack, the scent of bayberry mingled with that of balsam.

"Yes." He rubbed his eyes, focused on her. She had removed her death's-mask makeup. In the dim light her scars seemed to glow: they looked fresh, unhealed. After a moment he asked in an unsteady voice. "What—what time is it? Did someone call from downstairs? About a ride?"

"Not yet. I checked about an hour ago. We can try again. It's just past four."

Panic clawed at him. "Four? In the afternoon? Jesus! My grandmother must be frantic—"

"No—it's okay, someone got hold of her." The soft yellow glow made Nellie look childishly solemn, like a little girl up late on Christmas Eve. "I called downstairs to check with security. Apparently she's very upset but one of your brothers should be there by now—"

"Dennis."

"—and they're very anxious for you to get back. Of course," she added.

"I thought some cop was supposed to give me a ride." Anger and fear stoked his anxiety into something close to raw terror. "They kept me down there for two goddamn hours, and now they don't have the decency to help me get home? What the fuck is going *on*?" The ghost of another pale body flashed before him, its torso cleft like a wing shell. He began to shake again. "Who the *fuck* are *you*?"

"Shh shh shh . . ."

Nellie made a whistling sound and moved to one side of the futon. She put some books on the mattress and set the candlestick atop them. Flames hissed as she reached for something at the foot of the bed. "Here—"

It was a mug, tendrils of steam lifting from it and circling lazily. Jack thought of knocking it from her hand, sending it smashing against the wall and screaming obscenities—

"—this'll help you feel better."

—but of course he did not, of course he took the mug, gingerly—it was very hot—and held it before his face. He had thought, hoped, it would be coffee, but it seemed to be some kind of tea. The heavy warmth in his hands felt good. The steam had an odd smell. A rich herbal scent, like cannabis tea or nettles; but it also smelled like food, like good strong broth. He sniffed it tentatively.

"What is it?"

"Tea."

He took a sip. Tiny particles adhered to his tongue; they tasted reassuringly of packaged soup mix. But there was also a strong loamy taint, and the hint of something more pungent, even putrid. Jack swallowed and made a face. "What *kind* of tea?"

Nellie picked up another mug, identical to his, blue earthenware with a repeating pattern. Jack had thought it was cows, but as Nellie moved to sit beside him he saw that the blocky shapes were actually reindeer. "It's just some herbs and stuff. To help you feel better."

"Oh."

They drank slowly, in silence, only inches apart on the futon. Jack felt the warmth of her body, too close to his. The simple act of drinking calmed him. It was not so hot now, and as the heat dissipated, so did that earthy, rather unpleasant taste. He finished it and looked around for someplace to set the empty mug. Nellie took it from him and slid it across the floor, did the same with hers. She turned back to him, sitting cross-legged and so near that her thigh nestled against his leg.

"How do you feel?"

Feel? Jule's scorched eyes wavered in front of him, the cracked line of his jaw. "Horrible. I feel horrible." He shook his head: abruptly he felt nauseated. There was a dull tingling in his tongue and gums, as though he'd rubbed them with cocaine. "I need to go—Nellie. I want to go. I don't want to be here—"

Fury flared through his queasiness. How *dare* she show him her ghastly movie, keep him here when his oldest friend had just, had just—

"Oh God . . ."

He shuddered. The sensation rippled from his shoulder blades down his spine and outward, radiating through the alcove. The tingling in his mouth became part of that same elemental shiver. When he spoke the words came out convulsively. She had poisoned him.

"What is it? What did you give me?"

"It won't hurt you." In the tremulous light she looked more exotic, the slant of her dark eyes more pronounced, her sleek black hair thicker and somehow rougher, like an animal's pelt. He could see the inside of her mouth gleaming redly behind white peglike teeth. "It's something I learned about when I made my documentary in Iceland. They drink it there, during rituals—it helps the *no'aidi* on their journeys."

"*What?*"

"Shamans. They send the *gandus* out, the *no'aidi*—" Her hand traced an arc above the candles. "The shamans. It helps them fly."

He recalled the stave he had seen in a corner, the lewdly grinning effigy with its single antler. *I started in social anthropology, ethnobotany . . .*

"You—y-you *drugged* me—" He was panting, in disbelief and because the room had grown unbearably hot. "Wh—wh—"

She shook her head. "It won't hurt you. *Amanita muscaria*—fly agaric. It grows on spruce and birch trees. The reindeer eat it because it intoxicates them." She paused to give him an apologetic, loopy smile. "The active chemical is ibotenic acid. They excrete it in their urine. The shamans drink it, and then save *their* urine—the ibotenic acid is converted into a hallucinogen called muscimol. It's not toxic; not in these small amounts. It just helps inaugurate the effects of other drugs . . ."

Jack stared, then bent over and began to retch.

"No!" Nellie knelt beside him, her warm hand on his back. "It won't hurt you! I'm sorry—really. I—"

He gasped and looked up, too weak to push her away. Her pupils were big and bright as melon seeds. She swallowed, her mouth worked as though she had forgotten how to speak. "I was—so *shocked*—when I saw you down there. And your friend. And that little girl . . ."

Her gaze was intense, almost beseeching. Jack stared back at her, then whispered, "Rachel. You could see her."

Nellie nodded.

"You saw Rachel." He was not even sure if he had spoken aloud.

"I saw her," she said, slowly. "I see them, sometimes.

They're everywhere." Her face was dark and slick with sweat. She arched her neck, moving restlessly, as though her clothes scratched her; finally grimaced and pulled her dress off. Beneath it she was naked, her skin glossy-damp, gleaming in the candlelight. There were dark blotches like myriad aureoles, above beneath around her breasts: scars, the raised kisses left by petra virus.

"Everywhere," she repeated, and gazed at him with wide stoned eyes. "Everywhere, you can see them every-where . . ."

"Who?" Jack shivered luxuriously. His fear suddenly seemed very distant, detached and somehow observable—he knew it would be waiting for him, later. He felt bizarrely clearheaded, as though whatever he had ingested affected his body and not his thoughts. "Who do you see?"

"The dead. You've seen them, too."

"No."

"Yes. You've *seen* them, Jack. You saw *her*—the girl, downstairs—"

He shook his head furiously. "No no no—"

"I knew what she was. She's one of the dead . . ." Nellie rocked back and forth, slowly, her gaze drifting off from his. "And you recognized her, too. Who was she?"

He said nothing. After a moment he forced out the words, "Jule's daughter. She was his daughter. She was hit by a car and killed four years ago on Christmas Eve. He—before he killed himself, he told me that he had seen her. He said she didn't forgive him."

"Of course not." Nellie's voice was dreamy. "That's why they're here—because they don't forgive us. That's why we can see them . . ."

Jack began to shake. He felt a pulsing in the air, a chill as though a window had been thrown open, in that place with no windows. He yawned, mouth gaping wider and wider until his jaw ached: not from fatigue but from an awful uncontrollable hiation: as though something was forcing its way out, or in.

"It's true." Nellie's mad eyes lighted on his, her voice rose and fell in a sort of chant. "They've come to take it back. *This* is the world of the dead now. We gave them Verdun and Auschwitz and Chelmno and Sarajevo and Montreal, we gave them the forests, we gave them the oceans. We gave them fucking Antarctica. And now we've given them the sky, too . . .

"We killed everything, Jack. We made this world a dead world, and now the dead have come to take it. It is Ruto's world, now—"

She got to her feet, stumbling on the mounded blankets. Jack looked up and saw that she was holding the staff he had seen before, and the wooden mask. Though it was not a mask but her face, her tongue red and blood streaming from her mouth and her eyes staring as she grinned. "Ruto is the Sami goddess of the plague. If we don't say our prayers, she takes us from our beds and brings us to Tuonela, the Land of the Dead. She crosses Pohjola the wasteland and brings us to our graves. But *this* is Pohjola now—"

With a soft laugh she turned away, ghastly tongue lapping at the blood staining her lips and chin. Jack made a strangled noise and tried to stand, but before he could she looked back again. The gaping mask was gone. Only a slight dark-haired woman stood there, eyes shining as softly she began to sing. Her voice was throaty and off-key, but he recognized the tune immediately if not the words—

Nothing will grow but stones and thorns
Nothing will fall from the sky but as blood from a wound

They will cease not in their laughter until the end
They will watch as women suckle the dead
They will watch as enticing magicians are performing;
Fear the beguiling, hypnotizing phantoms of the Kali Yuga
Fear the end of the end.

She laughed and raised her arms. Jack staggered to his feet. She reached out to steady him and he took her hand, frightened yet comforted by her touch, the sense that something in the room was real.

"Oh, it's all really happening, Jack," she murmured, as though she read his thoughts. "It's all here—"

He nodded, staring at her for reassurance.

"That's how it works," she murmured, "when it doesn't kill us. We become gates."

"Gates?" He could scarcely form the word. "What—?"

"This." Her hand left his, fumbled for a moment at her jeans pocket. When she held it up again he saw a small bottle there, brown glass, little rubber dropper-bulb, white label with black letters—

Fusax 687.

"No."

Frantically he dug into his own pocket. His fingers closed around the familiar vial, drew it out. He stared at it in disbelief and terror, then slowly at her.

"Yes." Nellie nodded. "Me too. And more—more of us than you can imagine."

Jack shook his head. "But—how?" he whispered.

"Leonard Thrope. Among others." She bared her teeth in a grin. "He travels, he gives them to people he meets—"

"But why? *Why?*"

"So that we can change. Petra virus, hanta virus, AIDS, torminos simplex—they change our bodies and make us vulnerable. Even exposure to UV light can do

it. It all makes us *susceptible*, Jack—do you understand
what that means? It means we are capable of taking, of
receiving. The viruses change us, but they also open us,
so that things can get inside. They kill us—usually,
always, depending on what we have—but sometimes
they make it possible for other changes to happen
first—"

"*Fuck you.*" Rage burned through the cloud in Jack's
head. "You—what do *you* know? AIDS is not a fucking
gate, this is not some fucking—"

Nellie smiled, maddeningly. "*Fusax* is what makes us
gates, Jack. Do you know what it really is?"

He stared at her; suddenly, desperately, trying to
remember what Leonard had said about the drug.

What did he say? Christ, he must have told me something!—

But he dredged up nothing save the image of a grinning demon who held a staff impaled with human
skulls.

"It's a type of bacteria," explained Nellie. Her hands
moved as she spoke, drawing circles in the air,
arabesques, a helix. "A kind of spirochete: a symbiotic
microbe. We all have remnants of them inside our
brains. These particular spirochetes—the fusarium—
once they were just simple bacteria. But millions of
years ago they attached themselves to us. They merged
with our brain cells, they became neurotubules—part of
the passageways that transmit thought and sensation,
part of our neurochemistry. And now they're part of
us—I mean, *all* of us, not just you and me. They orches-
trate the way we think; they may even be what gives us
consciousness.

"*Fusarium* is a mutation. A—an independent
researcher discovered it, and then he—he decided to
share it, with people here, in the States. And in Japan.

At first they thought it might keep the petra virus from replicating. Because in the right individuals—people whose body chemistry has been altered by cancer, or UV radiation, people whose immune systems have been damaged by AIDS or petra virus or chemotherapy; sometimes with schizophrenics, or people who've had some kind of head trauma—In people whose minds or immune systems have already been changed, the *fusarium* attach themselves to proteins and—"

"You're fucking nuts," gasped Jack. He stumbled backward, trying to move away from her, and bumped into the alcove wall. "This is *crazy*, you're—"

Nellie shook her head emphatically. "*No*. It *works*. It threads itself inside us—within our brain cells, within our neurochemistry, our immune systems. There's no one place where it happens. The immune system is like a cloud, it's everywhere inside us. Like consciousness. It's not just in our lymph nodes, or liver—it's there, too, of course, but the immune system can move, just like consciousness can move. It can *all* move inside us—

"That's why people die from a broken heart, or depression. That's why sometimes we live, even when we should die: because our emotions and our T cells, our thoughts and our blood are all woven together. There are things dancing inside us, Jack—cells and bacteria and bits of light. They make a cloud, they form a web. And now, with *fusarium*, this cloud of—of *knowing*—it can move *outside* us. Our consciousness can move between us. Over great distances, between the living and the dead, even—"

He shook his head, trying frantically to shove a barrier between himself and her words. "*No*—"

"Yes! There are doors opening everywhere, Jack— too quickly, some of them. The world has changed. We must change, too, or die—and that's what the Fusax does. It changes us. It doesn't always work, but when it does—it's not crazy, Jack. It's evolution."

He shouted, *"Get the fuck away from me! You're a fucking lunatic—how would you even know—"*

"It's everywhere, Jack. It's on the fucking street, in IZE. Do you know about ice?"

Her voice dropped. "GFI holds the patent on the IT discs. Without IZE they're just 3-D TV. But *with* the drug—" She hunched her shoulders, shivering. "It's incredible. I did it a few times, before I met Leonard. The chemical effects produced by the fusarium aren't addictive—but IZE is. GFI owns E.C. Folham—that's the pharmaceutical company that developed it. It's not a street drug at all. GFI owns it; GFI has made it addictive; they're making it available now, through drug cartels. Eventually, once everything's restored, they'll market it. They've got the sky stations repairing the ozone layer, so they'll be able to continue broadcasting. They've got the IT technology to tie into TV and the web. And they've got IZE."

Jack stammered, "But—why?"

Nellie shrugged. "Why not? Why MTV? It's not a conspiracy; it's business as usual. If GFI really can repair the atmosphere, the rest will fall into place. Everyone will just pick up where they left off. The technology exists to retrofit televisions for IT, and GFI has already invested in front-end manufacturing sites in Malaysia. It's not such a big deal, really. Except that an incredibly powerful new psychotropic drug has been introduced all over the world, as part of a multinational corporation's five-year plan," she ended. "So you see that Leonard Thrope is just a very small messenger—"

"No." Jack struck her hand. "How do you know all this? Who told you, who started it, *how do you know*?"

She shrugged, then tilted her head toward the door. "The movie. The documentary materials—"

She ducked from the alcove, out of sight and then back again. "Here." She handed him a stack of legal-sized papers. "Look."

A rusted paper clip clamped them together, that slick heavy mimeograph paper he hadn't seen since childhood. He glanced at the top sheet. Japanese, but there were scattered English words in there too, amidst tiny smudged photographs—

!!Urgent Dossier!!
[[War Crimes Division]]
II: Unit 909
::
//Un. 731//
:Code: Cherry Blossoms At Night
UNIT 731

He frowned and turned the page, scanning down more columns of unreadable text until he found a list of Japanese names printed in English. One name seized him—

KEISUKE HANADA

—and he heard Leonard's voice, saying, *"He told me that he'd come to the monastery in 1946, right after the war . . . He had set up this sort of laboratory—"*

"Oh my God," breathed Jack. "He's a fucking *war criminal*—what the fuck are they *doing*?"

Nellie crouched beside him. "Maybe," she said, her eyes seeing something very far away. "Maybe he's making amends? Because this drug could be a fantastic thing, Jack. I mean, some day we may all think of him like Louis Pasteur or something . . ."

Jack shook his head, heart pounding; and thought of invasive bacteria that did not respond to antibiotics; of viruses that replicated hundreds of times in a heartbeat. He drew a finger to the inner corner of his eye, felt there the faint encrustation, grains of emerald sand . . .

"No," he whispered.

Nellie nodded. "That's what a lot of people think. Blue Antelope, all those fundamentalists. I mean, Blue Antelope thinks *we* should all just die—"

She touched her breast, the scarred aureole, and made a disgusted face. "—they think *that* would be making amends. They're *wrong*," she said with harsh vehemence. "I was with them for a while, but not anymore. 'Cause when I first got sick, I just wanted to kill people—do you know what I mean?"

Jack stared down at his hands. "Yeah," he said at last.

"But then Leonard contacted me about the documentary, and after we met he gave me the Fusax. And after a very little while I saw that it could be different; that it *was* different. Not all at once . . ."

She reached for the ripped T-shirt at the edge of the futon, picked up the tiny sewing kit stuck in its folds, and plucked something from it. A needle, Jack saw when a moment later candlelight sparked at her fingertip. "Look—"

She took the bedsheet in her hands, held it before her face and Jack's so that he saw the candlelight through it, showing the fabric's weave. "Here—" She gave him one end of the sheet to hold. Then she began piercing the cloth with the needle, deftly, methodically. Tiny perforations appeared. The candlelight shimmered, in one spot the fabric grew weaker, thinner, until at last a small hole gaped there and the flame glowed brilliantly, as though it had burned its way through the cloth.

"Do you see?" said Nellie. She took the sheet from him and held it taut, moved it back and forth to make a shifting cloud of light and dark against the candle glow. "Where there are enough of us—people like you and me, people who're taking Fusax, or ice—it can be like this. Our consciousness can weave itself together. We can make a new web, a new pattern; even if we are making holes in the *old* pattern. See?" Her voice rose, a little desperately.

Jack shook his head. "No."

But that was not exactly true. It *did* make a kind of sense, it was as though he could intuit her meaning on some submolecular level, without intending or even wanting to. Which angered and frightened him; because he did not see a web, but legions of alien creatures swarming in his body, microbial threads corkscrewing themselves into his brain.

It sickened him. He glanced down, spread his hands and saw how emaciated they were; could feel how his khaki pants flapped around his legs, his oxford-cloth shirt billowing from his shoulders.

"I'm dying," he said, and looked up at Nellie. There was wonder in his tone. "I'm dying."

She gazed back at him but it was as though her thoughts were elsewhere. Or, he realized, it was as though she perceived him another way, through another sense. The way blind Father Warren used to sit and listen to his grandfather: face tilted, intent on whatever tale was spinning out, milky gaze a million miles away.

"We all are," she said after a moment. "I know, everyone always says that; but it wasn't until I got sick that I really understood. I was reading this book—a really depressing book—and I thought, Why the hell am I reading this? All the people in here are dying.

"But then I thought, *But that's what we're all doing.* It's like we all have two jobs: living, and dying. We just don't like to think about the dying very much. You know, there's music that people have recorded, of what it sounds like to die—"

Her eyes upon Jack were so intense that he could hardly bear to look at her. "What it sounds like when your body starts to break up, when the cells all begin to decay. Leonard played it for me one night. And when I heard it, I freaked. Because, like, it wasn't *new* to me. It was something I'd heard before. It sounded like the wind, or the sea. Or like after you've been running, or working out, and you hear your own pulse in your ears . . ."

He saw where she touched his hand, but couldn't feel it.

"It's not something to be afraid of, Jack."

He said nothing. The mere thought of hearing such music filled him with horror.

"We are inside the engine of the end, Jack, you and I." Her entire body was trembling, sheathed in candle-light. "It doesn't heal us," she said at last. "All it does is change us. But maybe, someday—maybe change will be enough."

She leaned forward and placed her hands on his shoulders, then very gently pushed him down, until he knelt upon the mattress. He could not breathe; felt as though he were choking, this sheer mass of unbearable knowledge being shoved at him—

"Hush," murmured Nellie. She began tugging at her jeans, until she sat beside him, naked. "I'll help you, let me show you, shhh . . ."

He shook his head. The only other time he'd ever

felt like this was that night at Georgetown, when he'd taken a tab of windowpane acid Leonard had mailed him, and Julie came running to mind-sit him till dawn. The same edginess, the same whirligig of sensation, the same terrifying sense that the rind of the world was being peeled away to reveal a buzzing hive beneath.

But then Nellie touched a finger to his chin, just for an instant, and rested her hand upon his knee. Her touch—warm, slightly moist—somehow grounded him; that and her voice, wordless yet reassuring—

"Hush now, husshhh . . ."

He had not been so near a woman since he was fifteen. Her body was small and compact, narrow-waisted and wide-hipped, her skin the color of very fine amber. Like amber it seemed to hold many small precious insects: Jack blinked as a line of golden ants crept into the hollow of her throat, then pooled into a single droplet of sweat that spilled onto her breastbone. "Do you feel better?" she asked.

"No." His voice caught in his throat as she moved closer to him. Her breasts were full and rounded, dark-tipped, the nipples almost indistinguishable from the cicatrices left by petra virus. Displaced wonder settled upon him, a mist prickling his skin: why had he never noticed how lovely petra's scars were, the tiny darkened furrows where disease had harrowed flesh, what might they engender?

"God, no—" He looked away, covering his mouth with one hand. "Please—leave me—"

"I can't hurt you, Jack." Her face hung before his, the irises engulfed by black, her mouth parted in a smile. When she spoke her teeth sparked, flints rendering light. "You're safe, here . . ."

She touched his breast. Her fingers burned against his icy skin. He sighed, shuddering, and closed his eyes.

Her head dipped and she took Jack's cock in her hands. "Don't—" he cried, panic tumbling beneath his confusion and, yes, arousal. "I'm—"

"No. I'm immune, remember?" she whispered. And, of course, that was what the petra virus did, made you immune to the HIV virus while it infected you with another. "I'm not contagious, Jack. I can't hurt you."

He saw in her face nothing of desire, nothing at all he could recognize except perhaps a weird kind of joy, a look of such expectancy that it kindled him as well. His fear fell back. Not gone, but quieted, amazed at this arousal as by everything else—what was he doing with a *woman*? With *this* woman? He shook his head, not too wasted to feel astonishment, then raised his hand to touch her cheek. A moment later he felt her mouth around the head of his cock, and her tongue, constricting warmth as her fingers tightened around him. He was hard, but his desire was detached from everything he could see: the woman drawing momentarily away, so that he glimpsed her breasts, the sharp silhouette of her nipples as she turned, her narrow thighs. She smiled, a bright flash; but her hands never left his cock, and an instant later her head dipped once more, lips parted as she took him into her mouth.

His breathing quickened; he waited for his erection to fade but it didn't. When he shut his eyes he saw her still, gold-limned against the pulsing darkness. He could smell her, so different from Leonard or Eric or any of his lovers. Not the raw sweetish pollen scent of semen but musk and salt, disturbing because it was so much the sea so close.

"I know," she whispered. As her mouth left him he sighed, without thinking let his hand drop to stroke himself. "But I wanted to see what happens . . ."

She knelt before him and took his hands, drew them

to her waist and pressed them there, hard. He felt the spurs of her ribs, below them the hollow wherein her navel was a deeper declination. She made a soft urgent sound, and so he moved his hands lower still, until they stroked the inside of her thighs, muscular as a boy's, then slid between her legs to her cunt. Her pubis had been shaved; when she opened her legs her labia had the split sheen of an apricot. His finger found the soft node there and probed it, even as he leaned forward and nuzzled his face against her neck, pressed his open mouth against her. Tasting salt, a faint crystalline bitterness that made him think of fucking Leonard when they'd done too much coke. He closed his eyes and saw Emma standing in his bedroom, mouth tight as she gazed at emerald granules adhering to a tongue depressor.

The viruses change us, but they also open us, so that things can get inside.

He drew back, slowly, as Nellie moaned. She moved against him forcefully, reminding him that she was there—*that's how it works when it doesn't kill us: we become gates*—reminding him that her body was nothing like his, and that none of this was happening by accident.

"I—I don't know if I can," he murmured. "If *we* can . . ."

Though he was still hard, and when she took his hand and pressed it to her groin the skin there was soft and yielding as moist chamois.

"We can," she whispered. "This way."

She leaned back upon the mattress, guiding him until he lay curved beside her, his head facing the V formed by her outspread legs. The candle sputtered and flared brightly. He could see with acid clarity the scars upon her thighs, dark fissures that seemed to be strewn upon a landscape of smooth stone not flesh. He let his hand trail across her leg, then moved forward to kiss her knee, let his mouth linger upon one of the cicatrices, lips brushing against the small sharp ledge of skin. His other hand stroked her inner thigh, soft and unblemished; she made a low sound and took him in her mouth. Not his favorite sexual conjunction: he had always found it too distracting, too difficult to concentrate on his own response.

But now the symmetry entranced him, distant pulse of pleasure as she sucked his cock, his own inexplicable delight as he explored the unknown landscape before him, lingeringly, caressing her legs, inching forward until his face was pressed against her pubis. Heat and moisture, scent of ebb tide. He slid his tongue inside her, and she cried out; there was an intense explosion of warm liquid flooding his mouth. Some minutes later he could tell when she came, the muscles in her thighs rippling and a long slow coursing pulse in the fluid skin beneath his mouth; was less certain of his own climax, which he sensed first as a soft ruddy light, his lips prickling as at the taste of lemons; then suffused heat, a sigh as the woman drew her head back from his groin and somewhat awkwardly raised herself to kiss him. Her tongue small and hot and languid, the acescent taste of his come in her mouth. After a moment he moved away, one hand still clasping hers. She stared at him, wide eyes belying her calm expression. As he gazed back he felt a sudden vertiginous thrill, as of fear or bone-shattering cold. He opened his mouth to cry out, and once again that horrific yawning overcame him; he could feel the tendons in his jaw tightening, and then the muscles in his thighs, a violent shock of pleasure in his groin that made him gasp, echoing roar and he fell back against the bed, moaning.

"There . . ."

He blinked and took a deep breath, unsure how

much time had passed. The room was still dark, the candles seemed not to have burned down at all; but perhaps Nellie had replaced them. She sat leaning against the wall of the sleeping alcove. Her skin glowed dark creamy yellow, her short dark hair lay flat and damp against her skull. The cicatrices upon her breasts had opened. They glistened like the mouths of flowers, saturated with nectar; he could see silvery threads of moisture spilling down her abdomen.

"It's always different," she said dreamily. She lay one hand upon her breast and flinched, eyes shutting for a moment as though she were in pain. When she opened them again her gaze was heavy-lidded, as with fatigue or drink. "But I wanted you to see—to know what it can be like."

Why? he wanted to ask; but he was too tired. He closed his eyes and slept dreamlessly. When he woke the room was exactly as it had been before—candles burning, a close smell of flesh and unwashed hair—save that for the first time he noticed how terribly thin Nellie was. Before, the cicatrices had seemed like blossoms strewn upon her flesh, but now he could see her ribs thrusting out between them, and the smooth hollows of her cheeks.

"I am going to tell you something important," she said. She blinked and dabbed a finger at the corner of one eye. When she withdrew her hand he saw a very faint virent flash. "Because you'll be at the party tonight."

Tonight? Jack tried to laugh, but the effort was too much. Instead he nodded. When he licked his lips they were cracked and desiccated; his tongue, too, felt dry, hard and swollen as a parrot's. Nellie moved her hand as though to touch him, and shook her head.

"I can't go. I'm supposed to be there, but I won't be. But *you'll* be there—" She pointed at his hand. He looked down and saw the faintly glowing outline of a gryphon upon his palm. "—and so will Blue Antelope. They've planned a terrorist strike against the SUNRA dirigibles."

Jack did laugh then, wordlessly. After a moment he croaked, "Blue Antelope?"

Nellie nodded. "They think the sky stations are interfering with God's plan for humanity. Which is that we should die. Having poisoned His earth and destroyed His creatures, we all deserve to die. They're going to destroy the Fouga fleet." Her voice sounded clipped, as though delivering a speech from memory. "Assisted cultural suicide, that's all. Without the sky stations in place, the atmosphere cannot be repaired. We'll die, maybe everything will die, but then maybe other forms of life will be ascendant. Blue Antelope doesn't look upon it as a sin."

"How do you know?" Jack's laughter faded into a ragged whisper. "How do you know, how do—"

"Because I was the one who provided them with fifty-seven sheets of collodion cotton soaked with nitroglycerin, all of which have been incorporated into the Fougas' outer structure. That was after I got sick."

She coughed, a very soft rasping sound; and recited,

> So the angels swung their sickles on the earth, cut the grapes from the vine, and threw them into the winepress of God's engulfing rage. The grapes were squeezed out of the winepress outside the city, and blood came out of the winepress in a flood two hundred miles long and five feet deep. And it was this that washed clean the earth of abomination.

"But—" Jack stammered. He tried to stand but his exhaustion was too great; his legs collapsed under him. "The bombs—will they—"

"They'll do nothing except destroy eighteen months of work. And the Pyramid. And kill a lot of people. But that will be enough. GFI won't be able to rebuild the fleet—it was a miracle they could do it in the first place—and eventually most of us will die."

"But you're telling me this—*why?*" Jack's voice cracked. His face crumpled into weeping, though no tears came. *"Why?"*

Nellie's hand clawed across the futon to grab his hand. *"Stop them.* When I saw you downstairs, I saw this—"

She stabbed her finger at the glowing gryphon on his palm. "You'll be inside the arena. Tell someone about the terrorists. Stop them."

"You tell someone!" Jack cried, his throat burning. "You're—you're *lying*, this is some—"

"No. I am *not* lying. I was with Blue Antelope for three years, since before the ice shelf collapsed. The glimmering was the best thing that ever happened to them, and all those other Xian radicals. It gave them a focus. It made them stronger. When they learned I'd received the experimental AIDS vaccine, they threw me out—because I was thwarting God's will. Because if I was the sort of person who was running any risk of infection, then I was exactly the sort of person God *wanted* to die. But when I developed petra virus they took me back—because obviously His will was being enforced.

"And I was so enraged, I hated everyone so much, that I worked for them. In Atlanta and LA and here, in the Pyramid—"

She motioned at the walls. "I was a plant. There are a lot of us here. That's how Blue Antelope gained access to the Millennial Ball. And they had plants in the factories where the Fougas were constructed. Everywhere. Blue Antelope is everywhere. *Christians*—"

She shook with a spasmodic laugh. "—God's fucking people—they're everywhere. They're going to kill me, you know. Because I left. But I won't let them."

Jack swallowed, tasting bile and grit. His breath came in panicky bursts, and he turned, looking desperately around the tiny sleeping alcove for something, anything, that would give the lie to this. His gaze fell upon a silvery film canister pushed against the far wall.

"Leonard." The word exploded from him. "Does he—does Leonard know?"

She sighed and closed her eyes. "Of course he knows. He knows everything."

Jack gasped, amazement forcing through despair. "Leonard's a terrorist."

"No. He's *not* a terrorist. I mean, he's not a member of Blue Antelope—he *hates* Fundamentalists, but I'm sure he knows about the attack. His work, recording all the extinctions, donating all that money to the Noah Genome Project—he may not *belong* to Blue Antelope, but he *believes* in them. And he'll be at the Ball, as a guest of GFI. He plays both sides of the fence, Leonard." Nellie's tone grew bitter. "I think he's just waiting to see who'll come out on top. To see who'll win."

"No. You're wrong." Jack shook his head. "Leonard Thrope has never given a flying fuck about *winning*. He just likes total fucking *chaos*. I mean, in high school he was cast as The Lord of Misrule in some play, and it was so perfect—because that's what he is. That's why he'd be a *perfect* terrorist—"

"They would never take him," Nellie broke in. "He's a loose cannon. A security risk. Your friend is not a terrorist, Jack—"

He's not my friend! Jack started to cry out; *how could someone who tried to poison me be my friend?*

But then, as clearly as if he were in the room beside

him, he saw Leonard as a boy with a hot small mouth and eyes that broke too easily into tears; Leonard leaving him, a farewell fuck in Athens and that was it. Then years later Leonard drinking champagne at Jack's fortieth birthday party. Leonard in Jack's bedroom handing him a small glass bottle and saying *This is what's going to change fucking human history* . . .

Jack looked out into the dark hallway and thought of the postcard he had seen pinned to the wall there—

"I shall never believe that God plays dice with the world: the Lord God is subtle, but malicious he is not."

But Leonard *was* playing dice with the world; and so were Blue Antelope, and GFI.

"Stop them," whispered Nellie.

No, thought Jack, and closed his eyes. "No," he said.

Nellie's voice grew shrill. "Those solar shields are the only chance we have—"

"Why the fuck should I care? *I'm dying!* You poisoned me—you and Leonard, your goddamn pharmaceutical corporations! *Let* them die. Let them *all fucking die!*"

His words echoed in the tiny room. He could hear himself panting, hear the noisy slurring of Nellie's breath as she stared at him. He glared back at her, the moisture between the folds of her abdomen, sparks of green and gold there like tiny fish in a pool. When she raised her arm he saw, first, that the flesh hung loosely from her bones—not like flesh at all, more like moss, or lichen, or shimmering algae; and second, that her fingers— impossibly slender, spatulate fingers, gleaming like a fistful of silver spoons—now held something long and thin and metal—

A pencil, thought Jack Finnegan, and he began to laugh, the words a roaring avalanche in his head; *she's keeping score.*

—something she looked at very carefully, her eyes narrowed though he wondered how she could see, because the shimmering veil had fallen across her face now as well. There was the smell of wet leaves, a sharp glitter as she lifted the metal pencil to her mouth and her lips parted and he saw suddenly that it was not a pencil at all but some kind of elongated metal capsule.

"Stop them," she said. Something moved within the hollows of her face as with a grinding noise she bit down upon the shining tube. "Just stop them."

Stench of sulfur and almonds. Jack gasped, stunned, as the woman's body slumped sideways onto the bed. He started to move toward her, then stopped, seeing a fine white cloud of mist about her mouth. Holding his breath he staggered to his feet and stumbled from the room, bumping into walls, cracking his elbow against a table and crying out. It wasn't until he reached the door that he realized he was naked. With a groan he turned back, hesitating at the entrance to the alcove.

Nellie sprawled facedown upon the futon, motionless. Her body looked badly decomposed, but the smell that hung about the room was fragrant, rain-sweet.

Like lilacs, thought Jack, clenching his jaw as he grabbed his clothes and dressed, fighting horror and an exhaustion so profound it was like ice in the blood. *She smells like lilacs.* He shoved his feet into his shoes, turned, and fled.

CHAPTER FIFTEEN

Heroes and Villains (Alternate Take)

He had thought—truly stupidly, Trip realized now—that he would be able to see the Golden Pyramid from anywhere within the city. Such a gigantic structure, it would loom over everything else and he would set his course by it, make his way through the streets, how hard could it be?

I'm an idiot, he thought, and glanced at the harbor behind him. The *Wendameen* was gone. As far as he could see there was only viscous water, marbled red and black, speared with metal spikes and floating planks, a shattered portico like the prow of a sunken ship. To either side the shoreline stretched, endless, rotting piers and rusted scows, bridge girders and highway overpasses that had been bitten off in midair, eviscerated skyscrapers that tolled as the tide swept inside them. The sky shuddered, and flaming gouts of gold and violet spewed from horizon to horizon. After the silence and solitude of Mars Hill, after the weeks at sea with Martin, it was like waking in hell.

"Oh, Jesus," Trip murmured. He pushed against the first hard swell of fear: he was alone in a city, he was alone in The City, this had been a Really Bad Idea: *I'm a total fucking idiot.*

Wind ripped off the water. He shivered and buttoned the top of his anorak, conscious for the first time in ages of feeling cold—not the clawing grip of Maine's winter but a chill that seeped into him like poison, and seemed to diffuse outward from his bones. Surely it had not been this cold on board the *Wendameen*?

He shook his head. The memory of the last few months was fleeing from him, as though it had been a dream recalled in a noisy room. He knew it was not, he knew it had all been real, as real in its way as the shadow of another dream, the dream of drowning that came at him sometimes, a small dark animal nudging to be recognized.

But he did not want to remember that. What he wanted to remember, what he *did* remember, was the blond girl. Her image was inescapable: it might have been threaded upon the capillaries in his retina, stitched upon his eyelids. Her twilit eyes, her hot thrusting mouth; but more than those things her simple sheer *being*. The fact that she had *been* there beside him once, that he had touched her, that she had been real—

Do you remember nothing? she had asked him in a dream of flowers. Now, with the December wind pressing upon him like a cloak of ice, he remembered nothing else. He *was* nothing else: only a vessel, broken and halfheartedly repaired, holding her within him like a flame. He hugged his arms tight against his chest, forced himself to look out at the unpromising landscape before him. The smell of shit and decay was overpowering; he'd have to get away from the water or he'd be sick. He adjusted his backpack and stared glumly up at a derelict building that blocked his view of anything but itself. The walls had fallen away from its upper stories, so that he could see inside. Like gazing into a particularly horrible, mutated ants' nest. Heaps of rubble, in some places arranged in careful patterns, walls or rough barriers of wood and metal erected precariously on the sloping floors; in other places left as they had been when the building's exterior collapsed, the beams and joists twisted like coat hangers, insulation and drywall hanging from the metal like old clothes. The wind raked upward, sending a skein of crumbled mortar and gypsum dust and ash spinning down, so that Trip blinked and stepped back, covering his eyes.

Throughout the whole god-awful structure, people were living. He could glimpse them moving behind the makeshift barriers—lots of them, surely more people in there than any single building could safely hold, even if it had been sound, even if it didn't look as though a bomb had ripped through it. But then, of course, city apartment buildings and projects could hold hundreds of people, thousands.

The thought of myriad squatters creating a hive of that wasted spot made Trip's skin prickle. He looked up and saw a white-haired woman in black pants, no shirt, no bra, step across a gap in the wall she had made, sheets of plywood spliced together with chicken wire and electrical cord. She was shouting to someone he couldn't see, her white breasts moving as she stood on tiptoe and reached for an interior wall. He couldn't make out her words, but then she looked down, as though he had called to her, and her face twisted.

"Hey! Fucking asshole, get the fuck, what the fuck you looking at, you goddamn fucking—"

He took off. Not looking where he was going, so that he tripped and fell, cried out as his knee struck something sharp, but then he was up again, stumbling along the ruptured spine of what had once been a road. After a few minutes he stopped, not because he felt safe but because he couldn't breathe, his knee hurt too much. When he looked down he saw a rip in the white duck trousers Martin had given him, a leafy smear of dirt and blood.

"Shit," he said, blinking back tears of pain and hopelessness. They were the only pants he had. "Mother-fucking *shit*."

He'd never cursed like that before, not even once in his life. It felt good: made more raw rage flood his brain, like blood welling from a wound. He looked up and shouted at the woman in the building, though he couldn't see her anymore, couldn't even see the building.

"You fucking piece of cunt shit!"

He screamed, felt the words tearing at his face like wind. When he turned to walk away he saw a figure strolling just a few yards ahead of him, a young man wearing cowboy boots and a long patchwork overcoat. His face was heavily tattooed with spirals that had bled into his skin. The streaky purple light from the sky overhead gave his flesh a ghoulish cast.

"Yo, Happy New Year!" The man grinned, gave Trip a thumbs-up, and continued in his direction. Trip sucked his breath between his teeth and tightened his grip on his knapsack. The man stopped, rocking back and forth on his heels, and surveyed Trip with what seemed like totally unnecessary cheerfulness. "I'm looking for Avenue B. Know where that is?"

Trip stared at him, panicked, trying desperately to think of something to say that wouldn't reveal he was totally lost, totally without a single fucking clue.

"Actually," the man went on, "I'm looking for a place called Marquee Moon. It's supposed to be around here somewhere—" He glanced aside at a lightless alley that ran between two cavernously empty buildings, then back at Trip. "Ever hear of it?"

"No."

The guy nodded, kept on nodding, a speedy mindless mannerism Trip associated with hippies in those sixties biker movies he used to watch in the middle of the night with Jerry Disney. He was tall, broad-shouldered, not too much older than Trip—say, twenty-five or -six. A tiny golden placebit glowed above one eyebrow. His hair was dark and close-cropped, his face despite the tattoos and corpselike coloring amiable, even goofy. Trip had first thought the man's long overcoat coat to be shabby and much-repaired, the kind of thing you saw homeless people wearing, crazed veterans or crackheads. In fact it was very carefully stitched from hundreds of pieces of fabric—brilliant silks and brocades and jacquards, many elaborately embroidered—with here and there mirrored cloth, and prisms, and glass beads like eyes, jangly arrays of computer circuitry and feathers green and serrated as palmetto leaves. It was, Trip realized, a very expensive coat—it even *smelled* expensive, like the inside of a fancy store, perfume and unworn leather—and the man's boots were very expensive boots: alligator and totally illegal, of course.

"Yeah, well it's supposed to be around here," the man went on genially. He had a pronounced drawl. "A bunch of those places're supposed to be around here, in the same building even, Magyar and Hit and the Chancery."

Trip shifted his knapsack to the other shoulder. Enough seconds had passed, he knew he should either say something or leave, fast, before this guy drew a knife on him or decided to prolong the conversation.

"You're not from here, are you?" The man's gaze suddenly fixed on him. His hand moved, and Trip backed away, elbowing him roughly. "Hey, ouch! Jeez, calm down, buddy! I was just—"

His hand continued its arc until it touched Trip's knapsack, lightly. "I was just gonna *say*, you probably haven't been here very long. So you probably don't know where the fuck *you* are, either."

He gave him a rueful smile, revealing multicolored teeth like tiles. One of them winked, bright red.

Trip stiffened. Panic overflowed into a hot hateful memory: the guy reminded him of Leonard Thrope. "Fuck you," he muttered. He spun and started quickly into the alley, walking as fast as he could without breaking into a run.

"Hey! *Hey—*"

As footsteps rattled up behind him, he hunched his shoulders, made a fist, and turned. Fighting was something else he'd never done, but fear took over and he jabbed at the air breathlessly, his back colliding with a wall.

"Whoa! Hey, man—" The guy in the overcoat sidestepped, easily avoiding Trip's lame throw, and raised one hand palm out in a placating gesture. "Calm the Christ down, will you! I was just gonna *say*, this is *not* really a part of town you want to go wandering around in by yourself, especially on New Year's Eve."

As he spoke he moved carefully around Trip, holding his gaze as though talking him down from a ledge. "You look a little spooked, but *I* ain't gonna jump you. Hell, if I was, I would've done it already." He laughed, his mouthful of colored teeth gleaming. "Man, you're the first person I seen in a while looks more like a tourist'n me—"

He plucked at Trip's knapsack, the billowing sleeve of his anorak. "You gotta do better'n than *that*, man! C'mon," he urged, glancing to either end of the alley, "I can't leave you here, and I ain't staying."

The man shoved his hands in his coat pockets, balanced himself on a cement block, and cocked his head. When Trip said nothing, he shrugged. "Hey, suit yourself, man." He jumped off the cinder block and strode toward the far end of the alley. Trip watched him, and when the man stepped back out of the alley into the hazy red light, followed at a safe distance.

Out on the street the man was waiting, perched on the curb. There were junked cars everywhere, and on the other side of the road buildings in very slightly less ruin than those Trip had just left. Shuttered storefronts of corrugated iron, yawning doorways, walls pasted over with stripped-off posters. Two bald children hitting something with a stick, who gave Trip a curious glance and returned to their play. A rangy dog nosing at foul bright green water pooling in the sidewalk. He remembered a statistic he had heard once on TV, before the glimmering, something about there being a hundred million homeless people in the world, and untold thousands in New York City alone.

But if anything, the city seemed emptier now than it had even a few months before, when he'd been here with the blond girl. What had happened to everyone. Had they died? Been taken off to one of the life-enhancement centers that Jerry claimed were really prisons? He glanced at the man, whose clothes and incongruously amiable confidence disturbed Trip as much as the ravaged streets did, then looked the other way. A few blocks off he could see people crossing streets, the comforting yellow blur of a speeding cab.

I'll go there, he thought.

"I think it's that way." The man tilted his head back, chin aimed away from that feeble show at traffic. "Yeah, I know some of this now. There used to be this club down there."

He flashed Trip a Technicolor grin. "Princess Volupine used to play there, and Alex Chilton. Ever see them?"

Trip shook his head.

"Well, I'm going," the man continued, and started walking. "See you."

Trip stayed where he was. Once the man glanced over his shoulder, lifted his hand, and waved; that was all. Trip marked where he went. About three blocks to the south, the man slowed, stopped, looked across the street, then peered down an alley behind him; then he crossed the street and continued for another block, where he purposefully turned and disappeared down a side street or passage overshadowed by a very ornate old building. Trip waited several minutes, to make certain the guy wasn't going to pop back out again, and headed the same way he'd gone.

To either side buildings reared, their windows uniformly dark. A power line bearing a traffic signal sagged across the middle of the intersection. On one corner a bank of public telephones had been overturned; on another a man stood in the shelter of a phone booth's cracked plastic awning, smoking a cigarette and chanting as to himself.

"*. . . cat ice hash acid ice cat . . .*"

Trip walked by quickly, keeping his head down. He passed a few people. Two young women wearing black, their faces hidden behind cheap white masks. An older woman, also in black, whose eyes glowed plasmer silver. A man in cracked leathers, his face hidden behind a Mexican wrestler's mask, cantered past on a white horse and lifted his hand to wave at Trip. A girl walking an enormous dog: all with enough purpose to their movements that Trip felt somewhat reassured. There was order, somewhere. There was food, somewhere, for humans and horses, too. Life was going on.

Which meant it could be going on elsewhere, too; like at the Pyramid, where he had last seen the blond girl. He shoved lank, salt-corded hair from his eyes and

nodded to himself, determinedly, glanced up at the skyline to see if there was anything there like the apex of a
golden triangle. No; but he'd find it; if he had to, he'd
just take a cab, squander whatever cash Martin Dionysos
had given him, and that would be that.

Because if he could only get to the Pyramid, he
could speak to Nellie Candry, beg her to help him find
the girl so he could do what he should have done
before, what he should have done in the first place. He
would arrange to see her again, talk to her, spend time
getting to know her. He'd contact John Drinkwater and
figure out a way to take her home with him to Moody's
Island. He didn't care about touring anymore, didn't
care about the band, or money, or singing, or God. All
he wanted was to find the girl. All he wanted was to
take her to the Fisher of Men First Harbor Church and
marry her, the way he should have in the very beginning.

It didn't take him long to realize that he was lost. *Way*
lost: Meaning, he couldn't find the man he had set out
to follow, he didn't see anything that said Marquee
Moon, and he certainly didn't see the Pyramid. He
passed a small park, a woman selling water from a blue
plastic jug. Behind its lethal-looking wrought-iron fence,
the ornate old brownstone building proved to be a
branch of the New York Public Library. Raw wind stirred
drifts of dead leaves and papers that had piled up in its
corners. Broken scaffolding hung from an upper story,
and the remains of a banner. A large cracked wooden
sign, much defaced, proclaimed that due to funding cuts
this branch was closed, effective June 1, 1997, and that
the bulk of its collection had been transferred to the
Ottendorfer Branch at Second Avenue.

Still, the library didn't *look* precisely closed. A small group of people stood on the grand front steps, talking excitedly. They seemed to be about Trip's age, wearing long patchwork coats—it must be a fashion—over the kind of slashed finery and jangling carpenter's belts he associated with front-row seating at his shows; or conversely, dressed in very conservative, dumpy-looking men's suits with plain white shirts and somber ties. No masks, no protective implants or headgear; shaved heads for boys and girls alike, or else very long ostentatiously uncombed knotted hair streaked with garish colors. Plastic tubes around their necks that could hold water, or booze, or God knows what. Club kids, Lucius used to call them, derisively; and now Trip thought of what the man had said a little earlier, the names he had mentioned—Marquee Moon, the Chancery. Club names. He stared up at the library steps, unaware that he had stopped walking until a girl with torn red leggings and tunic looked down and smiled at him lazily. He started to smile back, then had an anxious instant when he thought, *She knows me! She knows who I am!* Imagining the devouring rush of fans across a stage, hands pulling at him—

But no, she was just smiling, already she had turned back to the others. He saw now that the pattern on her tunic was repeated on her flesh. The cloth had been torn so that one braless breast was completely exposed. Trip looked away, embarrassed, and hurried on.

He crossed the street and entered the park. The wind had grown stronger, and colder. It tore at his anorak, bringing with it the garbage-dump scent of the river. The sky had deepened from violet to an indigo that was almost black. Rents of glittering silver and crimson showed in it, as though some unimaginable

brilliance lay beyond; but Trip knew it was only darkness. He remembered the planetarium show he had seen
with the blond girl, her softly accented voice in the false
night. The stars so firmly fixed in the sky, how immov-
able they had seemed, how lovely and bright and true;
but there were no stars now, there had been no stars for
years. He stood, shivering, and stared up into a sky that
seemed to turn slowly, clockwise, like a weather image
of a hurricane, its central eye a deeper darkness that
revealed nothing, nothing at all. He squinted, trying to
imagine another kind of sky; but could not. And he
could not remember the stars; when he tried to picture
them all that came to mind was the girl's white face and
burning eyes, and behind her a shining banner—

WHEN THE WHEEL OF TIME SHALL HAVE COME TO THE SEVENTH MILLENNIUM, THERE WILL BEGIN THE GAMES OF DEATH.

From the street came a roar, an answering chorus of
shouts. Trip whirled in time to glimpse a car hurtling
past, and then a second, the first real traffic he'd seen.
From the shadow of a building children darted. They
took off running, purposeful as birds in flight, shot
down an alley, and disappeared. Trip shuddered, trying
not to think of what they might be up to.

*For the children of the kingdom shall be cast out into
outer darkness.*

The Biblical words came unbidden; they were no
longer connected to him. His memories of Christ, of
God, of suffering and redemption and mercy—all were
remote now as his memories of the stars. They had lost
all meaning for him, utterly. Without the world he had
known to frame them—without John Drinkwater, without his music, without the night sky over Moody's

Island or the sound of voices in a dilapidated clapboard church, without the girl—without *these* things, Trip saw now with a clarity that left him breathless, God and the stars could not exist.

He had always thought it was the other way around.

Something cold brushed his cheek. He blinked and saw a few stray snowflakes spinning down, not white but a pink-flecked grey. He pulled at the strap of his knapsack, wondering what time it was. Late, probably; night—New Year's Eve, the man had said, could that be true?—and he was alone in the city. He peered down the street to where he had seen a cab earlier, but it was empty. Echoing voices and the sound of breaking glass came from a block of shabby apartment buildings. He turned and walked quickly back the way he'd come.

At the edge of the park a bunch of children had gathered. Fifteen or twenty of them milled between two benches, sweeping back and forth on Rollerblades and skateboards, sometimes in tandem, playing an elaborate game that seemed to involve knocking down their friends. They were laughing, and swearing—he was a little shocked to hear the way they cursed; none of them could be more than eleven years old. As he drew nearer they began to look over at him, not furtively but with the same alert bright hunger he had seen in the eyes of feral dogs.

Too late he realized his mistake. Something came whipping past him, a blur of yellow and green, and pounded him in the stomach. He caught himself before he hit the ground, turned, and saw a mass of bodies rocketing through the twilight.

Trip gasped and tried to run, staggering behind a bench. A few yards before him was the open street, but already there were more figures there, zooming along the asphalt, jumping the curb and landing with such force that the wheels of their blades struck sparks from the gravel. "Oh, *fuck*," Trip groaned, flinging out his knapsack to sidearm a slight figure that grabbed his elbow.

"Motherfucking *prick*," a voice yelped, jubilant. Trip looked down to see a pale grinning girl with scabbed cheeks yanking at him. Her grin became a snarl as she twisted his arm viciously, pulling at the sleeve of his anorak; then savagely bit him.

"*Ow—!*" Trip shouted in pain, kicked at her as another child ran up. The air rang with shrieking wheels. Their hands were everywhere, their sharp knees digging into his ribs and blood trickling into his eye and this was it, he couldn't even gasp now because he couldn't breathe, one of them had his head in a hammerlock and was slamming it into the pavement—

"Fuck! You *fucker*—"

—and then there was an instant of shocked silence, as though all the air had been sucked away; followed by a deafening roar, a *ping* like rock striking metal. And suddenly the children were everywhere but on him; Trip was there by himself on his hands and knees, coughing and weeping, and someone was beside him.

"Whoa, buddy! Shit, they almost nailed you—"

Trip swiveled his head painfully and saw the man he had followed earlier crouching beside him, a gun in his hand. His patchwork overcoat flapped open to reveal an intricate holster holding another gun, some kind of compact assault weapon, and what looked like dental equipment.

"Whee doggy." The man whistled, then got to his feet. He looked around, the gun light as a toy in his big hand, and tipped his chin upward. "See there?"

Trip stood groggily and nodded; then looked. And

saw a small dark form lying prostrate on the ground at the far end of the park.

"Nailed her," the man said, with a kind of grudging satisfaction. He shook his head. "But she wasn't on wheels. Not that she wouldn't've taken you out," he added, giving Trip a sideways look. "Fuckin' A. But they nailed you BT, buddy—"

He slid the gun into the holster, flicked a catch, and let the overcoat fall shut across his chest, then made a gun with his finger and cocked it at Trip's forehead. "—B-I-N-G-O. What's your stats, pro?"

Trip swallowed. "Huh?" His jaw ached. He swiped at his face and saw a smear of blood on his hand. "Aw, shit—"

"Your status, man," the man went on impatiently. "You're fucking losing some bodily fluids there, don't you got a bandanna or something?"

"Oh—yeah, yeah—" Trip shoved his hand into the knapsack and pulled out a T-shirt, mopped his face with it. "It's okay, it doesn't really hurt—"

"Fuck if it *hurts*, man! Are you fucking negative?"

Trip stopped, looked at him through a fold of dark cloth. "Yeah, I'm fucking negative," he said at last.

"Well, here—" The man tossed him a silvery object. Trip caught it, looked down and saw it was a little sani-pack of sterile gauze treated with Viconix.

For Travel and Emergency Use. For When You NEED To Feel Safe, the label read, with smaller letters proclaiming, THERE IS NO KNOWN CURE FOR THE FOLLOWING VIRUSES. FOR PROPHYLACTIC USE ONLY, PLEASE CONSULT A HEALTH CARE PROFESSIONAL IF—

Trip tore the packet open, took the damp towelette, and swabbed his forehead with it, wincing at the cloying smell of vanilla and antiseptic.

"I'm taking your word on that, buddy," the man said. He cocked his head and watched Trip, nodding agreeably. "Can't suspect everyone, right? Plus it's only a scratch"—he squinted at Trip's forehead, grinning—"plus only a lily white tourist'd be out here by himself on New Year's Eve. Jesus Christ—"

The man turned and spit, surveyed the encroaching shadows, and shook his head. "Fuck this shit. Let's get outta here. Come on—"

He stood expectantly. Trip wadded up the Viconix pad and threw it at a bench, looked out to where that small form lay motionless on the ground. He took a deep breath. His throat hurt, he felt winded and a little bruised but otherwise okay.

"Thanks," he said. "Thanks a lot."

The man shrugged. In the gathering darkness, all coiling orange clouds and cobalt sky, the spiral tattoos on his cheeks glowed with a faint lavender cast. "Hey, it happens. Listen, I found out where that place is. Walked right by it. You probably did too—"

He headed for the street, coattails flapping, alligator boots clacking loudly on the asphalt. "My name's Clovis Tyner," the man said, grinning so that his placebit glowed indigo. "I come up from Houston, and you *know* I ain't gonna take no shit from some little fuckass kid like that—"

He thrust his chin in the direction of the park. "Used to come here on business two–three times a year, before the shit came down. Commodities. Pissed away more money'n my ma made her whole life, not that *she* woulda known what to do with it, 'sides buy a thirty-aught-six. You ain't even holdin' a piece there, are you?" he asked, giving Trip a curious look. "A gun? Fuckin' A. You're here in this part of town—hell, you're right here in this *city*, you must be the only little peckerwood here ain't holding. My my." He whistled again, then laughed. "You're pretty fucking lucky I came along, huh? This must be your goddamn lucky day!"

Trip managed a sickly grin. He kept waiting for the guy to clap a hand on his shoulder or make some other subtle/obvious move to touch him; but the man just kept on walking, so fast that Trip had to jog to keep up. They were across from the park now, heading back toward the abandoned library.

"So you gonna introduce yourself? I ain't gonna jump your bones, if that's what you're thinking," Clovis drawled. "Fuck no. You're too skinny for one thing. For another, you got a dick!"

He threw his head back and hooted, gave Trip a sly sideways look. "Admit it! You thought I was playin' for the pink team—well, fuck *that*! Yo, this is it—"

Trip looked where he was pointing: the library. "*This?*" he croaked.

Clovis paid no attention. He was peering over the wrought-iron fence at the crowd that had gathered on the front steps. Trip moved alongside him, trying to look nonplussed. There were more people here now. Tie-dye and crinkly plastic clothing in cellophane colors—pink, green, turquoise—glowed among the ubiquitous patchwork overcoats, sleek short hair, dreadlocks braided with long strands of glass and metal, shaven heads and foreheads branded with arcane symbols and the names of bands: Commanche Baby Music, Diskomo, 334. When the wind gusted it brought with it a haze of marijuana smoke, something that smelled like bug spray. Shrill galvanic music echoed from somewhere—an agitated noise, drum machines and what sounded like distant traffic. More people were crossing the street now, in twos and threes, animated groups all merging on the sidewalk. A few joined the crowd on the steps, but the rest jumped the fence and headed for the darkness that spilled around the building's perimeter, where the massive structure made its own night. At the end of the block four younger children on blades whizzed back and forth, yelping obscenities. Trip swallowed, feeling a stab of the terror he had felt before; but the people around him seemed pumped up with more attitude than anger. They reminded him of the crowds that had shown up for Stand in the Temple: college kids, kids who still managed to have money, whether it came from parents or hustling drugs or working at Mickey D's, student loans or rolling cars in the suburbs.

"Hey, let us IN!" someone yelled from the steps, and there was an answering chorus of shouts. A jar went whizzing past Trip's head; he ducked as it crashed onto the pavement behind him, sending out a whiff of raw spirits.

"Whoa, dude!" laughed Clovis. He grabbed the fence, gazed through twisted iron railings at the building's facade. "C'mon, we better go, else we won't get in at all—"

With a grunt he hauled himself over, cursing as his coat snagged on a finial. There was a metallic clank; Trip winced, imagining one of those hidden guns striking something and misfiring.

"Here," said Clovis, on the other side now and urging him to follow. "Give me your bag, you can climb over—"

In your fucking dreams, thought Trip; though in fact there was nothing of any value in the knapsack save Martin's sextant. Still, he checked to make sure the catch was secure, then hitched the bag tight onto his shoulder and clambered the way Clovis had gone, gasping as his hurt knee scraped against a jagged edge.

"—*awright*," Clovis sang out as Trip jumped. He

pounded Trip's back so hard he staggered. "Here we are now, entertain us!"

Clovis spun around and began to walk. Not, as Trip had assumed, toward the main stairs and what he thought must be the building's entrance. Instead he headed to where the crowd seemed to be heaviest, milling around the base of the library. Trip followed.

Heavy shadows fell across the ground, broken by columns of pulsing pink and crimson where the night sky streamed down. Kids darted in and out of the light. Some of them wore luminous coils around their necks; others had patterns etched into their skin or scalps that shimmered eerily when they dipped back into shadow. Trip glanced at Clovis: the swirls on his face burned ultraviolet. He looked down at his own clothes, the ripped white pants and old grey anorak.

"Hold on—" he muttered. Clovis stopped without looking back and bounced restlessly on his bootheels. Trip pulled off the anorak and shoved it into the knapsack, stood shivering in his flannel shirt and the thick navy blue wool sweater Martin had given him. He ran a hand through his hair, wincing, traced the rough outline of the cross branded above his eyes—he must look like shit, no one would recognize him now. He shrugged the knapsack back onto his shoulder and gritted his teeth against the numbing cold.

At least I can feel cold again. He smiled, imagining what anyone from Moody's Island would think of that; hearing Jerry Disney snorting, *You're a fuckin' nutjob, you know that, Marlowe? But Jesus loves you all the same!*

Damn straight, thought Trip, and elbowed his way through the crowd after Clovis Tyner. *Jesus loves me all the same—*

What a fucking asshole.

* * *

The way in proved to be not via the library's main entrance, which was blocked off with sheets of stainless steel and plywood, but through myriad service doors and windows that had been linked via a slapdash array of building materials—foam rubber, plastic bags, planks and Styrofoam insulation and hurricane fencing—to form an elaborate network of chutes and passageways, all leading into the basement. Dozens of solar panels leaned up against the building's exterior walls. Like the makeshift entryways they had a haphazard look, but people seemed careful not to knock into them. And while the crowd had grown pretty substantial—Trip guessed there might be a thousand people out there in the frigid wind, which seemed pretty good for an abandoned library in a city with no electric lights—once some secret signal had been given, and the doors and windows opened, everyone disappeared inside within minutes.

"Once you're in you can't get out till morning," explained Clovis. "Unless we get busted, I mean." Trip wondered if someone would search him and find the guns in their hidden holster; but when it was their turn to crawl through a rusted culvert, he found no one on the other side inclined to do anything except shout at them to move.

"G'wan! Keep going, keep going!"

A hugely fat bearded man in a caftan and surgical mask waved them on. He held a green lightstick, and waved it like a traffic cop's baton. "Pay inside!" he bellowed. "Pay inside! Keep *moving*—"

So they moved, but very *very* slowly. It was dark, and suffocatingly hot. A mechanical drumbeat throbbed relentlessly from upstairs, loud enough to make the room shake. Three muscular men in white caftans elbowed through the mob. They wore money belts, and each had a third eye tattooed on his forehead.

"Twenty dollars!" they shouted, breasting through a sea of rippling arms as people shoved money at them. "Twenty bucks, no barter!"

Trip struggled to reach his wallet, managed to pull out two tens. The bills were snatched from him, he hoped by one of the bouncers; then the three men were gone. The crowd's peristaltic motion carried him forward. Bass-heavy electronic music thundered directly overhead. Trip stiffened and braced himself, praying that he wouldn't fall.

"Stay tight!" Clovis shouted, twisting so Trip had a glimpse of violet coils and beacon tooth. "Stay tight—"

The room was black, save for the luminous tattoos and scarifications on the people pressing against him, the fat man's baton and, stuck on the ceiling, a few plastic light boxes. The crush of bodies exuded a thick rank smell—sweat and marijuana smoke and Viconix, patchouli and juniper oil, and a bitter chemical odor Trip almost recognized. A smell that was more like a taste, something that nudged the back of his throat, something he could almost name—

But then all at once the crowd surged forward, so fast that Trip grabbed frantically at Clovis to keep from being trampled underfoot.

"We're there, buddy, we're there!" Clovis shouted.

There turned out to be a broad ascending stairway. Deafening percussion raged down it like an avalanche. Trip bounded up behind Clovis, panting from the effort but also from fear.

"*Yes!*" Clovis yelled over the thunderous music. "You ready?"

Trip nodded, not ready at all. With a gasp he stumbled

into a vast space rent with flickering colored lights and
shadows, moving bodies, music.

"*That* way—" cried Clovis, and forced his way
through the crowd.

After the choking closeness downstairs it seemed
immense, the ceiling somewhere high overhead. Small
solar panels lined the perimeter of the room, flickering
jade, cobalt, scarlet beneath banks of empty bookshelves.
Between the shelves people stood or sat. Talking, drinking, selling things—T-shirts, silvery crescents and discs,
luminous drinking coils, fake tattoos . . .

"Hey, man—acid? X? Ice?"

A heavily tattooed girl in ripped tunic and leggings
stopped in front of him, swaying. Within her flat grey
eyes the pupils had almost disappeared; the corners of
her mouth were cracked and raw.

"Ice, man?" Her voice rose a little desperately; Trip
was unsure whether she was looking to buy or sell. He
glanced down, embarrassed, saw her bare feet shuffling
restlessly back and forth across the dirty floor. When he
looked up again she licked her lips and made as though
to grab him, her hand twitching ineffectually a good six
inches from his chest.

"*Eeeeyyesssss* . . ." She coughed, then wiped her
eyes. For a moment she stared at her fingers, her gaze
widening. With a beseeching expression she raised her
hand, so that Trip could see a greenish crust glinting
on her fingertips.

"*Izzit?*" the girl croaked, blinking. "*Whadizzit?*" Her
hand flailed, trying to grasp him again, but Trip turned
in disgust.

A few yards away he saw Clovis talking to a cluster
of dreadlocked men in long kilts and sleeveless flannel
shirts. Clovis dug into his pocket, handed one of them
a small object that sparkled; the man looked pointedly

away from him, his eyes locking for a moment with Trip's as he palmed something to Clovis. Trip hesitated, then began edging through the crowd toward them. Music flowed from unseen speakers, switching fluidly from techno to jackhammer to Japanese covers of antediluvian disco to enhanced versions of TV music—commercial jingles, theme songs—that Trip recalled from childhood. He edged past a sort of jury-rigged DJ's booth laid out across a long table, a tangle of power cords and speaker wire and stereo equipment, what looked like some kind of video projector. In the middle of it sat a woman, headphones threaded into her shaven skull, fingers stabbing at a knee top. Her eyes glittered metallic red, her cheeks were pierced with dozens of long silver needles. In the close heat he could smell her, patchouli and another smell—that weirdly familiar, corrosive scent he'd first noticed when he entered the library. Like hot metal or burning plastic or gunpowder.

He frowned, trying to place it; and stumbled over a knot of electrical cords.

"WATCH IT!" the red-eyed woman shouted.

"Sorry," he mumbled. He picked his way carefully back into the mob of dancers and stoned hangers-on, his eyes fixed resolutely on the floor. When he looked up again, Clovis was gone.

"*Shit!*" Trip clutched at his knapsack, trying to still the panic boiling inside him. "God *damn* it—"

Someone jostled his arm, a heavyset dreadlocked boy wearing a cropped-off velvet smoking jacket and very little else.

"Uh—sorry, hey man, I'm sorry—" The boy's eyes were preternaturally wide, and even in the mottled light Trip could see how flushed he was, how sweat blackened the velvet jacket and matted the tangled hair across his forehead. "Are you—you—?"

He leaned in close enough that Trip could smell him. Cigarette smoke, and that same sharply unpleasant odor again. The boy stuttered, gazing bewildered at Trip; then stammered something incomprehensible and shambled off. Trip watched him go, neck hairs prickling as he tried to place that scent—

—and suddenly he remembered, a surge of strobing white light and jagged music lashed him, an intermittent flash of phosphorescent green, and it came back. Leonard Thrope pressing an emerald ampoule against the crook of his elbow, hand splayed across the groin of his leather trousers. Trip bared his teeth in rage and revulsion. The smell was everywhere, and he knew what it was.

IZE. He was in an icehouse. All around the music soared and stuttered; someone else bumped into him, but this time Trip whirled and struck out savagely with his arm.

"Motherfucker—" he spit, staring at a frightened young woman who raised her hands protectively before her face.

"Hey—" she stammered, but Trip was already stumbling across the room, smashing furiously at flailing arms and kicking those dancers who didn't get out of his way.

"You *fuckers.*" He panted, pausing to catch his breath. His heart pounded, his sides were hot and damp with sweat, and his face; he had to blink furiously to clear his vision, focus on something besides glittering pinwheels and faces like exploded blossoms. His breath caught in his throat as he wiped tears from his eyes. "Jesus Christ, *stop* it."

Because suddenly the smell was no longer all around him. It was *in* him, it filled his nostrils like rank water and coursed down his throat, coated his tongue so that he retched, feeling that same liquid heat flashing through him, the same prickling of his flesh, as though the pores were opening like mouths to rain. He shuddered, clutching at his stomach; squeezing his eyes shut so he wouldn't see a garden of faces turned rapturously sunwise where there was no sun, softly moving hair like the pale tentacles of sea anemones. But even with eyes closed he still saw them: disembodied arms and legs writhing across a field of red and black, mouths and eyes swarming like plankton; a scintillance that was as much the brittle impact of ice exploding upon his flesh as it was light. And sound, too, that he felt as a thinning in his blood, skin thrumming taut between his fingers, a saline film clotting tongue and gums when he tried to cry aloud. A black-skinned girl with yellow scalp walked past him, laughing. Her eyes were wide and staring. Flecks of emerald glittered in their corners.

"I'm a hive," she said, grinning to show a cracked front tooth. "Buzz buzz."

Trip shivered. He clenched his fists, fighting another horror: the realization that his body could be so terrifyingly free of his control. The music grew deafening, strands of percussion and synthesizer fusing into a relentless high-pitched drone. His ears ached; the bitter taste flooded his mouth again and he spit, wiping his mouth on his shirt. Music hammered at his skull, and the scent of brimstone; he felt as though something were trying to force its way out from behind his eyes.

"—yo there, buddy, looks like you drank the wrong punch!" A hand clasped his shoulder, shook him gently. Trip looked up to see Clovis Tyner, his tattooed face creased with amused concern. "First time?"

"Ahh—" Trip gasped and shook his head. "Nooo."

Clovis nodded. His eyes were wide, a shimmering

pale blue; the pupils were all but invisible. "That can make it worse. You get the surge but not enough to carry you through. N' all this—"

He cocked his head to indicate the room around them—the quickening dance, speakers humming like wasps, abandoned shoes and empty bottles spinning across the floor. Within all the frantic revelry Trip glimpsed sporadic flickers of almost blinding white light, as though someone was aiming a laser at the crowd.

"—it just makes it worse. Contact high." Clovis laughed, a shrill uneasy sound that made Trip's skin crawl. "What you *oughta* do is take some more—now, before things get really crazy. Once they get the light show going—"

Trip shook his head so fast he felt dizzy; felt again as though he were perched above the whirlpool at Hell Head. "No! Just tell me how I can get *out*—"

"I told you, buddy: you're *in* here now." Clovis stood swaying at Trip's side, his gaze unfocused. "They never open the doors till morning. Especially tonight. Cops. Can't have all these fucked-up people spilling in the streets—that's a bad fucking scene, man, I saw it in Austin once, and here they don't even have anyplace to put you, I mean it's not like they got spare room in the Tombs or something. I heard sometimes they just like, dump you in the river. Bodies wash up—

"But you don't need to hear *that*, right? You've been in the scene, right?"

Trip shook his head.

"No? Well, shit!" Clovis whistled. "What the fuck you *doing* here? 'Cause I was gonna say it's like *that* scene, you know, even the way they describe it—rave, hive—the words are kinda alike—"

"Hive?"

"Yeah, man. 'Cause of the ice. I mean, you've done it, right? You know what I'm talking about. Contact high. *Contact . . .*"

Clovis repeated the word under his breath, as though he'd never said it before, after a moment nodded. "Contact—yeah, that's what I mean. Like X, you know? You get that rush . . ."

His voice drifted off. The music shifted, channeled into a familiar backwash of guitar chords and feedback and gongs, a shrieking dub version of a song Trip recognized but couldn't name. His skin yawned open, his mouth filled with saliva, salt; the scent of roses and lilacs. A girl's breathy voice plucked at his spine—

> *If you could just get your mind together*
> *Then come on across to me . . .*

And she was there, her kingfisher eyes a beacon and her words cutting through the skirling music, her small hands pressed against him, and he could feel them through his shirt, her fingers icy as they kneaded his skin, her breath hot and coming in quick bursts.

"Marz—" He groaned and tried to pull her to him, for an instant felt her hair running between his fingers like water. "*Marz—*"

She was gone. Another girl stood in front of him, long dark hair whipping around a heart-shaped face, eyes carefully outlined in kohl and gold dust. Skin glowing as though doused in flame. She was singing, and as she sang her arms threw off birds like sparks. But there was an odd perturbation in the air around her, a cloud of grey and white that was like a hole. Trip could see through it and glimpse the ruined library, flailing shadows. The dark-haired girl laughed, a sound thick with the scent of burning grass, and reached for his hand. He felt her fingernails drag across his palm and shook his head, took a shuffling backward step as she sang—

Around the world thoughts shall fly
In the twinkling of an eye.
Under water men shall walk,
Shall ride, shall sleep, shall play, and talk . . .

Her body shimmered. He could see vines tattooed upon her bare arms and a tiny green lizard skittering down one leg. She raised her arms, her voice rose into a howl as she twirled into a low thicket of flame. Behind her another figure knelt, a black-skinned man coaxing a blaze from something on the floor, smoke and scorched metal. Trip swallowed, blinking furiously as suddenly it all came together, words and music and a movie he'd seen once in a hotel room. For an instant the man raised his head. His eyes were yellow, like a cat's. Iridescent green beetles crawled inside them.

Then a shaft of brilliant white light ripped through the air. The dark-haired girl and the kneeling man blinked from sight, then back again. Feedback echoed like waves slapping at a pier. Streamers of lavender and lilac threaded down through the crowd. Trip sucked air between his teeth, trying to kill the taste of gunpowder. The dark-haired singer stared right at him, her eyes flexing like wings.

In the air men shall be seen
In white, in black, in red and green.
Iron in the sea shall float
As easy as a wooden boat . . .

She began to dissolve into blobs of yellow and orange and chartreuse. People were cheering and shouting. Trip stood openmouthed. Where the girl had been fiery letters traced across the air, like the tracks left by sparklers on a summer night.

HALEY OZ
"PROPHECY"
MUDFISH MUSIC 1999

"Whoooeee!" Trip turned to see Clovis Tyner punching the air with his fist. "*Now* we're eatin' biscuits!"

Trip took a deep breath, pressed his hands against his thighs. "What—"

The words died. Above him ripples of green and gold and violet lashed the air. There was a brilliant pulse of orange in one corner of the room, a sound like low thunder. Then it was as though the ceiling were abruptly torn away. Trip blinked, staring into the prismatic sky. All around him the room grew still, voices hushed, feet shuffling impatiently. There was a smell of the sea; there was the scent of lilacs. Something damp pressed against the palm of his hand, like an open mouth. He jerked backward, saw more words spinning in the air before him.

WHEN THE WHEEL OF TIME SHALL HAVE
COME TO THE SEVENTH MILLENNIUM,
THERE WILL BEGIN THE GAMES OF DEATH.

Small teeth tried to pierce his skin. Warmth probed at his ear, a woman's voice that made him go rigid.

"*Enticing magicians are performing; fear the beguiling, hypnotizing phantoms of the Kali Yuga. Enticing magicians are performing . . .*"

Something began to spin in front of Trip's face: a golden pyramid no bigger than an insect. As he watched it began to grow larger. Beams of light played across it, sending out a clamor of gongs and bells where they intersected. The sky was gone, and the hive of stoned dancers. There was only that monolithic golden shape, and within it a pulsing core that resolved into a vast irradiating eye. Its iris was sky-blue, the color so richly fraught with memory—hairs rising to warm wind, leaves etched across white clouds; the shimmer of sails on the bay—that Trip cried out in anguish. The eye wheeled away from him, growing smaller and smaller yet ever more brilliant, until it hung like a tiny perfect star upon the brow of a boy with glowing blue eyes and sinuously moving hands.

"I possess the keys of hell and death," he sang, *"I will give you the morning star: The end of the end . . ."*

It was the icon. Face tilted upward as it sang, eyes staring into the shattered sky as it danced. From its head reared a tall glittering ornament like a pagoda, that as it swayed sent forth dazzling sparks of aquamarine and ruby and emerald green.

> *Fear the beguiling, hypnotizing phantoms of the Kali Yuga*
> *Fear the end of the end.*

As he watched it Trip felt the same stirrings of bewitchment that he had in the studio at MIT—yet more than that he felt almost pathologically displaced. As though he were watching some utterly familiar videotape of his childhood—fifth birthday party at Pizza Hut or first day of kindergarten—but with himself, the erstwhile point of the entire enterprise, excised utterly from the stream of memory.

> *The end of the end . . .*

The icon grinned. It was *real*. Between the crowd of dancers and the earlier image of the girl singing there had still been a grey veil, the blinkered effect of senses struggling with what was before them.

This icon was different. It was Beautiful, it was Perfect. It was all but unrecognizable as an analogue of Trip Marlowe, even to Trip himself: if he hadn't experienced it before, if he hadn't remembered writing the words and melody it sang, would he have known it wasn't real? He wasn't sure; and the uncertainty terrified him. His entire body yearned for it, even as some spark of his consciousness recoiled.

He felt sick and feverish; revolted. The icon commanded desire and adoration and awe as effortlessly as a painting or a jaguar. It danced upon an invisible plane several inches above the library floor, and its dance made that unseen stratum more real than anything else. Something crashed beside Trip, nudging against his ankle. He wrenched his gaze from the icon and saw a weeping girl sprawled beside him, her eyes huge and black and staring, though it was not Trip they saw. She had tried to follow the dancer, and fallen.

I will give you the morning star . . .

The icon spun and flashed. Trip could hear individual voices in the crowd, people talking as to themselves, whispers of recognition; cries of grief. The music roared on, bells and clamorous gamelan; but now Trip could hear how insignificant the song was. Too clumsy, with its words and trumped-up tracking; too *corporeal*. Like the girl pawing pathetically at Trip's feet: an ugly reminder that despite the IZE, they were all still bound to earth by filaments of muscle and meat and memory. They were all still flesh, inherently flawed. And the icon was not.

A small frantic sound cut through the whirl of music. He glanced down, saw the girl moaning: she had been sick. The icon shimmered. There was a break in the image, a subtle rippling that for just an instant distorted its eerily beautiful face. Trip bit his lip, felt a brisk clarity at the sudden pain, the foul smell that rose from the floor behind him. He shut his eyes, but the impulse to see the icon was irresistible. He looked up again, at the same time bit his lip, *hard*, felt a soft spurt of blood onto his tongue. His mouth throbbed and he focused on that, tried to wield the pain as a barrier between himself and the chattering consciousness that filled the room.

"Make it stop," someone cried out. "Oh God make it *stop* . . ."

Trip swallowed. Fear nudged at him; too late he tried to wrest his gaze from the icon. It stood before him, one leg drawn up beneath it like a heron's.

Fear the end of the end . . .

A whirling arc of stars swept across its eyes, green trees and blue water, a rippling brown mat of living creatures racing across an emerald plain. The icon opened its hands. Within its palms golden-eyed frogs crawled, their throats bubbling up as they sang. They leapt into the air, forelegs extended so that he could see their tiny toe pads, their glistening skin. Where they had been an egg trembled in the icon's cupped hand, its shell a color that Trip had forgotten he ever knew, greening sky before a storm. Cracks appeared upon the shell, the clawed nub of a minute beak. As he watched something pushed its way free until it sat with lidless glaring eyes. Something like a tiny feathered dragon, eagle's curved beak and claws, pointed ears that flattened against its skull as it hissed at him.

Trip's flesh prickled. With all his will he forced himself to look away, to stagger in the other direction; and directly into Leonard Thrope.

"Trip . . ." Trip looked up to see the slight man standing somewhat unsteadily before him. "Trip *Marlowe*?"

Trip swung at him. Leonard blinked, moved backwards as a hand grabbed Trip's and yanked him sideways. "Oh, hey, Trip, nice to see you *too*—"

Flash of crimson as he smiled; another flash as someone struck Trip on the side of the face. He cried out, looked up through watering eyes to see a blond woman a full head and shoulders taller than he was, her body sheathed in pink latex, face hidden behind a Barbie mask. Her silvery plasmer eyes held no reflection whatsoever.

"Check him, Mikey," said Leonard.

Within the mask a mouth opened, showing white teeth filed to a point and tipped with gold. "Okay," she said to Trip. "C'mere, you—"

She spun him to face her, ran her hands expertly up and down his sweater and pants; found the wallet Martin had given him. She glanced inside, with a shrug handed it to Leonard and reached for his knapsack. At Leonard's admonitory glance she set it down. "Nothing on him but that—"

As she stepped away Trip slumped to the floor. His cheek throbbed where she'd hit him, his head felt as though it'd been pumped full of Novocain. He stared murderously up at Leonard Thrope, who only grinned and took the wallet. He opened it, raising his eyebrows at the amount of cash; then screwed up his face to examine the driver's license. "Old enough to drink yet, Trip? Let's see—"

For a second Leonard frowned. Then his appearance changed, melted from malign amusement into something Trip had only seen once before, when his mother received the news of his father's suicide. An utter void of expression, lines smoothed away, eyes blank. He looked at Trip, then at the license again. He perused it for a good minute, thumbed through the rest of the wallet, examining business cards, photographs, whatever was in there. Leonard held the driver's license between two fingers and stared at it, finally slid it into a pocket of his leather jacket. When he spoke, his tone was as devoid of mockery as his face.

"Where did you get this, Trip?"

Trip glared at him sullenly. He thought of lying, of saying he'd stolen it. Instead he got to his feet, squaring off with his fists at his sides. The Barbie Amazon edged closer to him, silvery eyes narrowing. "He gave it to me."

"Who gave it to you?" Leonard asked.

"*He* gave it to me." Trip said defiantly. He stuck out his hand. "Martin Dionysos. Can I have it back?"

"Martin Dionysos gave this to you." Leonard glanced at Mikey. He nodded and she backed away a few feet to lean against a wall, her eyes blank as pewter, her body giving off the scent of rubber and vanilla.

Leonard turned back to Trip. "Where, Trip? Here? In this club?"

Trip shook his head. The other man suddenly seemed uneasy, staring back at Trip with an intense, almost fearful, hunger. Trip felt a sting of poisonous exultation: so Leonard Thrope could be afraid of something!

"No." He grinned disarmingly. When Leonard ventured a wary smile back, he snatched the wallet from his hand, ducking as Mikey lashed out at him.

"You little *fucker*—"

"Mikey—no!" Leonard shouted. Like a snake recoiling for a second lunge she drew back, but did not strike again. "Leave him . . ." Quickly he turned back to Trip, who had grabbed his knapsack and was breathing heavily. "Is he here? Martin—is he in the city?"

Trip shook his head. "No." Immediately he regretted having said anything, but when he looked over he saw the Amazon turned to him, her pointed teeth glittering gold. Reluctantly he continued. "It was back in Maine. At a place called Mars Hill . . ."

Leonard nodded, eyes distant.

"Though actually, he did give me *this* here"—Trip held up the wallet, then shoved it into his front pocket—"on his boat."

"When?"

"Yesterday—" Trip frowned. "No, this morning."

"What were you doing with him?"

Trip hesitated. "He saved me. I—I tried to kill myself, up there. At home. I jumped into the water to drown. But I was washed up on shore. Martin found me."

Leonard's gaze shifted, focusing from whatever far-off thing he had seen to Trip's face. "This is after I saw you. After we made the recording." Trip nodded as Leonard continued. "Lucius said you'd do that—he said you'd split and go back to Maine. He thought you'd freak out on tour. He said you wouldn't be able to handle it—"

Leonard gestured vaguely, so that suddenly Trip was aware of jagged rays of light, people in the room around him.

"—he said you'd go home. Nellie thought you took off with her foster daughter." Leonard nibbled his lip; a ruby spark flared and died. "That's what I thought, too. But you didn't?"

The breath froze in Trip's throat. It was a moment before he dared speak.

"No. Do you know where she is?"

Leonard shook his head. "No," he said softly. "I really don't."

He sighed, ran a hand through his long mass of greying curls. He tugged at an intricate braid of gold thread and leather and tiny mirrors until it stretched before him; stared into the spectrum of tangled glass and metal as though divining something there. After a minute he raised his eyes to Trip's. "You said Martin gave you his wallet, here in the city. He left Mars Hill, then? He came with you? Where is he now?"

Trip shrugged. He fought to keep his voice steady, but couldn't. He had lost his balance: Leonard Thrope had moved his hand and once again the world had shifted under Trip's feet.

"Where is he?" repeated Leonard, urgently.

"He left," said Trip. The words tore at his heart. Because suddenly he saw the blond girl again, a shaft of bright pink disappearing through a revolving door. Smelled her, lilacs and salt and honey, felt her head between his hands and then watched her go.

"To where? Did he tell you?"

Trip could only stare, empty-eyed. "I don't know. He had his boat—we sailed down here, we left about two weeks ago—"

"But why did he leave?" Leonard's tone grew anguished. "He was so sick! The only thing keeping him alive was that he stayed up there—why would he leave?"

"Well—he brought me here. I mean, I asked him to," Trip said; then, with slowly dawning astonishment, "You *know* him?"

"I've known Martin Dionysos for twenty fucking years. We were at RISD together, I left my goddamn high-school sweetheart for him. Then Martin dumped *me*. We ended up at different galleries—"

He laughed harshly. "—we had, oh, different views about Art. Among other things. He hasn't left that place up in Maine for years, now."

"But he *wanted* to—" Trip's voice rose defensively. "I mean, I didn't, like, *force* him or something—"

Leonard stared at Trip. He took a deep breath, shut his eyes, and exhaled.

"Didn't you know how sick he was?" he asked. "Couldn't you tell? You stupid fucking kid. He was *dying*—"

"No! He *wanted* to do it—"

"Of course he wanted to do it!" Leonard laughed harshly. He grabbed Trip's arm and shook him. "Look at you! Little blond piece—he fucking fell in *love* with you, you little prick! Christ, he thought he *saved* you? Martin spent his whole *life* looking for stray dogs! You fucking asshole!" And Trip saw tears glowing in the basilisk eyes. "Didn't you notice anything? Didn't you see he was sick?"

"No."

For a long moment he held Trip's gaze. The boy stiffened, sure that Leonard was going to strike him. Instead he shook his head and glanced over his shoulder.

"Mikey," he shouted above the music. "Get the others. We're going. You—"

He turned to Trip and grabbed his arm. "You're coming with me—"

"The fuck I am," Trip spit, but before he could pull away another Barbie appeared, identical to the first—shimmering plasteen mask, effaced eyes, latex catsuit—save that her head was shaved.

"Bring him to the limo," Leonard commanded. "We're going. *Now*."

The second woman dragged Trip through the crowd, following Leonard as he pushed his way downstairs. By the makeshift doors the caftaned bouncers stood, talking. As Leonard approached one began to shout—

"Hey man, no one leaves till—"

—but then the others broke in.

"Leonard!"

"Yo, Lenny! Takin' off?"

Leonard nodded, not slowing his pace as the caftaned men pulled aside a heavy metal fire door. Icy air roared inside, a flurry of grey ashes.

"'Night, Leonard."

"Later, Leonard—"

They were outside. The grey ashes were snow; it coated the ground like dark fur. In the street a huge seal-grey limousine idled. A figure in black rubber and mouthless black metal mask stepped from the driver's seat and opened one of the back doors, holding it as Leonard slid inside.

"Fayal, this young gentleman will be accompanying us," said Leonard, jerking a thumb at Trip.

"Wh—" Trip began, but before he could say more was shoved into the seat beside Leonard.

"Shut up." The older man smiled coldly, reached to take Trip's chin in his hand. "You ought to thank me," he said, as the two Barbies and several other people clambered into the limo's backseats, laughing and complaining.

"Oh yeah?" Trip hunched against the window, trying to sound tough. He and Leonard had the middle seat to themselves, but he could see the others watching him with amusement.

"Sure." With a soft thump the last door closed. Warm air stirred at Trip's feet. "You're going to a party, Trip."

"A *what*?"

"A *big* party. And you weren't even invited." As the limo shot into the street Leonard gazed out the darkened window, to where the sky moved slowly overhead, gyring in upon itself. "You lucky kid."

Trip stared at him, trying to think of some sharp reply; finally just shook his head. He cradled his knapsack and stared resolutely at his knees. "What kind of party?"

"What *kind* of party?" Leonard raised his eyebrows. From the backseat came raucous laughter. "Don't you know what today is, Trip?"

The boy sank sullenly into the seat. "Yeah."

"So!" Leonard reached over and grabbed Trip's knee, shook it in mock excitement. His hazel eyes narrowed. He leaned in close as the limo roared around a corner. In the backseat his entourage shrieked delightedly. "Well, gee whiz, Trip, gee whiz—Happy fucking New Year."

CHAPTER SIXTEEN

The Chairman Dances

The elevator opened onto night. *Real* night, black night: thousands of stars thrown across the sky, tree limbs scratching at white streaks of cloud, silver moon–pinnace, snow. As Jack stepped out the cold struck him, but gently, birch twigs after sapping heat. Beneath his feet crunched a thin layer of snow, and beneath the snow the firm-mattress spring of earth. There was the perfume of balsam, so deeply fragrant that Jack felt as though his face had been thrust into a soft-needled bed, and underlying that the faint sickly smell of Viconix.

"May I see your ID, please?"

He was so enraptured of the sky, the icy dampness seeping up through his topsiders, that it wasn't until someone touched him lightly but persuasively on the arm that he realized he'd been questioned.

"Sir?"

Jack looked up into the smooth broad face of a veritable security giant, former linebacker or WWF hero in GFI's red-and-gold livery, the outlines of his formal jacket corrugated by the bulletproof vest he wore beneath, his head haloed with chatlinks: headphones, mike, beepers, vocoder, all alive and humming.

Oh: and *three* guns.

"Oh—uh, yeah, sure, wait—"

Jack nodded, patting anxiously at pockets for his wallet. He sensed the giant's impatience, shadows moving just beyond his vision, the premonition of many huge hands about to clap onto his shoulders.

"Oh! No—of course, wait," he stammered, suddenly recalling his hand, the image scanned there by the foot courier months before. "You need *this*—"

He grinned feebly and held up his palm. As though freshly branded there the gryphon glowed a brilliant red-gold. The giant smiled, nodding as one huge black-gloved hand encircled Jack's wrist, held it steady while the other hand drew a flattened disc across his palm. There was a softly reassuring chime. Jack felt a warm, not-quite-painful tingling, as though he'd been stung by tiny ants. Then the man did a quick pat-down, checking Jack's pockets, running fingers through his lank hair.

"You enjoy the evening, sir," he finally pronounced, beckoning Jack forward. Somewhere behind him he heard excited voices, the low *sooosh* of a revolving door. "Happy New Year."

"Right," Jack murmured. He stepped away; when he was at a safe distance glanced frowning at his clothes. *Shit.* He was still wearing what he'd had on at Lazyland when Jule kidnapped him—white oxford-cloth shirt, quite soiled; dark green chinos; very worn brown corduroy jacket. His temple throbbed, and he rubbed it gingerly, trying to make sense of time. It had been, what? Wednesday morning when he left Lazyland? The twenty-ninth of December? He was fairly certain of the date, if not the day of the week.

Nellie's words came to him then: *You'll be at the party tonight . . .*

He had lost a day; more than that, two days, squandered in a cell within the Pyramid. He had a flash of his grandmother sick with worry, his brother Dennis tending to her, tight-lipped; of the blond girl going into labor.

He groaned and pressed his hand tight against his temple. And recalled what Nellie Candry had told him—

Blue Antelope. They've planned a terrorist strike against the SUNRA dirigibles . . .

His hand fell away as he looked up; saw trees and night sky and stars, and behind them a faint cross-hatching, lurid pulse of green and violet. He blinked, then squinted, trying hard to focus. The stars blurred. When he tipped his head sideways, staring intently into the darkness, he could make out faint slender beams of light flickering through the air, like the traplines of a spider's web. He glanced up again, quickly, and could almost discern where the glittering constellations spun off from shafts of adamant.

Projections. He looked behind him and saw a huge glittering sweep of gold slanting upward into coiling light. That was the Pyramid. The lozenges of black and gold at its base were elevators, tunnels, revolving doors, glowing corporate logos. The myriad multicolored fig-ures—masked, helmeted, armored, sheathed—were other invited guests. He was in the staging area that adjoined the Pyramid, the atrium arena GFI had con-structed for the Millennial Ball. The entire vast space had been turned into a kind of cyclorama. White flakes whirled in those agitated arcs he associated with old movies and snowmaking machinery at Vermont ski resorts. Firs and leafless birch trees had been planted everywhere, receding into a silvery blur where he could just make out raised stages, arcades, pavilions, gold-and-red-clothed tables, promenades of emerald glass, house-sized video monitors, red-and-gold information kiosks, Red Cross tents, pillars and columns embla-zoned with logos. The sight of so much *stuff*, so many people, made his head throb even more painfully. His mouth was dry. When he blinked, phantom rockets spun and flared off into the snow, so that for a moment he thought someone had set off fireworks inside.

But no. A shiver went through him, and he yawned nervously, tasting copper in the back of his throat, and salt. His edginess swelled into anticipation, something very close to exhilaration, in fact. He thought of Larry Muso, his absurd hair, how surprisingly soft it had felt. What had he said about meeting him? A place called Electric Avenue, sometime in the morning . . .

Jack was fairly certain that he'd missed morning. At the very least, the folks here at GFI had gone to a lot of trouble to create the illusion of a midwinter night, once upon a time. He gazed down at the end-less tents and tables, fluttering pennons of gold and crimson and sky-blue, light-drenched trees, falling snow and video screens that showed GFI's dirigibles silhouetted against a slowly turning pinwheel sky. Slowly, he began walking toward it all. There were people around him, revelers in costume and black tie, kimonoed men and women, guests in formal robes, and some who were all but naked, save for gold-mesh caches-sexe and dominoes covering their faces; and almost as many uniformed security personnel.

"Let's find a goddamn place to sit," he overheard someone complain. A frowning white-haired man, maskless, tuxedoed, his eyes invisible behind silvery plasmer.

"Let's find a goddamn *bar*," his companion snapped. As they passed Jack she drew her breath in sharply. He looked over to see an elegantly spare woman with sleek blond hair, marquis-cut diamond earrings, bare shoul-ders thrusting from a column of hyaline silk and bugle beads. For an instant he thought she must recognize him, from some long-ago New York Public Library ben-efit or Fresh Air Fund barbecue in the Hamptons. But then he saw the quiver of fear in her eyes, a faint tremor in the too-taut skin around her mouth. She turned away quickly, in two long strides caught up with her companion. With a backward glance at Jack, she took the man's arm, steering him to where a cluster of security guards stood beneath a video screen displaying an aerial view of the Pyramid.

Jack stopped, brow furrowed; abruptly realized that the woman had been *afraid* of him. He stared at his clothes—yes, he was pretty disheveled—drew a hand to his face. Unshaven, too; and maskless; no expensive placebits or plasmer, no facial tattoos or identifying brands; nothing but skin. He traced the sharp outline of his cheekbone, let his hand drop, and looked at his wrist, his fingers like wands of dry bamboo. *Christ. I must look skeletal. I must look just like shit.*

He shivered. Snow brushed his forehead, and he wiped it away, saw that it left a greenish sheen to his fingers. He thought of what Nellie had told him of GFI's plans to distribute the fusarium bacteria, then shuddered as a wrenching wave of nausea went through him. He drew a long breath and tilted his head back, staring at the glass dome arching overhead. Cold wind played at his face, redolent of balsam; but he could also smell a very faint trace of acrid smoke, raw sewage, the wetstone standing-water scent of the city. If he focused and unfocused his eyes, stared beyond the scrim of stars and pared moon, he could see the structural grid of the dome; but if he stared beyond *that*, he could see something else lodged within the real sky like a bullet in a wound. A glistening golden shape, outlined with brilliant red lights that spelled out GFI and then melted into the image of a gryphon holding a globe in its claws; and not far from it another shape, and another. He counted seven of them, an unmoving school of skyborne leviathans, and as his eyes adjusted he made out the larger field of black that spread between them like a stain: the sky platform, or some other part of the pay-load that was scheduled to be towed into the upper atmosphere tonight. He blinked, pinched the bridge of his nose, and looked away.

. . . Because I was the one who provided them with fifty-seven sheets of collodion cotton soaked with nitroglycerin, all of which have been incorporated into the Fougas' outer structure . . .

In the distance he heard an orchestra tuning up, the echoing snarl of feedback and a voice booming from a loudspeaker. *Laughter. Music. Tears!* Jack bared his teeth in a smile, startling a liveried woman carrying a tray of champagne flutes.

"Oh! Champagne, sir?"

Her mask was a bit of Venetian frippery, orange-and-black feathers, sequined arabesques. Jack shook his head No, then said, "Oh, what the hell," and took a glass from her gloved hand. As she left, two security people passed in a haze of electrified chatter, glancing at him with detached interest but not suspicion. Jack sipped his champagne—Mumm's, what middle-class kids always ordered at the Plaza because it's what they always drank in movies—and within minutes began to feel light-headed. He hadn't eaten in two days. He still didn't feel hungry at all. The opposite, in fact, strung-out but intently focused. He wondered what would happen if he approached security and told them about the bomb.

The *putative* bomb, he corrected himself. He finished the champagne, was looking for somewhere to put it when the waitress reappeared. He set his empty glass on her tray and took another full one, sipped it rumina-tively as he watched more and more people fill *GFI's* winter palace.

Someone sure has a lot of friends, he thought, continuing

to walk toward the main-stage area. And probably they wouldn't like it if some emaciated, scruffy-looking, no doubt *virulent* guy, who didn't even have the decency to wear a mask, started raving about bombs. The thought of spending the night in another security pen made him grimace. He groaned, very softly, as he remembered Jule, and Nellie Candry's figure slumped somewhere within the Pyramid. He would be held again for questioning, an unknown man connected with two suicides.

Maybe she was nuts. He emptied his glass, gave it to a passing waiter. A conspiracy nut, spending all her time with that ghastly archival footage . . .

He sighed and glanced up, this time made no effort to focus on anything but the illusory stars. Orion, Ursa Major, Ursa Minor. He found Polaris, brighter than he thought it should be. He stared at it, frowning, and shook his head.

It's in the wrong fucking place. West, instead of north; he could orient himself to the street outside. *They can't even get the goddamn stars right.* He laughed in disbelief, and a group of brightly clad teenagers stopped to yell at him.

"Happy New Year!"

Something touched his face. He blinked, glitter pocking his hands and the corners of his vision. A creamy-skinned young girl, no makeup, no mask, tossed another handful of glitter at him. "Happy New Year!" she cried, and turned giggling back to her friends. He watched them go, thinking of flames raining down from the sky, broken glass and burning fuselage, ten thousand panicked people dying in a crush of fire and twisted girders; the world unredeemed by solex shields, all of humanity doomed because Jack Finnegan hadn't acted on a tip about a terror-ist bomb threat. Weighed that against the image of himself being questioned in a holding area, exhausted and sick, insisting on the veracity of a dead woman's ravings about terrorists and psychotropic drugs, while the party of the century went on till dawn without him, and he was finally released to stumble home to his brother's responsible, accusing eyes, having once again missed the ball. He thought of Leonard here, somewhere in his stained leather motley: the Lord of Misrule. He thought of kissing Larry Muso, of making love to him and then holding him afterward, the two of them laughing—*bombs*? what *bombs*? He thought of fucking Nellie Candry, of the web of connectedness between them all, how easily it could be torn but how that was how the light got through, sometimes.

I should leave, he thought. *I could escape now, I could get away from here, somehow get back to Lazyland . . .*

But that would mean never seeing Larry Muso again. That would mean never knowing how it might have all turned out. And for all his fears and illness, for all that he had given up on the world, he wasn't quite, *quite* ready to forgo the chance to see what might have been.

And suddenly, with a clarity that took his breath away, he realized that Leonard had won, after all. That after all these years they had all finally won, Julie and Leonard and the rest of them, everyone who had ever urged Jackie Finnegan to go for a dangerous drive, cross against the light, leap off the Brooklyn Bridge, fall in love with strangers.

Because all of a sudden Jack saw it was the *jump* that mattered: not the presumed safety of the cliff edge, nor the certainty of annihilation at the bottom. It was *Chance* that mattered, the dizzying recognition that somebody or something *was*, in fact, playing dice with the world, and had been all along.

The realization blinded him. He actually brought a hand to his eyes and covered them, blinking painfully.

When he moved his hand away again, phantom sparks glimmered in the air before him, green and gold and violet. He stared at them openmouthed, then glanced up at the ceiling, suddenly unsure as to where he was, or when; half-expecting to see the real and broken sky there, mirroring his own dislocation.

"What is it?" he whispered as the particles moved brightly around him. "What is it? *Tell me*—"

That was when he heard it: a soft roaring sound, a sound he recognized, a sound like something he had heard before—in the wind, in the sea, in the pulse of blood through his ears. It was, he realized, the sound of things falling apart.

He began to laugh, so hard that it racketed into a fit of coughing, and he had to clutch at the wall for balance. *Oh man*, he thought. *What a fucking joke . . .*

Because he had always thought the end of his life would come down to two questions: *Did he fall?* or *Was he pushed?*

But now he knew he had a choice. Now, for the first time in forty-two years, he realized that Free Will and Free Fall could feel very much the same.

So: Jackie Finnegan would go to the Ball. *He* would be the wild card.

Fucking A, he thought, sick and dizzy and filled with a kind of exultation. *Fucking A! I'm finally in the goddamn game!*

Then, as he turned and started toward the crowd—

No—

I am the goddamn game.

I love the sound of breaking glass, he thought.

And went to find Larry Muso.

* * *

It took him hours to reach Electric Avenue. Threading his way among costumed partygoers and sideshow freaks—fire-eaters, little people, a woman whose body was a mosaic of videocircuitry reflecting the faces of those gawping at her—pausing now and then to take in one of the stage shows. Overhead, corporate logos flamed and faded like Roman candles, their reflections rippling across the floor, trailing across faces and masks. An orchestra played "Begin the Beguine." The Jayne County Dance Theater performed excerpts from *Elektra*. There was a survey of the Broadway musical from its vaudeville origins to *Assassins*. And the Kronos Quartet, exhausted and halfway through Morton Feldman's String Quartet No. 2. Booths where you could create your own rudimentary IT images. A reunion of the surviving Beatles and some icons. Palm readers, an onychomancer. Clocks, analog and digital, that showed the time here in New York—9:48 P.M.—as well as the hour in every single time zone across the world.

And food—acres and acres of food, more food than Jack had dreamed was left in that fleeced world. He bypassed the McDonald's World Market, stopped to eat some caviar and an unpleasantly gummy slice of nova that tasted of petroleum. He washed it down with more champagne, aware now that he was getting slightly drunk. The alcohol seemed to intensify some of the effects of the fusarium, if that's what was causing the flares that pulsed just beyond his vision, the sense of a burgeoning sort of rapture that, like the phantom lights, was just outside his full comprehension. He put his glass back on the table, turned to walk unsteadily through what had become a huge crowd. People were mobbing the food tents as though they held celebrities—he saw one man filling the pockets of his morning coat with triangles of toast and foie gras—and more than once scuffles broke out, to be immediately put down by security and police in flak jackets. Overhead, the huge video displays showed scenes of millennial revels around the globe: blue-faced dancers in Delhi, drunken parties in Queensland, an ominously quiet Tehran street. The green silence of vanilla farms on Tafahi in the Kingdom of Tonga, the first place on earth where the new millennium would break. Now and then the video screens showed glimpses of the crowd below, indistinguishable carapaced figures swarming from table to table, stage to stage. Screaming would erupt then, and cheers, filling Jack with a sudden sharp unease. He glanced overhead, striving to see if the Fougas were still there; but all he saw was the shimmer of false stars and the spectral glow of reflected lights within the dome.

BONG.

A deafening gong, and more cheers. Ten o'clock. Jack blinked and rubbed his eyes, trying to disperse bright glimmers like dust motes or shining gnats. The snow had stopped—he overheard someone say the hydraulic system was clogged, dredging up God knows what from the New York City water supply—and what was on the ground had melted, making it sloppy going underfoot. Vast as it was, the dome had grown much warmer, whether from the mass of moving bodies (there was a lot of dancing) or an additional engineering failure, Jack was afraid to guess. His exhilaration wavered into anxiety; he was thinking about maybe finding a quiet place to sit for a while, maybe even trying to figure out a way home, when he looked up and saw the marquee.

ELECTRIC AVENUE

Blazing neon against a background of video confetti and flaking brick: a pavilion designed to look like a decrepit city apartment building. *An icehouse*, Jack thought with a pang. *God they're shameless*. But that didn't stop him from hurrying through the entrance, pushing past three ragged teenagers with pincushion faces and retro crew cuts and eyes like mill wheels, sprawled in the mud against the building's facade.

"Spare change?" one of them croaked. Jack stepped over her, saying nothing—paid extras or genuine article, they gave him the creeps.

Inside was a warren of dank hallways and crumbling rooms, emblazoned throughout with video screens that were doors into sunlight, ocean, mountaintop, sky. A few people milled about, watching the videos. A Japanese businessman, more stoned kids, an elderly woman whose plasmer lenses matched her cropped violet hair; a family group of husband, wife, adult daughter. They would look up perfunctorily when Jack entered a room, never taking real notice of him; certainly not any more notice than anyone else had outside. It wasn't until he found himself wandering back into the same rubble-strewn corridor for the third time that he realized that the elderly violet-haired woman was turning her head *in the exact same way* she had before. Light bubbled across her violet lenses in the same precise pattern, her hand moved protectively across the same breast, she looked at the screen again with the same lack of concern. Jack sucked his breath in; the woman continued to stare at a tape loop of erupting volcanoes. He stood there for another minute, trying to find the lie to the illusion; finally crossed to where she stood.

"Hello?" he said.

The woman ignored him. Very cautiously he moved his hand, until it should have brushed the flowing sleeve of her pleated satin sheath. There was nothing there. When he jabbed at her his hand momentarily flickered from view; and then he could see it again, floating disembodied within the folds of her dress.

"Jack? Jack Finnegan?"

Jack spun about, felt the sudden disorienting sensation of warm flesh and thick brocade. He recoiled as someone took his elbow.

"It *is* Jack, isn't it!" Delighted laughter. "I thought I'd missed you, or you'd missed me—"

It was Larry Muso. Looking even slighter than Jack had remembered him, and extremely pleased. He wore an elaborately brocaded ultramarine happi coat, embroidered with fabulous sea animals—cuttlefish, octopuses, sea horses—over a simple black tunic and loose black silk trousers. His hair had been coiffed into even more fantastic spires, a veritable chambered nautilus threaded with gold and deep blue wire, tiny seashells, gilt starfish. Gold dust powdered his delicate cheeks and mouth, and his eyes were carefully edged in kohl.

"I know, I look like the Sea Hag!" he went on, ignoring Jack's protests. "But I figured, what the hell—it's a party. So were you here earlier? Did I miss you? Are you *okay*?"

This last delivered with sudden anxiety as he peered up into Jack's face. "Jack? Really, you don't look very well, perhaps you should sit down—"

"N-no. I'm fine, I'm fine—" Jack swallowed, ran a hand across his forehead and felt sweat beaded there. "Actually, I am a little hot—this exhibit, I just figured out—"

"Aren't they remarkable? They've been in development for a while, but this is the first time we've actually run the programs in public. There are still quite a few bugs," he confided in his elegantly accented voice, taking Jack's arm and leading him through the hall to where a rickety staircase spilled outside. "Of course it doesn't work in the light, so that's why we've done it like this. Rather bad taste, don't you think?"

"Rather," Jack said, and laughed.

They were outside the mock-up now, treading carefully down the rotting steps until they stood side by side in a puddle of snowmelt and squashed grass and discarded cups. Larry stared up into Jack's face with disarming happiness, after a moment touched his hand gently.

"I *am* glad to see you," he murmured. "Are you hungry? Busy? I mean, do you have—plans?"

Jack laughed again, shaking his head. "You mean, what am I doing New Year's Eve? Nothing but this—" He swept his arm out, sending Larry off-balance. "Oh! God, I'm sorry—"

He grabbed at Larry's shoulder, feeling the surprisingly solid juncture of flesh and bone beneath his happi coat. As he helped him straighten he caught a breath of the same musky perfume Larry had worn to Lazyland so long ago. *Myrra.* He inhaled, dizzy, looked down to see Larry staring at him. For a long moment they stood there in silence. Jack's heart thrummed inside him, there was a soft roaring in his ears, ghostly sparks behind his eyes. He swallowed. When he let his hand fall away from Larry's arm, he heard the other man release his breath in a long sigh.

"So." Larry Muso cleared his throat. "Would you like to have dinner?"

"Dinner?" The thought of food made Jack feel ill, but he nodded. "Sure. I—"

"Wait—there's a catch. Because I have to be at GFI's private tent in"—Larry withdrew a pocket watch from his coat and cocked an eye at it—"oh, thirteen minutes.

This is the formal dinner for Mr. Tatsumi and our Board of Directors, also some very hush-hush guests, and maybe some surprises. I am required to be there, but I could arrange for you to be there as well—they've left a certain number of seats unassigned."

"But—Jesus, I'm not dressed for it, Larry." Jack looked miserably at his shirtfront, had a visceral surge of anguish as memory flooded him: Jule, the woman in the Pyramid. When he shook his head, fractal light exploded into black, the vision of a dirigible cracking open like an egg. "I mean, this has been a pretty horrible few days for me, a friend of mine—a friend of mine died, and—"

"Hush." Larry rested a finger against his lips, then leaned forward and touched it, gently, to Jack's chin. "I can find you a jacket and tie, my friend. They may even *fit*," he added, eyeing Jack's lanky frame before adding very softly, "You look very thin, Jack. And tired. Is it bad?"

Jack hesitated, then nodded. "Yeah," he whispered, tears welling in his eyes. "It's—I'm in pretty bad shape. Probably I shouldn't even have come . . ."

"No." Larry took his arm, his hand tightening as he motioned Jack toward a path. "I'm so glad you did. Come with me now—"

And Jack went.

GFI's private pavilion was walled with light, slender pulsing columns twenty feet high arranged in a great circle.

"A new kind of full-spectrum fluorescents," Larry Muso explained as they stopped at a checkpoint. "Very low wattage, very efficient. They promote serotonin production."

Jack grinned. "That's great." Larry's relentless enthusiasm was pure balm, Larry himself was balm, his ridiculous clothes and laughter, those lovely dark eyes. "That's really great," he repeated breathlessly.

"Yes, it is." Larry stepped aside, so that the helmeted security guards could search Jack, photograph and fingerprint him. A jacket had been found, an old black silk Armani, far too big: cuffs flopping around Jack's bony wrists, pockets deep enough to swallow his hands. He did the best he could, rolling up the sleeves, then took the foulard paisley Larry gave him and tied it loosely about his throat.

"Do I look like an idiot?" he asked at last, craning his neck to find some surface that might give back his reflection. "God, I must look awful."

"You look—very, *very* good."

Jack gazed down into Larry's face. And saw in his eyes what he couldn't find mirrored in the cramped security booth: he looked terrible. He really was dying.

But perhaps, in a way he had never imagined could be possible—perhaps it didn't matter. A few feet away the security guards hovered over a monitor, shaking their armored heads and saying something in Japanese. Slowly, trembling slightly, Jack lifted his hand and touched Larry's cheek. The flesh yielded beneath his fingertips, at once soft and salebrous, scented of sweat and myrrh. He leaned forward until that absurd pelagic curl of hair brushed his forehead, shut his eyes and breathed in deeply, heart thundering, the sea in his ears. He felt something shatter and fall away inside him, like an iceberg calving—a grief so profound and long-standing he hadn't even known he was frozen, hadn't known it was ice; had thought it was mountain, bedrock; granite.

I could love him, he thought. *If it's not too late.*

"Late?"

Jack started, saw Larry's head cocked questioningly. Had he spoken aloud?

"It *is* almost eleven," Larry went on, gesturing at the door as he made a farewell wave to the guards. "But the party goes on through tomorrow—it's not *that* late."

Jack nodded. "Oh. Sure." His heart continued to pound, and he turned so that the other man wouldn't see tears in his eyes. He didn't want to cause an international incident, breaking down in front of the CEO of one of the world's few remaining multinationals. "I'm just a little beat, that's all."

"Right. You'll feel better if you eat something."

They went inside. Passing beneath a glowing arch, where a holographic gryphon reared and clasped the sun to its breast, into a broad open space where tables were laid out with bloodred cloths, spare floral arrangements of black twigs, and golden ornaments shaped like sun and moon and stars, crystal glasses, gleaming flatware, and bone white chopsticks. Overhead the space yawned into the glittering uppermost reaches of the dome, the false stars twinkling, the moon now at full. Fifty or so people were scattered around the area, talking, a hushed mélange of English, Japanese, German, French. Men in black tie and robes and kente cloth, women in elegant evening wear, masks held in bejeweled hands. Jack recognized a few of them—a well-known stage actress of middle years, a television anchorman who had covered the war in South Korea; a video mori artist who'd been a protégé of Leonard's. There was a raucous burst of laughter from a bluff American who towered above several Japanese men in the group, and a woman videotaping their conversation. Clink of glasses, soft tread of waiters. No waitresses, Jack noted, only tuxedoed men bearing champagne, Scotch, trays of sushi and tiny fresh strawberries.

"Here. Now, I want you to *eat* something, Jack," commanded Larry Muso, deftly scooping several pieces of *uni* and *toro* onto a chilled metal plate and handing it to Jack. "I won't be able to sit with you, but I've put you at a table with—"

He broke off as an austerely dressed blond woman approached them. She nodded politely, then spoke in a low voice to Larry. He smiled, glanced sideways at Jack, and said, "Mr. Tatsumi needs to speak with me about a few things. I believe you're at Table Seven. I'll come and join you when I can—"

He bowed slightly, ultramarine factotum, and walked with the woman across the room. Jack watched them go, sighing, then looked up into the false sky. He experienced a twinge of unease, very much the bad fairy at the christening, Nellie's warning lodged like a poison dart within his breast. But, oddly, he had no real fear. Instead he felt very much the way he had the last few times he'd flown, in the wake of the Jihad 9 bombings: anxious but not actually frightened. At least, not frightened enough to forgo the trip. He took another glass of champagne—Kristal this time—but after a tentative sip drank no more; just held the glass as talisman and walked around thoughtfully.

At one end of the room a dance floor had been set up, smooth unpolished wood. A few yards away a technician sat behind an array of computers and projection equipment, and beside him six chairs had been set up in a half circle. As Jack passed, six black-clad women crossed the dance floor, carrying musical instruments. They sat down in the chairs and began tuning up. Two violins, two kotos, viola, and cello. After several minutes they started to play, a heartbreakingly plangent melody that made Jack's neck prickle. He stood, listening, until they finished, then turned away as they launched into a more familiar piece.

In the room around him people were getting settled at tables. Waiters moved gracefully, pouring wine, setting out small decanters of sake and cast-iron teapots on the scarlet tablecloths beside discarded masks. The encircling wall of lights dimmed, to a cool bluish glow. Jack smiled at passing couples, most of whom smiled back, and found Table Seven.

The other guests' names had been painted in gold leaf on small porcelain tablets. Jack glanced at a few of them, saw none that he recognized. His own was written in a swooping calligraphic hand—*Mr. John Finnegan*—on a square of thick handmade paper speckled with gold-and-lapis chips. He glanced at it wryly as he took his seat, leaned over to read the china place card at the setting to his right.

MR. PETER STILLMAN LOOMIS

He was wondering who Peter Stillman Loomis was, when a hand tattooed with death's-heads and flaming trees plucked the bit of porcelain from its holder and replaced it with another.

MR. LEONARD THROPE

"Leonard!"

He whirled, saw Leonard grinning as he stepped over to the neighboring table. There Leonard shuffled several more place cards, grabbed a bottle of champagne from a silver bucket, and ambled back.

"Hello, Jackie-boy." He yanked out the chair beside Jack and slid into it, leathers creaking, chains and amulets tinkling. "May I join you?"

Jack shrugged. "I guess so. Are you—I guess you're invited?"

"Before *you* were." Leonard raised a gold-bedecked eyebrow at Jack's place card. "Paper and ink. How quaint." He laughed, baring white sharp teeth like a fox's, and clapped a hand on Jack's shoulder. "So! You actually got here. Congratulations. I'm amazed. I didn't think you'd really come."

Jack shook his head. His eyes burned, but tearless now, as he said, "Leonard. Julie's dead. He—he—"

Leonard's grin tightened into a grimace. "I know." His gaze shifted, as though he saw something else in the air between them. He stared at his fingers, the network of scars and interlacing coils, finally reached out and covered Jack's hand with his own. "I know. Emma called me. To help her with some of the police stuff. They had him pegged as some kind of fucking terrorist or something. Julie. Can you imagine? So I called a couple of people, to help her out. To figure out what the hell to do with the body, how to get him back to Westchester. She was going to go to your house, Jackie—we could only get an ambulance to take him that far—"

"To Lazyland?"

"Yeah. I have no idea what'll happen from there. What a mess. What a goddamn mess." Leonard sighed, and rubbed the bridge of his nose. "Christ, Jackie. Just thee and me, now, and I'm not so sure about thee."

Jack sat in silence. In the background the sextet played, the conventionally mournful strings chased by the kotos' more plangent notes. The thought of Emma at Lazyland momentarily soothed him, despite his grief. Doctor Duck calming Keeley and Mrs. Iverson, tending to Marz even as she laid out her own dead husband . . .

"Oh God," he moaned, and covered his eyes.

"Poor Jackie—" Leonard put an arm around him. "It's okay, Jackie, it's okay—"

"Of course it's not okay." Jack let his breath out, looked at Leonard, and said, "Nothing's fucking okay. You know that—"

"Of course I know that. I've *always* known that." Leonard's eyes grew hard. He reached for Jack's champagne and downed it at a gulp. "It's poor idiots like you, just now catching on—*you're* the ones having a bad time." His placebit glittered as he poured another glassful and sipped it. "End of the fucking end, Jackie-boy. Might as well whoop it up."

Jack ignored his baiting tone. At the table around them other people were seated now, glancing companionably at each other and making introductions. Leonard ignored them, and for once Jack sided with him. "So." He coughed. "Are you alone?"

Leonard made a rude sound. "Am I ever alone? No. But tonight—you'll like this, Jackie, it'll remind you of Saint Bart's—tonight I found this poor lost soul, this Xian kid who thinks he's got a lawsuit or something against Agrippa Music for stealing his intellectual property. Broke my heart, let me tell you. I was going to bring him in, but then I decided, probably not such a great idea. So he's waiting out in the limo. Otnay ootay ightbray, if you take my meaning." He grinned and tilted back in his chair, adding, "But he's cute."

Jack gave him a disgusted look. "Glad I asked. But listen—" He lowered his voice. "There was something else, too, that happened. Someone named Nellie Candry—"

"I know Nellie Candry."

"She's dead."

Jack was rewarded by a blink: Leonard's green-flecked eyes closed, after a beat opened again. They would not meet Jack's gaze. "She's dead," Leonard said at last.

Jack nodded. Leonard flexed his hand, his expression fierce. "Blue Antelope."

"No. She—she killed herself, too. Some kind of—I don't know, a poison capsule."

Behind them was a soft clatter. The music soared, Shostakovich's Fifteenth with kotos. A plate was set before Jack, tiny curls of green and pearl pink, *nori* and an octopus no bigger than his thumbnail.

"Yummy," said Leonard. He picked up his chopsticks and pushed desultorily at his plate. "They would have killed her, you know. Because she defected—"

"Couldn't you have helped her?" Jack exclaimed, then winced at how shrill his voice sounded. He pushed his plate away, shot an apologetic smile at the young Asian woman to his left. Her skin was creamy orange from lichen supplements. When she smiled back at him, she showed teeth that had been capped to look like blue-veined marble. "I mean, you could have—"

"Couldn't do a fucking thing, Jackie-boy." Leonard grinned cheerlessly. "God's Mafia. And the young ones are the worst. All that energy they should put into drugs and fucking? Goes right into this other shit. Blowing up hospitals. Save the whales."

To his side, a well-dressed man with a greying ponytail frowned, stabbing at his octopus with a fork as he glanced at Leonard. Leonard lifted his champagne glass in mock salute, and pronounced, "'Curse God and die.' I say, *fuck Him.*"

Quickly the man turned away. Jack sighed and shook his head. "Some things, like Morton's Salt, never change."

"Admit it, Jackie. If it wasn't for me, you'd be bored out of your mind. You'd be—"

"Shut up, Leonard," Jack said wearily. "Just shut up."

Leonard rolled his eyes, but obediently focused his attention back on his food. Jack swiveled to look across the room. At the head table, a middle-aged Japanese man sat between two bland-looking Caucasian men in tuxedos and their wives. Several IMF types stood behind him, all flak jackets and plasmer eyes.

That would be Mr. Tatsumi, thought Jack. He wondered about Mrs. Tatsumi, recalling the news report he'd heard some time ago— that her death had been a suicide. He bit his lip, gaze traveling across the head table and its neighbors until he spotted Larry Muso. He was seated between two other young men more conventionally dressed in tuxedos and subtly luminous cummerbunds. The three of them smiled and nodded to one another, speaking cheerfully, oblivious to Jack's gaze. He watched them with something like amazement: that life could be like that, still. That you could have friends and coworkers, that you could sit at a table and talk and laugh and act like nothing's wrong.

At the dance floor the sextet took a break. The soft strains of a bland old Europop hit oozed from the speakers. Jack toyed with his chopsticks. When a waiter appeared and started to remove his plate Leonard snagged the octopus and popped it into his mouth. The waiter slid a new plate in front of Jack, this one with a traditional arrangement of salad greens.

"All hydroponics!" he heard a woman explain to her companion across the table. "Those same kinds of lights, you know, like sunlamps?"

"*Eat*," ordered Leonard. He made an exasperated noise and poked Jack with his fork. "Not even the Pope gets food like this. Eat your goddamn salad."

Jack ate. It did taste wonderful, the bitter greens sweet with balsamic vinegar. When it was gone he took a sip of champagne, and said, "She told me Blue

Antelope was going to blow this place up. She said there was going to be some kind of terrorist attack."

Leonard shook his head. "Not this place *per se*. Just the Fougas. They want to sabotage any attempt to interfere with the Big Guy's plan for us. Which seems to be not unlike His plan for T. rex."

"Is it true?" Jack put his fork down. "Is it true?" His heart began to pound.

"True? Yeah, probably."

"They're going to blow it up? They're"—Jack gave a barking laugh, pointed at the dome soaring high above them—"they're going to *do* that? I mean, she was telling me the goddamn truth? The drugs, and now this? WHY DIDN'T YOU—"

He started from his chair, but Leonard yanked him back down.

"Shut up, Jackie," he said evenly. "You want to get arrested?"

"I don't give a—"

"*That's* right! *That's* the attitude to take. *Don't—give—a fuck*," Leonard said very carefully. "Who knows what the hell's going to happen? Who *cares*?"

Jack stared at him. "*I* do. I mean, I care if I *die*—"

"Get over it." Leonard leaned forward to pluck a bit of willow twig from the table arrangement. "'Cause this is it, sweetie. Apocalypse *ciao*. Those Fougas?"

He cocked his thumb at the dome. Jack looked up and saw that the stars had dimmed, and the moon. Now he could see clearly the grid of glass and metal, and beyond it molten sky, a churning whirlpool of purple and green and blue speared by bursts of crimson lightning. Within it the seven dirigibles floated serenely, a pod of whales in a satanic storm.

"They're not going to do *shit*," Leonard hissed, and Jack's flesh crawled to hear him. "What, you think this is

Star Wars? You think you can save the fucking world by having it put on sunglasses? This is *terminal*, Jack! Goddamn cancer ward. The best we can hope for now is a good show. And good drugs."

Jack stared at him. It was a full minute before he could speak. "But—but how can you *do* this, then? Just sit here eating like—like—" He gestured futilely at the table. "Why did you *come* here, Leonard?"

Leonard pursed his lips and tilted his head back. After a moment he recited,

> *The sky is full of good and bad*
> *But mortals never know.*

Jack snorted. "What's that? Fucking Euripides?"

"Robert Plant. It's a *party*, Jackie. 'Here we are now, entertain us!' Why the hell not? What else were you going to do? Sit up there in the family mausoleum and watch the river rise while you wait to die of AIDS? I couldn't let you do that. At least this way you got a night *out*. I mean, isn't it better this way? Aren't you happy, Jackie-boy?"

Leonard grinned, took Jack's hand. "Aren't you glad to be with me, Jackie? Here at the end of all things?"

"Fuck you." Jack shoved his chair back. "Julie's right, you're a fucking psychotic—"

"Maybe. But Julie's dead, and I'm not. I'm here, now. I'm *alive*, even if it's just for another"—Leonard thrust his wrist out from the sleeve of his leather jacket and perused the moon-phase Rolodex there—"oh, another twenty-three minutes."

Jack slumped back into his chair. "What happens in twenty-three minutes?"

"Last call, last dance. Closing time. Or nothing, maybe. The Fougas are scheduled to launch at 11:55.

The fireworks start at midnight, along with all that other 'Auld Lang Syne' shit. We'll see," he said lightly, attacking the lacquered box of Kobe beef that had appeared before him.

Jack stared at him, waiting for something else: explanation, excuse, apology.

It was all a dream. And then I woke up, and my pillow was gone.

But there was nothing. He finally picked up a shred of beef speckled with dulse flakes. It tasted like the salmon had earlier, of petroleum and raw spirits. He set his chopsticks in the box and pushed it away.

All around him people ate and laughed, chattering in those overheated tones he recalled from winter cotillions and New York Public Library benefits, their talk punctuated by the *chink* of silver forks and gold jewelry, the swelling plaint of strings. Leonard was engaged in charming the man next to him, who was some kind of European investor.

"Security encryption devices for virtual private networks and intranets," he explained. Leonard feigned interest and kicked Jack under the table.

Waiters brought more trays. Green tea sorbet, some kind of clear soup, pickled beets, scallops the size of pencil erasers. Roast pork with green apples, quail stuffed with unborn eggs, smoked domestic elk. Another sorbet, anise-flavored. Finally there was a flurry of desserts—chocolate profiteroles, something puffy and livid pink, like a jellyfish—and coffee, *real* coffee, greeted with hushed excitement; not even the very rich could find coffee anymore. Jack took a few sips of his, trying not to show revulsion. It all tasted bad to him, almost poisonous.

"Well," announced Leonard, leaning back so that his chair tilted precariously on two legs. "That wasn't exactly Trimalchio's feast, but—"

A soft voice cut him off, amplified so that it sounded as though it spoke from directly overhead.

"My friends—"

The tide of postprandial chatter receded. Jack turned with everyone else, to see the spare figure at the center of the head table standing, hands clasped against his stomach. His body mike gave the carefully pronounced words an eerily hollow timbre. Behind him his bodyguards turned their heads slowly back and forth, tracking something unseen.

"This is a moment I have waited for, for a very long time." Mr. Tatsumi paused. His expression was somber, and he blinked several times before continuing. "To be here in company with all of you, in such fine surroundings, on such an important day. On what may be the most important day in human history . . ."

Leonard made the face and accompanying sound Jack associated with their days suffering through High Mass at Saint Bartholomew's. He frowned. Leonard ignored him.

". . . realize that in the last eighteen months we have made quantum leaps in the areas of resource management and environmental reclamation, as well as breakthroughs in medical research that will affect every single person in this room; that may very well someday affect everyone on this planet."

Enthusiastic applause. Jack swallowed bile and copper, felt Leonard kick his leg again.

"Hear that, Jackie? We'll all be tan and rested in *no time*—" Leonard's eyes narrowed as the chairman went on.

"We have made advances in entertainment technology that will change the way we see that world. Most importantly, in a few minutes you will all witness the moment when we move from *making* history, to *remaking* history, when we launch the SUNRA platform."

Tumultuous clapping and cheers. Jack pressed his
knees tightly together. *Why is he talking about it, why is he
even bringing it up, what the fuck am I doing here?* He shut
his eyes, feeling as he used to during the first moments
of takeoff: the same vertiginous horror of knowing it
was Too Late Now, the same silent primal recitation of
prayers to St. Jude Thaddeus, St. Christopher, the
Blessed Virgin. Catholic Autopilot, Leonard had always
sneeringly called it. Jack could feel him now, staring at
him with the same disdain he'd shown Mr. Tatsumi.
Didn't matter, didn't matter, didn't matter.

*St. Jude, pray with me, that I may receive the gift of faith
that moves mountains . . .*

"Thank you. Thank you all very much."

Jack opened his eyes a crack and saw Mr. Tatsumi
bowing gracefully, first to his tablemates, then to the
gathered diners. The CEO raised a hand, looking across
the room to where the lone technician sat behind his
banks of equipment. Mr. Tatsumi's mouth moved, and
his brow furrowed questioningly. Jack heard a scatter of
Japanese from the body mike. In the seats beside the
CEO, men and women leaned back and stared expectantly at the dance floor.

The applause died away, and the murmur of approv-
ing voices. Time to go. Jack sensed that pause for breath
that precedes the flurry of finding car keys, the crowd
heading for the turnstiles. Across the table from him
people nodded happily at each other, flushed and well
fed. Women reached for handbags, men stretched.
Dinner was finished, coffee drunk. Everyone was anxious to leave. Everyone was ready to find the *real* party.
For the first time since he'd entered the room, Jack
heard a cresting wave of sound from outside the GFI
area, cheers and shrieks and a voice bellowing from a
loudspeaker.

"ARE YOU READY? ELEVEN MINUTES AND—"

He looked over again at Mr. Tatsumi, still standing by himself. The CEO looked small and rather lost, and rather more impatient. A few tentative notes wafted from where the sextet sat very straight in their folding chairs. Around the perimeter of the dining area, the lighttubes flickered from blue to a soft lavender. People who had been standing looked around, then quietly settled back into their seats. The room grew deathly quiet as the strings' scattered notes, sweet as rain, resolved into the opening bars of "The Blue Danube."

At one end of the dance floor a single follow spot appeared. Mr. Tatsumi stared at it, frowning. Jack moved his chair back to get a better view, the hairs on his arms prickling. The follow spot bloomed larger, brighter, resolved into a man-sized column of blazing white, phosphorescent green rising from it like a wick. The column pulsed and trembled: something was taking shape within it. All at once the adamant brilliance grew still, as though whatever it held had suddenly come into focus, or being. The light did not fade so much as it coursed into the figure at its center, like quicksilver filling a glass. People gasped. Jack heard someone whisper a name.

On the dance floor a woman stood. Radiance streamed around her like water, pooled at her feet, and coiled there like smoke. She was small, black-haired, with a white face and burning black eyes. She wore what Jack at first thought was a wedding dress. But as he stared he saw that it was a fabulously elaborate kimono, glitteringly iridescent as a diamond, and so much larger than the woman it seemed as though she were impaled upon it. The waltz strains faltered; Jack glanced at the sextet, saw them gazing awed as everyone else at the vision in white. Very slowly, with tiny careful steps and head downcast, the luminous figure walked to the center of the dance floor.

"Holy Christ," breathed Leonard. "It's *Michiko*."

Jack shook his head. "Who?"

"His wife. The one who killed herself. Michiko Tatsumi. They made an icon of her—"

Jack gazed at the woman, then looked for Mr. Tatsumi. The CEO was bent double, clutching the edge of the table in front of him. His eyes were fixed on the icon. Several men clustered at his side, Larry Muso among them, but when they tried to help him Mr. Tatsumi frantically motioned them away. As Jack watched the CEO straightened, still holding on to the table's edge. Haltingly he walked away from it, until he stood at the edge of the dance floor.

In its center the woman stood, arms outstretched, the sleeves of her kimono spilling from her arms like wings. Her expression was beatific, her mouth parted in a rapturous smile. As the chairman approached, she moved her head very slightly back and forth, as though she were struggling to see him in a darkened room. When he stopped a few feet in front of her she cocked her head to one side, still smiling, and opened her arms to him. The waltz swept joyously on. There was a moment when they were absolutely still, the frail black-clad man staring down into that glorious nimbus of a face, the icon's mouth fluttering as though she were try-ing to speak. Then, slowly, with exquisite care, he took her in his arms and began to dance.

Jack blinked, struggling to see them; it was a moment before he realized he was weeping. He wiped his eyes, drew in a ragged breath, and glanced around furtively, as he had at his grandfather's funeral as a child, to see who else was crying. At his table, everyone. With the exception of Leonard, whose expression shifted from wonder to amusement to something Jack couldn't read. He turned and looked at Jack, opened his mouth, then shut it again, and finally shook his head.

Enough then, Jack thought. *Leonard Thrope is rendered speechless.*

For several minutes the room was still. All eyes were fixed on the two figures drawing smooth parabolas across the dance floor. Then, as the "Blue Danube" ended and the strings swept into another waltz, a couple from the head table stood and walked with scrupulous care to the dance floor. After a moment another couple joined them, and another, and more still, a zephyr of flowing gowns and coattails, until the entire room flowed with costumed dancers, men and women, men and men, women and women, Mr. Tatsumi and his luminous bride, all spinning and whirling like gorgeous clockwork toys. Jack watched them, so enthralled that he jumped when someone tapped his shoulder.

"Jack?"

Larry stood there, smiling, his piquant face flushed and radiant as the icon's. "Jack—Would you like to dance?"

Jack stared at him, then nodded. "Yes," he said, getting to his feet. "Of course."

There were so many waltzing couples that they could only move very slowly, and nowhere near the dance floor. Jack held Larry hesitantly, his hand poised lightly upon the smaller man's shoulder. He felt a little put off by the crowd; but then Larry tilted his head and stared up at him with such naked joy that it didn't matter. Nothing mattered but this, that he was no longer alone; that despite his exhaustion he could still dance, hear music, feel the warmth of Larry Muso's neck beneath his hand, the supple strength of his spine through his happi coat. They turned slowly, clockwise, counterclockwise, first one leading and then the other. Jack glanced up now and then to see other faces mirroring his own joy, white-haired women with their husbands, daughters with their fathers, lovers and businessmen, scientists and artists. Only Leonard Thrope seemed to be sitting it out, leaning back in his folding chair with legs crossed, watching the passing dance with an expression at once wistful and satisfied: as though finally, at last, after all these years, he had gotten what he'd paid for.

"Look," murmured Larry. He tipped his head back to stare upward. "It must be almost midnight . . ."

Jack followed his gaze. High above them the stars were still gone, but now the dome seemed to have melted away as well. The grid of glass and metal had disappeared. Where it had been an aperture was opening in the ceiling, a circle spiraling outward like a huge blinking eye, until it revealed the naked sky in all its livid glory, and within it The Golden Family's Fougas. They were blindingly lit, so that it was like sunlight spilling down onto the assembled waltzers, sun and the glimmering's bacchic pennons streaming across the heavens. The sounds of the waltz grew faint as couples clutched each other and cried out in amazement. From outside Jack heard an exultant roar as the Pyramid's ten thousand invited guests looked upon this crack in the dying century's defenses. From an even greater distance he heard the almost unimaginable thunder of the city's trembling revelry; the world's.

"They're ready," said Larry Muso. Jack could only nod, watching raptly as the Fougas began to move. A darkness blotted out the whirling sky, as though a cloud passed between the Pyramid and the heavens.

"That's the platform," Larry explained, pointing. He

giggled excitedly and grabbed Jack's hand. "That's what it'll look like again, soon—we'll see the sky again! We'll see the stars—"

Jack laughed shakily and shook his head. "It's—it's amazing." He was trembling, with fatigue and exhilaration and something he could only think of as rapture. "I mean, that they're going to do it."

Larry squeezed his hand. "*We're* going to do it. All of us. We're going to make it all right again."

The music had stopped. There was a nearly deafening wave of sound, but through it Jack could still hear the Fougas' steady thrumming. He stared into the open sky, felt icy air cut through the warmth of bodies, dispersing the thick scents of perfume and sweat and Viconix. The dirigibles with their heraldic gryphons began to drift in formation, the SUNRA platform a swath of darkness behind them. Jack's eyes hurt, he saw once more those luciferian flashes of emerald green; but he had no tears left, only wonder and transporting joy. He found himself shouting wordlessly along with all that multitude, one hand on Larry's shoulder, the other pounding at the air; cheering on the fleet.

Beneath one Fouga there was a starburst of white and crimson, sparks exploding into a Catherine wheel of orange flame. Everyone applauded wildly, and Jack laughed, exultant.

"Look!" he cried, delighted as when he'd watched fireworks from Lazyland's terrace as a boy. "God, *look* at it!"

He glanced at Larry. His doe eyes were wide and black and uneasy, his smile gone.

"No," murmured Larry Muso. "That's wrong, they've got the timing wrong, no, *no*—"

"What do you mean—" Jack began, but Larry only shook his head. "What do you—"

And then Jack looked up at the sky and saw that it

was not fireworks, not the dawn of a new age at all: not seven airships flying in formation but a conflagration, the night on fire:

Bombs.

Blue Antelope had struck.

Horrified screams as flame rained down and metal joists, burning fuselage and liquid fire. Glass exploded everywhere, there were bodies flying as people ran blindly, shrieking, trampling tables and chairs, bodies. The forest of lighttubes shattered into bolts of violet and green. Jack stood frozen, too stunned to move, only crying out when something slashed his arm. When he looked down he saw a piece of glass as long as his forearm protruding above his wrist. As in a nightmare he plucked it out, staring with wide empty eyes as blood welled from the seam of flesh and spilled across his hand.

"Jack! *Jack!*"

He raised his head slowly, blinking as oily black smoke filled his eyes; then was thrown back as someone barreled past him.

"*JACK!*"

He recognized the voice then. "Larry," he whispered. When he licked his lips they tasted of blood and ash. "Larry . . ."

Desperately he began to search, fear slicing through shock and the dull pain throbbing in his wrist. Finally he saw him, sprawled on the floor a few feet away.

"Larry!" he shouted. The other man lifted his head, stumbling to his feet. His face was dead white save where a black line smudged one cheek, but as his eyes met Jack's he nodded and raised his hand, palm out.

"I'm okay—*go*—" Larry shouted, then recoiled with one arm raised before his face. There was a roar as a slab of burning fuselage crashed to the floor in front of him.

Larry's voice echoed faintly, his form hidden behind smoke and leaping flame. *"GO!"*

Jack shook his head stupidly, clutching his arm as he staggered toward the blaze. His mouth formed Larry's name, but he couldn't say it, could no longer think of anything but his arm, the smell of burning metal, burning flesh, anguished screams; a woman made of light lurching toward him—

"Jackie! Goddammit, *JACKIE*—"

A hand grabbed him and roughly yanked him away. He saw only that infernal chiaroscuro, smoke and flames, forms like great scorched insects staggering through the murk. Someone shoved him through broken glass and smoking rubble, the heaped bricks of a fallen tenement. A video monitor opened onto the ocean's calm blue eye, then blinked into sparks and the stink of melting wires. Jack fell to his knees, gagging and weeping. He was pulled to his feet again and half-dragged, half-carried through a doorway into a passage dense with smoke, its walls radiating heat as though he stumbled through a furnace. He coughed, choking on poisonous fumes, his eyes streaming. Whoever had pulled him to safety was gone. There was only smoke and echoing screams, an airless passage funneling into a deeper darkness.

And then, as though he had plunged from a cliff, the world fell away. Smoke dispersed into icy air. The darkness broke like waves upon a rocky shore, sending up plumes of crimson and violet. Jack shivered uncontrollably, the cold flooding him as violently as the deathly heat had inside. He looked around, dazed, and saw that he was outside, in the street. There were people everywhere, thousands of them, the thunder of burning and myriad explosions; sirens, screams, shouted orders and the hoot of bullhorns. He saw a line of cars in flames, and overhead a vast pinwheel of green and violet, spinning slowly as smoke and flames roiled into its unmoving core. Before Jack could begin to make sense of it all, a figure shook him fiercely and began to push him through the crowd.

"Keep moving, Jackie, keep moving—"

Wincing, he turned his head and saw Leonard Thrope.

"Leonard," he whispered. "What—"

"Shut up." Leonard pulled Jack close, holding him so tightly it hurt. "Fuck, I hope they're—*here*—"

Leonard stopped, panting. His skin was dark with soot. His cheek had been ripped open; Jack could see a spur of bone beneath the blackened skin. Leonard turned his head, spit blood, and pointed down an empty side street. "They should be there. Come on—"

He began to run, and Jack followed, gasping with pain and the effort of breathing. "Who?" he wheezed, as Leonard halted impatiently. "Who—"

"My limo. I told them to wait for me—"

They ran the last few yards, to where the sidewalk ended in a vacant lot strewn with wrecked cars. On the other side of the street a grey stretch limo was parked. A man stood by the opened driver's door, his mouthless mask shoved onto his forehead as he punched frantically at a cellular phone. Another figure crouched beside the passenger door, face buried in his hands.

"Leonard!" the first man shouted, as Leonard and Jack came panting up beside him. "What the—"

"They blew 'em up!" Leonard yelled back. On the ground beside the limo the second figure looked up: a young man in an anorak, stringy green-streaked blond hair falling to his shoulders. "What the fuck'd you think, Fayal? Here—"

Leonard flung the passenger door open and reached inside. He pulled out several camera bags and tossed them into the street. As he did so he looked over his shoulder at his driver and pointed first at Jack, then at the young man. "Okay, listen, Fayal," he commanded. "I want you to take them to Yonkers—"

"*Yonkers!* The fuck I'm going to get to—"

"Just fucking *do* it!" Leonard thrust his hand into his leather jacket and withdrew a wallet. "Here," he said, shoving a wad of bills at Fayal. "That's for you. You've done a great job, now you're fired. Take the car, take it and *go*—it's yours, go wherever you want! Just take them first—"

The chauffeur shoved the phone into his pocket. He stared at the cash, finally took it and stuffed it into his coat. He sighed, running a finger along the edge of the mask propped on his forehead. "Shit. *Where* in Yonkers?"

"Hudson Terrace." Leonard cocked his thumb at Jack. "He'll give you directions. But go, *now*—"

He grabbed Jack by the shoulder and pushed him toward the car, then snapped something at the blond boy. The boy just sat there, shaking his head in disbelief until Leonard reached down and dragged him to his feet. "Get in the fucking car! No—in the front, with Fayal. Now listen to me, Trip—"

Leonard pointed at Jack, slumped against the limo's side. "He's bleeding, and he's HIV positive—find something to tie off his hand with, your sock or something, and then just sit tight till you get to Lazyland. There's a doctor there who can help."

"*Doctor?*" the boy repeated. "What do you mean, a—"

Leonard pounded the door in frustration. "Just get in the fucking *car*, Trip."

Trip nodded, and Leonard turned to Jack. "Okay, now listen, Jackie—can you hear me?"

Jack stared at him dully, after a moment shook his head. "Yeah—yeah. I hear you."

Leonard grasped his friend's upper arm and guided him to the middle seat. Jack sank into it, crying out at the pain, and gazed at his friend questioningly. Leonard pulled a soiled bandanna from his leather jacket and gave it to him. "Wrap this around that cut. Trip! For Christ's sake, find something for his hand!" he shouted angrily, then perched on the seat beside Jack.

"Now listen, Jackie. You know Fayal. He's going to take you to Lazyland, okay? He's going to take you home. Emma's there, she can help you. You'll be okay, Jackie. You hear me?" He shook him gently, until Jack looked up. "You're gonna be okay."

"What about you?" Jack whispered. It hurt to talk. Jack's tongue probed at his lips, the inside of his mouth, and found blisters there, scorched skin. "Leonard? Where're you going?"

Leonard's hand remained on Jack's shoulder. He turned to look back down the street, to where buildings like molten gems blazed against a churning violet sky. Above them pulsed an immense mountain of light, so brilliant Leonard had to shield his eyes: the Pyramid was in flames. Then, very slowly, the structure's apex bulged outward, like an ampoule giving way; and with a deafening roar burst into an enveloping cloud of black and scarlet.

"Holy shit," breathed Fayal, ducking into the front seat.

"Right," said Leonard. He reached out onto the sidewalk, pulled open one of his leather satchels. There was a videocam inside. He slid the strap over his head, clicked the camera on and off a few times, and played with the focus.

"Leonard?" Jack continued to stare at him. "Aren't you coming with us?"

"Coming with you? What, to Lazyland?" With a grin Leonard turned the camera on Jack's anguished expression. Sirens wailed behind them; there was the clatter of gunfire. "No, Jackie."

"But you *have* to, Leonard—you can't stay here—"

Leonard whipped the camera from his face and began to laugh. "Are you kidding?" he yelled gleefully, sweeping his arm out to take in boiling sky, flames flickering across buildings, the soft steady rain of ash that had started to fall. "*Leave?* And miss all *this*? No can do, Jackie-boy! Not for anything on earth—"

He grabbed Jack's hand. "Oh, Jackie—I *have* loved you, in my fashion. You know that, right?" Jack nodded weakly. "Okay. So you go on back to Grandmother's house, and I'll hang out at this swinging party."

Leonard stretched his legs out onto the sidewalk, chains jingling. As he turned to leave, Jack touched him gently on the arm.

"Leonard—" His blue eyes met Leonard's manic gaze. "Will I—will I ever see you again?"

Leonard looked at him and grinned. "Will you *see* me? Sure, Jackie—you'll see me again, we'll see everybody again, real soon. Really, *really* soon," he added. He stood there on the sidewalk, the vidcam nestled within the folds of his leather jacket. Then, unexpectedly, he leaned down, his eyes suddenly filled with tears. He let one hand rest upon his friend's cheek, and, very slowly, kissed Jack on the mouth. "I promise."

Jack gazed up at him. For just a fraction of a second he saw the other Leonard there, the boy with the bruised eyes and voice scraped raw by singing *How do you think it feels?* And then for another instant they were both there before Jack, the man who had saved him and the boy he had loved a hundred years ago, standing beneath the glowing sky in a rain of fiery ash.

"Leonard," he whispered, and raised his hand. "Leonard—"

But before he could say anything more, Leonard danced back from the limo and closed the door. He took a step toward the driver's door, tapped on its window, and shouted, "Get him home, Fayal, got me? You take care of him, Trip! Do your fucking Christian duty, okay?"

In the front seat the blond boy stared impassively, finally nodded.

"Fucking idiot," muttered Leonard Thrope.

Jack stared out his window as the limo's engine thrummed to life. "See you in the funny papers, Jackie-boy!" Leonard yelled. With a whoop he drew the vidcam to his eye and began taping. From behind the limo's darkened glass two small white faces gazed at him, bright flecks trapped in the lens and almost indistinguishable from the fluttering bits of ash falling everywhere. The cam's motor hummed as the recorded image flickered on the tiny monitor, dusted with jerking bits of electronic snow.

Then, very slowly, the limousine began to drive away. As it did so Leonard stepped backward, his camera fixed on the car, heedless of nearby gunfire and smoke billowing down from burning buildings. He moved deftly from the sidewalk into the middle of the shattered street, not feeling where embers gnawed through the soles of his boots or noticing the scent of his own scorched hair as he tracked those two faces staring at him from the car, recording them through the scrim of ash and video noise, the two of them growing smaller and smaller until they disappeared into the cloud of moving particles, flesh and flames and falling sky all exactly where Leonard wanted them.

And Leonard himself exactly where he had always wanted to be: dancing in the century's graveyard, laughing at the end of all things.

CHAPTER SEVENTEEN

Glimmering

I t took them six hours to get to Lazyland. Trip tore a
piece of fabric from his anorak and handed it to Jack,
being careful not to let their fingers touch and immediately hunching back into the front of the car. Jack
noticed the boy's fear, but he was too tired to care. He
wrapped his wounded hand, then slumped against his
seat and fell into uneasy sleep, an exhausted stupor
lanced with pain. Now and then he heard shouts from
outside, Fayal's heartfelt curses and pleas for divine
guidance, the sound of other vehicles, police sirens, and
ambulances. The boy in the front seat said nothing, and
Jack made no effort to speak to him; only offered directions to Fayal when after many hours they finally passed
Co-op City, the limo edging through the mass of cars
like a queen bee making her way through a broken hive.
When Jack peered out the window behind them, he saw
a city in flames: smoke rising from skyscrapers tinted
with the infernal dawn, flickers of gold and scarlet leaping from shadowy canyons and avenues. Watch fires
burned along the George Washington Bridge. On the
western banks of the Hudson he could see still more
blazes, and the air inside the limo was thick with the
scent of burning.

At last they broached the outskirts of the city of
Yonkers. They drove past crowds of people milling on the
sidewalk, revelers and rioters who moved reluctantly to let
the limo pass. Bottles crashed against the hood, rocks
bounced off the roof, and once Jack dived to the floor when

Fayal yelled at him, and automatic weapons fire echoed in the street outside. The car plunged through a sea of bodies. Jack heard a sickening thump, but Fayal just kept on going, until at last they were bouncing down familiar rutted streets, past Delmonico's and the ruins of Hudson Terrace, past gutted mansions where Jack could see figures capering joyfully beneath a sky like an open wound.

"This is it," he whispered hoarsely. He pointed to where his home's security gate hung half-open. "You—"

"I remember." Fayal shot him a bitter smile. The limo nosed through the gate, eased down the driveway, and came to a stop in front of the wide veranda. "You guys—out fast, okay? I'm gonna piss and get the fuck out of here."

Jack opened the door and stumbled onto the drive. He blinked in the spectral glare of—what? morning? dawn? When he glanced at his watch it said almost six. Morning, then.

"Jack!"

He turned and was nearly knocked down by Emma. "Oh, Jack," she murmured, hugging him so that his ribs ached. Behind her he could see his brother Dennis with both hands pressed to his forehead, his mouth an O of anguished relief. "Jack, I thought you were—we all thought—"

Emma drew back to look at him and cried, "Holy shit! You're bleeding! Get inside, come on—"

"Wait." Jack steadied himself, looked to where Fayal was zipping up his trousers and sliding back behind the wheel. "There's someone else—"

The blond boy stepped from the car, hands shoved into his pockets. He moved away as the engine gunned, and in a spray of gravel the limo shot back up the drive. With a desultory roar it turned out onto Hudson Terrace and disappeared from sight.

"Who is he?" Emma demanded.

Jack shook his head. "I have no idea. A friend of Leonard's, I think."

"A friend of—" Emma scowled, then clapped a hand to her forehead and sighed. "Jesus Christ. Well, tell him to come in—"

She looked at Jack's injured wrist, shaking her head as she steered him toward the porch. "I have to tell you, Jackie," she said in a low voice, and began to cough. "Things aren't good here, it's not good. I hope your friend can take care of himself. I'm not well, and—"

They walked inside. In the entryway Jack turned, saw the blond boy standing gazing up at the mansion's crumbling exterior, flaking shingles and broken windows and collapsing balconies, and beyond it all the venomous sky.

"Hey," Jack called in a low voice; then louder. "Hey—come on, let's go."

The boy looked at him. Finally he nodded and followed Jack inside.

The house was dark. Jack's brother cleared his throat. He was eight years older than Jack; in the months since he'd visited Jack in the hospital, Dennis's hair had gone white. His face was gaunt, his eyes red as though bloodied. He started to say something and began to sob. "I'm sorry," he whispered, wiping his eyes and turning away. "Fuck, I'm sorry—"

After a minute he squeezed Jack's shoulder. "I'm— I'm glad you're okay. I'm going to lie down for a while, though—it's been kind of tough, Jackie—"

"Where's Grandmother?"

"Upstairs." His brother's eyes were bleak. "She's all right. She's sleeping. But—well, Emma will tell you. I'll talk to you in a little while."

Jack watched him walk slowly up the curving stairs.

He turned to Emma. "What happened? Is she really okay? Where's Marz?"

Emma said nothing. Her face was grey with fatigue, and blotched with small raised spots, like acne. She smoothed a hand across her head, the blond curls dank and flattened. "She's dead, Jack," she said at last. "She went into labor yesterday morning—"

"Oh Christ—"

"—there wasn't anything I could do." She began to cry, shoulders heaving. Jack drew her to his breast, holding his injured hand out stiffly behind her. "She—it was twins. A boy and a girl. It would have been hard no matter what, she was so young, she was malnourished—"

"Twins? Did they—"

"They're okay." Emma laughed brokenly. "Can you believe that? Two mouths to feed. But I brought some Similac, and Keeley found some old baby clothes . . ." She started to cry again.

"Emma, Emma . . ."

He pressed his face against her scalp, smelled her unwashed hair, the acrid scent of disinfectant and isopropyl alcohol. On the steps behind him he heard soft footsteps. When he glanced up he saw the blond boy walking hesitantly upstairs. Before Jack could call out Emma took a deep breath and drew away from him.

"God. Enough. You should go lie down, too, Jack. Right now."

"Me?" He shook his head. "What about you? What about—what happened with, with—"

Emma sighed. "I don't know. Dennis was able to get through on the phone for a while, but the lines are dead now. They're supposed to be sending his body here, but—"

She waved a hand at the window, where skeins of

purple and gold and red threaded across the sky. "Who the hell knows. Dennis and I—we buried the girl outside. He made a sort of—coffin, out of an old table. But dogs kept trying to dig it up, and when Dennis went out to chase them off they came after him. She's—she's gone now."

She looked at him, her eyes haunted. "What else could we do, Jackie?" she whispered. "What else could we do?"

He shut his eyes, fighting off the images there. The girl in his aunt's bed, her pinched face above the coverlets; and then a mauled wooden box and broken earth. "Nothing," he said, his voice cracking. "You've done everything, Emma. You've done more than any human being could possibly do. Now you have to rest . . ."

She wept, and he walked with her upstairs, one hand on her shoulder, the other held gingerly at his side. On the second-floor landing he stopped and kissed her forehead.

"Where are you sleeping?"

Emma gestured at his uncle Peter's old room. "There. Dennis is in the other bed. Your grandmother and Mrs. Iverson are in there—" She pointed at Keeley's closed bedroom door. "And the babies—"

A sudden wail rent the air. Jack smiled in spite of himself, craned his neck to peer down the hall into Aunt Susan's room. The sheets had been stripped from the canopied bed. Two bassinets lay side by side on the empty mattress, and between them the blond boy was sitting, staring into one of them.

"I think I know where the babies are," said Jack. A second wail rang out. In the bedroom Trip leaned over, carefully picked up one of the babies, and awkwardly cradled it against his chest.

Jack shook his head. "Hey—"

"Hush." Emma raised her hands and gave a very small smile. "Look, he can't really hurt them. And I'm too beat right now to take care of them, and you shouldn't do anything till you're cleaned up. So just leave him, okay?"

Jack watched as the boy reached into the other bassinet for the second infant, straightened with them both in his arms.

"Is that doctor's orders?" Jack asked.

"Absolutely," murmured Emma. She patted his good arm. "Go try to sleep, Jack. That's the best thing any of us can do right now. Just try to sleep."

He sighed. "Okay."

For a few minutes he stood on the landing, watching as the boy sat playing with the babies. "Emma said there's some formula," he called into the room after a little while. Trip looked up. His face broke into a smile.

"They're so *tiny*," he said. "But they're really, really cute."

Jack smiled back. "Yeah, well, be careful. They're brand-new. Maybe you could figure out how to feed them."

The boy nodded. "Sure. Thanks."

Jack turned away. Outside his grandmother's door he hesitated, then cracked it open and peeked inside. Keeley and Mrs. Iverson lay side by side on the neatly made bed, mouths open, snoring loudly. Jack shut the door again, and went downstairs.

At the bottom of the stairway he stopped. The old porcelain holy-water font was there, as always, set into his grandfather's ancient clock. Jack stared at it wistfully, a burgeoning sadness inside him. Then, as he had a thousand times before, he dipped a finger into the little porcelain declivity.

Nothing, of course. But as he withdrew his finger it

brushed against something. An imperfection in the porcelain, a small raised ridge with a surprisingly sharp edge.

Jack swore and snatched his hand away. A neat red line had been drawn across his knuckle. As he stared blood oozed from the gash. Jack shook his head, shocked at how much it hurt, drew the finger to his mouth, and sucked at it.

"Shit," he murmured. Odd that in all these years, this was the only time he'd cut himself like that. His finger throbbed and Jack whistled softly at the pain. He dug into a pocket, found a reasonably hygienic bit of Kleenex, and wrapped his finger. Then he leaned over, his head bumping against the clock's glass facing, and peered inside the font.

Hard to see anything, because of course what *was* there to see? But he looked anyway, squinting and craning his neck, trying to focus on something besides that small circle of shadow, the glint of light upon its smooth curved sides. It was futile. He was just easing his head up and away from the holy-water font when it blinked at him.

He froze. Not daring to move, balancing on one foot with his eyes wide-open as he stared into the font.

An eye stared back. A round lidless orb like a damp marble, the cornea possessing the cloudy translucence of a partially cooked egg. Its iris was all but colorless; but the pupil glittered with a sort of brilliant malevolence, like a whole new kind of light: a black radiance that sparkled and gleamed. It was not so much suspended in the font, as it was as though the cupped shadow of the font itself had become an eye, horrible and avid, its gaze softened by neither flesh nor hair. Jack opened his mouth to shout, but the sinews hardened within his throat, the shout became stone as he stumbled backward, hands upraised. He made no sound, and no sound came to him, nothing save the echo of his feet upon the wooden floor. Two paces backward, and he stopped. He gasped, his chest heaving as though he'd been running. He clapped his palms to his cheeks, the skin cold and smooth as ice. Within its tissue sheath his cut finger throbbed. He stood, shuddering. After several minutes he felt no calmer, but his heartbeat slowed, the roaring in his head quieted to a dull fizz.

"Okay." He stepped toward the great clock. Before he looked down again he blinked. In that instant of darkness he had a revelatory flash: he saw the eye floating above him like an untethered balloon in the eternal twilight, like a hurricane turning slowly as it gathers strength. He knew that no matter where he went it would follow him, as the moon follows children. He opened his eyes and gazed into the font.

It was still there, staring up at him. He bit the inside of his mouth until it bled. The eye did not move. It did not blink. It did not disappear. It seemed to Jack that it might even have grown larger, the way a puffball mushroom expands, fed by damp and darkness. He continued to gaze at it, the grey striations of its iris and the pale bulbous corneal sack. Then with a grunt he turned and fled, racing upstairs so wildly that more than once he banged against the curving banister, until he reached the third floor, panting. He stood on the landing for several minutes, trying to calm himself, and finally went into his room.

It looked as it had when he left. Somehow he had expected a seismic change, the roof caved in, bedclothes strewn anywhere. But no. Only the window had been opened, and the door leading onto the morning balcony. He walked over to shut the window, paused, and stood for a moment by the open door. At last he stepped out onto the balcony.

The air was icy cold. After the city's rain of ash it felt pure as spring rain: it washed away the stale smell of Leonard's limo and the sickroom scent of the house beneath him. From downstairs he heard first one of the babies shrieking, and then the other. Then Keeley's frail plaintive voice crying out for Emma, and Emma calling back wearily, and Mrs. Iverson exclaiming, "Poor things!"

Then a deeper tone, Trip's voice commanding them all: "Shhh, hey, everybody be *quiet*—they're just hungry. I'll take care of them."

The wails grew louder but, miraculously, Emma and Mrs. Iverson and his grandmother were silent. Jack shook his head, imagining the boy pacing around the bedroom, trying desperately to calm the infants. But after a few minutes the babies quieted as well. Lazyland grew still again.

He walked to the railing, pressed his hands to the old wood, and leaned out. A film of ice covered the rail; as he stood there he could feel it melting beneath his fingertips, a cool thin stream falling about his feet and giving forth a smell like rain, like spring. There was a strange emerald clarity to the air, a sort of brilliance that he thought must be caused by ice crystals, or reflected light, one of those complicated atmospheric things he had never understood. He thought of the eye he had seen in the font downstairs, looked up into the sky, and saw it there, too, in the coiling clouds and haze of smoke above the Hudson. But now, for the moment at least, he felt no fear; only a sort of exhausted peace. A sense that he stood upon a battlefield where the war had been lost; but at least he was still standing.

"Happy New Year!"

From the riverbank far below a voice echoed, then many more. There was a rapid burst of fireworks or gunfire, cheers and what sounded like a trombone blatting.

Almost dawn, and the world is still partying, thought Jack. He yawned, rubbed his eyes, and indulged in the absurdly melancholy wish for more champagne. He breathed in sharply at a sudden stab of sorrow and anguish in his chest, recalling Larry Muso in his arms.

I should have kissed him, he thought; but then remembered Leonard's last words to him—

You'll see me again, we'll see everybody again, real soon. Really, really soon.

And oddly, he felt comforted. And he couldn't remember the last time Leonard had said anything remotely comforting.

He stretched, wincing. His arms hurt, and his wrist, and his chest. His mouth and throat ached from where he'd inhaled burning fumes. He could feel a pressure building in his lungs, the beginning of something that could be dangerous. He wondered if, by chance, Emma *did* have anything in that black bag for him. He scarcely felt strong enough to walk back to his bed. His arms dropped limply to his sides as he looked out for one last time into the night.

Beneath him the estate's overgrown lawns sloped into rank stands of sumac and alder, the ruins of all the other houses that had once stood guard upon the Hudson. Light shone through the tangle of trees and broken buildings—firelight, the watery flicker of a few moving headlights, myriad bonfires and a confetti of red and green marking the rowdy unorganized flotilla massed upon the river. The fires along the upper span of the George Washington Bridge still burned. Its struts glowed dull gold and citron yellow, and cast a saurian reflection in the black water below.

It's beautiful, Jack thought. *It's really beautiful.*

He lifted his head. For some reason—the cold; excessive moisture in the air; maybe just his blurred vision—the glimmering suddenly seemed less pronounced. *Or maybe I'm just getting used to it.*

He grimaced, still staring at the sky, then abruptly sucked his breath in.

For one moment—so quick a glance he was not even certain if it was real, or if he had imagined it, if it was just another remnant of the fusarium stirring in his sight—for one moment, something seemed to move in the vault above him. A profound and sublime darkness that might have been a cloud, or wings, or a mile-long pennon; the silent flank of a dirigible passing at an unimaginable distance through the heavens or the shadow of something else, spirochete swimming across his eye's inner orb, the silhouette of a face he loved. Something moved, and in those final moments he saw that vast cyclonic eye blinking as it turned slowly in the blazing heavens, and knew the sky was ready to burst at last.

But far overhead something else glimmered, faint as Jack's breath in the chill morning air, faint as a heartbeat, faint as dawn.

I see it! he tried to cry out, his burned lips moving though he could no longer speak aloud. *I can see it, it's there, they're all there, I can really see—*

And in that instant, the rush of wind and revelry dying into the sound of the sea in his ears, his fingers brushing against the rail as he fell and the first black raindrops mingled with his blood upon the balcony: in that instant Jack smiled; and thought he saw the stars.

AUTHOR'S NOTES

First and foremost, I would like to thank my brother Brian Hand, who was there at this book's conception, and who has shared with me unstintingly, at any hour of the day or night, his professional knowledge and experience of future technologies and rapidly changing environmental trends. Most of my speculations are based upon current understanding of the effects of the AIDS virus, global warming, and other ecological disasters looming upon the event horizon, as well as upon the work of Roger Penrose, Stuart Hameroff, and microbiologist Lynn Margulis, as well as the millenary musings of Italo Calvino and historian Hillel Schwartz: speculations intended to serve the ends of fiction, however, and not prediction. Any errors herein are solely my own.

To T. S. Eliot, all apologies; to Kurt Cobain, *shantih*.

The business success of the Finnegan family was inspired by that of F. W. Woolworth, who brought glass ornaments to the American populace. For this information I relied on Phillip V. Snyder's *The Christmas Tree Book: A History of the Christmas Tree & Antique Glass Ornaments*.

Unit 909 was inspired by the WWII atrocities of Japan's Unit 731, which engaged in extensive biochemical warfare in Manchuria and Mongolia.

My heartfelt thanks to the usual suspects: Martha Millard, who runs the only full-service literary agency in the country; my U.S. editors, Caitlin Blasdell and Christopher Schelling, and John Silbersack of HarperPrism; Jane

Johnson of HarperCollins UK; Richard Grant, for children, gardens, and the occasional loan of a tree house; Bruce Bouldry, for his knowledge of the sea and sailing, and for letting the *Magic Ghost* stand in for the *Wendameen*; Jim Hoffman for his cartological expertise and help in navigating New York Harbor; Ellen Datlow and Paul Witcover, who read this in manuscript and offered their invaluable suggestions.

Most of all to John Clute; for showing me True North.